FALLING
in a tulip field

SHIRA DE ROOIJ

Copyright© 2024 by Shira De Rooij

All rights reserved.

No part of this book may be reproduced in any form or by any electronic or mechanical means, including information storage or retrieval systems, without written permission from the author, except for the use of brief quotations in a book review.

This book is a work of fiction. Names, characters, businesses, organizations, places events and incidents either are the product of author's imagination or are used fictitiously. Any resemblance to actual persons, living or dead, events, or locales is entirely coincidental.

First edition: July 2024.

Sensitive Content Warning

This book includes:

The mention of the death of a loved one and dealing with grief, topics of mental health, anxiety and stress, explicit language, sexually explicit scenes

Should you choose to make this a closed- door read, feel free to skip over **chapter 27, 28 and 33** but please note you may miss some of the plot by doing so.

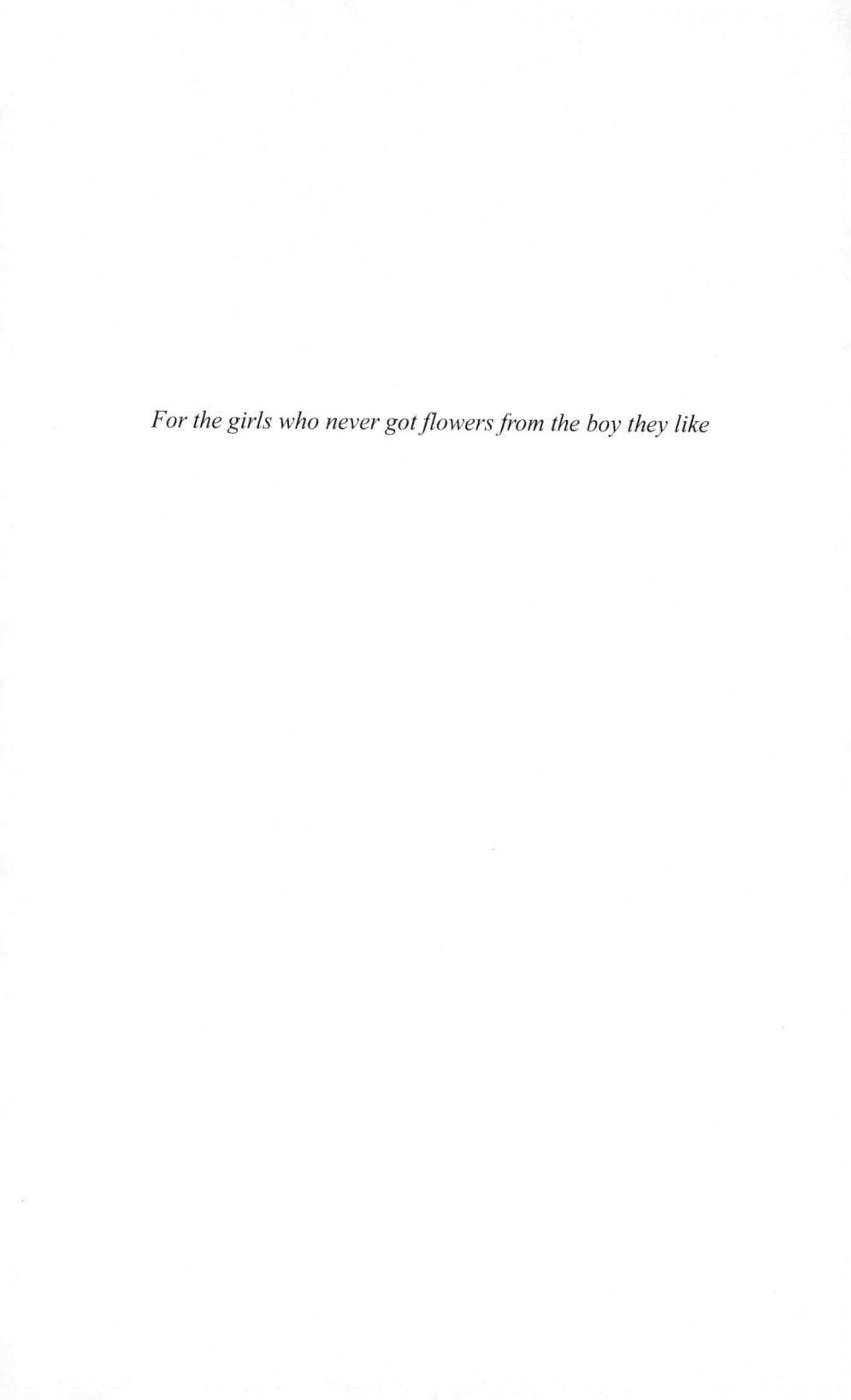

For the girls who never got flowers from the boy they like

CHAPTER 1
Nora

Amsterdam was known for her rainy days, and I was known as the girl who forgot to take an umbrella.

The heels of my boots clicked against the pavement quickly as I made my way through the rainy weather. I didn't need people around to stare to know that my shirt and skirt, even under my blue jacket, were completely soaked with water. I could feel my entire body shaking from the rain and blinked away the drops of water that were on my face. Even my hair that I braided earlier in the morning was drenched. For a moment, I was frustrated that I took my time to brush my hair and style it just for the rain to ruin it.

I wasn't the type to get mad at this kind of weather. I might be a summer child, but I always felt drawn more to the pouring rain and long walks under gray sky than to the heat of the sun.

I wasn't the type to get that annoyed in the morning, either. I was *definitely* a morning person. I always wake up early so I had enough time to run errands or cross off some of the checklists that I wrote down in my notebook.

But I hated *this* morning—my parents decided to lecture me about the choices I made in life. Apparently turning eighteen didn't immediately turn a person into an independent human being. I wanted to be treated like a real adult, like a person who can make decisions on her own, and as someone who can stand behind those decisions. Disappointment was a small word to define how I was feeling when I found out my parents weren't going to change their approach anytime soon.

When I entered Metropolitan Mugs, the coffee place near campus, it was already packed with students and people waiting in line for their order. I didn't need to look around to find the table in the corner, and I didn't need to wait long to get laughed at by my two best friends. I could hear them the second I walked in, and they were already snickering away about something.

Men sometimes had zero emotional intelligence whatsoever.

Luuk was the first to scan my figure, and as usual, he didn't hold back from making a comment about it. "At this point, I think the universe tries to send you a signal, Nor. You should listen to it more."

I sighed. "You know that I love when you read me my daily horoscope, but I'm really not in the mood to hear what the universe has to say about my life today."

"Rough morning, huh?" Xander, who sat beside him, smiled softly at me and gave me the coffee they already ordered for me.

I didn't always appreciate how well our friendship worked. I've known them since high school, and that's more than enough time for us to learn each other's best and worst sides, along with our habits. They knew I wasn't going to spill anything if I didn't get my morning coffee first.

The walls that were colored a warm shade of brown were covered with mugs in different colors and shapes, that God only knew for how long the owner had been collecting them. The workers moved quickly behind the counter; each one wearing their own white apron with a name tag. No matter what would happen in the world, three things will never change in this place: the aprons, the weather when you stepped outside, and the noise of the coffee machine that could drown out every conversation in here.

I took a sip of my coffee, and when I drank a good amount that managed to warm my body, I started with my story.

"My parents just don't get it. I thought that when I turned eighteen, they would be more understanding, and give me more freedom. Everyone posts about their life on social media, they look so free. I want to be free, too. It's not like I asked them to travel to Mexico for a year and drop out, I just want them to treat my passion to build a serious career."

Luuk's dark eyes scanned my figure again, and he nodded to himself as if something clicked in his mind. "You should've read the daily horoscope I sent you. It's not just the universe, even your horoscope says it's a difficult time for Virgo's. There's no wonder the conversation went that way, you're not supposed to make big decisions or have hard conversations right now."

That seemed to wake up Xander from whatever he was deeply thinking about. Since high school, he turned out to be quieter and more reserved. It was astonishing to see what family problems and one mistake could do to a person.

I could bet that before I showed up, he had his head in a book. It seemed like it was his only escape these days. Luuk and I wondered when we would see him happy again. Not the fake kind of happy, but the pure kind. Where his blond hair and everything around him could be a mess, but you'd still see where his face creases when he smiled. Now, I barely saw that.

"You can't expect her to live her life based on horoscopes, or what you feel the universe is telling you to do, that's ridiculous, " Xander commented before taking a sip from his water bottle. "Besides, when it comes to parents, no time is a good time to have these kinds of conversations."

Luuk and I switched gazes, wondering if we should try and ask him more, or if it was one of those times we should've just let him be. Luuk has known Xander way longer than I have, they've known each other since they were kids when Luuk was into wearing baseball hats even though he was a terrible player—or so I've heard.

He knew better than me what to do or say when your best friend was going through not just a tough morning, but a tough year.

"So, your parents aren't that excited about you turning into an event planner?" Luuk tilted his head. "I thought your mom would be more open-minded about this. I mean, she plans events herself, she knows how satisfying it can be when you plan the perfect party or event, and—"

"She also knows how much time it takes to organize one event, how much effort and energy it can take from a person," I interrupted. I had so much frustration left in me since the worst breakfast ever with my parents. We were sitting together, and after giving it enough time and thought, I tried to propose the idea of me working. I thought it all out, wrote all the pros and cons of making this kind of move. But they didn't just dislike the idea, they *hated* it. I had to sit there at breakfast, staring down at my bread and omelet, hearing them go on and on about how bad of an idea it was.

"It's not like she's against me doing it eventually, but she doesn't think now is the right time. They want me to focus on my studies and finish my degree, and then when I finish my communications degree, I can see if I still want to do it in life."

Luuk stopped. "That actually sounds logical."

"Are you saying that because of my astrological map, or because you really think so?" I asked. "Sure, it sounds logical, but I don't want to wait three years until I can start a career. Why waste time when I can apply for jobs now and start gaining that necessary experience?"

Xander leaned his head on his hand. He blinked during the conversation, like he was trying to hold himself together before he collapsed and fell asleep. Before I could ask him if he made sure to check his sugar levels, or if he ate enough this morning, Luuk already got on that.

"Have you eaten enough this morning?"

Xander glared at him, and then rolled his eyes before he turned back to me. "I think you should do whatever you can to prove your parents wrong. You should look for a job as an event planner and pave your own path in this world. Sometimes parents act like they know better, or they think their kids are just like them. It's not supposed to be this way, we need to prove them wrong."

It was hard to ignore the bitterness in his voice. Neither of us needed to ask him why he said it.

"So I take it as a *no*," Luuk continued. "I get that you don't mind fainting, or finding yourself in the hospital, but we care, so you can't keep treating your health like it's some kind of a game."

"I'm taking care of myself just fine," he mumbled.

"It's your dad, isn't it?" Luuk pressured. "He said something?"

"Jeez Luuk, you're more annoying than my English professor. No, nothing happened, I'm just not hungry." He put the books he had on the table in his bag and got up from his chair. "Now if you'll excuse me, I need to go to English class. We are studying Moby-Dick today. A real treat."

In a matter of seconds, he left Metropolitan Mugs. Luuk was following his figure as it disappeared in the campus and went back to look at me. "Can you believe him; he's acting like a child. I feel like if I don't remind him he has diabetes, he'll keep acting like it's nothing."

"Luuk, you know it's not just the diabetes, it's everything else that happened around the time he found out," I said. "You know him better than me, I'm not the one to judge, but I think we should give him space."

"Yeah, sure, let's give him space and watch him lock himself in the house for months again, fantastic approach if you ask me."

He ran his hand through his dark hair. "I just feel like as his friends, we should do more, you know?"

"I know." I wrapped my hands around the mug, feeling the warmth of the coffee. I had zero intention of facing this stormy weather today, and every intention of staying in my bubble that was warm and fuzzy. "But we also need to respect his decisions. If he wants to talk, he will," I said calmly. "You should focus on your date with Bram. You said the first date was fun, I haven't heard you talk that way about any other guy you went with lately."

He looked around at the people, like he was looking for something specific. "You know, Nor, I was sure that finding my twin flame would be an easier journey. Even though this guy is nice, I don't feel the sparks, I don't feel like he's the one."

"Isn't it too early to decide if someone is the one or not?" I raised a brow.

"Finding your twin flame is supposed to have a very specific feeling, I didn't get that feeling yet."

"What feeling?"

A small smile appeared on his lips, like he waited for someone to ask him that exact question.

"Like getting lost in the galaxy. When you're walking around space, surrounded by millions of stars, and whether you're near the sun, or the planets like Venus or Uranus, you can still feel the presence of that one star. Whether it's smaller than any other, you still know that that star was meant just for you."

Then he looked dreamily at the gray sky outside, like even in that weather he could imagine stars, galaxies and everything and more.

"That kind of a feeling," he whispered.

"You'll find it someday," I smiled. "If not with this guy, then you'll find him at one point or another."

"You know, I'm kind of mad at you," he said, which made me giggle.

"Are you now?" I asked as I checked my Instagram page.

Since I've started my degree, I started posting more. I believed that if I put enough effort and creativity into it, I might get noticed by someone who'd want to hire me for a job. It might be a long shot, but I needed to start somewhere.

"The stars are not by my side for years when it comes to love life, even the universe is testing me, but you don't have to work so hard for love. Your Venus house, it's full of opportunities this year, but instead of going out there, you're busy being in your career mode."

He scanned my face all over again, still couldn't get over his annoyance. "I'm still shocked you're not a Capricorn moon, or at least rising."

"I thought you said it's a bad time for a Virgo? Aren't you the one who said two minutes ago about how I shouldn't make life changing decisions and all of that?" I asked, and couldn't help but giggle. I didn't mind hearing about the topic, it was quite fun, but at some point, my brain would stop to comprehend all of this information.

"I was talking about today specifically, not this year. Besides, even if you meet someone today, it's not like you can decide to get into a relationship in an instant. As long as you don't jump into someone's bed today, or decide to get married, you'll be just fine."

"Oh, what a shame," I laughed. "I really wanted to have a winter wedding, and I already showered so that would be such great timing."

He shook his head and checked his mug to see if he had any drink left. The look on his face when he didn't find any was priceless.

"You and Xander are impossible to talk to in the morning. You with your full-on career-oriented mode, and Alexander acting like a child because God forbid, his friends are worried about his health; mental and physical." He folded his arms and pretended to get offended. "But no, no one listens to the guy who actually listens to the stars and the universe."

I did a miserable job at hiding the smile that crept onto my face. I put my phone back in my bag and got up to sit next to him.

He watched me carefully as I sat by his side and took the magazine he had near his empty mug.

"It's still raining outside, and I have time until my first class, so what do you say we start this morning properly. I'll buy us more coffee and you can read our horoscope; we can't go on with our day without doing that, don't you agree?"

His smile found its way back to its face when he opened the magazine.

Yep, that was a much better way to start this rainy day.

CHAPTER 2
William

Rainy days were my favorite kind of days, and thankfully there were many of them. There was something about the way the winter covered the entire city and somehow the best of customers came to the restaurant when they were caught up in a storm or wanted a warm drink.

I knew that I should've wished for sunny days, because sunny days brought more customers, and maybe then my parent's restaurant would get the miracle it needs, but nothing, not even money, could beat the rain. Nothing sounded better than having an old couple that watched the view through the glass windows, and believe me, they've been sitting at their table for a good amount of time.

"Will, what are you doing here?" I heard my dad ask as he walked right towards me to the bar. He was all dressed up in one of his best suits, his blond hair was slicked back, and his enormous round glasses covered the majority t of his face, making his brown eyes look a few times bigger than they actually were. "Son, go home, we're not going to get many customers with this kind of weather," he said, putting his hand on my shoulder, then looked down at my books that I left off to the side of me. "I don't understand why you're trying to study in here, young minds need a quiet place to focus, your mother read that in an article once."

"I'm not going home, Pa," I said calmly. "You go, you can't be late to the bank, I'll close up soon."

"Will," he sighed. "That's not what's going to save the place, we've done everything we could, but now we have to start acting rationally about this," he said and patted my shoulder before letting me go. "I know you love that place, we all are, but sometimes it's time to face reality."

"Pa, you can't actually think of closing it? What do you think grandma would say?" I asked, trying to sound rational as I possibly could, but how could I when I had memories running around, when I knew how much effort my grandparents and then my parents put into this place.

I looked around at the almost empty restaurant. Our place wasn't big or super modern, but it still had a special story behind it, it still had its own magic, and I refused to believe magic could fade that fast. It was a small oasis in a big city, with plants scattered around, paintings of tulips on the walls and big enough windows to look outside at the rest of the world. On rainy days, you could watch the rain fall but it could never reach you, and on sunny days, the whole place lit up. It was a good place to escape the world and grab a cup of coffee or a warm meal, and a good place for me to hold onto the past. And those memories were magical, even more than Oasis itself. Yep, my grandma wasn't just a poetic soul, she knew how to pick the right name for a restaurant.

I cleared my throat when I took a notebook out of my bag. "I know it's a long shot, but I think if we make a few changes to the place, we might be able to save it. I had a course in business and I wrote down some ideas, if you just take the time to look at it—"

He pushed my notebook back to me and all he did was shake

his head. He didn't have to say much for me to know what he thought, I was getting used to this kind of conversation. I was proposing my ideas, but in my parent's eyes, coming up with alternatives always seemed like I was holding onto false hope that things could change. They both became pretty pessimistic when it came to the restaurant.

"Son, I know you mean well, but no, we can't afford to put any more money, or time, in trying out these ideas that you came up with. I know you don't agree with us, but someday when you grow old, you'll understand."

But I didn't understand. Not now, and I doubted that I ever would..

"Maybe you didn't notice, Pa, but I'm not a kid anymore. I sit in my business courses every day. Maybe I'm not the owner, but every day of studying, or being here, I have a clearer view of what it means to have a business, to own a restaurant. That's why I also know that with the right plan, the right resources and actions, it's possible to make this place shine. If you could just wait a second and listen, then we might—"

He put his hand in the air and I leaned back on the wall, because I knew it meant end of discussion.

"What do you think grandma would say if she knew we were selling this place?" I asked him and folded my arms.

When I was a kid, my parents never told me about the debts, the loans, the struggles they went through to keep the place. I still felt like that kid, the kid no one was going to try and hear his opinion. After all, what can someone young do to change things?

He's gone quiet, and just when I thought he was going to leave, he smiled wearily while he looked at the wall behind me. I followed his gaze and watched the painting of the tulip on the wall, it looked quite similar to the one my grandpa gave my grandpa when they first met.

"You know what your grandma used to say?" he asked.

"I don't know." I shrugged my shoulders, still wounded a bit by not being heard. "She could publish a whole book of quotes from the number of things she had to say. She could've been the Oscar Wilde of her generation if she wanted to."

"Will." My dad stared at me.

"No, I don't know," I mumbled and looked down at the clean tables. Even the servers stayed home today, because with no customers, there's no need for them.

"As you know, she loves flowers. One day when I helped her with her garden, there was a flower there. It was dry, small, it was a matter of time before it would die completely. You know what your grandma did?"

"Started to read from the bible and prayed for its health?" I asked, though by my dad's stare, I understood I was wrong.

"She cut it."

"Grandma cut a flower?" I raised my brows.

"She loves flowers, but she was rational too. She told me that it had no part in the garden anymore, but she could still use the soil to create something new, stronger, more beautiful even," he explained, and then looked back at me. "You see where I'm going with this?"

"That grandma should've really written a book, or something."

"She said that to me when I was just a kid, and still, forty years later and it's still one of the most memorable things I remember. It stuck with me. I think your grandma would support this decision, with all the love she had for Oasis. We had some great memories here, we hoped that you could own the place one day, but things don't always go as planned."

He sounded so at peace with his words, like he knew in his full heart he was making the right call, like my grandma came here herself, flesh and blood and said it to him.

"We're going to cut the flower and let something else grow. It's going to be hard, but we'll get through it as a family, okay?" he asked.

I looked over at the old couple who were smiling at the rain after I served them warm soup. There could be so many other couples just like them coming in if we had the right tools, the right plan, if we could make the right choices.

Why cut something if you could save it?

"I'm staying." I opened a beer bottle from the counter nearby.

"As you wish." He held onto his bag. "Just don't stay here too long, it's getting cold and your mom is working on a nice dinner for all of us today, you can't be late."

"I have an umbrella." I reminded him, but nodded when he kept looking at me. "I won't be late, promise."

I watched him walk out the door and went back to my books to study. Once in a while, I lifted my head to look at the rain falling outside. It was getting wilder, louder, and I knew that if we hadn't had any new customers for hours, we weren't going to have any now.

The old couple left, and the longer I stayed alone by myself at the restaurant, I realized how stupid it was of me. I was waiting in this empty space, hoping that in some way my ideas could change this sad reality, believing that it was too soon to cut the flower.

My grandparents put way too much effort into this place just for it to be shut down, replaced by something meaningless like some fancy restaurant with even fancier meals listed at crazy prices.

The thoughts weren't leaving my mind while I was putting the books back in my bag, knowing I would have to keep studying once I got home. When I went to turn off the lights at the bar, the door opened up, and I heard someone walk in.

I looked up at the clock on the wall before I turned around to tell that person the place was close but stopped the moment my eyes were met with wild green ones.

Standing there at the door, she looked about my age, but more importantly, I noticed that she had been caught up in the middle of the crazy weather. Though she was shivering from the cold, she didn't act like she was fazed, she only moved a few strands of her dark- brown hair behind her ears and walked towards the bar until she sat on the stool.

She pulled off her wet jacket that clung to her body and put it on the stool near her before looking at me.

"Can I have a cup of coffee?" she asked. I still haven't moved, I scanned her figure again.

I didn't know if I was more shocked by the fact that a customer walked in, or that this girl looked so cool, calm, and collected, though her entire body was shivering from the rain.

"God, please tell me you have coffee. Every place I went to was fully packed with people, or had long lines, or just plain closed. I don't get it, it's raining, it's a cold day; is it really too much to ask for a good coffee?" She asked out loud. "And I know, I already drank coffee this morning, but I can't settle for one mug a day."

"Sure…" I mumbled and looked back at the coffee machine. I couldn't hide the smile on my face when I took out everything I needed to make her coffee.

"What is it?" she asked. "I can see you smiling, you know."

I chuckled and turned towards her, running my eyes over her body. "It's just…"

She looked down at herself like she just noticed how wet she got from the rain.

"Oh, that." She smiled and fixed her hair that was styled in a tight braid. "I know, I look like a mess, but that's an ordinary look for me on days like today. I have the tendency to walk out of the house and forget my umbrella. Bad habit, I know."

"I don't think you look like a mess." I put the cup of coffee carefully in front of her. "You look very…"

I stopped to think of the right word to describe it. After hours of being by myself and going over material for class, my mind wasn't working as fast as it usually did.

"You look very radiant."

"Radiant?" she scoffed out of disbelief.

"Yeah, like the sun," I shrugged.

It took me a few seconds after to realize how weird that sounded.

Why did I just say that?

Yep, I definitely needed to get back home and take a nice break from studying.

"It's a shame it's hiding today, but I think I remember what it looks like."

I laughed. "I like rainy days; you never know what they may bring."

"That's a good point. All of this did bring me one of the best coffee I've had in a while. You know how much a good coffee can change someone's day? My morning started with the worst breakfast ever, and then I had this boring class when the professor nearly killed me because I was late, but do you see me complaining? No, you don't, because you just made me a great coffee so I could forget all of the shitty parts of my day. So, thank you…" She dragged out her words.

"William, though most people like to call me Will." I smiled and put my hand forward for her to shake.

She looked down at my hand and let her hand shake mine. "Thank you, William." When I raised my eyebrow, she had a childish gleam in her eyes. "You should know, William, no matter if I know you for a second, minute or a year, if there's something you should know about me, it's that I'm not like everyone else."

I opened my mouth, but no words came out. I never met someone that confident in herself in my life.

"Very well…"

"Nora Tuinstra," she said. "I know, it doesn't roll out the tongue easily, but I'll find my way to market myself one day. And when that day comes when I become an event planner, people won't find it so hard to say it anymore. But until then, you can call me Nor, that's how most people call me."

"Very well, Nora," I replied back, which made her laugh. "So, you want to be an event planner?" I asked and put my bag back on the counter to give me space to sit in front of her. I poured myself a drink as well.

"It's always been a dream, though today, it feels like an awful dream. I went to every place I could to find a job, because in my head, it couldn't be that hard to find a job, to gain experience. I don't even want to do it for the money, I just want to work and get to plan events. But no, they don't want a first-year student who has no actual knowledge in the field." She sighed and then lifted her head up again. "It's okay I'm spilling it all to you, right? Every time I went to a bar, the bartenders or waiters never told me they were bothered to hear my stories, and some of them had really good advice to give."

"You want some advice?"

"I want to find a job that could prove my parents wrong, but sure, some advice would be a nice start," she replied, which made me smile all over again.

I pulled back from the chair enough to take off my yellow sweater and be left in my t-shirt. She blinked her eyes when I put my sweater between her hands and motioned her to wear it.

"That's my advice, Nora. Get warm first so you don't get sick, and then think of all the other steps to move forward," I said.

She looked at the sweater, and then back at me.

"I already told you, I've gone through many rainy days this way, I never got sick."

"There's always a first. Besides, you wouldn't be able to organize any event from bed."

She looked at the sweater again and took it slowly from me. I held back another laugh when she put the sweater over her body, and as expected it was huge over her body.

"I never got a sweater from a bartender before."

I scratched the back of my neck. "I'm not a bartender."

"A waiter then?"

"No, not that either," I said. "Let's say you can't really define my role here, I'm kind of doing what is needed from me at the moment. One day I'm helping in the kitchen, other days I'm serving, and when there's no one at the bar, I'm the one making drinks, but that happens on very rare occasions."

She wrapped her hands around her drink. "But you just made me a coffee."

I leaned forward on the bar. "As I said Nora, very rare occasions."

She went quiet before turning around in her chair. Her eyes were roaming on the empty space, at the empty tables, at the quiet that surrounded both of us. I hated this silence; it reminded me how bad the situation was. It wasn't like I've gotten used to it now, but I learned to accept it, accept that our situation was far from ideal.

"Why is there no one here?" she asked. "Are you closed, and I just barged in?"

"I wish," I muttered.

Then the silence was creeping in again, reminding me of how long it's been since this place was full of people, since it felt alive.

"Hey, William?" she asked.

"Yeah?"

"I know it makes sense that as a customer, I would just go to the bar and spill my guts out, but I think bartenders-waiters-people with unspecified jobs should be able to spill their guts, too," she said quietly.

When I finally lifted my head to face her, my lips curled up when I saw her struggling with the long sleeves of my sweater.

I gently helped her lift the sleeves up so she could move her hand freely.

"It's a long story Nora."

"Luckily for you, it doesn't seem like the rain is going to end anytime soon."

I looked at her, then at the rain, and then at my bag. The decision was made pretty fast when I grabbed my phone and wrote to my mom I was going to be late for dinner.

CHAPTER 3
Nora

Long story was one way to put William's story. William laid back against the chair and looked over the empty restaurant as the rain fell hard outside. I held onto my second cup of coffee while I scanned his face.

I just met the guy, but even if I wasn't some talented art student who was looking for the smallest of details and even if I didn't know William's horoscope or zodiac sign, I could tell how much the future of the restaurant was weighing on him.

He wasn't the one who came out from the storm, and still, his light brown hair was messy. He didn't bother to move the strands of hair that fell on his forehead, but in his defense, it was a cute look. I didn't even question the fact he could have been a barista or a bartender when I entered the place. Most of the people I ordered drinks from were attractive people with some charm to them, with beautiful blue eyes and a tall frame. Though William didn't have a confident guy kind of charm, but of a shy guy with a golden heart. Luuk had a way to know people by the stars, and I had a feeling about people, call it intuition, call it whatever, I just knew when something was true.

This time I was proved right when he told me about his

family shortly after, and the history of the place, and how much he was willing to do to save it.

"Is it stupid that I believe things can change?" he asked quietly into the space only we've been a part of. "I know money is an issue, and that my parents are getting older, and it makes sense they're tired of trying, but I don't think we've tried and considered all of the options. I just wished that one time they listened to me, truly."

"Believe me, if there's one thing I know about parents, it's that it's not enough to say something, but sometimes you have to act on your own and show them you mean your words, prove them with actions instead of words how serious your intentions and ideas are." I mumbled and looked down at my drink, which spread a sweet aroma in the air. "Look at my parents for example, my own mom is working in the field, but instead of actually helping or guiding me, she insists that I'm too young, and that at my age, I should focus on my degree."

"It doesn't make sense," he said. "Come on Nora, I'm sure there's a bigger reason for your parents acting the way they do than just your age. I don't agree with my parents, but they have their reasons. What is yours?"

"Hey, I told you what I know," I lifted my hand in the air but held on tight my mug with the other. My best bet was to play dumb, as if I don't know their reasoning. Because sometimes it feels like I don't.

"And yet, I feel like there's more," he said calmly. "Remember when I told you about my grandma? Well, she had this talent, she always knew when someone was holding back the truth or lying to her. When a customer didn't like their meal or drink, she just knew."

"And you're like that too?" I sighed, knowing I had no way of holding things back from him.

"I want to believe so," he chuckled. "But even if I don't, since the moment you walked through that very door, I could tell you're not afraid to go after what you want. If you want something, you'll work to get it. If you want coffee, you'll find a way to make a guy who hates drinks make it for you."

He looked at me, and I couldn't help but smile back at him for saying that.

"I find it hard to believe that your parents won't let you start working because of a degree or how young you are. There are many ways to multitask between a job, university, social life and much more in life without neglecting any part."

"Is this coming from personal experience?" I sipped from my coffee. "Let me guess, you don't just work in every position possible in this restaurant, later at night you go to some secret club, dancing the night away as some stripper."

His chest rumbled and he laughed so loud that he put his hand on his chest.

"You know, if you never told me, I would've guessed you study creative writing or something, because your mind is definitely creative." His lips curled.

"So, no stripper then?"

"Unfortunately, no." He smiled. "I don't have an extra job, it's just hard sometimes to be a business student and then come here to see a business fall apart right in front of my eyes." He stopped to look around us. "I just don't want to feel like I'm neglecting this part of me."

I put my hand on his shoulder. "Well, it's not too late to try and save it."

He nodded to himself before raising his head. "Enough about me, back to your parents. Do you have another reason in mind?"

I could tell he didn't like having the attention on him, so I went back to my drink. I pressed my lips together. I didn't want to go back and look into the past; I wasn't that kind of person. But when he brought it up, I couldn't hold it back.

I glanced at him hesitantly. "I think eventually our family, our parents, they know us better than anyone else. They know how ambitious I am, and more importantly, how ambitious I *can* be and how much I want to achieve. They…They know how in the past I have let these ambitions blind me in a way."

"How did that happen?" He turned his head so his full attention was now on me. "How did it blind you?"

I let out a shaky breath, blind was a small way of describing it. I laughed to hide the heavy weight that appeared in my chest and turned back to him with a smile on my face. "You know, if you want to be a bartender someday, you definitely got the whole listening to customers and giving advice part down."

He didn't buy my act though, he just looked at me under the dimmed lights of the restaurant, like he was busy thinking of how to pass my sweet talk. "I'm serious, I gave you a whole half an hour-long story about my grandparents and family and this restaurant," he stopped to clear his throat, his cheeks were covered in a pink shade. "I usually don't talk that much."

"And I usually don't drink that much coffee, but here we are," I muttered as I sipped again from the coffee.

I really didn't understand why he wasn't a full-time barista; it was a waste making him wait on people instead of creating that delicious magic.

"That's a lie, isn't it?" he chuckled.

"A very tiny one," I replied and we both laughed.

Then we heard a phone ring. William reached for the phone in his jeans pocket and smiled awkwardly as the ringtone got louder.

"Is that Noah Kahan?" I asked immediately as *Mom* typed out in big letters flashed on the screen.

I started humming to the melody, following the words I recognized the lyrics. Slowly my humming turned into a singing, and when I felt William's eyes gaze at me I smiled at him.

"You set up the song 'Call Your Mom' to let you know whenever your mom calls?" I asked. "That's pretty creative of you."

He scratched the back of his neck. "It's a good song…"

"I know it is, I heard the entire album and it's one of my favorites," I told him, and just like that, he let his hand down and his muscles relaxed.

"You did?" he asked, while his lips curled up.

"Yeah, and we can talk all about it some other day, but right now, I think you should answer your mom," I giggled while he was still looking at me like I revealed some big truth.

"She's so going to kill me," he muttered before he accepted the call and pressed it to his ear.

He sighed when he heard the voice of his mom on the other line, and nodded as he kept listening to her.

"I know I promised, I'm sorry. I'll close everything up and be there soon, fifteen minutes max."

When I heard that, I saw it as my sign to leave as well and gathered my stuff. I picked up my jacket from the stool, frowning when I realized not only was it still wet, but it also looked exactly as it did when I just came here. There was no way I was putting it on again tonight.

I looked down at the sleeves of William's sweater. I didn't feel like taking it off. It was nice, and warm, and it smelled nice, like coffee and cinnamon. But as much as I wanted to keep it on me, I wasn't going to let him walk out in the rain in a t-shirt. I reached with my hands to the hem of the sweater, but right before I lifted my arms to take it off, he put his hands gently on mine.

"Don't," he said and left my hands slowly when he made sure I was keeping the sweater on.

Then he glanced at the view outside and I followed his gaze. The skies turned dark, there was a glow on the pavement under the street's lights. It must've been nice working in the restaurant an entire day, seeing how the sky changed color and the rain disappeared and came back along with the customers.

"It's your sweater," I mentioned.

"Yeah, I'm aware of that, thanks." His eyes gleamed in

amusement. "I live close by, a ten-minute walk to be exact. I can handle the cold weather until I get home, but I bet you have a little more than that to get to your house."

Well, I couldn't argue with that. One of the reasons I found myself with William in the first place was the need to take some time away from my parents. I didn't want to spend an entire afternoon in my house, knowing they still had more to say after that awful breakfast we had this morning.

"Fine," I huffed out.

Though honestly, it wasn't that hard to agree with him, I was the one left wearing a warm sweater.

There was a short silence in the air, and I could sense he wanted to say something but decided against it. I stayed silent and gave him the time to work through the thoughts in his mind until he had a clear idea what he wanted to say.

"I'm sorry for dumping all of my problems on you tonight," he said quietly. "You just came here to grab a coffee, and then you got a short version of the story on my life, and—"

"You know something, William?" I asked him, because as with all people, I could see him too. "You have every right to complain or feel the need to share. You don't need to carry on this weight and pressure all alone, and I say this as a stranger that met you less than an hour ago."

"I'm usually not that open with anyone, I don't know what happened to me today." He ran a hand through his messy hair. "I felt like I was talking with a friend."

My lips curled up, because I knew deep inside both of us felt that way. "We can be friends if you want."

It was funny, I already felt like we were friends when I said that.

"We can?" His blue eyes got this new kind of spark in them underneath the lights.

"I mean, I already have two best friends. One is a big bookworm, and the other could read horoscopes to me every morning, but I still don't have a friend who can make a magical coffee, so I guess you could be that friend."

"Horoscopes?" He raised a brow.

"It's a longer story than your long story," I laughed.

He gave me his phone and I typed down my phone number. When he reached to take it back, I pulled it closer to my chest. "I'll give it back to you on one condition."

"Oh, I can't wait to hear that one out," he said, but I could tell he was more than curious to hear what I was about to say next.

"I want a song at least as good as 'Call Your Mom' when you see my name on your screen."

The smile on his face was unmatched to any other I've seen before.

"You got it."

CHAPTER 4
Nora

"So let me get this straight. You met a random guy in a restaurant, you both talked, exchanged numbers, and you didn't bother to ask him what his zodiac sign is?" Luuk asked me as we sat around the dining table in my house.

My parents were busy cutting vegetables in the kitchen to add to our meal while Luuk was busy investigating me.

"I'm sorry Luuk for not asking a guy for his zodiac sign when I just knew him for an hour," I mumbled and tried to avoid him by putting more bread on my plate.

"Yeah, go on, keep on eating that bread, you're going to need a lot of energy for later when we both stock his Instagram account." he muttered, and took some bread as well.

"You won't find him, I already tried any social media platform. Facebook, Instagram, even Twitter, there's nothing. I guess I should've asked his last name."

"What about the restaurant?" he asked. "Didn't you find him through the Instagram account or site of the restaurant?"

I pressed my lips together. Since I met William that day, I couldn't help but think about Oasis. It had so much unfulfilled potential. The restaurant was beautiful, and I could definitely find it beautiful and homey, but without the right marketing and social media presence, no one was going to experience this beauty, because no one would know of its existence in the first place.

"They don't have any social media presence," I said.

"Say what now?" he raised a brow and I sighed, because of course he was going to make me repeat it.

"They don't have a site or anything like that. From what William told me, his parents are very old school, to respect and honor what his grandparents built many years ago, so they keep the atmosphere really homey, with traditional meals and recipes. Instead of having decorations, they keep it small and sweet, with paintings on the wall or some vases with flowers," I said as sadness took over my body when I thought of this place getting shut down. "They will never make it if they don't change things around."

Luuk knew me long enough to recognize what I wanted to say next. "Don't tell me you're actually thinking about it. I've heard your description of him, the guy sounds cute, really cute, I would've probably swipe him right for sure if he was on any of the apps I use." He looked sideways to make sure my parents couldn't hear us and leaned in closer. "There's a big difference between wanting to help a cute guy that made you some coffee on a rainy day, and volunteering to be the event planner or marketing expert of a restaurant."

"First of all, it's not some coffee, there was something magical in the way it tastes, and there's something magical in that restaurant, too. You weren't there Luuk; you didn't hear the story behind the place, or how much heart and soul was put into this. I don't see what's so wrong with wanting to help people with the knowledge I have."

"Nor, you more than anyone should know what happens when you go too far with some goals and ambitions. I'm sorry to be the one to blow your bubble, but you should focus on your degree and being a bit more realistic about it."

I put down the bread and leaned back in my chair. I looked at him, hoping that I didn't hear him right. But I did. He looked at me intensely, like he actually believed what he was saying was the right thing.

"I thought you agreed with me that I should follow my dreams, find a job, show my parents I can do anything? What happened to that?" I asked.

Then I gazed at my parents. They just finished a long day of work, my mom was sipping from her glass of wine and laughed at the way my dad cut the cucumber, because it reminded her of that episode in the Kardashians.

"Did..." I breathed out. "Did they talk to you about me? Did they ask you to tell you to say all of that?"

"Nor, come on."

"I'm serious, Luuk."

He folded his arms. "So am I. If you want to go and get any other job that can help you gain experience and knowledge, and more than all make you happy, then I would be the first to support you. But I don't want to watch you go and give your all to a place that isn't going to survive no matter what you do."

"You can't know that," I said bitterly.

He shook his head." But I do. It will end up with you being broken and feeling like a failure for not achieving your goal, while you give good people false hope that you can change a future that has already been decided."

"What if it's not false hope? What if I can make a change in people's life?" I asked him. "Is it so wrong that I want to help a friend?"

That seemed to throw him off. "A...a friend?"

"Yeah, a friend. Like I have you as my friend, and Alexander..." I stopped to look out for him.

He disappeared for what felt like ages to look through the

library in my house for some book to lend. Alexander had the habit of going over the books in our library every time he came here. Most of the time, he really was looking for something new to read, and other times it felt like he was looking for distraction from his own life. I couldn't tell which one of these reasons was today.

"Yeah, I know what a friend is, I just can't see how you're going to keep with that crazy plan of yours without being more than friends."

"It won't happen," I shrugged my shoulders and wondered if my parents were ever going to join us to eat, because the food probably got cold at this point. "I'm a professional, Luuk, okay? If I'll take this on myself, I'm going to be professional about this. I don't see why you're worried about me developing feelings, I'm not worried."

He chuckled. "Yeah, that's because you're in some weird state of delusion. If Xander was here and not getting cozy with books, he would've said the same."

"I'm not delusional," I said.

I might have been delusional about things in the past. Like that time, I made up my own crazy theories about Taylor Swift's songs, or that time I thought I could organize a huge event instead of my mom when she got sick. I might have pushed myself too hard without realizing the boundaries of reality, but it was going to be different this time, and I was going to not only prove it to my parents, but I was going to prove it to Luuk.

"You still haven't touched your food because you believed your parents would join us ten minutes ago, though you know it happens every single time they invite me and Xander over for dinner. You also believed Xander would be here with us, chatting and telling us about his feelings for once instead of looking for more books in your dad's office. That's delusion right there." But by the smile on his face, I could tell he was quite happy with his observation.

"It's not the same thing." I pinned my fork in the piece of cheese on my plate.

"Nor, come on, we all know, including your parents, that you had an enormous crush on Zac Efron when he played Troy Bolton, and since then, you always fell for the same type of guys. I can see a guy that fits your exact type when I see one," he said.

"You just forget one part; William doesn't play basketball," I whispered when I heard my parents getting closer to the table.

"You don't know that yet," he whispered right back. "I think you should be realistic, that's all."

"Says the guy that believes he's going to meet his twin flame," I said.

It took me less than a second to regret blurting that out. His eyes turned into a lighter shade of brown and he looked down in hurt.

"Luuk, I'm sorry, I didn't mean—" I tried to reach out to him, but he had created some distance between us.

My mom put the salad on the table along with a bottle of wine before she sat by my side. "So, what did we miss?"

My dad sat down by Luuk and offered him a glass of wine, which Luuk accepted immediately. He sipped from the glass and put it down while he was watching me from across the table.

He smiled towards my parents and leaned back comfortably on the chair. "Not much, just your daughter starting a new job."

They both went to look at me. I played with my hands under the table as I felt them staring at me.

"Come on, Nor. Don't be shy, tell them," Luuk said as he kept eating from his plate calmly.

Having best friends was great, most of the time. And the rare occasion that it's not as great, they could be annoying as hell. My friends felt more like siblings, and Luuk was acting exactly like that, he was acting like a big brother that was giving me a hard time.

"Nora?" my mom asked.

I played with a strand of hair that slipped from my braid. "Yeah, umm, I found a job. Well, not really a job, more of a gaining experience kind of thing."

"Okay," my dad said as he adjusted his glasses. "Tell us about it?"

"Are you sure we should talk about this right at this moment? I think we should focus on the food before it gets cold. I can go look for Xander, make sure he wasn't swallowed by one of the books." I tried to get up from the chair but my mom stopped me, putting her hand on my knee.

"Nora," she said.

Her quiet tone made a clear message, I wasn't leaving this table until I gave them what they wanted to hear.

"It's not even settled yet, so I don't see why we should be even having this conversation. It's not as big of a deal as you might think. I have a new friend who works in a restaurant and I want to help him market the place a bit, making it more known and approachable for the public." Before they could try to snoop some more on the subject, I continued. "It's nothing you should be too worried about, I'm still very focused on my degree, and if you don't believe me you can see my grades or have a chat with my professors, especially the one we have in that journalism course I take. Apparently I have the potential to be a journalist, will you believe that?"

My mom cleared her throat. "Sweetie, didn't we tell you that we want you to focus on your degree? We don't want you to put extra pressure on yourself, a job can wait."

"There's no pressure, do you see me stressed out right now?" I asked her. "I'm good, everything is more than good. I have extra free time, so I only want to help a friend, I don't see how that could harm anyone."

My mom switched glances with my dad, like she was asking him without saying anything to contribute to the conversation, too. They didn't understand that I knew what I wanted, and nothing that they could say would stop me.

"We didn't want to bring up that subject again, because we trust that you're older and wiser this time, but maybe we should talk about what happened. You were acting like everything was fine back then too, but—"

"Dad, please don't." I raised my hand to stop him from going any further. "Can we just not talk about this and have a nice dinner for once?"

After another switch of glances, he nodded, and everyone at the table started to eat.

"I'll go look for Xander." I rose up from the chair, and this time no one tried to stop me.

When I reached the end of the hallway, I leaned my back against the wall, closed my eyes, and took a deep breath. My parents didn't need to say one more word, I got the answer I was looking for. William was right, there was more to it than I thought, they were still stuck on what happened to the overachiever teenager I was.

"Nor, are you okay?" Xander asked as he opened the door of my dad's study room.

He had a pile of books in his hand, and if I didn't know any better, I would think he snuck out to a local library and took any book in sight. We had another library in the living room, but my dad always kept his best books close to him.

I looked towards the big space that led back to the kitchen, but just the thought of being back in a place that sucked all the air out of my lungs made me feel anxious again. I was so not in the mood to dig right back into the discussion we had. I knew my parents well enough to know they would keep going from the same place we stopped in.

"Did you happen to see alcohol in my dad's room?" I turned to Xander. "Whiskey maybe? He for sure has some whiskey left there somewhere."

"I..." he frowned. "I didn't really look, but maybe—"

I passed by him and pushed through the room, scanning the desk and papers till I found a glass with some liquor. I brought the glass closer to my nose, and when the strong smell hit me, I drank what was left in the glass.

"God, that's strong," I muttered.

"Nor, what happened out there?" He closed the door, and when I stared back at him, he motioned with his head to the door. "At the table."

"Remember that guy I told you about?" I said, though I knew he remembered, I told them about him two days ago. Even then I could picture Xander creating a whole story in his mind, like he could envision this one meeting on a rainy day to the smallest of details.

A smile crept onto his lips. "The cute one, with the dark blond hair and dreamy blue eyes that looks exactly like young Zac Efron?"

"What is going on with you two, he looks nothing like him," I said while he kept laughing. "And I didn't say the word *dreamy*, you said that."

"No, I think Luuk was the first, but you have to admit, it's pretty accurate," he went to put the books on the desk and leaned on the wall. "We just like to mess with you. It's been so long since we've seen you hanging out with any other guy but us, you can't blame us for thinking it could lead to some romance."

"It hasn't been that long," I clarified.

He chuckled. "Hey, don't look at me like that, it feels like forever since we've been in high school. A lot has changed..."

But we both knew that he was saying *everything* that needed to be said without saying anything at all.

"Yeah, like the relationship between your parents. How do you do it, Xander?" I asked him, hoping I might get an answer to all of my unanswered questions. "How are you dealing with your dad for example? When you have disagreements and not seeing eye to eye?"

He gave me a sympathetic look. "Your parents again?"

I bit my lips. "I thought of helping William with the restaurant, taking over the marketing side, listening to his own ideas about the place and maybe save the place before it's too late."

He nodded to himself. "Let me guess, your parents and Luuk aren't so thrilled about this?"

"You don't seem super thrilled yourself," I mumbled out and looked around to see if there was any other drink left in the room by any chance.

"I just know what pressuring yourself can do to you, and I don't want to see you in pain again because you didn't succeed in something as you expected to," he explained.

"Luuk said something similar," I nodded. "I know it's a bad idea, really bad to set these high goals but—"

"But your heart is all in already," he finished.

I sucked in a breath when his words sank in.

"It is," I whispered.

"Then it's settled, you should do it. Let's be real, no matter what any of us say, once you make your mind about something, none of us can stop you," he said, and smiled at me, which made me smile back at him.

"It's funny, there's so much mess around this topic, and I didn't even bring up the idea to William. I mean, he could say no, he could hate the idea, he could say that it's too late," I sighed.

I scanned the cover of the book at the top of the pile. Unsurprisingly, it was one of my dad's old editions of Shakespeare's plays.

"I wouldn't be too worried about that part if I were you," he said, and when I frowned, he laughed. "You made him give you his sweater on a cold night and make you coffee when you told us yourself he's not a fan of making them, so I doubt he would say no, you can be pretty persuasive when you want to be."

"First off, I didn't make him do anything. But you're right, I can be. Besides, he said he has his own ideas, which shows he isn't one to give up, and neither am I, we can be a good team," I said, and when I heard Xander laugh again I folded my arms. "What?"

"Nothing, I just find it interesting how a few days ago William was just a stranger to you, then an hour later he became your friend who has now become your teammate in all of this." He put his hand over his mouth, holding back another laugh. "What do you think comes next in this order?"

"Oh, shut up," I said and picked up a book in his stack. "If you'll say another word, I'll hurt your little poetic friend over here."

"Fine." He quickly wrapped his hands around the hardcover and put it back on the pile.

He didn't say another word and went towards the door with the books. I watched him walking carefully down the hallway, making sure not to drop any of them.

Even after everything happened this evening, I couldn't help but laugh. I couldn't ask for a more annoying, yet amazing best friends.

CHAPTER 5
William

It was supposed to be just another day in the restaurant, but no day was *just a day* when Nora had anything to say about it.

I haven't seen her for a couple of days since that night we first met, but when I raised my head, I noticed her again. She walked into the restaurant, didn't even bother to recover from the rain or ask for coffee like the last time. Right as her foot passed the threshold, she walked straight towards me. She wore a similar outfit to the one she wore on the other day. By her quick steps and determined look on her face, I had a feeling she had a genuine purpose to be here.

While I placed the plates on the tables and smiled at the little girl that sat next to her mom, I could feel Nora gaze at my movements carefully.

She roamed her eyes over my body and smiled. "You look cute as a waiter."

That caught me off guard and made my cheeks warm up. It didn't help that the girl and her mom could hear us. "I.. I am?"

She folded her arms, pretty amused by my reaction. "Come

on, don't tell me no girl has ever come over here and said you look cute."

I only shook my head, because I had no other clever way to reply.

"No girl has flirted with you while ordering something, or wrote her number on a napkin, or—" she pressed her lips when I kept looking at her with wide eyes. "Oh, I thought it was way more fun to be a server. You know, I once thought that if I didn't get a job as an event planner or something in that field, then I could be a waitress, but I guess I'll have to rethink it if it's not as fun as I thought."

"Fun?" I chuckled. "Well, I love it, and maybe it's just me because I used to help here since I'm a kid, but…"

I went quiet when another thought ran through my head.

She noticed that immediately. "What is it?"

I chuckled, and my cheeks flushed when I met her eyes again. I lowered my voice so the customers close by wouldn't hear me. "What you said when you saw me, was that flirting?"

I heard a laugh but it didn't come out of Nora's lips. It was the little girl who was watching us even though we weren't standing that close to their table anymore. Nora shook her head and put her hand on my arm, dragging me towards the bar, not leaving me a choice but to follow her.

When I put the tray aside, she sat on one of the stools. I leaned to look at her, and she smiled softly at me. "Some compliments are just that—they're compliments, okay?"

I nodded.

"I just might give more compliments than average," she continued.

Now that I wasn't walking around tables serving customers anymore, I could look at her properly; she looked as alive as the first night that we met, with wet clothes and wide eyes.

Before she could stop me, I reached my hand and traced the strand of hair that fell on her forehead. I tucked it gently behind her ear and smiled when I realized that small action didn't help her situation.

"So, tell me Nora, what is it that brought you here on this lovely rainy day?" I asked, curious to see what would come out of her mouth this time.

"You didn't get my message?"

"Nora," I laughed and motioned my head to the tables, where customers were eating their nice lunch or late breakfast. "We're having one of those rare, *good* days, I had to work extra time."

"So, you didn't get my message?" she pouted.

I shook my head again.

"That's a shame, I used emojis, some of my favorite ones, actually. I don't make that extra effort for anyone," she mentioned.

"Let me guess, your favorite emoji is the one with that big smiley face, that the smile is so big that you can feel someone's excitement through the phone," I said, and I was actually pretty confident in my guess until I looked at her. I frowned. "A red heart maybe?"

"Do I look to you like a simple red heart kind of girl?" she asked, and then moved her head to look at the few mugs on the shelf behind me.

I sighed. "Fine, I'll make you a coffee."

When I turned my back on her, I could hear her saying a little "yay" which made my lips curl all over again.

When I finished making my coffee I was about to put it in front of her, but pulled back when I took a second glance at her. "Are you sure you should drink coffee? You seem pretty wired without it."

"Just gimme the coffee," she pressed.

I clearly didn't do it fast enough in her opinion because she quickly brought her hands forward and took the mug from me.

"Lovely," I muttered and watched her content smile as she took a sip.

While she was doing so, more customers walked through the door. I looked for my dad who loved taking the job of the host and directed people to their table while chatting about the history of the place and recommending everyone the same dish from the menu, but he was nowhere to be found.

I took some of the menus near the bar and walked towards them. "Look Nora, thank you for coming here, but is it okay if we talk later?"

"How much later?" she asked, and I smiled as I was playing with the menus in my hands.

"You don't like waiting, do you?" I asked.

"Not really, no," she answered.

I chuckled. "Okay, so hear me out. Maybe you could stay here, have a nice meal on the house, you can use the time to do your assignments or whatever you need to do, and when there's less people and the other waiters have everything under control, we can talk?"

"So what you're saying is you're offering me free food?" she asked.

"It's a privilege saved for friends only," I told her, and when she didn't argue, I took it as my chance to take her to one of the free tables and made sure to get her the best dish on the menu, in my opinion at least, and went on with my job. I told her how bad the situation here was, how much we prayed and hoped for days like this, we couldn't afford ourselves to hand around free meals, but if we were already sinking, did it really matter?

The time passed by fast as I walked between tables, serving customers, and smiling at some more little kids that ate lunch with their parents.

When I was about to serve another table, I felt someone tap on my shoulder. I turned around to be faced with my dad who looked at the dish in my hand, and then at me. He looked like he wanted to say something, I knew that look all too well, but he just kept his eyes on me, like he expected me to figure out his internal thoughts on my own.

"What?" I asked and then looked down at my dish. "Is it cold, or something?"

He shook his hand and took the dish from me. "You're taking a break."

"Pa, I can't take a break." I tried to take the plate back, but pulled it away. "We haven't had this many customers in weeks, and I know we are missing a server today, so—"

"You're taking a break," he said again, leaving no room for discussion. "You haven't eaten anything since you came here from your class, and I believe you let your friend there sit on her own for way too long."

My eyes followed him until they landed on Nora. She was sitting at one of the nicer tables that had a perfect view on the street, she was sniffing one of the tulips that was scattered near the glass windows to see if it was real. She frowned in disappointment when she realized it was made of plastic.

I chuckled when I tried to imagine what would happen if I left her alone for a while longer. How long would it take for her to go completely crazy on her own with no one to chat with until she'd drag me over again.

I could feel my dad staring at me again, but this time, it felt like he was trying to bring pieces together, the kind of look he had when my grandma told him to put a random ingredient in a meal and he just had to go with it and think later as to why it was a good idea.

I decided to save him the time from doing that. "She's just a friend," I interjected.

"Maybe you should spend less time in the restaurant working and spend more time with friends, huh?" he asked. "Take some time away from this place."

"Pa, I know you've given up, but I haven't. I'm not going to take a break until I know things are doing well again," I sighed.

I was tired, so tired, but I didn't want to let my dad see it. I knew I was trying to fight my body but staying awake for so long, for doing so much without taking a break. But it was like I was driving a car, and I couldn't press the breaks. I knew way too well that if I stopped the car I might not get to drive on it again, so I just had to keep on driving. Even if I was tired, even if my eyes were fighting to stay open and my body signaled me to sit down and eat properly.

"Everything is under control, and they'll stay this way even if you're taking a short break to eat," he explained, and then looked at Nora again. "I know you don't want to talk about the future of the place, so at least let me talk about your future. You're young, you're supposed to live a little, hang out with friends in clubs or bars or I don't know where. And yes, I think you should sit with that girl, because she came all the way here in this weather, so I am sure she has something important to say."

"She always has something to say," I mumbled.

"What?"

"Nothing Pa," I cleared my throat. "Can we maybe not have this kind of conversation right now? Just trust me, that for now, that I'm pretty content with my life."

"Being content is not the same as being happy," he commented.

I could feel my heart clench by hearing him say it. Thinking about it was one thing, but hearing my own dad say it was a whole different story. My parents tried to find different opportunities to talk about my future and my life, how important it was for me to have a life beside the restaurant, to have fun like most people my age. But what could I say? I couldn't see myself living any other way.

My dad's voice woke me up from my own deep thoughts as he put his hand on my shoulder. "You know, you should be glad I'm the one who's standing here and not your mom. When she hears I saw you with a girl and didn't dig for information, I'm the one she'll come to with complaints."

That made the both of us laugh. We knew one of my mom's favorite hobbies was to gossip with the neighbors, or watch the best reality shows just so she could find more to talk about. So, to get intel on her own son's life? That was a real treat.

"Or, and I'm just suggesting something here, you can decide not to share that information with her," I said, though I knew it was a lost battle.

"I can't hide anything from your mom," he said, and my smile widened when I knew exactly where he was going with this, because I heard that sentence way too many times. "Honesty and transparency, it's part of the reason our marriage has worked for-"

"Twenty years, yeah I know. I celebrated your anniversary with you. Remember when you had me help you bake that cake?" I laughed. "It was a terrible red velvet cake that I tried to make. Maybe I had a future as a waiter, maybe even a barista, but definitely not as a baker."

"It was a delicious cake," he corrected me.

Then he gave one of the waiters the dish and turned back to me, putting his other hand on my shoulder. "Now go to her."

"What about the food?" I asked, trying to fight my dad's strong arms that were leading me to Nora, who thankfully was focused on her phone and didn't see anything that was going on between the two of us.

"I already asked them to make you your favorite pasta, with extra cheese of course." He gave me one last look before he went back to his work.

I scratched the back of my neck and walked slowly to the table near the glass windows and plastic tulips.

I guess a short break couldn't hurt.

CHAPTER 6
Nora

The restaurant looked even more beautiful in the light of day, it felt more alive, too. William looked alive, too. I could see his eyes lighting up when he saw all the customers flood in. It seemed like he had been waiting for this moment for a while, and from the short version of his story, I knew that he was. When my phone rang, I took a deep breath before I answered Alexander's call.

"Hi," I answered, not even bothering to sound excited.

"I expected a bit more enthusiasm," he said.

I knew he didn't take it to heart, but he knew my reasons.

I could hear him walking around, probably in his room, organizing his own private library for the hundredth time maybe.

"From 1 to 10, how mad is he?" I asked while I was playing with my little spoon. It's been three days since Luuk and I last spoke. We never went this long without talking.

"You tell me, I'm the one who's spending the last three days with him reading our morning horoscope, not you," he said, which made me even more upset that I made that stupid comment at dinner.

"Nor, you know I care about you both, you two are my best

friends in the entire universe. Even though we met you later in life, it doesn't feel like it, you just fit right in and we became this unbreakable trio," he said.

There was a *but* coming, there was always a *but*, and I didn't need to be a big reader to know that part was next.

"But sometimes it's tiring being in the middle every time you argue. I swear, you act like two children that need an adult to shake you up and be the voice of reason. I know he can be a bit dramatic, okay? He can take one word and make a bigger deal out of it than it needs to be, but I'm on his side this time."

"I'm on his side, too," I whispered. "I didn't mean to tell him that, I'm just…I was mad that he didn't support me."

"So maybe you should have a talk and get past it? You can apologize, he can tell you he couldn't live without you as his horoscope partner, and I can get back to eating breakfast peacefully, what do you say about that?" he asked, and just by hearing his voice, I could tell he was more eager than all of us to let this stupid situation be swept under the rug.

"Fine, I'll join you two for a drink tomorrow morning," I said. "Happy now?"

It was unbelievable how Xander was a part of a fictional world half of the time, because he was more aware of the reality around him then Luuk and I would ever be.

I could hear a sigh of relief from the other side of the phone. "Yes."

I sipped from my basically empty drink. Unfortunately, William was too busy with customers to make me another one. But maybe it was for the best. "So, tell me… What did my horoscope say I should expect from today?"

"I'm sure that even if you read it, you would still be sitting in that restaurant, using your never-ending stubbornness to convince them to take you to work for them," he laughed. I wished I could tell him he was wrong, but my friends knew me better than anyone.

"Well, I have more than stubbornness to offer. I have charms, I have wits, I know how to get to people, you know?" I said proudly as I smiled to one of the waiters as he passed by me, the smell of the dishes he held got to me and made me regret the fact I finished my dish so fast.

"I didn't say you didn't, I just think you can be hell stubborn when you want to be. Whoever this guy is, take it easy on him," he explained, then I heard someone talk to him in the background. I didn't hear him for a few moments, till he reached the phone again. "Hey, Nor, I gotta go, but we'll talk tomorrow morning, okay? I'm dying to hear how it all went down."

"Okay, bye." I ended the call and put my phone back on the table.

I used the rest of my time alone to write notes in the green notebook I brought with me. I always had a thing with lists, I felt like my mind couldn't contain all the information and ideas I had in my head only. When I wrote it down I found order and could think clearly.

No more plastic tulips, need to find good real ones ASAP!

Try ~~more~~ all dishes from the menu because that chicken was amazing Valentines Day event at the restaurant?

Find out if William's coffee has a secret ingredient. Cinnamon maybe?

Just when I was about to write the next point, I heard steps coming closer and looked up to see William who had stopped by my table.

He looked at the notebook and pen I was holding before he went back to stare at me. "I was about to ask if you want company, but it seems like you always find a way to entertain yourself, don't you?"

I closed up my notebook and motioned to him for the free chair in front of me. "You're right about that, but I rather be entertained with people, than be by myself."

He chuckled, but didn't argue with me and sat down. When I scanned his face, I noticed the same marks and details I saw the first night. He had beautiful blue eyes but they were a little more tired looking. The same shade of worry and uncertainty appeared behind them, and all throughout his body. He might've been tall and strong, but when he sat on that chair, we were basically at eye level. He let out a sigh, as if he hasn't had the chance to sit for any amount of time.

My heart ached when I realized the situation of the place was no joke. He didn't take a break when customers appeared, he tried to hang on the momentum no matter how he was feeling physically.

He thanked the person who gave him a dish of pasta with what seemed like an endless amount of cheese. When he felt my gaze on him he stopped twirling his pasta. "What?"

I tried to ignore the nice smell and focus on him. "You weren't kidding when you said the situation is bad, didn't you?"

"Nora," he let out a breath. "That night...I was tired from the day, and my studies, and after the conversation with my dad, I just needed to let everything out. Everything is okay, really, don't worry about it."

I smiled bitterly. "You know, the last time I told someone *everything was okay* with me, I had a complete breakdown a few days later." When he looked at me in question, I shook my head. "Long story. What I'm trying to say is that it wasn't a one-time thing, seeing you tired. You seem more tired than you did that night actually, and no matter how good your coffee is, I can still see it."

"Nora..."

"What I was trying to tell you in that message was that I want to help you," I said, and motioned with my hand to his plate. Though he was confused, he complied and started to eat, while paying attention to what I had to say.

"Look, when I entered this restaurant, I didn't know a thing about it, not until you told me parts of your story, history, your family...I could see how much it all means to you, and how much potential this place has. I mean, I've been to many bars and restaurants in my life, believe me, but I don't get to see many places like this one. A place that pays respect to family and tradition."

Something told me that my words took him by surprise, and struck him—straight to the heart. He put down his fork and his eyes met mine, his voice was close to breaking. "Thank you for saying that."

"You don't need to thank me, I only tell the truth." I smiled genuinely at him. "I don't want to see you and your family lose something that you clearly love so much. You remember when I told you briefly about my parents, that they don't want me to have a job right now and that I should focus on one thing in life at the moment?"

He nodded. "Yeah, of course I remember."

My lips curled up a bit. "Well, I thought about it, and it would be kind of hard for them to be against me working for something, that I'm not getting paid for and it doesn't officially identify as a job, right?"

"I mean, I guess." He took another taste of the pasta. "I'm sorry, Nora, but I don't see where you're going with this."

I laughed and tried to slow down, caught up in my enthusiasm. "I think your restaurant has a potential to reach so many people, but you didn't use the right tools and ways to reach them. I'm offering my help to use these tools. As you know already, I have classes in marketing and social media, and all of that. I can open an Instagram profile for your restaurant, upload stories about it—dishes, pictures, everything. Obviously not just Instagram, we'll open an official site or the place, a TikTok account and the best part is that I can plan events here and use my abilities for a good use." Before he could think of denying that idea, I cleared my throat. "Just imagine this, Valentine's Day, romance is in the air, loving couples are looking for the best meal to eat on this special day, and then bam!"

"*BAM?*" he chuckled, but by the way he looked at me with a gleam in his eyes, I knew he was too deep in this conversation to walk away, he was too intrigued, and might even want to hear the rest.

"The search is over, they found a beautiful restaurant in the middle of the city, with amazing chicken and-" I stopped and took my own fork. "Excuse me for doing this, Can I...?" I asked when I motioned to his plate.

He pushed it closer to me. I took a bite of his pasta and when I put it in my mouth, I closed my eyes in utter joy. It was better than the pasta I ate in that Italian restaurant I went to with Luuk and Xander.

He smiled and put his hand under his chin when he looked at me while I was trying to put into words how that pasta made me feel.

"And they taste this incredible pasta, just like this, with all the cheese, and then they enjoy a curated playlist we pull off with all sorts of romantic songs. We scatter a few balloons, or some pink tulips, and there you go: you have a way to reach an amazing number of customers. Of course, I'll post everything to social media after with the best hashtags."

"Of course," he repeated, and I could tell he wanted to laugh again.

"Laugh if you want, but this shit works. I wouldn't have that many classes about social media if it didn't bring results," I said. "Besides, you said you had ideas of your own, just think of both of our ideas combined."

He looked through the big glass windows, at the old buildings, some local restaurants and people riding their bikes as if it didn't just rain ten minutes ago.

"When my grandparents opened the place, the business went so well. The customers weren't just customers, it felt like they surrounded themselves with a community of their own. It was beautiful to see, especially as a kid with a lot of extra energy, there was always someone around or something to do," he said with a certain sadness in his voice.

"What happened?"

"It wasn't enough anymore. My grandma passed away, my grandpa was determined to keep the place alive in her memory but he died from his own grief only two years later. My parents promised to keep this tradition and this place alive for both of them. At the beginning, it was easy, the restaurant thrived with people who knew my grandparents, but as the time went by, people passed away, people grew up and left the city for all kinds of reasons, and then new, young, and ambitious people opened their own restaurants nearby."

"It sounds like a lot to deal with," I said and moved my chair closer to put my hand on his shoulder to try to comfort him.

He looked down at me and put his hand on mine before he let go. "Look, Nora, I appreciate everything you're trying to do, but I can't let you do so much for us, especially when I know there is a slight chance of it working at this point. I think it's better for me to deal with my parents and this entire situation on my own."

"I know we have only known each other for about a week, but I expected you to realize what kind of friendship you got yourself into. I'm not letting you deal with it on your own, especially when I know your parents have given up and it's only you who keeps fighting for this." I looked at him, trying to figure out what was running through his head. When he stayed silent, I sighed. "I don't mind helping, I'm basically a bored student that has nothing to do but study and hang out with my friends. I'm dying to have something else to do, something to post or market. You will be helping me more than I'll be helping you, actually. You will help my friends, too; they can't deal with me anymore."

"Is that so?" he asked quietly. "I can see why."

He side eyed me to see how I would react, and his tense muscles relaxed under my hand when he heard me laugh.

"Oh, would you look at that, he has a sense of humor," I joked. "Come on, what do you say? We can give it one week of trying to see how it works out. If it's a complete disaster I promise to leave you alone and not bother you about this ever again."

"Ever? Sounds like a bold choice of words."

"Sometimes we need to be bold to make a statement," I said back. "I wouldn't have come here and offered you help if I didn't think I could do it."

"I believe you," he mumbled while looking at me. "We barely know each other, but I believe you."

"Good," I whispered.

His eyes roamed over the restaurant and stopped on a man who was talking with one of the waiters. By his light brown hair and facial features that reminded me of William's, I could easily assume that that was his dad.

"Okay, let's do it," he turned back to me.

Charm and wit. Never doubt these abilities.

"But I get to decide when my parents know about all of this," he continued. "They have a hard time accepting new ideas, so we'll have to do it in secret at the beginning. They'll need to see results in their own eyes to believe anything can change."

It felt like he was talking more to himself than me, as if it was his way to convince himself that it was a smart way to go, that he did things right.

"Things we'll change," I promised him before I could remind myself there were promises that shouldn't be made so lightly.

"Thank you, Nora." He turned to look at me for a second

before looking down at his pasta again. "I know that it might not seem like I'm grateful for all that you just said, but I really do appreciate it. I have a hard time showing on the outside what I feel inside."

"You don't need to show me anything, I can see everything I need to." I smiled at him, and when he smiled back, I knew it was just the beginning of a beautiful friendship.

CHAPTER 7
William

I should've felt bad, even a little bit for lying to my parents and being secretive. I was never this type of person. I was always a little more quiet of a person, but I didn't know how to hide or bend the truth. But now, instead of feeling nauseous, I felt relieved. When I was standing in line with Nora to pick up tulips from the Museumplein's constructed garden, I couldn't imagine spending this day differently, or wasting any time feeling guilty.

Later, I reminded myself. *When things work out, and the business is saved, they'll understand.*

Standing close beside me, Nora looked around at the different tulips in wonder. "Why January?"

"Huh?"

"Look, I know I'm not a florist, or an expert about flowers, but aren't most flowers supposed to bloom in the spring?" she asked. "It's a money thing, isn't it? All of these beautiful colors are just a way to make us buy more flowers or something. I have to say it's a good marketing plan." Her eyes lit up. "We should do it with the restaurant, too. We should let people have a free taste for them, they get addicted to the food, and just like that you get new customers."

I was tempted to keep quiet till it was our turn to go and pick free tulips, just to see what she might have to say next, what idea will pop out of nowhere. We were standing in a long line that you could see only on national days like this, or when someone handed out free stuff.

"You only drank that one cup of coffee I made you in the morning, right?" I asked, and when she folded her arms, I laughed. "Hey, I'm just checking."

"So, it *is* a money thing?"

I smiled when I discovered once again how persistent that girl was. "This whole event is organized by the Dutch tulip growers; they want to promote the start of the tulip flower season. Though, you are right. If you go to a tulip field in the spring, it's a whole other kind of experience. Tulips are always beautiful, but in the spring they have a look that is indescribable. I can promise you that much, I've seen it more than once."

I thought of myself as a kid, riding a bike, watching the tulips blooming under the summer sun. God, what would I give to go back to that exact moment in time.

"You went to see tulip fields with your grandma, didn't you?" she asked quietly.

Just like that, the memory, the colors, my grandma's smile disappeared in an instant and I went back to reality, to standing in line to get a free bouquet of tulips.

I shifted my attention to her, trying to figure out what gave it away.

"Your eyes," she said softly, not tearing her eyes away from me. "They're brighter when you talk about your family, but your grandma specifically. I could tell you were tired when we talked for the first time, but the moment you started talking about her, your eyes lit up."

I took in her words, feeling how the air came out of my lungs slowly.

"I haven't gone to see tulips since she passed away, not even with my grandpa," I admitted, not stopping to wonder why I was doing that. "It was too painful to think of going without her."

"But you're doing it now." She slightly leaned into me, and our shoulders brushed.

There was a short silence between us, like both of us could sense the shift of conversation. It wasn't light and fun like I hoped it would be, like this day was supposed to go.

I cleared my throat and put my hands in the pockets of my jeans. "Well, you started it. You said that you can't stand the plastic decorations, and that if we chose to go with a certain theme for the restaurant, we need to commit to it. If we use flowers, we better use real ones."

"Or..." she said. "You looked for a good enough excuse to get out and experience the wonders of the world and live a little for once. You can't be in that restaurant all day, and then spend the rest of the day stuck in your head, or in your books while you study for hours. Do you even have time to see your friends with your busy schedule?"

"Not all friends need to see each other every day," I said, and when she tilted her head, I shifted my legs from side to side. "Or...week."

"Sounds like an excuse," she commented.

We walked a few more steps forward, and when we stopped again, I turned to her. "Well, if you're such a strong believer in maintaining a close relationship with your friends, then why did you come here with me instead of meeting with your friends this morning?" I asked, and before she could ask me where I got that information, I pointed at her phone. "I heard you talk with your friend earlier at the restaurant. Xander I think? You made some excuse for being busy with an assignment and that you would meet him the day after." She turned quiet. And when she looked at the ground, I bit the inside of my cheek. "Sorry, I didn't mean to meddle, it's none of my business."

"No, William, you did nothing wrong," she said in a weak voice. "I was supposed to apologize to my friend today, we had a silly argument, I said something I didn't mean. I…I was mocking him for wanting to find his twin flame."

"Twin flame?" I asked. I was trying to think if I ever read about it, but most of the things I read were numbers and business related.

"It's an astrology thing. Twin flame is supposed to be a soul connection. It's a strong and intense connection with a person who's your other half, like a soulmate, or so my friend Luuk believes. He thinks that when you meet this person, all of the stars will disappear, and that will be the only person in the universe you feel drawn to."

"Your friend Luuk sounds like a hopeless romantic," I said, finding myself eager to learn more about him, about her other friends, of all the people and stories that related to this special human called Nora Tuinstra. Yeah, I remembered her full name from that one time she mentioned it.

"He is. God, I can't even count the number of dates he's been on his short time on this earth. He's very active on many dating apps, but it's never because he is the kind of guy that wants to sleep around with the men he meets or have short flings. He wants love; a real, romantic one. I admire this quality about him, I don't want him to think that I don't, or that it's stupid in any way, because it isn't."

I nodded, while listening carefully to her. I could tell she meant it with all her heart, I could tell every time we talked that she was a genuine person, and if not genuine, then an honest one. I didn't need weeks or months of friendship to know that it was written all over her.

"Then explain it to him like you just explained it to me," I told her.

She looked around at the tulips, as if she found comfort in them. And understandably so, because the world knows that I found comfort in them, too.

"You're right." She nodded. "I guess I just feel bad. It feels like I projected my own view on love when I said what I said, and the stress over my parents and their thoughts on me working didn't make me want to consider the delivery of words all that much either."

She got so lost in her own thoughts that she didn't notice the kids who were running around the line, chasing each other. I put my arm around her and pulled her to me so she wouldn't trip over. She looked down at the kids that passed by us and then up at me, till her eyes met mine. They looked greener than usual today. Maybe it was because of the flowers around.

I knew I shouldn't ask more; I wasn't the guy who asked many questions, and looked for answers, but for some strange reason, I always looked to hear Nora's answers. She was so good at getting information out of me, she barely had to try, I wondered if I could do the same.

"So...what is your view on love then?" I asked.

Her lips curled up, and despite what I might've thought, she didn't hesitate to answer. "Different from Luuk's, but not that different." She laughed when my eyes narrowed. "I know I've been very open with you, I am open about many things, but we'll need to know each other for a bit longer if you want to hear the real answer."

"I'm okay with that," I said. That was interesting. She didn't mind opening up about her friends, or her parents, or her hopes and dreams, but when I mentioned the word *love* she took a step back.

I let down my arms from her body and stepped away when they told us we could go in. Nora walked quickly inside; there was a gravitational pull between her and the pink tulips. When she reached her destination she turned her head to me. "Are you coming?"

Even though I knew Nora was the one standing there, my brain was pulling its tricks on me again. Maybe it was because it was the first time in years that I've been in anything similar to a real tulip field, maybe it was my tiredness, but instead of Nora, all I could see was my grandma. I saw her standing here, with gray hair and light blue eyes, but still filled with so much life and the will to pluck the tulips, and she wasn't going to let her weak bones stop her.

Are you coming?

That was my grandma's way of telling me I was much younger than her, so the least I could do was keep up with her before we had to go back home.

"William?" I heard Nora's voice, much closer.

I blinked my eyes shut.. Just like that, my grandma was gone, the open field was gone, and I was back in Amsterdam. I looked down at Nora, she pressed her lips together in worry, like she didn't know what to say.

"Maybe it wasn't such a good idea coming here, we can go to a regular flower shop and buy some tulips as a beginning. It won't matter to people if it came from a field or a shop. You won't even have to come; I can go by myself and-"

I put my hand on her arm. "No, I want to stay and pick up tulips like I said we would." I stopped to look down at the white tulip behind me. "What about white? Very classy color."

She tilted her head. "I like classy, I have no problem with classy. Or white, but I feel like we should get something more colorful, you know? Something that catches the eye of a person walking on the street, or a color that looks nice on an Instagram story. Something that gives off a certain vibe, if you get where I'm going with this?"

I chuckled, she was trying so hard not to offend my poor choice. "Something like pink?"

"Pink, purple, yellow. Oh, yellow is fun and cheerful, we definitely need a yellow," she said.

"So, people will get a cheerful vibe through their phone screen or looking up as they're walking the streets and they see some yellow tulips and think, *wow, we should try this place*?" I asked to see if I was understanding how she wanted to approach this whole situation.

"I swear William, I'm going to turn you into a marketing genius by the end of this," she promised as I followed after her to choose nice pink tulips.

"The end of this?" I asked.

"You know, when your restaurant is thriving again, you are able to have some time to live and stop waiting tables, and me..." She sat on the ground when she found the tulips she wanted. "Well, I guess I don't have a plan of where I'll be at the end of this. Hopefully my parents will realize how serious I can be when I commit to something. I guess you won't need me anymore when our secret plan works out as we hoped."

My heart ached that she talked about the end when we were only at the beginning. Maybe I had my own plans, and I could understand this ideal future she was picturing, but I couldn't picture myself not needing her help with marketing, or choosing the right type of tulip, or the right thing to say to new customers. I learned a lot already in my business classes, but it was obvious she was the creative one between the two of us.

I brushed my fingers over the delicate petals but stopped when I noticed she was switching her glances between me and the flowers. "What is it, Nora?"

She opened her mouth and closed it, then did it again. "I have more to ask you." She paused. "But I don't know if I should, because it's about your grandma. After what you said, and after seeing this place, I don't want to bring anything up that you're not ready to talk about."

I looked at her through the petals. "You can ask, and if I don't feel ready or comfortable to answer, I won't."

That seemed to ease her mind. She nodded and picked up one of the tulips. "Your restaurant, there are the plastic decorations at the tables, but there's also a painting of tulips hanging on the wall. The whole place has a sweet, floral scent to it. Out of all of the flowers in the world, why did your grandparents choose tulips?"

She thought her question would bring back sad memories, but it only made me smile when I was reminded of the romantic and pure side of my grandparents' love story.

"My grandpa, he courted my grandma for a while. He used tulips to show her his love, and she finally said yes and agreed to go on a date with him, or I should say *go steady* with him. But even when they were seeing each other, and then eventually engaged, and then married with children, tulips continued to play a big part of their life."

My lips curled when I was reminded of all the times my grandpa snuck a kiss to my grandma, thinking no one noticed, or brought her a tulip after a long day of work.

"I always say it's a shame that my grandma didn't write her quotes down somewhere. She had wise, philosophical things to say about everything, especially when it came to flowers. She used to say that love can go two ways."

When I paused to pick up a tulip, Nora kept staring at me, as if she couldn't believe I dared to stop at this point of the story. "What did your grandma say about love?"

"She said love can go two ways. It can be like a battlefield, where the flowers you grow die out because of the lack of effort and the will to work on the relationship. When you don't show up and pull out the energy to grow tulips, they'll eventually die, like the relationship itself."

"Was your grandma a poet by any chance?" she asked.

"Cause this shit sounds dark. Not that I don't agree with her, relationships can die more quickly than we would think."

My body froze as I heard the sadness in her voice. She kept on picking tulips and enjoyed the bits of sun in the sky, but I could still hear it, I could notice it, even if she didn't plan to, she just confessed something.

"Yeah, they can," I agreed quietly. Whether I liked it or not, I knew what an end of a relationship looked like.

"What is the other way?" she asked.

I let out a breath and motioned to her to look around us, at the colors, and people, and blue sky above us. "Like a tulip field."

"Battlefield and a tulip field, your grandma sure knew how to play with words," she laughed.

"Yeah, she does..." I cleared my throat. "She did."

"Anyway, she said that the right kind of love is the one where your willing to work for, put effort into, it might take time, there might be arguments, but in the end you learn to grow, and before you know it, you grow old together and find yourselves in the middle of a tulip field."

Nora looked around and smiled, like she saw the place we were standing at in a new, different way. Her eyes gleamed when she turned back to me. "It's beautiful, it seems like your grandma was kind of a hopeless romantic."

I nodded, seeing through my mind all the flowers, all the bouquets, all the small and big gestures, all the hard work that was put into one relationship. "A true hopeless romantic."

"What about you?" Nora asked. "What is your view on love?"

I smirked, because of course after all this story she had a way to bring the question back to me.

"Different from my grandma's, but not that different."

"Very funny." She rolled her eyes.

I looked through the tulips and picked up the one that stole my attention the most, it wasn't in the boldest shade or the tallest, but it was beautiful. I handed it to Nora who was looking down at it in confusion.

"Who knows, maybe you'll get the real answer one day," I said, and kept staring down at the tulip.

My fingers wrapped around the stem, my hand shook a little from the slight worry it was stupid, offering her a tulip, thinking she would take it that lightly.

But before I backed away and took the tulip with me, she held it and then pulled it close to her nose to let the sweet smell wrap all her senses.

"I'm okay with that." Her lips curled and she put the tulip in the bouquet she created, one out of many more.

CHAPTER 8
Nora

Xander and Luuk weren't at our usual hang out place in the morning. It didn't stop me from drinking my coffee and saying hi to some friend from class. The only difference was I didn't read my daily horoscope. Instead of trying to figure out what my two friends were up to that none of them could answer the phone, I walked towards Luuk's apartment. These two loved spending some of their time there, whether it was to talk, or for Luuk to try one of his new cocktails on Xander, just for the fun of it.

His place was located in one of the hotspots of the city. He literally woke up in the morning and saw the entire city through his windows, with the perfect view on the Dam square and all the tunnels and city life as we know it, with people riding their bikes during the day and going to bars for a nice drink in the evening.

It's not like I wasn't appreciative of my own life with my parents, we lived close to the beach, which I was grateful for in the summer season. It was about jealousy and adoration all at once. I wished I could be more like him, more independent.

I knew that I should live in the moment, not think too far

into the future, but I couldn't wait for the time I lived in my own apartment, where I could decorate it as I pleased, living with a roommate or maybe even a future boyfriend, and I'd wake up in the morning to work the full-time job I waited so long to have...

I put my bike at its usual spot and picked up the bouquet of tulips I had bought this morning, and then knocked on the door.

I had to knock a few more times before I heard steps approach. When the door was finally opened, I got to meet Luuk in my own eyes, a very tired version of Luuk. Despite the hour, he was wearing PJs and held a mug in his hand with the quote "*Good Morning Sunshine*" that he got on sale.

"You are aware it's ten in the morning, right?" I asked and entered the apartment before he could stop me, not that he could in his current state. He leaned against the wall as if he was going to fall if he wouldn't hold onto something. "You'll miss your class if you won't get ready anytime soon."

"I don't need class. Who needs to study when nothing matters, when love doesn't even exist?" he asked in his own dramatic way. "I don't need you here either, you were right. Finding your twin flame is impossible in this city with all these gorgeous blue-eyed boys with heart of stone."

I put my stuff on the small round dining table near the kitchen and took the mug he held.

"Hey, what are you doing-" he tried to steal the mug back when I took a sip of what I predicted to be his terrible mixture of leaves he made to deal with hangovers.

"How drunk?" I asked him.

"It's none of your business," he muttered, and when he saw I wasn't going to give him back his mug, he went to look for another mug to prepare a new drink.

"Why don't you deal with a hangover like a normal human being, you know you can just drink water and take a pill to deal with it and the effect would probably be much more helpful than this weird herbal tea. What did you put there anyway? It tastes like crap."

"Don't mock my tea, there's a secret ingredient. The strong taste can make any hangover disappear," he said as he prepared it all over again, and I had to back away to not smell it.

"Or it can make you lose any will to live, but I guess if it helps you... Who am I to judge?" I mumbled as I looked around his messy apartment.

His place was often messy, he always had dishes or clothes scattered around, but this time it was messy, even for him.

The floor was covered with clean clothes, some were still on the hangers. There were glasses with what seemed like a homemade cocktail, and an open bottle of wine near them.

Maybe what confused me most was his small blue sofa, where Xander was sleeping. Because the sofa was too small for his figure, his legs were hanging in the air, like he was a character in one of the stories he loved to read so much and found himself in the middle of the strangest scene I encountered lately.

I turned sharply back to Luuk, but he held up his hand. "Before you say anything, I didn't let him drink. I was maybe sad and had to cheer myself up, but I'm not stupid, I know he prefers not to drink because of his diabetes, and I wasn't going to start calculating how much sugar these cocktails contain."

"Oh, cocktails, how nice," I muttered. "Why didn't you call me? It seems like you had a fun party of two over here, it's a shame I had to miss all the fun."

"Because I didn't want to hear you say I told you so, happy now?" he asked and checked on Xander to make sure he didn't wake up from the noise. He took another sip of his tea and sighed. "I didn't want to hear it, I just wanted to hang out with a friend and say whatever was on my heart at that moment without having to deal with judgment or pettiness."

"I wouldn't have judged you, Luuk," I said softly and stepped closer to him.

"Yes you are," he stepped back, like he was offended by it. "You're judging me now; I can see it in your eyes Nor. You are many things, but you were never the best at hiding emotions."

I pressed my lips together and looked around us, trying to think how to navigate in this situation. "What happened, Luuk?"

He sat on the counter and moved his legs back and forth while wrapping his hands around the mug. "He said he wanted a future with someone, but that someone isn't me. How did he define it? Oh, yeah, he said I was too much, too extra, and that I was too high maintenance for him and he couldn't breathe. We were supposed to have this romantic night here. I tried all these outfits and made him these stupid cocktails to make it special, but he didn't even bother to show up, only had the nerve to call me on the phone to end it."

He looked down at his tea, he blinked his eyes to hide away the tears, but I could see a few slipped away down his cheeks. I hated seeing him like this, so…devastated.

I went to sit by his side and put my arm around him. To my surprise, he didn't fight it and let his head fall on my shoulder.

"I feel so stupid, Nor." He let out a shaky breath.

"You're not stupid, you just haven't found your person yet, and that's okay. You're only eighteen Luuk, all of us."

"Hate to break it to you, Nor, but we're almost nineteen, and nineteen sounds so much less fun than eighteen."

"If you're going to be this bitter, I'll leave you alone here to clean this whole place up and wake up Xander." I smiled when I noticed his lips curled up into a smile. "Luuk, you have no idea how amazing you are, you really don't."

"Keep going," he mumbled.

I laughed. "I'm serious. I know we had that stupid argument, but I realized I said what I said because I could never be this way. I could never love that hard, be some type of hopeless romantic who wants to do everything to make a single person happy. You set all of this up for a date with a guy and made fucking cocktails for him. The only guy I've had in my life left because I couldn't be that person. I was always career focused, even as sixteen years old, and I'm just as career focused now as I was then. Sometimes I feel like that's the longest relationship I'll ever have, that I'll ever know."

"So, no romance with the Troy Bolton clone?" he asked and I pulled his head away from my shoulder instantly.

"I'm trying to apologize here, can you at least pretend to have a sweet friend moment and hug me before you switch subjects like this?" I giggled. "He's not his clone, and you two have to stop with that, I don't want you to call him Troy by accident when you meet him."

"What about on purpose?" he asked and I rolled my eyes.

"We're talking about you now, not me." I stopped to look at the mess around us. I pointed to the floor. "What is this? What happened? Why is the floor covered with clean clothes, and why is Xander sleeping on the sofa and not on your extra mattress that could actually contain his whole body. He looks like Alice in Wonderland after she had too much tea with The Mad Hatter."

"I took a few pictures of it when I woke up," he laughed, but stopped when I stared at him. "I know it sounds ridiculous now, but after a few drinks, I started to pull out clothes for my room and showed them to Xander. I tried to use his help to decide which clothes to throw away and which to keep for my future dates. I ended up showing him all of them, and then I drank one of the cocktails. I don't remember much, but at some point he fell asleep and I passed out on my bed."

"Wow, you really know how to keep things entertaining when you're drunk…" I kept staring at the floor.

"Sorry for not inviting you, Nor, but I guess we needed to have our own guy's night. Besides, I'm sure you had a great time with—" He paused.

"You forgot his name, didn't you?" I laughed. "You called

him Troy so many times in your head that you forgot his real name."

"In my defense, it has been emotional 24 hours, give me some slack," he said and when he finished his tea, he took the mug I held and started drinking from it as well.

"Emotional is one way to describe it," I whispered as I stared at Xander, wondering if he would need us to find him a princess to wake him up from his sleep.

"Oh, please, do tell." He sipped from his drink. "I can't wait to hear all the tea I missed."

I stared at the mug, and then at him. "Funny."

"Come on, what happened? Did you turn the restaurant upside down? What did you make the poor guy do for you, besides coffee?"

I chuckled; Luuk really did live for the gossip. The heartbroken guy that opened the door for me was long gone. "I'm helping him, but I promised to do it in secret for now, until he's ready to tell his parents."

"Secrets, oh, I like it, so mysterious. There's something so sexy about mysterious guys," he said.

"He's not mysterious at all, actually." I smiled when I thought of the few times we hung out together to talk about future plans for the restaurant and get his approval on posts I made. "He claims to be shy, and I can see him being quiet at times but he was pretty open with me, even though I could see it was so hard for him to share parts of his story. God, Luuk, if you were there with us when we picked those tulips, his eyes lit up, his blue eyes got so bright."

"Wait, hold on, you went to pick up tulips?" Luuk asked, and just then noticed the ones I brought with me. He jumped from the counter to look closely at them.

"Beautiful, aren't they?" I said. "I picked a few white ones, but it's only because of William. He says it's a classic color, though I don't really see it."

"You went to pick up tulips?" he asked again.

"Yeah, I saw these plastic decorations in the restaurant, and I told him that to show something really authentic and part of the story of the place he has to use real ones, at least for the rest of the week. We're doing this kind of a contest to see if I'm right or not, though I think it's obvious that in this case I'm totally right. People love flowers. Besides, you should've seen how beautiful the tulips were when we went to pick them. So much color, and beauty, I could understand why some people find tulips so romantic. Just think how sweet it is to give someone a flower to show them your feelings for them without expressing it in words." I spoke up so fast that I barely noticed the weird expression on Luuk's face. "I know it's not like your tea, but I guessed it would be a nice gesture to make instead of just saying I'm sorry."

"No, it's not that," he said and walked towards me. "I just never saw you talk this way."

"'This way' how?" I smiled. "Like a true marketing genius? I know, I'm still at the start of my career, and I know you're worried that I'm getting too ahead of myself, but it's going to work. I trust my ideas with my whole heart."

"I never heard you talk this way about flowers," he said while examining my face. "You always saw flowers as a decoration for your events or parties, but you never cared too much about their meaning, how romantic they can be. Honestly, I haven't heard you talk about romance in what feels like forever."

"It's not me, it's William. And his grandparents. They showed each other their love through tulips," I explained. "Since I came home yesterday, all I could think of is how I could show this story in the restaurant itself. The whole place started because of his grandparents. Sure, they use family recipes for the meals they serve there, but I wish there was a way to show more of who his grandparents were, more of who his grandma was. I wish…" My eyes stopped on the mug he held in his hand.

"What?" he realized I was staring again. "I know I was pretty grumpy this morning and not so sunshine-y, but if you come here tomorrow..." he kept on talking, but at this point I wasn't listening to him anymore.

I jumped from the counter and went to look in my bag from my notebook. I started to quickly sketch the idea that went through my head before it disappeared and wrote down my notes.

"You can at least warn me when it happens, so I don't end up talking to myself," he commented, and when I tried to peek at my notes, I already had closed my notebook and put it back in my bag.

"I can't control it," I giggled.

When I put my bag over my shoulder, I went to give Luuk a big hug. "I really am happy we solved everything, it was a nightmare not talking, and spending my mornings alone with my coffee."

"Yeah, I'm happy too..." he mumbled. "Now can you explain to me what's going on or are you going to keep me guessing?"

"I just got an idea," I walked through the door.

"Yeah, I got that part, but what was it?" he asked as he followed me with his eyes.

"I can't, I have to go plan everything before I offer the idea to William," I opened the door, "Good luck with waking up the sleepy beauty over there. My advice, don't let him try out the tea."

"If you offend my tea one more time—"

I closed the door before he finished that sentence.

CHAPTER 9
William

It was weird sitting in the restaurant on Sunday morning to eat breakfast with my parents, but my mom wanted us to have family time together, and it seemed like she knew that I wouldn't show up if we weren't going to actually sit down and interact with one another.

It wasn't like I didn't show up or cared about our time as a family, I loved the idea of us sitting together, but lately it was tiring. The fun, innocent talks about my studies and life in general eventually all led to talks about the future of the restaurant and them trying endlessly to show me they were making the right decision by potentially selling.

That's why this time I asked my best friend to join me so they wouldn't be able to go too far into the topic, which saved me from lying more than I already do the planning going on with Nora.

I looked down at my phone screen and smiled when I scrolled through the pictures she sent me for approval before posting them on any social media account. The first ones were pictures of the interior of the restaurant and the different dishes we make, the kind of pictures you could find on any restaurant site or account, but when I kept scrolling, I realized she managed to take a few pictures of me working. I zoomed on one and chuckled.

All this time, I thought she waited patiently for me to prepare her coffee, but apparently it was her perfect chance to take pictures of me. Some were of me making the coffee, some focused on my hands or the mug I was holding, but most of them focused on my face. I bit my lip as I tried to fight my smile. No one ever took photos of me before, and the thought of seeing how happy and calm I was through her eyes, made my heart flutter.

I didn't blame her for taking pictures without telling me. I know that if she asked, I wouldn't be too eager to cooperate.

"I know what you're thinking Nora, the answer is no." I typed quickly and looked up to make sure none of my parents noticed that I was busier on my chat with Nora than our family breakfast.

My mom had a strict no phone rule, and though I was old enough to argue on the topic, I was trying to respect this one rule.

Nora answered quickly.

NORA

Don't you see the potential we have over here? Statistics show that people are more likely to buy a product, or in this case go to a restaurant, if they know the face behind the business.

ME

I get your view on this, as a marketing student and all of that, but I hate to see pictures of myself. You should've seen how quickly I grew annoyed with graduation pictures; it was a nightmare sitting in front of the photographer with that blue background, I just wanted to run away as fast as I could.

She typed back in an instant.

> **NORA**
> How did that picture turn out?

> **ME**
> If I could burn it, I would've.

> **NORA**
> I'm sure you looked cute, like you look in the photos I took. Well, no, on second hand, you don't look cute, you look handsome, okay? There's nothing more appealing than a guy who can cook, or make a good coffee, or serve you a dish with a charming smile. Luckily for you, you can do it all.

My cheeks flushed when I read her words carefully, once, and then twice. I knew she said compliments were just compliments, I had to remind myself of that, because I could easily find it as her way of flirting with me.

But when she talked about me that way I had a whole other thought in my head, and they were leading me to treacherous paths. It made me think like it meant more, like she felt more than she showed, that we could be more than we were.

"Did I make it too spicy again?" my mom asked as she handed me a cup of water, which I gladly took from her.

I coughed. "What do you mean?"

"Your cheeks are red," she pointed out.

My mind went blank when I went to sip from the cold water.

"William, is everything okay with you?" my dad added as I kept drinking, desperate to get more of the cold drink.

"I'm fine," I shrugged.

"You've been quiet the entire breakfast. Is it because of the restaurant? Are you still mad at us?" she asked, and in her own motherly way, I was this close to confessing everything to her like I did when I was a little kid and had a bad day in school or got a bad grade. "I thought you saw our side on this, your dad told me about the girl that started showing up here lately, the sweet girl with the braid. What was her name again?"

"Nora," I said as I stared at my dad, not that I thought he would be able to keep that one piece of information from her.

I hoped for a salvation, and maybe for once my prayers had been answered, because my best friend walked through the door with a bag of food in his hand. His dark curly hair was messy, like he was rushed. It wasn't an unusual case with Ethan, showing up late, because he often got caught up with his astronomy research and books.

"Hey, everyone. Sorry I'm late, been watching stars all night for one of my astronomy classes," he said and went over to hug my mom and shake my dad's hand before he sat near me. "I know you're the food experts in here, but I hope my cheesecake could make a good enough apology."

"Ethan, don't be silly. You didn't need to bring anything, we're just glad you could join us. Seems like it's been forever since we saw you and Will spending time together," my mom smiled at him, and then her eyes opened wide, like she was having a revelation. "Is it because of the girl?"

I groaned when I realized my mom wasn't going to let that one theory go, and now neither did Ethan. Like the only reason Ethan and I wouldn't hang out was because of girls, and dates. Like Oasis didn't become my second home.

"There's a girl?" Ethan joined her enthusiasm. "That's why you've barely hung out with me lately, because of a girl?"

"It's not like that," I mumbled. "Dad, please tell them she's just a friend."

"I don't know about that son, I saw how you were looking at her, and you gave her tulips."

"Tulips?" Ethan prepared himself a sandwich with some chocolate. "I thought you stopped going to a tulip field since…"

"I did stop," I clarified before any of them could reach the wrong conclusions. "It was the National Tulip Day, and she…she wanted to see real tulips, not like the plastic decorations we have here, so I took her to see them. Besides, how could I miss such a great deal of having a bouquet of tulips for free?"

"Well, whatever is going on between you two, I'm glad you have her by your side. Besides Ethan, of course." My mom's blue eyes softened. "You've been in a bad mood because of the restaurant situation, but since she came you've been smiling more, you've seemed more at ease at home. I know it's hard to understand our decision, but we're glad to see you've been mature enough to support us, you'll see it's for the best."

I looked down at my plate, because how could I look my mom directly in the eyes and tell her I didn't get over it, I would never make peace with their decision. This restaurant was everything to me, it was the last thing we had left from my grandparents, and I was going to fight for this place for as long as I could.

"Yeah," I muttered, and from that point forward let them chat with Ethan while I ate quietly.

The food was great, like everything my parents cooked, but I had no appetite. Instead of focusing on their talk, I focused on my chat with Nora. In her own special way, she made me feel at ease even when she wasn't around. She made me forget that I could lose this beautiful place sooner than I thought.

ME
> So how are you spending your Sunday morning? Let me guess, you have a hundred things on your to-do list and you've been up since 6 AM or something?

NORA
> 7 AM, and no, I actually said no to all my plans, and I'm on my way to Luuk's apartment. He's been dealing with some emotional stuff and could use some company.

> So you're talking again? I told you he would understand.

> Yeah, I have to admit, a lot of it happened thanks to you. I just had to get a small push to do it. Thank you, William.

> Always.

She was typing again, but I didn't see her message. Ethan touched my shoulder, and I lifted my head up as I pushed my phone into my pocket, nervous that I might've got caught by my mom.

But when I looked up, my parents were busy trying out the cheesecake Ethan brought, and it apparently was so delicious that they forgot anything else existed around them.

"Come with me," he said.

He told my parents we were going for a short walk and we'd be back soon.

We walked quietly outside, and just when we reached far enough from the restaurant, he turned to me.

"So, now that we're not sitting with your parents, will you tell me what has really been going on with you lately?"

"What do you mean?" I asked, though I knew I couldn't hide anything from Ethan. He knew me better than he knew the stars he's researched about all his life.

"About all the lies you told your parents over breakfast. I knew we didn't get a chance to meet much, we haven't had a chance to hang out properly since you've taken an active part in the restaurant, but I still know you, I'm still your best friend. I can tell when you're hiding something, and I know for a fact that you would never give up on your grandparents' place, no matter what your mom, your dad, or anyone else has to say about the matter."

I rubbed the back of my neck, as I tried to think of the proper way to tell him everything.

"Just say it, Will, I won't judge," he promised.

"Remember that girl my parents were talking about?" I asked.

Nora seemed like the best part to start with, in some way she was the best part of the story.

"The one you haven't said a word about so far? Yeah, I remember." He folded his arms. "What about her?"

I took a deep breath, because I knew that one was going to take more courage and time to explain. "I met her two weeks ago, she showed up at the restaurant, I stayed late and there was no one around, we talked, I ended up telling her about the situation, and the ideas I had to save the place, I just spilled out things I probably shouldn't tell a stranger."

I chuckled when I realized how crazy it all sounded out loud. "But it felt right, she's just so easy to talk to, she can make even a shy and awkward guy like me spill anything."

His lips curled. "Go on."

"We became friends, and then before I knew it, she showed up at the restaurant a few days later with her plan to save the restaurant. She's a communication student, so she has so many ideas to work with, she already made a site and social media accounts." We barely knew each other but she was so happy to be able to help me, she wanted to be there for me, for Oasis. "She even made me go to pick up tulips with her, I don't know how the hell she managed to make me do it, but one moment I was taking orders, and a moment later I was telling her about my grandparents love for flowers in a field."

Ethan chuckled as he looked over my face in amusement. "Who would've thought William Vanderweide had the ability to talk so much?"

"You can't tell this to my parents, they can't know I've been making plans to save the restaurant as they make their own plans to close and sell it."

"You really think I would ever think of telling them?" He cocked a brow. "I might not agree with your decision not to tell them, but I don't know what it's like to lose a family business, what it's like to lose the only thing you got left from your grandparents."

"Thanks, Ethan," I said. "I'm sorry for not telling you earlier, I didn't want to put you in an uncomfortable position with my parents."

"They're great people, and we have great talks. You're right about that, but you're my best friend." He put his hand on my back. "I just want to be able to help you from now on, whatever you need. I have no idea about marketing, but if there are things that don't acquire any specific knowledge, I'm your guy."

"Thanks man," I said.

Then, when we walked around the city we grew up in, I realized how silly I was behaving. We called each other best friends, but we never got to see each other; I was so caught up with saving something that means so much to me, that I was sort of neglecting responsibilities and relationships that were just as important. I already lost one relationship because of my over dedication to the place, I couldn't risk losing an even more important relationship because of it.

"I know I haven't been such a good friend because of everything that happened, but what do you say we'd hang out soon?" I asked with slight hesitation.

"I have a better idea," he proposed. "We should hang out with that new friend of yours, I think it's only fair after you kept her a secret, too."

My heart was beating out of my chest. "Nora?"

"Nora," he repeated, and then nodded. "She must be a very special girl if you took her to pick up tulips and told her about your grandma."

I wished I could explain to him how she made me feel, but I couldn't. She clouded my brain with emotions so much so that I couldn't even express it to my best friend, or to myself. Just like the sun, she caught my attention without having to do a single thing but be there. But right when I thought of a way, I noticed her, right on the other side of the street, riding her bike.

She must have felt my gaze on her cause her eyes wandered to our direction, and when her eyes landed on me she stopped the bike and put her legs on the ground.

She walked towards me, wearing a tight blue skirt and a jacket of the same color, her hair braided as always, but now that my best friend was right beside me, I had to fight the urge to fix the strands of hair that fell on her face.

"Nora," I said.

She walked away from her bike, and instead of just welcoming me with a short 'hi' and a sweet smile, she wrapped her arms around me and pulled me towards her. My body relaxed as I put my own arms around her and breathed in her sweet smell, something that reminded me of coffee and something more, warmer than this weather.

"You know, it's going to sound ridiculous, because we literally just saw each other a few days ago, but I missed you." She smiled against my chest.

"This might sound even more ridiculous, but I missed you too," I said, and we both laughed like we were sharing our own inside joke.

When we heard Ethan clearing his throat, we backed away from one another.

"Umm, Ethan, this is Nora." I turned to look down at her. "And Nora, this is my best friend."

"Damn, and I thought I had the chance of becoming your only best friend," she pouted, but right after went to give Ethan a short hug. "It's nice to meet you. I was telling William he should hang out with his friends a little bit more, see the sunlight outside, stop walking around the same walls serving customers."

"I like serving customers," I answered.

Nora turned to look at Ethan, and Ethan turned to her, before they stared at me.

"William, you're a good-looking guy, you really are, but the bags under your eyes aren't doing you any justice."

I blushed and lifted my hand to touch the skin close to my eye. I knew she tried to make a point, but all I could hear was the first part of her sentence.

"You know, we were just talking about hanging out this week. It's going to be a chill evening playing Monopoly. Well, not so chill if it's going to be like last time we played, but there would be drinks and snacks, and you might get to see Will losing in monopoly. He might seem relaxed and collected now, but it all disappears when his competitive side comes out. You should come."

"Ethan," I tried to stop him from making maybe the worst decision ever. I preferred her to think I was a reserved and shy person rather than impossibly competitive at board games.

"Can I invite my friends?" she asked.

"The more the merrier," Ethan answered. "Right, Will?"

"Right," I hissed.

It was his way of getting back at me for not hanging out for so long, I just knew it, and I hated every second of it.

"I'd love to come," she said, and then looked at her phone when it buzzed. "I have to go, but text me the details and we'll be there," she said and right when I thought she was going to leave, she turned to me. "Oh, and William?"

"Yeah?" I swallowed; I didn't even know why I was nervous to hear what she had to say.

"You're not the only one who's acting way too competitive when it comes to Monopoly, so let's just promise each other that whatever happens at this game, we keep on working with each other like nothing happened, okay?"

"Okay," I breathed out in relief and chuckled a bit.

I watched her go back to her bike, waving at us as she was riding towards the other direction.

If Ethan wasn't talking, I would've probably kept looking at her figure fading away in the distance.

"Now I understand everything," Ethan mumbled.

"Understand what?" I asked.

He wasn't willing to give me an answer. He shook his head with a smile, like he knew something I didn't.

"Come on, *William*, let's go back before your parents won't leave us any of the cake."

I followed him, though that cheesecake was the last thing on my mind.

CHAPTER 10
Nora

I walked into the restaurant in a better mood than I usually do. I always felt that way when I woke up with an idea I worked on for a few days on and I wanted to show and tell another person about it, just to have them share the same excitement I shared all by myself.

I waved towards the man I learned was William's father who I already shared a few conversations with. I already managed to learn some facts about him. Despite the complicated situation of the business, I could tell he was a good father, he always made sure William took breaks and ate properly. Every time he saw me, he tried to show interest in my day, just because he knew I was his son's friend.

"Weird to see you here," he joked and looked through his glasses for William, who was taking orders from a family of four that sat close to the back door. "I don't know what I did that I got such a hardworking son, sometimes I need to bribe him to have him sit down and eat something."

"If you want, I can try to find an excuse to walk outside. It's not that cold, the rain had stopped a while ago. I can take him to eat something new for a change," I offered, and was quick to clarify. "Not that I hate the food here, all the dishes I tried are amazing, but I think a change of scenario can do good for him."

"How are you planning on convincing him to go outside?" he asked, his eyes still following his son's movement; William smiled shyly when the mother of the family was complimenting him on his devoted service.

"I took some acting classes in high school; I can be pretty persuasive when I want to be. Besides, I study communications, it would be a shame if I wouldn't use techniques that I learned to help people I care and love," I said. He stared at me when I said it and I cleared my throat. "Care and love in a friendly way, of course."

"Of course," he repeated, though I could sense his suspicions..

It didn't go away even when William was walking towards us. He put the menus on the desk close to him and stood by me. He lifted his hand but put it down when he sensed his dad looking at us.

"Hi, Pa," he cleared his throat, hinting at him to leave us by ourselves.

"You're taking a break," his dad said back.

"I just got here an hour ago, I have so much energy today. Pa, just look at all the people. Can you believe it? It's been this busy the entire week," he said, and frantically waved his hands over everyone to emphasize the crowd. It was sweet how he was acting like a child that couldn't hold in his excitement about the simplest things.

"Yeah, I've noticed, but don't let it fool you, one good week isn't going to save the place, we'll need much more than this to turn things around. Now go outside, take your friend with you, and eat something nice." He gave him a few bills from his wallet.

"Pa, I'm not going anywhere, you need me," William said, still not taking the money his dad just offered.

"William, we have other waiters here to do the job. I don't want you to waste your time here. Instead, use it wisely, by focusing on your studies and spending time with your friends." He put the bills into the palm of his hand and walked away from us.

William looked down at the palm of his hand, and right before he was about to throw it in his dad's direction, I put my own hand around it. His hand was shaking, and I didn't need to look up at his face to understand the frustration he wanted to get out of his system.

"Come on, William." I tried to drag him after me, but he didn't follow. His body was frozen in place as he looked at me in disbelief, his eyes didn't radiate the same warmth that I've grown to know.

"Not you, too," he muttered.

"William," I stepped closer and put my hand gently on his chin, turning his face back to me. "I know it's frustrating. I know the last thing you want is to take a moment and stop everything but take it from someone who knows what it's like being burnt out, you don't want to get to that stage. Even if you worked an hour, it's still an hour, a break couldn't hurt that much, right?"

He pressed his lips together, still keeping his silence.

"Besides, I plan to go for a short walk, and it might rain. If you walk with me, we can find shelter together when it starts raining. I know how much you hate it when I come here without an umbrella and say that you wished you could protect me from it."

"I hate it because you might get sick. I get that you love wearing short skirts with sweaters as part of your fashion statement, I always love this look on you, but I almost wish your fashion statement was a few coats and endless layers of warm sweaters," he stated as he let his eyes roam my body, his eyes stopped on my skirt. He swallowed slowly and went back to look me in the eyes. "I want to go with you, but I don't want to make it seem like I've given up, like I agree with my parents that the future of everything we built is hopeless." He chuckled when my eyes never wavered. "Stupid, right?"

"No." I shook my head. "I know the feeling."

His breath was shallow as he looked at me intensely. I knew what he was thinking, he never thought that someone could understand what he was going through. It was confusing learning that someone could share your feelings.

I offered my hand to him. "Come with me, and I'll tell you all about it."

That seemed to be exactly what he needed to hear, because he put his hand in mine, no questions asked and followed me outside of the restaurant to the fresh cold air, which already felt like a small win.

"So, where are you planning on taking us?" he asked, not letting go of my hand. It felt nice, knowing he trusted me that much to lead him whenever my heart desired.

"I don't know if I should pick some cheap place, I mean, you're the one paying after all, I should be really smart about this," I joked.

"Technically, my dad is paying," he corrected. "But I'm telling you right here, right now, if we were on our first date, I would be paying."

"Because you're a gentleman?" I asked.

He squeezed my hand lightly. "Yes, but also because I was raised that way. I learned how to look at love, how to act when I meet a girl I like. I'm the kind of person that would want to open the door of the car, pay for dinner, do simple gestures like that."

"So, you are a gentleman," I said in full confidence. "He can cook, he can make coffee, and he's a gentleman. What more could a girl ask for?"

"*He* would love to know where you're taking him," he chuckled. "Though you can tell me while you continue giving me compliments, I really wouldn't mind that."

I laughed.

"It's your love language, isn't it?" he asked out of the blue. "You love words of affirmation."

"It's my way of showing love, sure, but it's only because I've always been very vocal with my opinions and thoughts. But in relationships, it's not the first language that would pop to mind."

"So what would pop to mind?" he asked, and when I smiled to myself and kept walking peacefully he laughed. "Let me guess, another question you're not ready to answer yet?"

"I bet you learned how to cook and make coffee and serve tables pretty quick, you're a fast learner," I mused. "The answer to your other question is Italian. There's this one restaurant near the Dam Square I ran into by accident with my friends. We looked for a new place to eat for once, and because no one in our friend group is decisive, I just walked into the first restaurant I saw so we could just eat already. It turned out to be an amazing Italian restaurant with great pastas and pizza, it became one of our favorite places to eat since then."

In our friend group, we always had our rules. When it came to our usual stomping grounds, we didn't usually bring other people. It was usually just the three of us, but here I was, taking William to one of those exact spots.

When we walked through the doors and selected our meals from the menu, I realized I barely put any thought into that decision. I also didn't put any thought into whether to have a chill, or not so chill, night with our friends together. I was barely thinking when it came to William these days, and that realization itself was scary. Sure, we were friends, we were helping each other out, but still... I never let go of my plans so much for someone, and I was always thinking twice about my actions.

One minute we were at Oasis, and ten minutes later, I was sitting with him in a place I never went to with anyone except Xander and Luuk. I was the type to plan, and write down everything in a notebook, and here I was, staring at a sweet guy that became a permanent part on the pages. That conclusion was terrifying, it was treacherous for someone like me.

I tried to shake all of these thoughts from my head and moved my attention to William who was taking in his surroundings. He looked behind us at the kitchen, where we could see the cook working with the dough for the pasta. He worked on a surface that was covered with flour and moved his hand quickly.

I scanned William's face, and just then I realized something I should've seen much sooner. He was so caught up in work, and studies, and trying to save his family business, that he didn't get to go to any other restaurants. I wanted to ask him what the last place he's gone to eat that wasn't Oasis, but chose not to. I didn't have anything against his rosy cheeks from witnessing everything going on around him, it was cute seeing him blush from being flustered, but I didn't want him to think about any of it right now.

"So, how does it feel?" I leaned forward. "Was it that bad going to eat and take a break from work?"

I could see a hint of a smile on his lips. "How would I know; I haven't tried the food yet." Then he turned to me and let his smile show. His voice was quiet and grateful. "It's nice Nora, this feels nice."

I reached my hand over the table and gave his warm hand a light squeeze. "Good."

I let go of his hand as we got our meals, and I didn't touch my food until after I watched his reaction from tasting the pasta he ordered covered in parmesan. He hummed as he kept twirling the pasta around his fork. He barely said anything since the food showed up, he just kept eating. When he realized that, he put the fork down and lifted his head to me, noticing I was still eating my first slice.

His cheeks got covered in a familiar shade of pink, and he cleared his throat. "Sorry, I didn't realize I was that hungry."

"I don't mind," I smiled, and slowly put the half-eaten slice down. "William, I don't want to sound like your dad, but I do agree with him that you need to take a break, find balance."

His voice turned quieter, maybe even wounded. "Don't tell me you've given up too?"

"That's how you know me, as a person who gives up easily?" I asked, and as I encountered the fear in his eyes that I would turn out to be like his family, I wanted to get up and hug him, just to give him some reassurance.

"I wouldn't have come to you in the first place and offered to help if I didn't believe in myself, and you," I said gently, because using a gentle approach was the best approach to use right now.

He didn't need me to lash out at him or tell him what to do and treat him like an irresponsible kid, because he wasn't.

He knew exactly what he wanted and what was important to him, it was one of the best parts I learned to see in him as a person.

"I always think of new ideas that I can market that will help the restaurant. I basically ran away from Luuk's apartment just because a new idea came to my mind and I had to plan it out, I'm far away from the giving up zone."

"What idea?" he asked, his voice back to normal.

"I was eager to tell you about it after I wrote it down, but now I understand that it can wait. There are more important things to talk about, at least right now," I tilted my head to watch him better as the light entered through the glass windows of the place, lighting up his face. "Don't you think?"

He opened his lips but closed them, his eyes haven't wavered from mine as he nodded shortly.

After we both went back to eating and he finished his meal, my eyes wandered to his mouth, to the way his lips were as pink as the color of his cheeks. I was fixated on them until I saw them moving. I knew that I shouldn't have been paying attention to them.

"You…" he started. "Back at the restaurant, you said that you understand how I feel."

"I do," I admitted. "But I think that it will make the most sense if I start at the beginning. I don't think I've told you this yet, or maybe I did, I can't remember, but I'm an only child born into a family of hard-working parents. Both of them succeed in their line of work."

"You haven't told me that," he said calmly, "I'm not surprised though, that your parents ended up with such a hard-working and ambitious daughter."

I smiled at that. Compliments didn't often stick with me, but it was nice hearing a compliment come from William's lips.

"Anyway, as I grew up, I always had the drive and motivation to prove myself, to show my parents that I'm exactly like them. Maybe it's because I knew I'd be the only child they were ever going to have, so as the years went on, I think it turned into me wanting to prove something in general. I tried to be the best student, the best daughter, I wanted to be the best in every way possible."

I played with my own napkin as I relived all of the memories, all of the effort I've put in over the years.

"But you know, if there's one thing I learned, it's that you can't risk your own health and self-care to prove something. There were times where I put too much pressure on myself, I forgot to eat at times and preferred to skip dinner to focus on an assignment, or I wanted to use my free time to see how my mom works, what being event planner meant and was all about."

"Nora…" he whispered, like he knew where I was going with this, and in some way, he did.

"I kept going down this lane, and in my high school years, when all the talk about college and designing my own future would become too much, when I started to feel the pressure, There was all this anxiety surrounding what was to come, it became a bigger issue. It was no longer just about what I needed to prove to my family, but what I needed to prove to society, that I can do everything I've planned to. I didn't want to get to my twenties and not achieve any of my goals. So, I worked so hard on everything, until I ended up collapsing under the pressure, literally." I paused. "And physically."

I was finally ready to meet with his eyes again, but when I lifted my head, he wasn't sitting in his chair. At some point, he got up and moved the chair near me. He was close now, closer than he's ever been. His expression was soft, though with Willaim, he always had this soft demeanor.

He lifted his hand and moved away a few strands of hair that fell over my face. He used to do it a lot, and every time he did, I felt shivers travel through my body, and tingles along the side of my face where his fingers were.

"I wanted to do that since I saw you enter our restaurant today," he whispered.

Then he opened his arms to me. He didn't need to say a thing, I already let myself fall into his arms, and put my head over his shoulder.

"Taking a break to think things over and recharge doesn't mean you've given up, William," I said. "I hope you know that."

"I know that, it's just not so easy to do," he said quietly, still looking down at me. "Thank you for bringing me here, I needed some time off from everything."

"If you ever need to take time off, you have my number," I told him. "But you should know there's a price to pay."

"What price?" he asked.

I looked down at the few slices that were left of my pizza. "I never finish my food."

He followed my gaze, and when he realized what I meant, his chest rumbled from laughter.

"I'll help you finish the food later," he said and tightened the grip of his arm around me.

"Later?"

"Yeah, later." He smiled down at me. "I don't know how to explain it Nora, but us being like this...it feels nice."

Nice. Seemed like every time William was around, everything felt this way.

William was a different kind of nice.

"It is," I said.

CHAPTER 11
William

Every person has a few sides to them. Shy people could suddenly gain confidence while going on a stage, and a confident person could lose all faith in themselves while talking to a crush. And in my case, I turned completely competitive when it came to a silly board game named Monopoly.

I wanted to hit Ethan the moment he invited Nora, the last thing I needed was for her to see me this way. I tried to be the well collected guy, the guy that helps in the family business and makes coffee occasionally, but games like these deleted all those facts about me. I was sitting in the kitchen of Ethan's apartment, his roommate was gone, so we were all able to sit around the living room and make as much noise as we wanted.

Nora showed up right on the dot with her friends by her side. Luuk, who I've got to hear a lot about already, showed me how to make cocktails on the island in the kitchen. I tried to listen to his explanation when he put the alcohol into the drink but couldn't help but look back at her other friend, Xander. He was sitting next to Nora, both of them had a small chat with Ethan.

"Don't take it personal, he's going through shitty time right now. Complicated family dynamics, childhood friend he misses, boring as hell assignment in English courses," Luuk said, and I was kind of surprised he managed to focus on the drink and everything that happened around us at the same time. "We should be thankful he even bothered to show up here," he mentioned. "I've known him since we were kids, and never once have I seen him this troubled."

"So it's nothing against me?" I asked to double check, still worried I wouldn't get along with Nora's friend. Sure, her friends didn't have to be my friends, but I preferred us to all get along, for the sake of Nora, I knew that was one of the reasons she invited them tonight, for all of us to bond.

He chuckled as he cut a piece of lemon to add the cocktail. "He isn't scared of you stealing our friend from us if that's what you're implying."

"What?" I breathed. "No, no, that's not what I was implying, I…I would never—"

"Dude, chill, I was just joking." He put a bottle of beer in front of me. "If you're nervous now, I don't want to see what will happen when Nora beats your ass at monopoly, well, all of our asses."

That seemed to wake all my senses up. "Huh?"

"I still remember the first time I lost to her," he put his hand on the upper side of his left arm. "Still hurts."

"Well, I'm sorry you had to lose, but that's not going to happen to me," I said.

I meant every word, he could see that, and yet, he laughed right at my face like I told him the funniest joke he's ever heard.

"What?" I rubbed the back of my neck. "I don't mean it in a condescending kind of way, I've just played Monopoly for a long time, and I've always been competitive. Okay, really competitive, and—"

"You think you can beat Nora?" he asked. I could feel him testing me, how far I was going to go with my statement.

"It doesn't matter if she's my friend, or if I like her, board games are like any game, it's like soccer. Outside the field you can feel whatever you want, but on the field, you do what you need to win." I paused when I looked at his arm. "Without hurting anyone physically, of course."

He put the knife on the counter and stared at me. I knew we were all friends here, but talking to Luuk was much more intimidating than what I imagined or prepared for.

"You like her?"

I felt my cheeks warm up, and in an instant, that warmth spread. I hoped that he couldn't see it show on my face. "I didn't mean the 'like' that you think, it's not that I don't like her, just not in *that* way."

I was more of an introvert, so it always was a bit harder for me to connect and meet new people, awkward interactions were part of the deal, some nervousness too, but I didn't expect to feel sweat under my shirt.

His face turned from serious to friendly and sweet in five seconds. I hoped he wasn't going to laugh at me again.

"You're joking with me again, aren't you?" I asked him.

He put the drinks on the tray so he could carry them to the living room. "I have a feeling tonight's going to be fun."

He walked around the island and stopped next to me. He motioned to me with his free hand to step closer, and when I did he spoke quietly so no one else could hear. "You seem like a nice guy Will. I can call you Will, right?"

I nodded shortly.

"Just because you're so nice, I feel obligated to warn you. If you keep with that attitude, my loss would look like nothing compared to your loss tonight. When it comes to Nora, my advice is: Don't fight it."

"Fight what?" I asked, but he already walked ahead and put the tray down in the living room.

I followed the same direction in slower steps, realizing they left me a place to sit near Nora. She must've noticed the way my muscles tensed because she put her hand on my back and moved it in circles.

"What is it?"

"I have a question," I said. Everyone around us was so busy drinking and talking that none of them paid attention to us, which was a perfect opportunity to ask what I was wondering since she said yes to Ethan's invitation to come here. "Why did you say yes to Ethan that day, you didn't have to join. With how busy you are, you must have better things to do than…"

"Rather than spending my night with you?" she asked, finishing my sentence, and somehow coming from her mouth, it didn't sound as innocent as it was supposed to. "I don't think so."

I pressed my lips together to hide the big smile that was about to appear on my lips.

"Is it Luuk? Because whatever he told you, it was probably a joke or a way to test you," she said, her hand still on my back. "Don't even ask me why, I guess it's a guy thing."

"A guy thing?" I repeated.

"Yes, believe me I've spent everyday with these two since high school, I gave up understanding how their mind works a long time ago." She glanced at her friend and then turned back to me. "I can tell Luuk likes you."

"And Xander?" I asked her.

Just from observing the three of them together, I could wrap my hand around how their dynamic worked, but more importantly how much she cared about the two of them equally. And if I wanted Nora to stay in my world, which I did, I wanted both of them to like me—or at least like me enough to have me around.

"Don't worry, he will warm up to you eventually," she promised. "He warmed up to me, and I was a pain in the ass when we met."

"You're not a pain in the ass," I chuckled. "You just have a strong personality."

"Which is the same thing, but a nicer way to rephrase it." She smiled and let go of my back when she saw me relaxed again. "Anyway, whatever it is, don't think about it. If I'm going to win tonight, I want it to be fair, and not because you were distracted."

"And if I win?" I blurted out.

She held a straight face. "Then I would still like you."

My heart skipped a beat.

"Because that's what you're afraid of, isn't it?" she asked softly, and made sure our friends were busy with their own conversations before she continued to talk. "I know you're more of an overthinker. But if there's something you shouldn't worry about, it's us, this friendship, this connection we have. I'm not going to give up on all of this because I discovered you're extremely competitive."

When she phrased it like that, it did sound ridiculous.

She leaned closer until I could see deep into the green of her eyes. "If anything, it will only make me like you more."

Our eyes were locked, and I could see how her smile reached her eyes. I wondered how it was possible, that she was the most energetic person I knew, always filled with ideas, always had somewhere to go and something to do. Yet, she was calming, like a relaxing voice that stood out of all the voices in my head.

"Are you guys just going to keep talking the entire night, or are you ready to play?" Ethan asked, pulling us both out of our own peaceful moment.

We looked at one another, like we knew exactly what was going on in the other's head.

"Ready to play," she said, and went to pick up the cubes, though she was obviously too slow. I was holding on to the cubes and rolled them between my hands. "Oh, definitely ready to play," I said playfully.

From that point forward, things escalated—and fast. I tried to keep calm, I tried to pretend I could act like a gentleman even when I played a game, but I couldn't keep it up for even five minutes.

"Give it to me, William, this hotel is mine," Nora was chasing after me as I ran away from her. "I already had plans for this hotel."

"Did you now?" I held the card of the hotel close to my chest, like I could protect it if I held it close enough.

"Yes!" she passed the sofa. "I have the money, I have the workers, I was going to invite celebrities and plan events there, and because you can't admit that you lost it, my plans are put on hold. Now. Give. It!"

She jumped forward till she wrapped her hand around the back of my t-shirt. She pulled it towards her and closed the gap between our bodies. Her chest was pressed against mine, and her small body appeared to be much stronger than I thought.

"If you want it, take it." I smirked when I put my hand up in the air. She was maybe stubborn, but I was just as stubborn.

She huffed and put her hands on her hips. I could see how she calculated her odds in her brain, the odds were against her, whether she wanted it or not, I was taller, and the only way she could reach my hand was—

"W…what are you doing?" I asked.

One moment she was standing on the floor, and a moment later her legs were wrapped around my waist. I had to put my hand down and wrap it around her back to make sure she didn't fall. My other hand was still in the air, holding the precious card she wanted, and by the spark in her eyes, I could tell she was going to do anything she could to get it, and a part of me was more than curious to watch her next move.

She put her hand on my shoulder to stable herself as she lifted herself, climbing further up my body like a little monkey. I could feel the fabric of her long shirt tickling my neck. She was close, I could feel her body pressed to mine, I could feel her breathing against my skin, and I could feel her looking at me.

None of us moved, none of us did anything when we were wrapped around each other. I forgot my competitive side, maybe because there was another one that came to life. My eyes wandered down slowly to gaze at her lips; she was so close that it was the natural thing to do. I usually used to see it move, because she always had something to say, but it was closed now, her lips were pressed one to another, covered in a pink lipstick.

Just like that, I realized the way I was feeling right now, was the exact same feeling I had at that Italian restaurant when I hugged her, when she put her head on my shoulder.

It was *nice*.

And just like the restaurant, the feeling of holding her close was too nice to let go of.

"William?" she asked quietly, the smirk on her lips was gone.

I closed my eyes, because if I looked at her face for a second longer, I would just feel even more confused, more bothered by the fact it was hard for me to let go of her…for reasons that were beyond my understanding.

I put her down gently back on the floor and settled the card in her hand. I couldn't help but chuckle at her when she lifted her head, stunned that I gave up so quickly.

"The hotel is yours, Nora," I said. "You won."

"William?" she asked, not even looking at her hotel. "What just happened?"

I looked at the living room, it was empty. We were so busy fighting over cards that our friends decided to quit and go to sleep. I turned back to her. "I think it's time for us to go to sleep too. You can take Ethans' roommate's room. I'll sleep on the couch."

"You're not sleeping on the couch, you're much taller than me," she said.

Of course she had to fight with me on this.

"Nora, please." I didn't want to beg, but I was certain my voice sounded like I did.

"I'm not going to sleep before you tell me why you're being weird with me. One second we were running around the living room and fighting over a hotel and…"

"And now you can plan events in that hotel and have guests and do whatever you want. I'm sure they'll leave five-star reviews." I paused to laugh at that. "You could've been a great hotel owner, I can picture you giving the staff orders, making sure everything runs as it's supposed to."

I sighed and walked to her, I pulled her by the arm and wrapped my arms around her body, bringing her close to mine as we were moments ago. Though this time, I kept it short, so there wouldn't be any overthinking over any actions.

"Good night, my dear friend. See you in the morning," I smiled.

She raised her brows but said nothing else as she walked slowly into the room.

When I heard the door close behind her, I laid on the couch and put my hands on my face, as if it could erase what I said.

"My dear friend?" I sighed against my hands and curled up to the side. "Ugh."

I sure knew how to be awkward when I wanted or didn't want to be.

CHAPTER 12
Nora

I stared at the ceiling and then watched the clock near the bed. It was one in the morning, and I still couldn't fall asleep. It wasn't one of those nights I was familiar with, where the ideas were twirling in my head and I had to write them down before they vanished away. I wasn't in my own bed, or my own house, and the only thing my mind was focused on was on William.

It was supposed to be a fun night, full of good spirits that are built off of innocent competitiveness. But I didn't feel like a winner, I felt like I lost something.

I played with the card in my hand and looked at the details of the hotel. I used to do a lot in order to achieve the goals I listed so carefully down in my notebook, I used to do a lot to win, Luuk and Xander suffered enough time of me throwing cubes in the air, or running after them to get the fake paper bills of the game they weren't so eager to give, but something was off with me tonight.

I could keep pretending the only reason I was so close to William was to get that card, but the truth was, I wanted to be close to him again, I forgot about what I was fighting for the minute I was wrapped around him, seeing the blue in his eyes from up close.

I threw the card away on the desk near the bed and curled to the side, my eyes were focused on the closed door of the room that was covered with stickers of different musicians from the eighties.

I wondered what Willaim's room looked like. Was it covered with stickers too? Probably not, he was all into classy things, he liked to be organized and maintain order when he worked. If I had to guess, I'd say that he made his bed in the morning to keep a routine, and maybe the most predictable thing in his room were probably family pictures. He talked about his family so much, especially his grandma, that he must've framed old pictures of him as a kid with her. I just knew it.

Maybe I should blame Luuk and Xander for not being able to sleep, and making me think of William. All the way to Ethan's apartment they made all sorts of comments, asking me how long I thought I could play pretend being "just friends" with William and wondered if I could hold back from kissing him. I was fighting to defend myself to them. It was such a stupid mistake to tell Luuk about the tulips.

When I decided I had enough of all of these thoughts, I got up from the bed and opened the door slightly. As I was walking on my tip toes in the hallway, I stopped to glance at the boys sleeping in Ethan's room. Ethan was sleeping in his bed as Luuk and Xander were lying on mattresses on the floor, their hands almost touching despite the distance between them.

How sweet.

I closed their door completely and went to the kitchen to look for a night snack. It was dark, so I had to use my phone to light up the different cabinets and drawers.

"Looking for a night snack?" I heard a voice in the darkness.

I looked up from the drawer and was met with William who was lying on the couch. His phone shed a light over his face.

"You can't sleep either?" I asked and watched him as he put his phone in his jeans back pocket and walked towards it. He stood by me and smirked when I put my phone forward to light up his face.

Then he put his hands on my hips, causing a feeling of tingles to rush up my body. I lifted my head, watching him closely as he moved in front of me, and it didn't matter where my thoughts wandered, I realized how stupid they were when he chuckled and moved me gently aside to push the switch. The kitchen lit up in an instant and I was faced with an amused William.

"I was looking for a snack, but I can't find anything," I exhaled slowly as he put his hands on the counter behind me, boxing me in.

"I know something better than a snack," he said and pulled away to walk to the refrigerator.

His movements were fast and confident as he opened it, took out what seemed like a cake, and then opened one of the drawers and put two spoons on the counter.

"Come on," he said when he felt me staring.

He took the cake and spoons in one hand and held mine in the other. When we reached the coach, he gave me my spoon and motioned to me to try out the cake.

"I promise you'll love it. Actually, I hope there's some left for our friends in the morning after we devour it," he said, and when he put the spoon in his mouth and hummed in content, I took a bite too.

I closed my eyes the moment the sweet cheese flavor filled my mouth.

"It's Ethan's famous cheesecake. It runs in his family for decades, and even though I tried it hundreds of times I'm still addicted to the taste, and I'm not much of a sweet tooth," he smiled to himself when he saw me taking another bite. "It's actually the reason Ethan and I became friends."

"It is?" I leaned back on the couch to get comfortable.

"When I was nine I think, yeah eight or nine, I was playing soccer with the guys on school break, and one of the kids hit me so hard, my leg hurt like crazy. I even cried."

"You cried?" I pouted.

"Yeah, I know it's not the manliest thing to do," he laughed. "Anyway, I went to sit on the bench, and then Ethan came over. He ate his lunch and then handed me his lunch box; it had a cake inside. He said that the cake had magic powers to heal me and I would feel better the moment I ate it. I didn't believe him, but I wasn't going to say no to a cake."

"And then what happened?" I asked as I kept eating, treating the cake as my replacement for popcorn.

"I felt better immediately, we kept on talking, and eventually I went back out to play. Since that day forward, we started hanging out together, and the day after I took him to my family's restaurant to introduce him to my parents, and—"

He paused and put his spoon down.

"What?"

"No, nothing, I haven't thought about it for a long time. It's like there is this part of my brain that prefers not to think too much of the past, because there's this sadness that can overshadow what used to be a happy memory. My grandma liked him, she said that she can already tell he's a friend for life. She was right, as always."

"At least he got to meet her," I said gently.

"I wish she could meet you too," he said back, his eyes warmed. "I don't want you to take it the wrong way, but you remind me of her."

"I am?" I whispered. My stomach felt fuzzy inside, like I got the sweetest compliment I've ever heard before.

"Women in my family are very independent and confident, but my grandma especially. She was a rare spirit, very strong too, she stayed that way until her very last moment. You have a strong spirit too, same confidence, maybe more confidence in your goals and dreams then even she did," he sighed, and shook his head. "Sorry, I didn't plan to go there."

"Please don't apologize, I feel flattered," I said. "Not just because of what you said, but because I'm glad you feel comfortable telling me about her in the first place. I haven't dealt with much grief in my life, but I can only imagine how hard it was for you."

He pressed his lips together, and after a slight hesitation he took out his phone. He ran his fingers through the screen and when he found what he was looking for, he turned it to me. I put down my spoon and took the phone gently from his hand, and by how vulnerable his expression was, I could feel he was going to show me another side of him.

It was a picture of an older woman and him as a kid. They were standing at the restaurant, as she was wearing a floral dress with her arms wrapped around him. His hands were covered in flour as he smiled proudly at the camera, revealing a missed front tooth.

"That's the reason I couldn't sleep," he said quietly. "Sometimes I'm scared that I might forget how she looked, sometimes I caught myself at the end of a busy day and realize I wasn't even thinking of her. So, I look at pictures and videos we used to film as a family, it helps me find some peace."

I lifted my head from the phone screen, he turned around to wipe away a tear he didn't want me to notice and cleared his throat before he turned back to me.

I tried to think what was the right thing to say, what he could possibly want to hear in such a fragile stage.

"She's beautiful, William," I gave him back his phone. "Now I know why you're so beautiful, you got all your good looks from her."

There was a hint of a smile on his face.

"With or without a front tooth," I commented, and then I heard a faint laugh.

We kept on eating from the cake, and when I looked down to see how much we already managed to finish, I laughed.

"What?"

"Doesn't it remind you of something?" I asked him.

"It reminds me of all the times I ate in the middle of the night but stopped when I realized I needed to wake up early and had a whole new day ahead of me," he mentioned. "Though I never had much company at any of those times."

"It reminds me of that chapter of 'Friends' when Rachel and Chandler ate that cheesecake that wasn't meant for them," I said. "I doubt the cheesecake on the show was anything like this one."

He tilted his head. "So, you like 'Friends'?"

I licked my lips when I felt the sweet taste on them. "Of course, don't you?"

"Yeah," he said, and left the spoon aside when his eyes narrowed, like something else was on his mind. "What would you say is your favorite show to watch?"

I laughed. "I don't know William; do you think we're at that stage of our friendship to talk about such deep stuff?" I leaned a bit forward, ready to make another one of my lighthearted comments that could still leave him blushing. "Talking about interests like favorite shows are very *intimate* as they tell you who the person truly is."

He shrugged his shoulders, though his cheeks were covered in red. I liked when he turned shy all of a sudden, leaving me room to tease him. "I feel like we're supposed to know these things about one another. Somehow we talked more about the heavy stuff, than light stuff. Like, I never got to tell you I'm an only child too, or what my favorite color is."

"I already knew you were an only child, I talked with your dad about it," I smiled, because I couldn't handle how sweet he was being. "And it's white, your favorite color is white."

"How did you..." He frowned.

"Out of all tulips, you wanted to pick the white ones. You always wear at least one white clothing item, and you complimented me when I did my nails," I lifted my head to show him the white color that covered my nails. "So, you might think we don't know the light stuff about one another, but I bet that if I asked you right here, right now, you would know my favorite color."

He was shaking his head, his shoulders moved from his laughter until it died down when he went to look at me. "Your favorite color is pink."

I wanted to tell him my favorite shade of pink had nothing to do with tulips, or clothes, or anything like that, but it was the shade of pink that covered his cheeks, his lips, and his skin when he was cold. But it seemed dangerous going in that direction.

Sure, we were friends, but all you needed was the right switch to turn it into something more.

"It is," I whispered. His eyes wandered to my lips, like he tried to figure out by himself that shade of pink.

"So, what is your favorite series?"

I decided to challenge him more than he already was. "I'm more of a movie kind of person."

"Of course you are," he sighed.

He looked at me like he hoped for a clue, but all I did was cross my legs and hug them close to my body.

"The Notebook?" he asked.

"I have a feeling it's more likely to be your favorite than mine," I said. "Not that I hate it, it has some great scenes, good story line, but the ending makes me sad."

He put the cake aside to move his body near mine. And when I moved closer to him, our shoulders brushed.

"What is your favorite scene from that movie?" he asked.

"I was right, it is in your top three at least, isn't it?" I asked and leaned backwards until my back met with the soft material of the couch. "It makes sense for you to like it. After all, it's a classic movie from the early 2000's, sweet guy plays as one of the main characters, I should've guessed it..."

"You're right about that, now stop dodging the question," he turned his head, leaving me no choice but to look at him.

I tried to ignore the shivers down my spine from the touch of his arms pressed to mine. "I like the scene when she's about to leave his house, but they get into a fight near the car. I like what Noah says. 'You fight in a relationship, you argue, but you still love one another.'" I let out a deep breath and hugged my body. "Your grandma is right, William, love is either a battlefield or a tulip field. It can't be both."

"What makes you say that?" he asked, and I slowly shut my eyes when I realized that he wasn't the only one who didn't mean to go to darker and sad places, but ended up going there anyway.

"I had someone, we used to fight, we used to argue, but he didn't choose to stay. It wasn't just a battlefield William, I felt like I was at war, I just kept waiting to hear the final shot."

My body turned cold, thinking of it, talking about it. When you're in a relationship, you don't think it will end, and if it does, you hope it ends as amicable, short, and as painless as possible. But his grandma was right, there was nothing dramatic or poetic in saying love could turn into a war, into a ground made of ashes. I've seen the ashes, I've heard the words loud and clear, I was left hanging there, waiting for the shot, and I did hear it, eventually. I was so close to letting out a whimper, followed by tears, but then I felt the soft touch of William's hand on my face. He brushed his thumb on my cheek, erasing a tear that slipped away.

When I felt more tears coming up, I moved down and rested my head on William's knees. He lifted his hands in the air, like he didn't know where to place them, until I wrapped my hand around his wrist and put his hand on my head. He got the message and stroked my hair in his gentle touch.

"My favorite movie is 27 dresses," I said quietly, trying to think of a way to change the subject, to think of anything else.

"A romance movie about a woman who helps her friends with wedding planning." Even though I couldn't see him, I knew he was smiling. "I can't possibly see how you of all people would like this kind of a movie," he said in a sarcastic and playful tone.

I nudged his knee gently.

"It's your turn now, what's your favorite movie?"

"Actually," he lowered his head and whispered to my ear. "I'm more of a TV series kind of guy."

I rolled my eyes and smiled, knowing he couldn't see it. "Of course you are."

"Do you have a guess?"

"Maybe one of those baking shows, or cooking shows. Oh, I know, you probably watched that show that you need to guess which one is the real cake out of a few options," I said, somehow I had a feeling that even if he didn't watch this show, he would be good at it.

"No," he laughed. "My favorite show actually used to be Game of Thrones."

I didn't care about how puffy my eyes were or how much my tears stained my cheeks; I turned around so I could look up at his face. His hand was still in my hair as I looked at him with clear shock.

"You mean that show where people get slaughtered, blood is spilled everywhere, people die, heads get caught off... You mean that series?" I asked to make sure I heard him right.

"Don't forget the family relationships, the politics, the romance, the—" He stopped talking when he looked down at me. "Why do you seem so stunned?"

"Because you're such a sweet guy. It doesn't make sense that such a sweet and genuine guy like you would watch it. Not that I didn't watch all seasons myself, I just…"

His eyes darkened as he watched me. His body turned rigid; his hand stopped moving but stayed in my hair.

"William?"

His chest rose and fell. "You can't keep on doing that."

"Is it becoming uncomfortable for you that I lay on your knees?" I tried to lift myself up, but he put his hand on my shoulder to stop me from moving away.

"Nora, I know you said that some compliments are just compliments, but for me it doesn't work this way," he sighed. "If you keep on saying all these sweet things about me, I…"

"You what?" I asked.

My stomach was turning, I felt a rush going through my body, I wanted, no, I *needed* him to finish that sentence.

His eyes looked down at me, till they gazed at my parted lips. It felt like he had his own fight, trying to decide if he should say something or keep quiet, if he should move forward or stay where he was, if he should keep being the sweet guy, or show me a whole other side he had.

"Go to sleep, Nora," he said.

"What?" I sighed; my heart ached in disappointment. The energy shifted instantaneously.

"Close your eyes," he said more gently. "Try to sleep, I'll carry you to bed when you do, okay?"

I should've listened, but I couldn't close my eyes without knowing first. "But you haven't finished your sentence, you wanted to say something."

"I also remembered that we have classes tomorrow, and I don't want you to get tired," he went back to stroking my hair. "Come on, go to sleep."

I folded my arms and kept staring at him.

"I'll make you coffee in the morning," he tried again.

I sighed. "Fine."

He smiled down at me, and when I closed my eyes, he pressed his lips to my forehead in a kiss.

CHAPTER 13
William

After that night talk with Nora, I've been trying to ignore whatever I felt and focus on work.

"It wasn't that bad you know, that night playing Monopoly, it seemed like you and Nora had a great time." Luuk sipped from his mug, enjoying the warmth of a hot chocolate in this rainy weather. "I know Nora is my friend, so I'm not objective about it, but how did she win in the end?"

I stopped cleaning up the table when that night crossed my mind all over again. Nora's body against mine, our late talk, the number of times I looked at her lips like we were more than just friends.

Friends. I needed to remind myself of that word each day now if I wanted to act normal around her. We were friends, and even if I was interested in something more, she wasn't. She planned to go on with her life when she was done helping me with the restaurant, she wasn't going to stick around.

Whatever happened that night, it was part of a silly and childish game, and whatever we talked about, it was a friendly chat—nothing more and nothing less.

"She used that tactic of showing up out of nowhere, right?"

he guessed, "When you don't see her coming, but then she appears in front of you and you have no place to run. She's smaller than all of us, and still can win in a face-to-face match, funny, isn't it?"

What was funny is that Luuk knew what he was talking about and I was left stunned, trying to put together his hidden messages. She did come out of nowhere the night we met, and even if I had a chance to run, I wasn't planning on it.

"Have you ever watched High School Musical?" he asked when I didn't talk for a while.

"Huh?"

"High School Musical, the movie with the basketball guy that falls in love with the sweet nerdy girl that he met on New Year's Eve, it's a classic," he continued.

I chuckled and turned my entire body to him. I didn't know where he was going with this, but I was intrigued. "Yeah, sure, I saw it when I was a kid. Why?"

"Who's your favorite character?" He asked.

"What?" I scratched the back of my neck. "Wait, is it some kind of a test to see if I'm right to be friends with Nora or something?"

I didn't know how that was a way to test anything, but from the short amount of time I got to spend with Luuk and heard what he had to say, I knew there was some logic behind his questions, I just had to look for it.

"No," he shrugged. "Do you really think I would get out of my house, get dressed, take the metro, and make all this way up here to chat if I didn't think you were a good company for Nora to have? I could tell you're a good guy when I met you at your friend's apartment. Even if I didn't think that way, I'm not planning on telling Nora what to do. I've known her long enough to understand that I should respect her decisions," he stopped to look around the restaurant. "Even if I don't agree with some of them."

"You didn't want her to help me here, did you?" I asked and when I made sure all the customers were taken care of and no one needed my help, I sat on the chair, and Luuk sat in the chair next to me.

He sipped from his mug, taking his time before he looked back at me. "I know you think Nora is this fun and easy-going person. I'm not saying she's not that kind of person, but you usually get to see one side of her when she's here with you, throwing ideas around, ready to save not only the future of this place, but ready to save this entire universe."

"She is this person," I smiled as I thought of all the times Nora entered through the front door, with her unique energy, with endless ideas and things she wanted to do to contribute to the place.

He put his hand on my shoulder to catch my attention. "But she's not just that person, Will. I don't want to be dramatic over here, because believe me, I can be a drama queen, but I don't joke or exaggerate when I say she's been through a lot in high school, mental health stuff, her ex wasn't the most understanding of that, it was…a mess. When we got to university it was a fresh start for her, and I want it to stay that way. So, no, Will, I'm not here to test you. I'm here to ask you to look after her, to make sure that when Xander or I are not around, she has someone she can count on. I need her to have someone that will make sure she doesn't carry too much on herself again."

My heart ached, not the usual kind of ache, but I could feel actual pain running through my veins when I imagined Nora going through darker times. Even though she told me a bit about her past, how she took one step too far to achieve her goals, it was different hearing about it from someone who was a close friend of hers. It was different hearing it from someone that knew her before and after.

I was grateful that he made all this way to talk to me, but I couldn't focus when all I could think about was Nora.

I might've had my own doubts, I might've been confused when it came to her, but one thing I knew for sure was that I cared. I cared about her well being more than I thought I did.

"I'll look after her," I promised in all seriousness.

"Good," he nodded. "And please, don't tell a word about this to Nora, she would tell me I worry too much."

"Okay," I said with a slight hesitation.

I didn't like hiding things; I wasn't much of a good liar either. But if I managed to hide the truth from my parents for the sake of saving the place, I could hide the truth for Nora's sake.

"Now that we got that over with, who's your favorite character?" he asked again.

I looked back at the restaurant and felt the same urge I always had to run to customers or help in the kitchen. I was sitting for way longer than I was used to.

"Luuk, I really appreciate you coming here. I don't want you to think I didn't enjoy all this…guy talk and seeing how much you trust me even though you met me once, but I have work to do. Since Nora started helping out, we have more customers, almost on a daily basis, and if I want to show my parents that this place has a future, I gotta go help out."

"So, you don't want to answer?" He raised a brow, still sitting comfortably on the chair.

"What do you say about this, we can hang out some other time when I finish work, and you can ask me any questions you have in mind, okay? Whether it's movies, or horoscope stuff or-"

"That has been bothering me since I met you. From Nora's stories, I got an earth sign vibe, but when I met you face to face I suddenly thought that you can be a Pisces too. I'm talking about your sun sign of course, it's harder for me to guess the moon and rising."

"Of course," I muttered. I could say I didn't know what the hell he was talking about and what was the difference between all these words, but I had a feeling it would extend our talk, and I couldn't get distracted at work.

"Well?" he asked.

I should've known Nora wasn't the only stubborn person in her friends' group.

"I..." I tried to think out loud because I obviously wasn't an expert on any of this. "I was born in the summer, start of July, so if I'm not wrong I think I'm a Cancer?"

"I should've known," he said, as a pleasing smile came over his face. "Of course you're a Cancer, it makes total sense now."

"What does?" I asked, and looked back at the other table to see if anyone needed me. I had no idea how I was supposed to handle Luuk scanning my face, like he was in a search for something.

"You're independent, yet you're not too practical. Nora said you have ideas of your own, which means you're creative too. You work in your family restaurant which shows you're a family oriented, and—"

"Luuk, I don't want to stop you cause it's seems like you're enjoying yourself, but I don't believe in that stuff like you do, not that I don't respect your passion and love for it, and from what I heard, Nora loves starting her morning with those daily horoscopes," I said. "But I need to get to work now, so I guess I'll see you when-"

"Do you know her zodiac sign?"

"Know who's zodiac sign?" I asked.

I got so confused with this whole conversation, and maybe I should've slept longer last night.

"Nora," he said, and smiled when he saw my confused expression. "She's a Virgo. That's her sun sign."

I had zero knowledge when it came to astrology, horoscopes, all of this stuff, but lately I learned how much I loved learning new facts about her, whether it was a favorite color, favorite movie, or her zodiac sign.

"It means she was born in the summer too, right?" I asked.

Somehow the idea we were both born in the same season made me feel lighter, like we were different, but still had small things like that in common.

"You're not completely hopeless in astrology after all, huh?" he chuckled. "She was born on August 29th; in case you feel like writing it in your personal diary."

I didn't have a diary, or a notebook, but I already knew that after he left I was going to write that date down on my phone.

Then the front door opened, and Nora walked in. She was fixing her dark hair and lifted her head to look around for me, but her eyes stopped when she found Luuk and I together.

"Hi," she said slowly, and switched glances between us. "Is there something I should know about?"

I moved to look at him, because he seemed much sleeker with words than I was.

"I was walking around the area and thought of visiting your friend over here. We had a nice chat, right, Will?"

"Right," I nodded and watched Luuk stand up before he gave me a short hug with a tap on the shoulder. "Don't forget what we talked about," he whispered to my ear when he glanced at Nora before he completely let me go and moved to give her a side hug.

"Nor, see you tomorrow morning at our usual spot."

Then he left the restaurant, disappearing in the rain with his umbrella.

When I went back to look at Nora, she was already looking at me. "So, what did you two chat about?"

"About…guy stuff," I said shortly. "Boring stuff, really."

I was more than ready to get back to work, but Nora was still standing there, and by the frown on her face, I knew she didn't buy anything I had to say.

I pressed my lips and tried to think of what I was able to tell her without feeling bad for hiding something away. "High School Musical."

"High School Musical?" she asked.

"Luuk wanted to know which character I liked most," I laughed. "Strange, isn't it?"

"And what was your answer?" she asked.

I chuckled when she kept looking at me, waiting. "Is there something about your friend group I should know about? You like watching this movie, and its Luuk's strange way of seeing what I think?"

She shrugged and followed me as I passed through the tables. "It's not necessarily a thing, it's more of Xander and Luuk thing they like to tease me with."

I stopped walking and turned to her, suddenly feeling intrigued to know more. "Continue."

She ticked her tongue. "First, give me your answer. Don't think about it much, who's the first one that comes to mind."

I switched my weight from side to side before looking at her again. "Troy, I guess. I'm not an athlete in any way, but I can relate to his competitiveness, and the pressure he might feel to not disappoint his dad and himself. I wish I could go to an empty auditorium and scream too from time to time; you know?" I stepped forward, looking closely into her eyes and lowered my voice, so just she could hear me. "And of course, how can anyone not love a guy that loves this one girl and wants to prove to her, despite everything they went through, that they belong together. They have belonged together since that one random night they met."

We were looking into each other's eyes for a long time, until she broke eye contact and put her hands together as she revealed one of her smiles. "Yeah, they did."

"What's so funny?" I asked when she giggled to herself. I had hoped it didn't mean my answer was a bad one, because I gave it a lot of thought, as I gave anything in my life. "Is it something I said?"

"It's nothing you said, promise." She put her hand on my arm to calm me. "I just...I should've guessed you'd say that. You see, Xander and Luuk have been telling me you remind them of his character, and I tried to deny it. But they were right, they were so right...."

I felt my skin heat up when she looked at me again, like she saw a whole new side of me she just managed to figure out. "Is it a good thing or a bad thing?"

"A good thing, definitely a good thing," she whispered. And after her eyes were roaming my body she went back to my eyes. "But as much as I love talking about it, I came here to talk with you about something important."

I glanced down at the green notebook she pulled out of her bag and how she hugged it against her chest. "Right, you said you wanted to show me your newest idea."

"Is it a bad time?" She looked behind me. "I can come in later, or I can get back there in the kitchen and learn how to cook one of your infamous dishes. I always wanted to know how to cook, and not something basic like an omelet with bacon, but something that only a cook would know, something... professional."

I smirked as I pictured her running around in the kitchen, it felt like she could be a natural at everything that had to do with bossing someone around or having a list of things to check off.

"Nora, I actually wanted to talk to you about that. You're here almost every day, you manage a few accounts at the same time, taking care of content and marketing, and in your spare time you come up with all sorts of ideas," I started.

It wasn't like I didn't think of all she has done already, but Luuk put things into perspective for me. She used to not only look after my family's place, but she looked out for me, and I felt like I wasn't doing that enough, I didn't check up on her as much as I should've.

I know," she said. "I'm having a blast."

"But you would've told me if you stopped feeling that way,

having a blast I mean," I said carefully. I didn't want to cross any boundaries, or push or to talk, but I felt like I needed to at least ask her. "You would tell me if you wanted a break, or wanted to quit this whole thing, right?"

Her expression softened when she heard the worry in my voice, that wasn't as stable as always.

"William..." she cupped my face gently. "I've told you how I felt since the first time we met, it's never going to change. If I wanted to leave, I would've, but I don't want to do that."

"So you will tell me if it all becomes too much for you?" I asked again, just to make sure.

"I will, even if it means I don't get to have your coffee as much as I'd like," she answered, and slowly let me go from her hold. My face was hot from where her hands were.

"So you're my friend just because of the coffee I make you?" I lifted a brow.

After the weight was lifted off my shoulders, and I got the answer I needed to hear, we were back to being us. She was her confident self and I was back to breaking out of my shell, just for her.

"That, and a few other reasons," she winked.

What other reasons? I wanted to ask her, but pressed my lips together instead. I loved the way she teased me, but it was killing me at the same time.

Then she threw away the cloth I was wiping the tables with and led me behind her to the backside of the restaurant, where it was empty and more quiet for us to have a chat.

I had a feeling that if her idea was anything like everything else she's done for this place, I was going to love it.

Absolutely love it.

CHAPTER 14
Nora

As we were sitting in Oasis, I opened my notebook, looking at all the sketches and notes I wrote down before I turned it over for William to look over. His eyes scanned the pages before he lifted his head. I tried to act like I was cool about this whole thing. I didn't mind if he said no to my ideas, but in reality I wanted to see the same spark of excitement in his eyes as I felt when I came up with the concept.

"So, let me see if I got this straight. You want us to start selling coffees to go, like they do at typical coffee shops, but to have cups with quotes printed on them with a picture of a tulip?" he mumbled, and looked down again to check he didn't miss anything.

"I remember what you told me about your grandma, that she could publish a book filled with quotes because she had that intelligent and poetic soul. Why leave all these quotes locked in your memory and not out there for people to see while they drink the best coffee ever?" I asked him. "I know you might've expected me to say something else, but if I learned anything so far from my marketing courses is that not all ideas have to be crazy and big to make an impact. Sometimes going simple and direct is the hardest thing to do."

He nodded as he kept looking through the pages.

"It's okay if you hate it, I can always think of other ideas, or we can develop one of yours. I do feel like it might be time soon to plan events, you remember when we talked about Valentine's Day?" I asked, though it was more me who brought it up.

He nodded slowly, a small smile appeared on his lips. "When you said you would like to scatter the place with big pink balloons, yeah, it was pretty hard to forget."

"Well, I thought about it, when you said it felt like too much for this place and we need something more quiet and subtle. Like adding a chocolate desert to the menu for just that day or putting fresh tulips out. You can have your white tulips, and I can bring up pink ones," I offered.

I had to press my lips together and stop myself from continuing on and on, because he could already see it all in my notebook. He could see everything I envisioned when it came to my hopes and dreams, and all the events I wanted to plan in the future. And some other stuff, a bit more personal.

Then I realized I didn't tell William any of that, he just continued flipping around the pages thinking it was filled only with concepts for Oasis.

His hands stopped when he came across something he wrote, and his chest rumbled before he looked at me. "Nora, I feel like it's a good time to tell you I don't have any secret ingredient for my coffee. Definitely not a cinnamon."

"What?" I took the notebook from him and stared at notes I made a while ago, where I tried to figure out the secrets for the perfect coffee.

"The only secret I do have is using fresh coffee beans and cleaning my coffee maker regularly, if that even counts as a secret," he shrugged his shoulders.

"It's not the exciting secret I was looking for," I pouted.

"Maybe the secret is not the coffee beans, or machine or how you brew something, but the person making it. Maybe you're the secret."

He laughed at that. "Believe me when I say this, Nora, I have one secret in my life and that's more than enough for me. I can't wait for the day I could just talk to my parents about everything, show them that there's more than one way to survive this challenging time. You have no idea how guilty I feel every time I tell them a white lie or make up an excuse. I was always a good kid, I was always honest with my family, even if we have disagreements, but look at me now."

"I am looking at you," I said. "All I see is a guy who's desperate to save something he cares about. Do I think lying to people and hiding things is okay? Of course not. But if it's the only option you have, and that's how you'll save your family business and what your grandparents worked so hard for, then you should give yourself some slack. You're doing your best."

In some way, I didn't feel like I was talking about him, but about me—like I was trying to convince myself that I wasn't a bad daughter. I was only doing my best under the circumstances.

"Nora," his voice sounded quiet, more serious. "I love your ideas, all of them. Maybe the type of cup of coffee won't make a big difference sale wise, but it can show more of who my grandma used to be, what kind of person she was. She was a big coffee fan as well."

"The real question is if she loves it as much as I do?" I leaned forward.

He chuckled. "No one is like you, Nora. I don't think any person can contain that much coffee in their tiny body without having an adrenaline rush 24/ 7."

"Well, that's not accurate. The Gilmore Girls can do that, especially Lorelai."

"I don't mean fictional characters on a tv show, but real people, ones you see on a daily basis," he commented. "With all my respect to your abilities, you can never beat The Gilmore Girls when it comes to coffee. Though, it would be a very close fight."

"Aww, William," I put my hand on my heart. "I think it's the sweetest thing you ever told me."

He laughed, though this time, it wasn't just a soft sound of laughter, but it was a hysterical one, till I was sure he had a few tears slip away from his eyes.

"I'm just..." he pressed his lips like he was trying to think how to explain himself. "With other people I have talks on my degree, or most of the conversations goes something like *hi, how did that assignment go for you* or *how was lunch*, but with you, it quickly gets to balloons, and tulips, and the capacity of coffee a human being can contain in a body, and this."

I held the notebook in my hand and went over the pages, some filled with notes, some still white and empty, waiting to be filled with new ideas that I could bring to life. I closed it and put it back on the table next to my empty cup of coffee. "Remember when I told you a bit of what I was going through in high school, of the pressure I felt and how I needed to learn how to deal with it?"

"I remember," he said.

By the look in his eyes, I could tell he was concerned, like he didn't expect things to turn serious that fast again.

"What I told you was the very short version of the story. After I was completely out of control of myself or knowing what I needed, I went to therapy, and I got a notebook similar to this one, and she told me to write down how I was feeling, and the moments where I felt pressure and anxiety. Long story short, after months of writing down, it became part of my routine. I started writing checklists for every day, but not too long or too complicated, to make me feel like I'm productive enough but not putting too much pressure on myself. It's kind of my way to feel like I have control over things, even if in reality it doesn't work that way." I played with my hands under the table. "I know it might sound ridiculous-"

"It doesn't." He shook his head in an instant. "It isn't."

"I know there's more awareness of mental health these days, and everyone deals with something in life, big or small, but no one knows about this except my close friends. There's a lot of judgment going on out there, I already met people who didn't want anything to do with me because of it, because they couldn't understand it," my voice was shaking.

I knew William was nothing like people in my high school, and he was nothing like my ex, but that fear was still there, reminding me that I could never know that for certain.

"I use mantras," he said, making me turn my head at him.

"Huh?"

He smiled and took his phone out of his jeans' pockets. "I use an app. When I'm stressed out over life or feel anxious, I go to this app, and a random calming quote or mantra pops up when I open it. I used to have my grandma around to tell me the right thing at the right time, she always knew what to say, but now that she's not here, I had to find a new way to deal with life. So, Nora, if anyone dares to call someone like you ridiculous because of a notebook, then they can call me ridiculous too."

My heart felt all fuzzy and warm inside. I had Xander and Luuk by my side, but it felt much sweeter and heartwarming to have William there too, that he had my back.

"Someone like me?" I croaked, almost not recognizing my own voice.

His lips curled up, but his eyes were still tender. "I thought words of affirmation weren't your love language."

I looked at him, completely stunned. Who knew the shy guy I met what seemed like forever ago, would turn out to be cheeky?

The longer I got to know the real William Vanderweide, I realized he hid a lot behind shy smiles and blushing cheeks. Our friendship too was more than a friendship based on a joined interest. I couldn't pinpoint why I felt something different with William than I felt with any other person I met, but I knew I didn't want it to ever be over. It felt as if moments like that were only the tip of the iceberg to how cheeky and playful William really was inside.

I leaned in and crossed my hands above my notebook. "When a girl is wearing a nice dress, and she knows she looks good in that dress, she would still smile when someone tells her she looks beautiful."

He tapped on the table. "Is this your way of telling me that if I ever get to see you in a dress, you want me to call you beautiful? Because Nora, you don't need to ask, the first night we met I said you were radiant despite the rain, I'm sure that when I get to see you all dressed up, without rain or other natural forces in the way, you'll be…"

"I'll be…" I tried to make him continue.

He seemed to catch himself in a deep thought, because his cheeks blushed in a slight pinkish color. He shook his head like he brushed that thought away and went back to me. "I need to get back to work."

"Are you being serious right now?" I asked when I watched him get up from his chair.

"There are things better left unsaid, Nora."

"I'm not getting up from this chair until you tell me." I folded my arms. "I'll just sit by myself, alone. I'll just stay there until closing hours, and—"

"You know, I can see why you and Luuk are friends, you both can be dramatic when you want to be," he sighed.

He scratched his arm and looked around, like he wanted to see if anyone else was seeing what was happening.

"Stunning," he said.

"What?" I asked with crossed arms.

"You will look stunning in a dress, more beautiful than you

already are. You would make everyone look at you, whether they wanted to or not, they wouldn't be able to not look at you," he took a deep breath. "That's what I was going to say."

"So, why didn't you?" I whispered.

"I don't know what other friendships you had in life Nora, but from my experience, friends never talk to each other that way," he said, and after his eyes roamed my face once more, he turned to look aside at the framed tulip field we hung up on the wall last week.

He was right, friendships worked on close connections, but also on boundaries. And moments like this, words like this, they blurred those boundaries.

"I wanted to brush it off, but then you talked about sitting on your own, and the two of us know that you go crazy if you sit for more than ten minutes without walking around or being in movement. I also know how stubborn you can be and if you say you'll sit here all day, you actually mean it, so…"

I smiled to myself, for some reason it brought me joy knowing that he knew me that well. And oh, I would absolutely have kept my word and stayed here until the last customer left the door.

"I always mean what I say." I put my notebook in my bag and stood up. "So, now that we had time to talk over business stuff, and *other* stuff, will you teach me how to serve?"

His glare was priceless when he watched me putting my hands on my hips, waiting.

"I remember you said you wanted to try being a waitress, but I thought you'd give up on that idea," he said. "Is it a checklist kind of thing?"

"It's always been on my checklist trying to do something new every day, but I think that if I get to help you with customers and talk to them face to face I can see this place from a different point of view, you know?" I said as I looked at the tables around us.

"Should I even argue on this with you and tell you to go home and rest or should I just roll with it?" he asked.

"Roll with it," I said. "Always."

He laughed. "Fine, but on one condition."

"Oh, now I'm intrigued."

"I'm the boss today. If I decide you need a break, you take a break, if a customer is being rude to you, not that it happens here that often, but if it does, you tell me and let me take care of it, got it?"

"Yes, boss," I said sweetly and watched as his eyes darkened.

"Okay, so-"

"Wait," I stopped him. "I have my own conditions, too."

"Now, *I'm* intrigued," he said. "Okay, I'm listening."

"If I decide you get too tired and need a break, you take a break, and if a customer even dares to be mean to you or say something rude, you tell me and I'll take care of it, got it?" I asked, and when he blinked and said nothing, I put the palm of my hand on his. "You look after me, and I look after you."

He looked down at our hands, and in what felt almost natural, he turned the palm of his hand so his fingers traced my own, till they were laced together. "I like that."

Then he cleared his throat, as if he thought I didn't understand him correctly. "Looking after each other, I like that."

When I looked down at our hands, it put a smile on my face.

I liked that, too.

CHAPTER 15
William

I was sitting on Ethan's bed as I watched him go through some of his notes for his course. He folded his sleeves, which gave me a glimpse of the tattoos he had on his arm, all the planets in the galaxy were attached to his skin, along with stars like the sun that was the closest to the palm of his hand.

When people looked at Ethan, at first glance, he seemed like a cool guy who could start a conversation with anyone. But since he was a kid, he was a true geek. He was always that boy in class that knew more than anyone else about the stars and about the universe we live in.

When he told people in high school he was going to pursue that love, and study astronomy and physics, some of them thought he would go through some change, some transformation and realize it was an unrealistic idea, too boring, but I knew he was never going to stop looking up at the sky. Then every month from then on, a new tattoo appeared on his arm, not too big, but not too small, they were in the perfect size to notice.

He adjusted the glasses on his nose when he finished writing, and turned to me, just to see that I was busy with my own writing process.

"What are you working on?" He closed the book he was using for his assignment and put it aside along with his notebook and computer. His room was an entire mess these days, he wasn't in his apartment much because of his studies, but if there was one thing that stayed clean and organized, it was his desk.

"Just an assignment for one of my business courses, nothing interesting, just numbers and more boring stuff," I said.

I was trying to think of all the boring things to say that would make him lose interest so he wouldn't figure out what I was actually doing.

"I've never seen you this focus when you made an assignment for one of your boring courses. Come on, Will, I'm your best friend, you can tell me everything." He scratched his arm and tilted his head to the side like a new idea came up in his head. "Is it porn?"

I stopped writing at once. "What?"

Though it was cold and raining outside, I felt warm. "It's not porn."

"Is it the new Netflix show you started watching a while ago?" He frowned like he was trying to remember. "What is the name again?"

I sighed, and turned over the computer to him, because I knew there were literally no limits to Ethan's curiosity. He took the computer from me after looking at me again to make sure I was okay with it and read the document I opened.

After a quick reading on his part, he looked up at me. "It's a list of movies."

I took back the computer and put it aside on the bed. "It's a list of movies for a movie night at the restaurant."

"Movie night?" He crossed his arms and leaned in on his chair.

"I spent time yesterday helping my dad cleaning out our attic, and I found some things in there that belonged to my grandparents, black and white photos of the two of them, and some love letters they wrote to each other. When I think of my grandparents I always remember the tulips. Maybe I just love the idea of showing love to someone through flowers, and even if gifting flowers was their form of communication, their love language, they still found other ways to show their feelings, you know?"

I smiled as I thought of the days when I got to see this life-changing love as a kid, there was something innocent in those small gestures, something so pure.

"Anyway," I cleared my throat. "I got to thinking of all the movies they got to watch, and the movies I always liked watching with them, and because of them, and I came up with the idea of having a night a week when we can show movies at the restaurant. I mean, my grandparents always cared about the community they created, and the people surrounding them, and watching movies together as people, I think it can be our way to create a new community."

"Will, that's…"

"I know, I know. It sounds like a lot of work, my parents will probably think the same, but I have to try. I mean if that works, we can make it a regular thing." I shrugged my shoulders; I didn't think of the difficulties of putting it into action, I just wanted to do it. "You know, I didn't go to that attic for years. I always thought it would be too painful to look at old pictures or think that much of my grandparents and who they used to be, but even though it hurt, it didn't hurt as much as I thought it would."

He sighed. "Well, grief isn't linear, it takes time to learn how to continue with your life and deal with it in your own way. I mean, I remember how you were when it happened. You were only twelve when your grandma passed, and if someone even mentioned her name, you would run and hide on the top of a tree or something."

When we were kids and I told people Ethan was my best friend, they told me to wait till I grow up, that we'll change as people, and go through hard challenges in life. Losing my grandma was a real test on our friendships because we were comfortable with each other. We had the chance to see if we were friends for a short period of time, or if we were friends for life. Dealing with that huge loss showed me it was a forever type of thing.

Ethan had to deal with a lot of crap on my part. He had to handle my bitter mood, and constantly tried to help me get out of my comfort of my own bed and walk outside, even if I didn't say a word. He gave me homework every time I skipped school because I didn't want to deal with the real world. He was there, during the storms, the grief and the tears, and he was there for me now. So, no, it had nothing to do with comfort and easy circumstances.

"Why are you looking at me like that?" I asked when he looked at me behind his glasses.

"It's been a long time since I heard you talk about your grandparents, especially this way," he said. "You don't like to talk about them, so the fact that you're doing this now…"

I smiled, because he was right, just the thought of them was painful for so long, so talking about it was a huge step for me. I made a lot of those lately, *big* steps. I wanted to say it had to do with growing up, of coming to terms with loss and deciding to open yourself up, but it wasn't just me. It was Nora. Since that night, since that rainy night, I kept on making all these big steps, and they all led to her. "I think it's Nora."

"Nora?" he asked and sipped from the glass of water that was hidden between all the papers and books on his desk.

"She's the first person I talked to about my grandparents and what was really going on with Oasis," I said. "I didn't give much thought into it; I just told her everything. She has that effect on me, I always feel comfortable sharing things with her, things that I might feel embarrassed or scared to confess to anyone else."

"I thought I was the only person you share everything with, now I'm jealous," he joked, and then leaned towards me and rubbed his hands together. "So, do you feel ready to tell me what really happened that night when she was here with her friends?"

I've gone quiet. Sure, he was my best friend, and sure we were already in this session of sharing. But yet, even though I knew all these facts, I couldn't say anything, because what would I tell him? That the innocent competition spirit between us turned into something more? That one moment we were standing near the couch and a moment after we found ourselves on the same couch? That we were just talking, but all I could think about during our talk was how much I wanted to kiss her? Sure, I wanted to tell him, but I couldn't say it, not when I was still wondering what went through her head during that time.

As if I wasn't embarrassed and confused enough, he continued. "You two almost finished the entire cheesecake I prepared earlier that day, and in the middle of the night, I was thirsty and went to the kitchen, but then I stopped in the hallway when I saw you looking at her as she was falling asleep in your lap."

My heart skipped a beat when he looked at me. *He knew.* He knew exactly what happened that night.

"So, you do know what happened," I said slowly.

"Yeah, I know. The question is if you do?" he asked, and when I kept being quiet, he smiled at me. "Look, Will, I know you prefer being quiet and keeping things to yourself, maybe you think it's easier this way, but I'm actually worried for you that if you don't say it out loud at least once, you won't feel any better, and it will only get worse."

"Could it get any worse than that?" I sighed when I realized how right he was.

He knew I didn't show up here in the middle of the day because I wanted to chat about the weather or his cheesecake recipe. He had enough studies to do and I had enough responsibility in the restaurant.

I took a deep breath and licked my lips. Instead of saying it slowly, or allowing myself more time, I just said it, because fast or slow, quiet, or loud, my confession hit me the same way it did, every time. It hit hard, right to the core.

"I like her."

"You like her," he nodded, like he could see on my face the relief I felt for finally saying it.

"I'm an idiot," I laughed, and my laugh became even harder when he offered me the cheesecake he had on his plate and hadn't touched yet.

His cheesecake was good and creamy and everything a cheesecake was meant to be, but it couldn't make me feel less of an idiot.

"Because you like a girl, Will?" he chuckled. "I think you will need to do much more than that to be considered an idiot."

"No, I'm an idiot for not doing something about it sooner. Maybe if I just asked her out at the beginning like I wanted to, then—"

"Wait, hold on, what do you mean?" he asked. "All you told me about her at that time was that you met a nice girl at the restaurant, you never told me *that* part."

"Trust me, you don't want to know more parts, like the part I told her that she radiates like the sun, or that she heard the song I put on my phone when my mom calls me."

"Radiates like the sun?" he repeated and put his hand on his mouth to stop himself from laughing, like he just realized how awkward his best friend can actually be.

"Stupid, I know."

"It's original, I'll give you that."

"I wanted to ask her out, but it's been like, what, two years since I properly dated someone? And that relationship ended up miserably," I groaned. "Then it all happened pretty fast, she told me we could be friends and I said yes, because I thought that I might realize we really are good as friends and nothing more. Besides, since the moment I met her I knew I wanted to know more about her, it wasn't supposed to matter in which way I'd get to do that."

"And then you realized you have feelings for her and been overthinking it all this time," he sighed and put down his glasses. "Damn, how didn't you go crazy from keeping it in for that long?"

I was known for keeping things in, I kept these feelings hidden for about a month. I knew he wasn't mad for it, he was used to it, but I was sure he expected me to give in a lot sooner and let the words out when I figured out I start liking this girl.

"I've been focusing on work, you would be surprised what it can do to a person," I said. "Now that you know, I feel much better. I can just keep on focusing on work and pretend I like her as my friend."

"Will, do you remember what you did when you found out your grandma was sick?" he asked me. "How you focused on helping out the restaurant and changed the subject every time someone mentioned it? How you ran away from the waiting room the moment she passed and stayed in your bed for weeks later? Do you remember?"

"Of course I remember."

Was it even possible to forget the five stages of grief? Was it possible to deny less, and accept the loss more? Just thinking about that time made me want to curl up. I hated thinking of that version of me, looking back at things now, I felt sad for the little kid that just kept on running.

I laid down on his sheets after finishing the cake. "I don't understand how it has anything to do with it."

"I don't think running from your feelings again is the best way of dealing with the situation, that's all," he said, his voice was gentle enough to get to me, but stern enough to make me listen. "You should tell her, Will."

"No, I really shouldn't," I said.

"Will…"

I put my hands behind my head and looked up at the ceiling. "Even if I tell her, even if in some other universe she says she likes me back, I can't do that to her. You remember what happened last time I was with someone. I was trying so hard to make the relationship work, but I was too busy with my own grief and helping my parents with the restaurant that I didn't care for her enough, and she left. I don't want the same thing to happen with Nora, she already does so much for me and my family."

"The relationship didn't end because of you Will," he commented and sat with me on the bed. "You just didn't fit together, and sometimes the reason for a breakup is that simple."

I wish that was the reason, I wish it was that simple.

"Stay," I whispered to her in the middle of the empty restaurant. Everyone left Oasis as I was left to clean the last tables before I was ready to 1 head home. She was standing there, looking at me with sad blue eyes.

"Will, you know I can't." she fumbled with the fabric of her dress, barely able to look back at me as she was about to go.

Don't go.

Don't leave me.

"I can't be with a guy I barely get to see outside of these walls. I've tried to be there for you, you know? I tried to give you time, I tried to be patient, I tried to be understanding. I tried everything, but I feel like you never did. You're so blind to your grief that you don't see me anymore."

I nodded, because what could I say? She wasn't wrong.

I took a deep breath before I went to look back at her. "You deserve more, I know that."

We looked at each other for a long moment, and then I looked at her as she walked towards me. She kissed my cheek in one long and sad kiss and stepped back. "Goodbye, Will."

She moved towards the exit door, but stopped with her hand

on the handle when she heard my shattered voice. "I tried…I really did try."

She gave me one of her weaker smiles. "I know you did."

I closed my eyes, because I couldn't look at him when I didn't believe what he said.

"Nora deserves a normal relationship, with someone who'll treat her right," I sighed, and I could feel my heart aching with each word that came out of my mouth. Luuk's words echoed in my head when I thought of what Nora needed, what I wanted her to have, what I knew she deserved.

I'm here to ask you to look after her, to make sure that when I, or Xander are not around, she has someone she can count on with her, someone that will make sure she doesn't carry too much on herself again.

I knew that if she was with me, she would always have to carry more on herself. She would have to carry my darker parts, the stress and pressure of keeping my family business together, my terrible habit of overthinking, the list could go on and on.

"That's what she deserves," I whispered, more to myself than to Ethan. Just to convince myself one more time that I was doing the right thing.

CHAPTER 16
Nora

I was sitting with Luuk at our usual spot as people passed by with different coffee and drinking orders. Luuk opened the horoscope page right away. He cleared his throat before looking directly at me, as he did each time he was reading me all about my future.

"What do you want me to begin with?" he asked me and sipped quickly from his green tea. Luuk was a bit cold due to the weather, and still, he wasn't willing to stay in his apartment the entire day. He said it made him feel lonely and lifeless. His words, not mine.

"We've got career, health, relationships, finances, though in my opinion it's the most boring part of it all, and we got the general energy of the day," he said as his eyes were roaming the page. It always made me laugh to see how serious he was being when it came to the way the stars viewed our paths in the world.

I wrapped my hands around my cup of coffee, and even though I ordered it a while ago, I wasn't drinking much of it. Despite what I thought in the past, it wasn't one of the best coffees in the city. It was fine, just meh. I wished I could call

William; tell him I was on my way to him so he could prepare me his special coffee.

"Nora?" he asked again when I didn't answer.

I blinked my eyes when I realized I was in some weird trance. "Um, I don't know," I played with a strand of hair.

Usually, I was all in for this kind of game, guessing what happened next, what of all these options was the most intriguing one, but a part of me felt off today. Maybe it wasn't just a matter of general energy that could be fixed with the right coffee with the perfect balance of sugar and coffee beans, maybe it was more than that.

Since I met William and started helping him, I started to feel more like myself than I ever felt. Writing down plans and brainstorming about ideas were probably the best parts of my day, it made me believe that I could prove my parents wrong and that I could do great things with my passion.

I was in control.

After a long time of feeling lost under the pressure, I was in control.

But the scariest part about control was the fear of losing it in a matter of seconds.

I was trying not to get in my own head, because I wasn't that kind of person, not anymore. But then all these thoughts ran through my head, like the way William's blue eyes beamed with joy as the customers kept filling out the restaurant, how fun and easy it was to serve and take orders and believe like we could always work together like we did that day.

"So do you think you can handle table five, or should I go?" William asked me as we were sitting side by side, looking toward the big round table with exactly eight people sitting around it. Two elders who sat with a few adults and a kid.

"Can I ask you something first?" I turned to look at William who already had his eyes on me.

"Yes, you have to wear this apron, it's a requirement," he said as his eyes roamed over the white apron he gave me as part of my so called "training". I eyed him and he chuckled. "Okay, maybe it's more for my own personal amusement."

"Shocking," I hit him gently on the chest. "What I've been meaning to ask is why do you number tables that way? I mean I always watch these shows and you hear someone yelling, take this chicken to table 6, and this cake to 4." I tried to imitate the people I heard in the movies. "I get it, you need order and you just showed me an hour ago that seating chart, but I always pictured you as the kind of person to remember people by face, not by a table number."

"You got so much more to learn, rookie," he mused and smiled as he walked towards that table to take the order from the family.

If I was being honest, I knew I wasn't a good waitress. I was mixing up the tables in my head and dropped one plate in the way, and almost another one would've fallen if William didn't catch it on time, but I wasn't going through a bad time, I was enjoying going around and talking to people as William explained everything to me in the most patient way.

But maybe more than working together, I loved seeing him in his element, he was as natural as this. Not at being a waiter, but at communicating with people, making them feel at home in his family's restaurant. Like he made me feel at home the first night we met.

He came back from the table and put his small notebook behind his back. His eyes twinkled when he stood back next to me. "Nora, how do you feel about seeing our kitchen?"

"You're kidding right?" I asked. "I've been helping you for so long, and you never let me into the kitchen, what changed?"

"We don't really let many people into the kitchen, our cooking is based on our family's recipes, and with ingredients my grandma loved to use. My parents are not strict parents, but they're strict about that rule," he explained. "But I think even my dad couldn't say no to you when he realizes how much you've helped us already, and what a good friend you've been to me."

My heart fluttered.

"Also, I kind of promised that kid over there that I'll make him a sandwich with hagelslag. It isn't part of our menu, but I couldn't tell him no." He looked back at the kid who was surrounded by adults and then at me. "Are you up for making a kid smile?"

A kid that wanted to eat bread with chocolate sprinkles. Damn, I could relate to that.

"Show me the kitchen," I said, and he didn't waste time to hold my hand and lead me into the place where I wondered so many times how it looked from the inside. We moved between the cooks, avoided the hot pans and the meat on the grill before we found an empty corner.

William was moving fast as he was looking for bread and hagelslag, and eventually he came back with all he needed to make the perfect sandwich.

I watched his hands move as he made it.

"William."

"Hmm?"

"If you could choose any career in the world, and you didn't stay here and help your family, what do you think you'll choose?" I asked.

I sat in a high stool to watch him better. Just when I was sitting down I realized how much walking around and taking orders ended up being more work than I thought it would be.

Then I turned back to look at him, and he didn't even pause or hesitate when he said, "I wouldn't choose anything else." When he felt my gaze on him he probably felt the need to explain. "I know some people whose parents or family had a business, don't necessarily feel that eager to run that business in the future, they might have other dreams and wishes in life, but it was never my case. When I was a kid I was looking for the moment my dad would let me learn recipes and help out, and all my life I saw myself running the business one day, continuing what my grandparents started."

He talked with such honesty that I wanted to hug him and tell him it would happen, nothing bad would happen, but it wasn't my place to promise such a thing.

"I never dreamed of doing anything else, I never thought of it, I would never choose something else," he said and looked around at the meals that went out to customers. "Not if it was up to me."

"Hearing you talk like that, it's beautiful," I said, though I didn't know if it was enough to convey all I thought of him at that moment. I always saw him as a sweet and genuine guy, but many moments I spent by his side I found myself astonished by how strong his love for his family was, and how kind he actually was.

"I know I've been a waitress for only an hour or so, but I loved watching you from the side, you seemed really happy today, like you were in your natural element," I said.

"You know, I haven't felt happy for a while," he looked up at me. "Even when we started having more customers, I was still feeling anxious, like it was all a dream and the next day I came to work, it would be the same way as before. But getting to serve with you today, and talk with people, it made me realize something."

"That I don't have a future as a waitress?" I joked.

He laughed. "That things can feel easy too, that it's possible working without thinking 24/7 about the scary unknown future. You make me feel a bit more hopeful, Nora Tuinstra."

I felt something lighting up with me when he called me by my full name. I knew I was playing a dangerous game, I shouldn't care that much about William, I definitely shouldn't have felt like his problems were my problems, because it made it clear that I shouldn't bother myself with this more than I already did. But here I was, caring, worrying, thinking how I could turn the bit hopeful guy in front of me to hopeful.

I left the stool and wrapped my arms around William's body.

I could feel his chest rumble and shoulders shake when he wrapped his arms back around my body. "What is that for?"

I didn't know how to explain my actions, I just wanted to feel his touch.

I shrugged my shoulders.

I could feel him smiling when he kissed my forehead and then gave me the sandwich he made.

"What about the kid?" I asked, but still took it from him.

"I'll make him a new one," he said. "You might not be a kid, but everyone loves hagelslag, and you deserve it after trying out being a waitress for a day."

"Say no more," I muttered and took a bite from the sandwich, as I heard him laugh while he was making a new one.

"Nora?"

I heard Luuk's voice again, and that memory from the restaurant faded away and brought me back to Luuk who was still waiting for my answer.

"Maybe I'm completely healthy and you're the one who got a cold?" he asked. "You've been acting weird this morning, Nor."

My gaze wandered over the people in line and stopped on a man eating a chocolate cake with sprinkles on the top of it. "Believe me, Luuk. I know."

"So, what would it be?" he asked and waved the paper he was reading from to bring me back to our original topic.

"Surprise me," I said.

I wished I could show a bit more enthusiasm, but a part of me wished we didn't do this today, I didn't need to get more confused or weird than I already felt.

He made a dramatic cough like he was about to announce something life changing. "Dear Virgo, when it comes to your energy you would probably feel that something is off but wouldn't be able to put in words how you feel." He paused to look at me, like despite his fate in the stars, he couldn't believe how accurate the horoscope was this time. "It would be wise to take a step back, not rush into any decision. Try to wear light and soft tones like pastel, gray or white that would keep your energy in balance."

I glanced down at the white sweater and pink skirt I was wearing.

"You sure you haven't read the horoscope today before we met here?" he asked.

I shook my head and he sighed and went on reading, because even he had nothing to say about it at this point.

"When it comes to relationships with others, you will feel off balance with a person you care deeply about. Your nature as a kind and loyal friend would be up to the test when a new force threatens the stability you have with that special someone. Remember, the key to pass the storm coming is hidden within your grace and intelligence." I lifted my head towards Luuk, and he put his hand in the air like he knew what was going through my head. "Hey, don't look at me, nothing could threaten our friendship Nor, you know that already."

"Remind me again why astrology always has to be so vague?" I asked. "Grace and intelligence, what does it even mean?"

"Ask the stars to be clearer the next time," he suggested.

I tried to take another sip of my coffee, but it was bitter, and cold and didn't help in making me feel any less irritated.

"Sorry to break it up to you, Luuk," I said while I threw the coffee to the trash, "but the stars don't seem to be on my side today."

I put my things back in my bag, and just when I was about to get up and leave the place, my phone was ringing and Luuk stared at the name on my screen. "Well, maybe they didn't completely abandon you either."

"Huh?"

Before I could take my phone back, he answered the call and pressed it to his ear. He smirked at me as he answered the person on the other side of the line. "Hi there, Will. How are you feeling in this lovely cold and freezing weather?"

I reached my hand forward, but Luuk already got up from his seat and took his bag with him, walking towards the exit door.

"Luuk, I'm really not in the mood for this, give it to me," I muttered behind him as I put my small bag around my shoulder. I was feeling frantic.

I was sure the entire campus could hear the heels of my boots hit the ground as I was trying to get my phone back.

"Oh, Nor?" he asked and glanced at me again. "I don't know if you want to talk with her right now, she might be sick, we will have to check on that, and her eyes are crazy green today. Did you watch Harry Potter, Will?"

"Are you seriously going to compare my eyes to-"

"Yeah, so not specifically the color of Slytherin, but more like...hey!" he turned sharply when I grabbed the phone from his grip and walked away from him.

"You should go if you don't want to be late, again," I commented, and it might have put some sense into him, because he was already walking away to class.

"Sorry about that," I said, suddenly feeling embarrassed that Will had to go through with Luuk's nonsense. "Let's start this conversation properly. Hi, William."

"Hi, Nora," he said in a low voice that made me shiver. "How are you today?"

I pressed my lips together, trying to think of something to say that wouldn't make him worry for me for no valid reason.

"Do you want to talk first about what Luuk just told me?" his voice was more hesitant this time.

"My eyes are nothing like the color of Slytherin. Besides, it was rude of him to say it while he knows my house is Ravenclaw."

"You're right, your eyes are nothing like that, even when you're upset or lost in some deep thought, they're more similar to grass after the rain, or the color of a meadow on a sunny day. Depends on your mood." He explained it as if he had given a lot of thought before to give such a specific description.

I was flattered to think it was true.

"Nora, are you still there?" he asked when I hadn't said a word.

"Forgive me, William, I've been feeling a bit off this morning," I said as I was walking around the campus with no goal of where I was heading to.

"Yeah, Luuk has been mentioning that you might be sick," he said. "Maybe you should go home and rest? Or if you want, I can make you a soup, it's my grandma's recipe. I hope you like vegetables and chicken."

I smiled as I pressed the phone to my ear; he really was the sweetest guy I've ever known, wasn't he? He was willing to leave everything just to make me soup and make me feel better. I wasn't sick, but part of me hoped I was just to see what else he would offer.

"I adore chicken and vegetable soup, but you should know I'm not sick. I'm afraid I'm just having one of those days. I was staring at my notebook this morning and couldn't write anything, and then I had this bad coffee, and ugh, sorry, I'm sure you have better things to do right now instead of listening to my stupid complaints."

"Don't say that Nora. When it comes to you nothing is stupid or a waste of time, okay?" he assured me.

"Okay," I whispered as I was fidgeting with the fabric of my sweater.

"Do you have any other classes today?" he asked.

"No, I had one earlier before I met with Luuk, but that's it," I said as I was looking at the people passing by, all dressed with multiple layers and walking on their way to the different classes. "What about you?"

"My professor canceled our class, he had a family emergency," he explained, and after a short pause he said, "Would you maybe like to spend the afternoon with me?"

There was a bounce in my step, but I tried not to get my hopes up too soon.

"You want to see me pretend as a waitress for the day again?" I asked.

It wasn't like I didn't want to spend the day in the restaurant like usual, but today was different. Something in me wanted to be in the fresh air, whether there was a storm coming or rain about to fall, I couldn't stay in a close space that would make me question things with William any further.

"Although I would love to wait tables with you again, I don't think that's what you need right now."

"What do you think I need?" I asked, though I had no doubt that he knew me enough to know that answer.

"You need fresh air, and maybe I could use some of that too," he admitted timidly. "I thought of going to a market close by. I need to go buy supplies for the restaurant, anyway, and then, maybe some tulips. No fake ones, of course. Then we can find a good soup."

"I already told you I'm not sick," I said, but couldn't help but smile at his offer.

"Is that a yes?" he asked, and if I knew any better, I would've said he sounded nervous.

"William, haven't you learned already that when it comes to you, it's always a yes?" I asked and didn't ponder too long over what I actually meant by that. "I would love to spend the afternoon with you."

CHAPTER 17
Nora

When I reached the spot William sent to my phone, I realized he wasn't kidding when he said it was going to be packed with people and that it would take me some time to find him. Despite the gray sky and the frigid air, people were spending their day buying groceries, flowers, or old books. The old residential buildings that were around fit the atmosphere and the canals close by were the perfect addition to the view.

I wondered what would happen if I could spend every day like this, not having to deal with my responsibilities or my worries and just walk around, pick whatever I liked and could enjoy my day without having somewhere to go.

William and I didn't spend much time outside of the restaurant. William was trying to help his family, and I wanted to help him and get better in my own abilities, but even if I enjoyed doing that, I still felt like my soul needed those short breaks from everything. I wanted more days of eating at an Italian restaurant with him, or walking around together and spending the day talking about stories we might not be able to share with someone else.

"Where is he?" I muttered to myself and tried to step on my tip toe to look past the people, but all I saw was more people and more stands with sellers.

I sent him my location because he had a better chance finding me than I did him, and when he answered me I opened the phone immediately.

WILLIAM
Hang in there, Nora. I'm on my way.

I walked near a stand with cheese, then another one with vintage decorations where the seller was nowhere to be found, until I stopped near an old book stand. The seller was an old lady with gray hair who read a book through her round glasses. My eyes scanned the books, some were in a better condition and others were missing a letter on the cover or little details, but out of all the books, my eyes landed on one with a yellow cover and flowers painted on it.

"The Language of Flowers," I read from the cover.

The old lady must've heard me. She put her book down and lifted her head to look at the book I was holding.

"Wonderful choice," she commented.

I flipped the book to look at the back cover and then flipped a few pages, something about the way she said it made me suspect it was in a worse condition than I thought or that it was of the least popular one in her stand. But it was in a good condition, maybe even a perfect one, I could easily see it in a library or a bookstore.

"Is it meant for gardeners, or something like that?"

She laughed. "Oh, no dear, flowers aren't meant only for beauty, or to look at from afar. In the Victorian era, they could deliver coded messages," she said.

"Like love?" I asked her when I was reminded of what William told me about his grandparents, how the tulips were their way to show love for each other, their tool to grow as a couple.

"Flowers can be a declaration of love, but not all flowers mean that, and not all meanings are that beautiful. Did you know you could use flowers to warn your enemy?" she asked.

"Like in a battlefield, when two enemies fight against each other and each one of them is trying to win?" I chuckled. "It seems absurd that someone would send flowers to a person they despise instead of some threatening letter, or I don't know what people did those days, maybe an invitation to a duel or whatever."

She looked at me calmly, like she already heard that kind of opinion in the past. "You laugh now, but you can't know when you'll need to warn your enemy. Just think of the flowers as a way to send a message without having to utter a word. When you think about it, that's the perfect way to say what's on your heart and stay graceful at the same time."

"No offense, but I don't think modern day politicians or officers in the military would use a flower to warn someone."

"Who said anything about a literal battlefield?" she asked. "The battlefield of love might be the cruelest of all. Some would say the fight to gain someone's heart is the hardest of all fights."

I stared at her as she kept explaining to me how ladies of the Victorian era used flowers to court their suiters, and how they wore their flowers, but it was hard for me to listen to her. I was still stuck on the *enemies'* part and the *battlefield of love*. I thought that if I left campus and went for a walk outside, this day would become less weird, but that old lady just proved me wrong.

I felt someone touching my shoulder lightly and turned to see William. "Sorry you had to wait."

"That's okay," I smiled. "You know I always find ways to keep myself entertained."

He looked down at the book I was holding and tilted his head as he tried to read the cover. "Good book?"

"It's a good book for any couple of lovers," the old lady said as she switched glances between us.

I gazed at William, whose cheeks were already pink from the cold, but got a deeper shade as he heard the conversation between me and the old lady. I, on the other hand, wasn't going to let my thoughts wander to that place, because when it came to us, compliments were only compliments, tulips were only tulips, and our friendship started to become as important as the one I had with Xander and Luuk.

If I really had feelings for him, somewhere deep inside, I wasn't going to admit it, especially not in front of some lady who thought she knew who I was from a few minutes of small talk.

"Oh, no," I said. "You're reading it all wrong."

She looked at William again before she leaned forward to take a better look at me.

"Are you sure I'm wrong, dear?" she asked, her voice low but certain.

"I...I think we should go, seems like it will rain soon," I glanced at William. "Thank you for all the information about enemies, and lovers, and coded messages. It was definitely... interesting."

I put the book down and nodded my head, ready to go, but after I took a few steps, I realized Willaim wasn't walking with me, he was still there at the old book stands.

"I'll take it," he told her and took out his wallet from the pocket of his jeans. "How much is it?"

"William," I tried to warn him, but it was too late.

She put the book in a bag and told him something that made him laugh before he left the lady and came back to me, handing me the same back. "For you."

"William," I whispered as I watched the bag in disbelief that he had just done that. "Why?"

"You seemed to like it, so I wanted to give it to you, it's not a big deal," he said and when he saw I still hadn't moved, he took my hand gently and put it in my head.

My heart was beating briskly as I accepted his gift.

"Just to clarify, I didn't like it, and I didn't like that old lady either. It felt like she looked right through me, and I'm pretty sure she read 'Love and War' way too many times with all this talk about love and enemies," I said, and when I turned my head to look back at her from a distance, I was almost certain she was looking at us. "Or historical romance, that's an option, too..." I muttered. "What did she tell you when I walked away?"

He laughed, like he was holding back a secret.

"William?"

"She said," he cleared his throat, "she told me that she's been selling books for longer than she can remember. She can recognize if a person is a hopeless romantic or not when she sees one, all by the books they pick. It's her way of picking up on their character."

"Okay, and...?"

"She told me you're more of a hopeless romantic than you let on."

"Because of a book about flowers?" I asked.

I would've said it was ridiculous if I hadn't known any better, but I've known myself enough to know she was right.

"What did you say?" I asked him.

He answered with no hesitation as his blue eyes met with mine. "That I know that already."

It was funny how I kept being surprised by how much he knew me already, by how we managed to figure each other out without having to talk, what was unknown to others was a common knowledge between us.

"Come on," he said when he sensed my silence. "After what you told me about your morning, we should get you a normal coffee."

"Oh, this morning," I sighed as we walked ahead. "I feel the need to apologize again, I didn't mean to rant that much, and Luuk—"

"He's a funny guy," he said before I could apologize about him, too. "If I couldn't tell earlier, I can tell now what a close friendship you have."

"Yeah, we are," I said. "The three of us are, I don't even know how we became a trio. They were best friends from kindergarten and somehow I found a way to slip in and they had to make room for me."

He laughed and put his hands in his jacket. "You? Are you sure? It doesn't sound like something you would do."

I hit his shoulder lightly as his laughter kept going. He slowly made me feel at ease again and forget all the things that bothered me when I woke up this morning.

"I do have one question though," he started. "Ravenclaw?"

I immediately laughed. "Out of everything you heard me say through the phone, that's what you wanted to refer too?"

"It got me curious to know more. I mean, I'm not saying you're not an overachiever, or witty or insanely creative, I just pictured you as a Gryffindor."

William Vanderweide. He always knew how to catch my attention. One would think it was because of his good looks, because of his pair of magnetic blue eyes or shy smile, but it was more than just that, these were his words and actions. The way he called me by my full name, or complimented me in ways no boy ever did before. It was the way he gave me a tulip, like it was the most natural thing to do, giving me flowers I could keep safe in my room when I get home.

"Did you now?" I asked. "What made you think that thought?"

"Your daring heart," he said, and pressed his lips together like he just realized he said that without having to put any thought into it. Almost like a reflex. "It's one of the things that make you stand out of all people, or so I think," he said and went to look up. "It's like the sky. There's gray, there's blue and then…"

"There's the sun," I finished when my eyes noticed it hiding behind a cloud.

"You really do love comparing me to the sun, don't you?" I asked. "You did that the first time we met. Why is that?"

He avoided my eyes as I tried to make him look at me and kept looking up instead. "It's nothing. I spend a lot of time with Ethan, you met Ethan."

"Yeah, I did…" I said, confused by how weird he was behaving.

Please don't get weird on me too William, I had enough of that for one day.

"He loves the stars, the planets, did I tell you he studies astronomy and physics in university? I think all his talk about the galaxy made me start looking at people as ones."

"Oh, that I understand," I smiled. "I spend so many mornings reading horoscopes with Luuk that every time I meet a person, I can't help but wonder what their zodiac sign is out of curiosity, you know? I mean, some people believe it, some not, but even if I look at it as a fun thing to read and nothing more, I still feel like when I find out someone's zodiac, I learn so much more about them at that moment."

"So, why do you read the zodiac then, if you don't believe it?" he asked.

I could understand why he wondered, Xander wondered the same thing too when he found me and Luuk reading together.

"It feels like a fun game, guessing what could come true and what is just written there. This whole thing started because of Luuk's sister actually, Jupiter."

"The fifth planet?"

I stopped to take a good look at him. "Look at you William, knowing stuff about the galaxy."

He shrugged his shoulders, but by the smirk on his face I could tell he was proud of himself.

"Anyway, their family is really into astrology, palm reading, tarot, all of this stuff is a big part of the way they grew up. Luuk and Jupiter used to read horoscopes together, it was their thing, until she decided she didn't like that world anymore. She left to travel somewhere in Europe, and Luuk was left by himself."

My heart sank every time I thought of Jupitar leaving. I didn't have a sibling, but I knew that for Luuk, Jupiter wasn't just his sister, she was his best friend. Despite his efforts of brushing things off and acting like her going away for an unknown amount of time was nothing, I knew he missed her.

"So that's why you started reading with him?" he asked when he put the pieces together. "So, he wouldn't do it by himself and feel alone."

"They're still the best of friends, I'm just filling her place until she decides to come back. Besides, I never had siblings, Luuk and Xander are the closest I have to that," I explained. "I'm sure you feel the same way about Ethan."

"I do," he nodded, before he went to smile at me. He didn't say anything else, just smiled to look at me.

"What?" I giggled. "I'm warning you, William, if you tell me there's no place that sells coffee here, I will kill you."

"Lying to you about coffee?" he asked. "I know better than that."

Good to know.

Despite the crowd walking the streets of the market, the atmosphere was serene, quiet, like nothing could ruin it.

"I have something to tell you, something I've been keeping away for a while," he said, and had no intention of keeping my curiosity at bay, because the pause was too short for that. "I know your zodiac sign."

"You…you know my zodiac sign," I repeated.

His childish smile on his face made me smile too. He wasn't

happy just because he learned something new about me, but he was happy he got to discover it on his own.

"You're a Virgo," he said, and as if that didn't surprise me enough, he continued. "Sun. It's your sun sign."

"Luuk told you, didn't he?" I asked, though I was secretly impressed he got that information. Luuk wasn't me, he believed in the stars in the most genuine way, and he wouldn't share this kind of fact about me to anyone.

I smiled when I understood it was just another one of Luuk's ways to show me he was more than supportive of the relationship I was establishing with William. If I had any doubts about Luuk's thoughts about him, they were all gone now.

"I can't reveal my sources," he said as he crossed his arms.

I laughed again. "Fine, as you wish. What is yours?"

"I'm not telling you," he said. "You'll have to figure that out on your own."

I wondered how long we could keep going back and forward like this, playing with facts and questions like it was another game. I almost wanted to test it out just to see how far we could go, just because I was having so much fun being around him and talking with each other this way.

"You don't need to tell me, I've read horoscopes on a daily basis for a while. I will figure out your zodiac sign soon enough," I commented and took a step closer to him. "For now, I'll enjoy the fact I know your Hogwarts house."

"But I didn't tell you my house," he mumbled as his eyes scanned my face when I made another step forward.

I didn't need to step that close, I didn't need to close the distance, but for some reason, I wanted to hope I could make his body shiver or warm up like mine did when he stood close.

"Exactly," I said. "Come on William, you're one of the most loyal, hardworking, kind and compassionate people I know, if not the *most*. Why do you think I love being around you so much?"

"Nora," he breathed out as he stared down my face, his eyes roaming down to mine until they landed on my mouth.

Boundaries. I needed to remind myself that any friendship needed boundaries, clear lines you shouldn't cross, but here I was, enjoying the fact I made him act this way. That one sweet word on my part could make him want to lose control. I could feel it, I could see it all over his face, and part of me wondered if I'd ever get to feel it too.

"You're a Hufflepuff," I said and took another look at him. "Definitely a Hufflepuff."

He let his eyes roam on my lips for a second longer before he went back to my eyes. "We...we should go get you coffee."

"Are you sure that's what you want?" I tilted my head.

"Let's go inside, Nora."

I didn't think he would say something else; he was a *gentleman,* after all.

Then he put his hands back in his jacket's pockets and we kept on walking.

I suppose it wasn't a good time to tell him I wasn't sure coffee was the only thing I wanted anymore.

CHAPTER 18
William

I stared down at Nora as we were walking the streets of our city, knowing it was a matter of time till the rain started to fall and we would have to make our way back. I played with my hands as I waited to hear what she had to say about my movie night's idea.

We both had that thing in common, having ideas, but Nora was much braver than I when it came to expressing them out loud. I was used to hearing so many no's from my parents, that even if Nora had a different approach to it all, which she did, I was still a bit hesitant on what, when and where to share my ideas.

"William, I love this idea," she said, her eyes got the same spark they had every time she was excited about something. "I mean, who doesn't love movies?"

"I want you to plan the event, you can pick up any decorations you want. The color palette, the ads for socials, whatever you want. As long as it works with the budget," I said.

She looked at me with big green eyes, her mouth was parted as she processed what I meant. I expected her to jump from joy, knowing one of her main goals of helping me was to gain experience as an event planner and show people how creative and dedicated she really was.

I moved a strand of hair from her face and curled it behind her ear. "What is it?"

"I never actually planned an event before. My mom is the event planner in the family, she's the expert. The closest I got was planning birthday parties for cousins or friends, but it was never anything that was too over the top, and not in a restaurant that's for sure," she said, and maybe for the first time ever, Nora wasn't just the girl with the daring heart I knew, she seemed scared. "I don't want to let you down."

"Nora," I put both my hands at the side of her face. "You won't let me down. You're incapable of that."

"How are you so sure?"

"Because I've seen what you're capable of. Before you showed up at Oasis the first time, I spent most days with almost no customers, things felt hopeless, and now the restaurant is full of people like it never before, and it reminds me of the days my grandparents were still here, when everything was good and simple. Think of this movie night as a fun experiment. You can write your checklist, plan out what seems right, and even if in the worst-case scenario no one comes or people don't show interest, we get a fun movie night."

"Just the two of us?" she asked.

I swallowed hard as my hands froze around her face.

I wish that could be an option. Since our late night talk I imagined in my head what it would be like to watch a movie together, sit on the coach or go on a nice date to the cinema. We would probably watch a romantic movie, something light and fun, something that would fit us. But even if the movie would be good, even if it would be the best movie of the year, I would gaze at her every once in a while, wondering when is the perfect time to kiss the girl I liked.

No, watching a movie together was a whole other definition for a bad idea.

"No," I let my hand slip from her face. "With our friends."

"Right, our friends," she said slowly, and sounded almost *disappointed*?

No, that couldn't be.

"If you don't want to do it, then you don't have to. I don't want you to put pressure on yourself or be in a stressful position because of me, that's never—"

She put her finger on my lips and smiled kindly at me. "William, I want to do it."

"Oh, that's good," I said against her hand that hadn't moved from my lips yet. "Great, actually."

"But I want you to pick the movie."

"Me?"

"I might be the planner, but it's your family's restaurant, your grandparents' story, your idea, it only seems fair you'd get that part," she said. "Besides, let's be honest, you have more knowledge than me when it comes to romantic movies."

"What makes you say that?" I asked.

I knew why she said what she said, but I wanted to hear more of how she perceived me. If I couldn't confess my feelings to her, I was going to enjoy what I could have.

She opened her mouth and closed it, like she wasn't sure with which direction she wanted to go with this.

"You watch *the Notebook*, by choice," she said at last. "I think that sums it up pretty nicely."

I laughed and pulled her in for a hug. "That's a good point, Nora."

"Wait," she pulled away. "What about your parents?"

"They are going on a romantic trip. I honestly thought they would cancel it with everything going on in the business, but they haven't had that quality time for so long, so who am I to judge them," I shrugged. "While they won't be here, we can have the event without causing any suspicions. And after that, well, we'll deal with it as it happens."

"You really thought of everything, didn't you?" she asked.

"You write lists, and I overthink everything," I smirked and when I felt a drop of rain fall on my cheek I looked up and so did she.

"It's going to start raining soon, we should go," I said as I kept watching the gray sky.

I put my hand on her back to lead us to a safe place, but she put her hand on mine and moved away from me gently.

"No..."

"No?"

She wanted to get completely wet in the rain again and scare me at the hundredth time that she might get sick, didn't she?

"There's one more thing on my list that I need to do." She brought me her bag with the book. "I'll be quick, I promise."

Then she stood on her tip toes and pressed her lips to my cheeks in a gentle kiss. I was standing there like a schoolboy, putting my hand on my cheek as I watched her walk away.

I was so stunned that I barely managed to take my phone out of my pocket and answer it. "Hello?"

"What's up? You sound weird," Ethan questioned.

What I was about to say would probably sound ridiculous through the phone, but I didn't care. "She kissed me on the cheek."

"She?"

"Nora."

"So, that's why you're not in the restaurant right now, because you spent the day together?" he asked, and just when he mentioned it I could hear the voices and noise around him.

"You're at the restaurant?"

"Yeah, I know, I'm supposed to study, learn about the stars some more, but I did learn something new today. I learned what a supernova is today."

"Supernova?"

"It's a powerful explosion of a star, it sounds sad, but believe me Will, it's one of the most beautiful sights I got to see in class. I'll show you pictures later, maybe this will be what convinces you that astronomy and physics can be beautiful," he explained, and I knew that if I wasn't going to stop him now he was going to forget why he called in the first place.

"Come back to earth, Ethan."

"Yeah, right, umm there's a girl looking for you at the restaurant," he said. "Tall, blond hair, blue eyes, red dress and she has a tattoo of a tiny croissant on her arm. Ring any bells?"

"I think I would've remembered if I knew a girl with a tattoo of a croissant," I chuckled. "No, I don't know her, did she say why she was looking for me?"

"No, she didn't say much, she didn't say anything at all actually. Since she got here she sat at one of the tables and ordered the pasta, you know, *your pasta*," he said the last words in a whisper like he was afraid someone would hear him.

"Many people like to eat pasta, Ethan," I said as I looked ahead to see if Nora was coming back, but there was no sign of her.

"You know, never mind, you'll figure out what she wants when you get here, I think we have something better to talk about, don't you think?" he asked, and when I didn't answer I heard him sign. "Will, what exactly are you doing with Nora right now?"

"I took her to the market, she needed fresh air," I said and looked down at her bag, where the book was kept safe. "It's getting harder to hide what I feel for her, Ethan. I…I hoped that if I spend a day with her, acting like friends are supposed to act and do normal things like drinking coffee or buying books, then it would make it easier to pretend, to push back everything and see that it's so easy to be friends."

"Let me guess, this fantastic plan of yours didn't work," he sighed. "Will, why are you doing this?"

"I already told you Ethan, she—"

"If you're going to start telling me this crap about her deserving normal man, and normal relationship again, then I'll hang up the phone," he said. "Will, I have known you since you were kids, you're not this kind of guy."

"This kind of guy?" I asked quietly. It was easy thinking I did things right when I kept them to myself, but to hear it from my best friend was a whole other story. It blew out the perfect plan I schemed in my head, all the rights and wrongs, it pulled me a bit farther from those sad beliefs I held onto for a long time and a bit closer to some self-reflection.

"The guy who lies to the girl he loves about his feelings, the guy who lies to his parents about his dreams and plans, *the guy that runs away*," he said.

"I never said I loved her," I whispered.

"Will, I don't want to start this conversation on the phone, but maybe it's what you need to hear right now, and it's only going to get more involved the longer you spend time alone with her. You compared her to the sun, she's the only person who makes you get out of this restaurant and remember to live a little, and on top of everything, you told her about your grandma. I don't think you need me to tell you what it means, you're emotionally intelligent enough to figure it out on your own," he said.

I pressed my lips together and took a deep breath. "She deserves better."

She deserved a healthy relationship, and to go on dates with a nice guy. She deserved the whole package, something she can write about in that notebook of hers. I didn't know how much my name deserved to be written there, or how worthy I was to even go on one date with her.

"I guess I was right... we shouldn't talk about this on the

phone," he sighed. "I'll see you later, Will. Don't forget to get here soon."

"I won't," I answered and finished the call.

I kept staring at the phone, getting into my deep thoughts again until I saw Nora approaching me with her hands behind her back.

"What are you hiding in there?" I laughed when I saw how content she was with herself.

Her lips curled even farther when she put her hand forward and revealed the white tulip she was holding. "For you."

"For me?" My voice was raw as I took it from her and pulled it closer to my nose to smell it.

"It's just my way to show you how grateful I am for today. I told you this morning I've been feeling off, and from that moment you tried your best to do anything to lift up my spirits," she explained. "So, yeah, I bought you a tulip."

"Did I succeed?" I asked as I looked at the tulip. I tried to hold the delicate stem in my hand. "Did I lift up your spirits?"

She lifted her eyebrows and crossed her arms, making me laugh once again.

"Thank you for looking after me," she said.

I could hear my heart, and it was beating, and beating, and beating hard.

"Nora, I'm sure that anyone else would've done the same for you. I'm sure there are many people who could look after you… better than I do."

"What…what makes you think that?" she asked, her eyes full of worry.

"Just trust me, one day you'll see I'm right," I told her. "I'm not good at this."

"Okay, so let me also say something," she stepped forward. "One day you'll see you're wrong, and I'll be more than happy to be the one to prove you that."

My body froze as she looked up close at me, making all my

muscles tense up as I tried my best not to lean forward and wrap my arms around her.

"Today was the best day I had in a long time, William, at least believe me on that."

"Even after you met that weird old lady who reads historical romance and *Love and War*?" I asked the first thing that came to my mind.

"Even after that," she laughed. "Now I think we should go back to the restaurant; I can see in your eyes how anxious you are to go back there. I've kept you out for far too long."

I was anxious, it was true, but for the first time in a while, it had nothing to do with the restaurant.

I was anxious that she might figure out how I feel.

I was anxious she would see everything I've been trying to hide.

I was more than just anxious.

"You're probably right, we should go," I said.

Before I lose control.

CHAPTER 19
Nora

It was already raining outside when William opened the door for me to enter the restaurant. I laughed when I looked at William that ran a hand through his wet brown hair locks and then ran it over his face as a few drops fell from his hair on his face.

"What?" he asked as he heard me giggle, though he didn't sound mad, he was rather amused by the whole situation.

"Nothing, it's just nice seeing you experiencing the winter in full force. You have to admit it keeps you awake and alive." I moved my hand over a few locks of hair and moved them behind his ear to fix it.

"I can't believe you managed to convince me to leave my umbrella behind," he chuckled and wrapped his hand around my wrist as I fixed his hair. "I thought it was my thing making sure your hair didn't get in your way."

"It is," I felt my cheeks blush at the thought. "But I made you run in the rain while trying to protect a book and a tulip. So let me look after you now, alright?"

"Is looking after me including making me a nice hot chocolate?"

"That's what would make you happy, a mug with nice hot chocolate?"

"Prepared by you," he clarified. "I'll show you where you can find anything you need to make it, it's right where the bar is."

"You want me to take over the bar?" I tried to hold in my excitement, though I failed miserably. "Look at that, I started as a waitress and I got a promotion to be a bartender, and my parents thought I wouldn't be able to survive in the career field."

He chuckled. "Easy there, it's just for a while to make one drink, like you were a waitress for one day. Things like this take time to learn."

"Okay, any other special requests I should know about?" I asked and watched his long sweater. It wasn't soaked with water, but he could use a change of clothes. "I would've tried knitting you a sweater, but I don't know if I have the talents for those specific *qualities*."

He laughed and roamed over my body once more, it was as if he was trying to decide if I got too caught up with the rain and he had to worry about my health.

"Hot chocolate is more than enough for me," he commented.

"Good," I said and leaned closer so no one around could hear me. "Because I don't know how to make anything that isn't hot chocolate or coffee."

His chest rumbled from laughter.

"So what you're trying to say is that every time you get me under the rain, or caught in a storm with nothing to shield me with, you would do that?" he tilted his head as he watched my hand move.

I didn't know if he referred only to the drink or the way my hands fixed his hair, but I didn't mind doing both, it felt pretty natural doing it.

"William Vanderweide, are you trying to use my kindness so you can get me to do things for you?" I noted.

"I mean, I love to drink something warm in the winter, makes me feel all happy inside, but on the other hand, I would rather see you protected inside, all dry and warm," he said, his expression turned serious as he looked at me. "If you knew how much you've done for me..."

"What are you..." I stopped when I noticed a pair of blue eyes looking our way. A girl in a long red dress was sitting on the stool at the bar and drank from a glass of red wine as her gaze was focused on us.

"William, don't turn around, but there's a girl at the bar that's looking our way," I said, and as if I didn't tell him *not to*, he turned around right away and looked at the girl who waved his way.

"So, that's the girl," he mumbled.

"Wait, do you know her?" I asked as I tried to read his face.

"I don't know her, but it seems like she knows me," he said.

He let go of my wrist, and then pulled my hand away from his face. So far I haven't felt the cold of the weather or the rain drops that found their way under the fabric of my sweater, but his small action made me feel cold.

"I'm going to find out," he said and then motioned to me with his head toward Ethan who was at one of the tables eating lunch. "Go eat something, all we got to eat was a quick snack."

I wanted to tell him I wasn't hungry and I was more eager to know who that girl was.

"Or I can—"

"Nora, table, Ethan, food, go," he said. When I reached the table, he walked over to her.

"Hi, Nora," I heard Ethan's voice as I watched William going to the bar and talking with the girl.

"Hi," I answered shortly. I tried to keep my tone light, though it was hard to hide how uncomfortable I felt with William talking to someone I've never seen before.

"You know Nora, people usually say hi while looking at each other, it's kind of an unwritten rule," he commented.

I sighed, and turned my head slowly to him and forced a smile. "Hi."

"You don't like the girl."

I didn't even bother to deny it. "You know her?"

I always wondered what things Ethan knew and just didn't say, maybe that was one of them.

"No, I wish. She came here an hour ago, said she was looking for William and then went to one of the tables there and ate. She hasn't talk with anybody since, she asked for William," he explained as he watched them too. "I mean, I'm his best friend, am I not allowed to know whatever she has to say to him?"

"Maybe she's in one of his classes?" I proposed.

"Nah, she doesn't look like the type."

"Oh, there's a type now?"

"She has a tattoo of a croissant on her hand, and out of everything on the menu she picked the pasta, *William's favorite pasta*. She has something to do with food, I would be willing to bet on it."

"Will you?"

He chuckled as he leaned at the back of the chair. "What is it with you and Will's love for games and bets?"

"You don't need to understand, it's our thing." I shrugged my shoulders and tried my best not to look at William's direction.

I didn't personally have something against the girl that made me feel like I needed to stay alert. I wasn't used to seeing William talk to other girls in here, it felt like our place, our special place we helped to grow and save together. But then there was a girl, a beautiful girl, sitting at the same stool I sat the first night I got here, wearing a beautiful red dress.

All I could think about was what William told me when we talked about what would happen if I wore a dress.

You will look stunning in a dress, more beautiful than you already are, you would probably make everyone look at you, whether they wanted to or not, they wouldn't be able not to look at you.

I wanted to be the only girl he would say those things about.

I needed to think about something else, because here I was thinking bad things about a girl that could turn out to be the sweetest girl in the world. I took out my notebook from my bag and opened it in the page I marked in a dogear colored with red.

Words of affirmation - almost 100% sure
~~quality time~~
Physical touch??? Too confusing
~~Acts of service~~
~~Receiving gifts~~ receiving tulips?

I looked down at my list and played with the pen.

Maybe I gave up acts of service too fast? He opened doors for me, and he bought me that book at the market. He makes me coffee without me having to ask, and I mean, all the other small gestures he does to help and support my big goals that are related to work and event planning can be considered as acts of service. Right?

"What is it?" Ethan asked me.

"My own kind of a game, though I play it only with myself, it helps me focus on things and find order when I feel like I'm about to overthink everything," I said and glanced at William. "I'm not sure how good I am at this game anymore."

"If you teach me the rules, maybe I could help you," he suggested and took another bite from his ham sandwich.

"Part of the rules is that only I need to deal with it, if you help me with these kinds of lists specifically, it would be considered cheating," I said. "And I don't cheat, Ethan."

"Specific lists?" he asked. "What does that even mean?"

I shrugged my shoulders again and started to sketch random shapes on the paper.

"Okay, if you're not going to tell me, can I tell you something?" he asked. "I've been sitting in this place for hours because I thought it would help to change the scenery when I study, but it didn't. Then I was in the mood to talk with people, but the mystery girl didn't want to talk to anybody, and William's parents are both busy and they didn't let me help them. So, I was stuck in here, thinking about a supernova."

"I'm almost sure I've heard that word before," I mumbled. "It has something to do with the stars, right? The way they burn or die or anything in that area of definitions?"

"How do you know that?" he leaned forward.

"Luuk and his endless talk about the stars, though he talks about the stars when it comes to zodiacs and the effect of planets in your houses. You know, he believes that by the placements of the stars in your birth chart, or just their place in the sky or during a retrograde, they can influence your life or behavior. He doesn't know about it in the way you must learn about every day in your degree," I said, and I could feel an idea born as I looked at Ethan. "When was William born? Don't give me the actual month and day because that would be cheating, but a season."

"Wait, hold on," he put his half-eaten sandwich down and cleaned his hands with a napkin. "You want to tell me the things you're struggling with are about William?"

"Not all of them, most of this notebook is filled with checklists about things I want to do and to help myself control my daily routines and pressure I put on myself, but it also helps me have order about other stuff…"

"Other stuff like William?" he smirked.

"Ethan, you can't tell him I write about him, it might give him the wrong impression."

"Oh, and what impression would that be?" He crossed his arms.

"That I might like him," I blurted the second I made sure there was no one around.

"Friends like each other, friends are more than allowed to like each other. I mean we're friends, I like you as a person Nora, there's no reason to be embarrassed."

"You know it's not what I meant," I whispered. "I'm not even supposed to talk about this, he's your best friend."

"Which is exactly why you *should* talk to me. I have all the info. I've known him since we were kids. Do you know how much I know about him?" he asked.

"You know so much about the galaxy that I'm almost scared to ask how much information you're capable of holding in your brain about William," I said. "If you give me a season, it would get me a step closer but wouldn't consider cheating. You know, I don't even want to know the season, just tell me if it's warm one or cold."

"What do you think?" he asked.

"Well," I played with my pen and twirled it between my fingers. "He doesn't like walking in the rain without an umbrella, he loves tulips, and from what he told me they look beautiful in the spring. He is a warm person to be around, he has a warm personality, very warm. If I had to guess, I would say he was born in the summer or spring time."

He smiled, like I've said everything he needed to hear. "Look at that. You two have been friends for about a month, and then some, but from the looks of it, you know him pretty well."

"I was right," I whispered. It was a 50-50 situation, but still, I felt proud that I didn't need his best friend's help after all.

"You know William better than you think you do, Nora," he said when he looked at William. "Don't forget that."

I blushed at the thought. I did, didn't I? Maybe I had a lot more to learn, but I already felt special from knowing his family stories or getting to see pictures of him as a kid. "I won't."

He started to pack up his books and computer and took his

sandwich. He got up from his chair and pulled the back over his shoulder.

"Where are you going?" I asked. "It's still raining outside."

"It never stopped you and William, did it?" he grinned, and then it hit me that all along I felt that I was in my own world with William, but Ethan had caught on. "If I don't leave now, I'll never get to study and I really need to get a good grade on this assignment."

"So, you're leaving me alone?" I pouted.

I didn't normally have an issue staying here, hanging out while I people-watched or working in my notebook,, but this time it was different, and Ethan knew why I needed company.

He pressed his lips as he thought of the right thing to say till he saw something behind him. "Something tells me you won't be as alone as you think. But hey, if you get to learn anything about the mystery girl—"

"I'll let you know, Ethan." I put my pen back down. "It's okay, don't worry about it. Good luck with your studying."

He said goodbye and then waved to William his goodbye too and went outside of the restaurant, right into the rain. That small talk with him made me realize he wasn't just William's best friend, or a guy that liked to study and learn more, he knew more than he let on. He observed people like he observed the stars, and he observed my connection with William in the same way.

I looked over the menu, because after all, I did promise William I would eat, and after walking around all afternoon, I needed to.

"Want any recommendations?" I heard a feminine voice approach me.

I looked down at the feet that stood near the table and lifted my head till I was met with a woman with kind eyes and a sweet smile. It took me a few seconds to scan her face to realize who she was.

"You're William's mother," I said.

When she pointed at the chair in front of me I nodded quickly and watched her sit. She laughed. "What gave me away?"

"Your eyes, your smile, the resemblance is definitely there," I explained, but couldn't help keeping staring at her.

"Is something wrong?" she asked.

"No, everything is fine. It's just...I spend a lot of time here, my parents and friends would even say too much, and I've never seen you here. I mean, I met William's dad, but when I asked William about you, he said that you started a new job. I can't imagine how busy and complicated it must be."

"Yeah, my husband and I talked, and decided he would stay to take care of the restaurant, and I would start following my own dreams. I might be forty-five years old, but it's never too late to start, you know?" She smiled at me. "But until we sell the place, I like to still come here to visit my husband and son, and lately I've been curious to meet you, too."

"Me?" I asked.

"Will is very fond of you, he talks about you every time he comes home and we have the chance to chat," she explained, as I tried to act as if it didn't affect me. The thought of William talking about me with his mom made me feel flattered.

"I'm fond of him, too," I whispered. Though it didn't feel like I said enough. She was his mom, and even though I didn't have to prove myself to anyone, I wanted her to like me. "Believe me, I wouldn't have spent days on end here and walked through the rain to get here if I wasn't fond of him."

"It's good to hear," she said. "You know, with everything going on with the restaurant, and the future of our family business, it's nice to know Will has such good friends who can support him. When the place closes down, he will need people like you and Ethan to remind him that it's not the end of the world."

"Can I ask you a question?"

"You can ask me anything you want, Nora," she said.

I bit my lips, hoping William won't be mad at me for bringing up the subject. I knew I shouldn't meddle and ask too personal questions, *especially* when it came to the restaurant. I spent enough time with William to know it was a sensitive subject. But I had to know more. "I got to talk to William about this place, a lot, and he has many ideas in mind that he would love to try out to help you save the place. If you're thinking of selling it and shutting it down, then why won't you let him try out one of his ideas?"

"You think we're being mean by not letting him do that."

I shook my head. "I think he would end up going crazy if this place won't exist in a month or two. But he would definitely deal with it better if he'd get to at least try doing things his way," I said. "I'm sure you're trying your best to be good parents, but with all due respect, I think you should have an honest conversation as a family, find a middle ground."

I could tell my words got to her, because her voice became more fragile, like it hurt her saying them out loud. "What Will needs is to focus on his future."

"If you'll watch him closely, you will see that's exactly what he's doing," I said softly. "I don't judge your decision; all I'm asking is for you to open your mind. You have no idea how creative and intelligent your son really is and how much he cares about your family's history and tradition."

She narrowed her eyes and looked at me for a while. She had a strange look, I couldn't tell if it was good or bad. "Can I ask you something, Nora?"

"You can ask me anything you want."

My heart was beating louder as I waited for her question. Somehow I was nervous to have a chat alone with her, and who knew what she wanted to know. A part of me felt like she knew, like she knew I was helping him without her knowing.

But I was nervous because she knew *other things* too.

They say mother knows best, and I was certain that was true when it came to the heart.

But just when I thought it was going to be another serious question, her lips curled up. "Why do you call him William?"

I blinked. "Huh?"

"Everyone who knows him, calls him Will, but you call him William. Why is that?"

"Oh, that," I smiled in relief. "That's…a long story."

"I'm sure it is," she said knowingly.

"So, what would you like to eat?" she asked after we finished our talk and she was about to go.

I turned around to look at William, who was still busy with the *mystery girl* and went back to his mother. "Do you have soup maybe?"

"A soup?" she smiled.

"Yeah," I said. "But not just any soup, the one with chicken and vegetables, the one you make with William's grandma's recipe."

She studied my face like she didn't expect me to know such detail, but instead of saying more, her lips curled wider. "Oh, that soup. I'll let them know your order."

"Thank you," I said. "And thank you for keeping me company for a while, it was nice to finally meet you."

"It was nice meeting you, too," she said, but didn't walk away. "Nora?"

"Yeah?"

"Can I ask you for a favor?" she asked. "About William?"

"Is there something wrong?"

I was about to ask more, but she was quick to calm me down. "No, nothing happened. His dad and I, we're going on a short trip we've had planned for a while, which means William will stay here. It might be only my motherly concern, but we are used to have dinner as a family at least once or twice a week, and because we won't be here for a few days I don't want him to spend in the house alone for days and-"

"I would love to invite him to have dinner with me and my parents," I said before she would have time for more worry. "I'll make sure he won't be alone."

I didn't even know how to feel about that talk. She thanked me again and reiterated how nice it was to meet me after hearing my name so many times. I should've been relieved that we got along and that she answered one of the questions I've been dying to ask her or her husband. I should've maybe felt guilty for helping William but keeping his parents in the dark for such a long time. But even if I did feel those things, all I've been thinking about was William, and the fact he told his mom about me. It was a simple thing, short fact, almost too easy to brush off and let go off. But I didn't, I didn't let go.

CHAPTER 20
Nora

I was busy the entire week with prep work, advertisements, and even checking the logistics to see which movies had public performance rights and any other legal things we needed to know about. I didn't want to risk putting a movie that wasn't allowed to be shown in our loud environment and circumstances. Instead of Leonardo DiCaprio and Claire Danes, there were unknown actors before 1996.

It didn't ruin the movie for anyone, or for me. At the end of the day, people knew what they came to see, a Shakespearean inspired movie.

I was sitting in my chair with a bucket of popcorn as I looked over the people who watched the movie in Oasis. They were eating popcorn or having a nice warm drink as the rain was pouring outside. When I looked at the screen too, I wasn't too shocked to look at the characters of Romeo and Juliet starring in it. When I wanted William to choose the movie I had a feeling it was going to something hopeless romantics like him would adore.

"Can I join you?" I heard Ethan's voice as he pointed at the chair next to mine.

"Sure, go ahead," I said, though I couldn't hide my lack of enthusiasm.

It wasn't Ethan's fault I was reacting that way, he was a great person to talk with, the longer I spent time with him, the longer I understood why he was William's best friend. I just wanted William to sit by my side so we could have time to talk.

"Jeez, don't sound too excited about it," he commented, but I could tell he was trying to joke with me to cheer me up.

"It's not you Ethan," I shook my head and put the popcorn aside.

"Let me guess, it's about that guy at the bar with the blue eyes who's making drinks for everyone while he's talking with that mystery girl," he said slowly and glanced at Williams' direction once again. "Nora, you have nothing to be jealous about."

"I'm not jealous," I said, maybe a bit too quickly than I should have.

"Yes, you are Nora, and it's completely normal. I would've felt the same if some guy suddenly showed up out of nowhere and spent all her time with someone I care for. You think I'm not jealous either? We were supposed to play basketball yesterday because it was a nice day, no rain whatsoever, but he had to organize things for today. Then I show up here for Movie Night and he's busy with work and some random girl none of us knows. It's okay to admit this situation sucks, Nora."

I covered my face with my hands to try and hide my annoyance and groaned when I dragged them down my face. "It's not just that, Ethan. I understand he's busy, I understand it more than anyone else, I didn't have much time for myself this week either, but it's not the only reason I feel frustrated. I just..." I sighed, because I didn't know how to put it in words, or I did know, but I didn't want to say it yet.

"She's not his type, Nora. Even if she was, he's not interested in her that way, it's pretty easy to tell when it comes to Will," he explained. Maybe it was because he was his best friend, he could see things I was still blind to.

"Do tell." I turned my entire body to him.

I wasn't even paying attention to the screen anymore, or to people's reactions to the movie night we planned for them.

"Will is a hopeless romantic, like his grandma, like his grandpa, like his entire family basically. If he feels something for a girl, he will just feel it, he won't give it a second thought. If he liked that girl, he would try to find any way to be around her or talk to her. But from my perspective, the time I see him talking to her is while he's working." He said, and leaned closer to mark his words. "He's just being friendly with her, like he's friendly with any other customer who comes here to have lunch or a nice drink."

I knew he was right, but the pit in my stomach didn't go away when I watched the girl lean a bit too close to William, laughing at something he said. I just wanted to have a fun night where I watched an old film with my friends and had some quality time with William. But in reality, Xander and Luuk weren't here, and William was busy.

"I know that," I whispered.

"Do you?" He lifted a brow and ate some more of the salty popcorn.

"I do. I just think I just imagined this whole night going differently. I mean, it's my first ever official event that I got to plan, and my two best friends aren't here, and William is here physically, but...ugh."

"Luuk and Alexander didn't show up?" he asked.

"It's not because they didn't want to support me, they always have," I tried to defend them before he'd get the wrong impression. "Luuk has a date, he wanted to cancel it because of the movie night, but I didn't want him to miss it. Who knows when he'll meet his twin flame, maybe it will happen today?"

"And Alexander?"

"He's going through a...complicated time right now. On usual circumstances he would be the first to show up here, he loves reading Shakespeare. If he didn't show up, it means he really wants to be alone." I explained. "Maybe I should check up on him tomorrow, make sure he's okay."

"You should," he nodded. "Sometimes being a best friend means you need to run after them when they try to run away from their problems and everything going on in their life."

I bit my lip and looked into my lap. "Is that something you had to do? Run after William?"

He pressed his lips together and looked at the screen to think it over.

"If I'm right about you, and I'm pretty sure I am, you won't have to run as much as I did, maybe you won't have to run at all," he said as his lips curled at the thought. "I'm going to make myself something to eat, you want something too, a sandwich maybe?"

"Nah, I'm not that hungry, but thanks," I said and watched him walk away to the kitchen. He probably didn't want to bother William with more work and orders when he had full permission to be in the kitchen.

I kept on watching the screen by myself, and when I got tired of eating the popcorn, I looked over at my very empty mug.

Then someone tapped my shoulder and I lifted my head to see William near my chair with a new mug with coffee he made.

"I figured you'd need a refill at some point, this was a long day, after all" he said, and when I took it from him carefully, he sat beside me.

"Thank you," I said quietly as I sipped from the coffee. For the first time I didn't know what to say to him. I wanted to ask about that girl or tell him how frustrated I felt about tonight, but I just couldn't express it to him. I didn't want to be seen as the jealous type, especially when he didn't own me anything and let me organize my own movie night.

"I'm sorry," he said as he scanned my face, looking for my eyes. "I didn't expect to be so busy this week or be at the bar for that long. You were right, people do love coffee, and the idea of the mugs been working better than I even imagined."

I looked at my pink mug with the image of the tulip on it.

"William, you have nothing to apologize for. You've been busy, I've been busy, the most important part is that the restaurant will get more recognition and have customers that will help the business." I tried to reassure him, and at the same time I tried to remind myself why we made this night in the first place, what was our end goal.

"But it's not true Nora, it's not the most important thing." He shook his head, and then surprised me when he reached for my free hand and held it. "Our friendship is more important than this, *you* are more important. I've let myself get so caught up with work this week and I didn't get the chance to spend time with you, and honestly, I really missed that. I missed eating lunch together and talking about our day like usual." He blurted it all out as if he was scared that he would forget it if he didn't say it quick enough..

It was ridiculous. It's been only a couple of days where we didn't get to see or talk to one another, and still, his confession made me feel relieved that I wasn't the only one who felt that way. "I missed that, too."

"I really didn't plan on waiting tables and serving behind the bar until this late," he said apologizing and ran a hand through his thick hair.

"Well, you were busy," I said, trying to think of a good way to bring up that girl I was curious about, wanting to know what her intentions were with William.

"I planned to come over here earlier, but this *girl* showed up here again, and it wouldn't be polite of me to ignore her."

I cleared my throat and glanced at him, doing my best to pretend I didn't know who he was talking about. "What girl?"

"The one who has been here since we've opened. Do you remember that day we stopped in after the market?" he asked, though I think he knew very well he didn't need to ask, that day at the market was memorable for me for all kind of reasons, and I was sure he felt the same.

"How you made me smile when I felt like meh? Yeah, I remember," I squeezed his hand.

He grinned, like he needed to hear that validation. "Well, when you went to buy that tulip, Ethan called me and said there was a girl waiting to talk with me. When we talked she introduced herself, apparently she's a food blogger, she has an Instagram account with like 20k followers, and I know that's the exact number because she couldn't stop mentioning it."

"A food blogger?" I asked, suddenly my stress was replaced by excitement. Out of all the options, I didn't expect this one.

"Yeah, she wanted to film videos of the food here, she even asked if she could put me in one of her videos," he laughed. "She said I was good looking and it might make girls want to come to the place and try the food."

He laughed like he heard a good joke, and I wondered if the reason he blushed so much from my compliments was because he didn't get many of them from other people beside me.

"She's right about that, you are good looking guy," I mumbled, not missing the way he blushed to my words.

My compliments usually came naturally, there were no second's thoughts on what they might mean, but the air felt thicker when William looked at me with his blue eyes, like we both felt that it was more of a secret confession than a friendly compliment.

"So, what was your answer about her offer?" I tried to change the subject.

I made my best effort to sound as supportive about it as I could, though on the inside I couldn't help but feel intimidated.

The last thing I wanted was for William to work closely with a beautiful girl who was clearly more advanced and helpful than I was for his family business.

I mean, it wasn't like I was doing a bad job, I was working hard on the posts I made and gaining genuine following, but I also knew my tools and knowledge was still limited.

"I said no," he said.

"You did *what?!*"

"I said no," he chuckled at my state of shock. "I said it the first time she offered, the next time she offered, the third time, and five minutes ago."

"But...but William, she has 20,000 followers, and she's a food blogger, and-"

"I don't care about any of those things," he shrugged, still amused by my reaction. "I want you. I mean...The only person I want to keep working with and switch ideas with is you."

My heart soared. Getting such a confession for him meant more than anything I could ever write about. I didn't want to exchange ideas with anyone else either. I didn't want anyone else.

"But William..." I mumbled as I looked at the scene of Romeo calling Juliet under her balcony. *How romantic*...I never knew much about Shakespearean plays, I never understood much of poetry, but I had to admit there was something so romantic in a guy coming under your balcony late at night and calling you his sun. I put my mug on the table and turned to him. "The restaurant is in a great need of some more exposure, and it doesn't matter how much I try, I don't think I'll ever manage to give that to you in the limited time we have. Do you know how viral food bloggers can go? One reel posted by someone with that many followers could get so many people interested in the restaurant, you have no idea how much power social media can have."

"I get it, I've seen how many people have showed up since you've started to manage our social medias accounts."

"Then imagine what would happen if you find someone with even more knowledge, and following, and content ideas about food, just imagine," I said.

I didn't like the idea of him working with this girl, I loved our dynamic, I loved talking with him over fresh ideas and having the chance to help him while developing my own skills at the same time. But I needed to put my feelings aside and think of what he needed. I couldn't let him miss out on such an amazing opportunity because he was trying to be a good friend and support me.

"William, we need to face the truth. It doesn't matter where I got you so far, or how many people learned about this place because of a post or a reel or whatever it was," I took a deep breath and faced him. "I don't know if I'll be able to save this place, I don't know if what I do will be enough, not with the limited time your family has."

I could feel it coming—the pressure, the anxiety, wanting to be enough but not knowing if I'd actually get there. Maybe Luuk was right when he told me I shouldn't do it, because I did exactly what he warned me about, I was blaming myself for not doing enough. I was getting more emotional and attached to what Oasis had to offer to people, I was getting attached to William, and my brain was getting attached to all the bad scenarios that could happen if I didn't try hard enough.

"Hey." He put his hand gently under my chin to make me look back at him. "Don't do that, don't take the blame. You're doing more than enough, you're going above and beyond for me."

"How did you know that I—"

"You have that look in your eyes," here moved his hand from my chin to caress my cheek. "I didn't know what you meant until you told me about how you handle pressure in the past. But now I recognize it, and the last thing I want is for you to be stressed because of me, okay?"

"But what if we don't get there? What if your parents end up selling the restaurant?" I asked. I didn't plan on going there, not on a night that was supposed to be fun and light, but I knew that I wouldn't be able to feel at peace if I didn't ask this.

"As long as I get to keep seeing you here everyday and work together, I'm ready to take my chances." He smiled and after looking at me a few more moments he went to look at the screen. "Damn, I was so busy with customers that I missed the first time they met."

"I'm sorry we didn't get to put the 1996 version, I know you wanted the one with Leonardo DiCaprio," I said. "Though I am curious to hear why you wanted that movie out of all the movies out there. I mean, you do know how many people die in this, right? Or how many people die in general in Shakespeare's pieces, I mean, have you read Hamlet?"

"You read Hamlet?" He raised a brow. "What more don't I know about you, Nora Tuinstra?"

"It's not me, it's Xander. He's the one that reads Shakespeare, he even had an assignment about it. I never read any Shakespeare so I saw it as my opportunity to learn something new. I was kind of disappointed to hear how many characters died."

"If I'm being honest, telling you to show this movie was a bit selfish of me. I was less thinking of the customers and the restaurant, and more about me wanting to watch this movie again. It's been a long time since I've seen it and I was feeling nostalgic." He started to explain put his hands on the back of the chair when he turned to me. "When you talk about romance movies, one of the first one to pop in my head is *Romeo and Juliet*. Some of the scenes in there are just…"

"What is your favorite scene?" I asked while I rested my

head on my arms that laid on the back seat of my chair too, imitating his actions.

He laughed as he looked back at the screen, his cheeks changing their color to pink.

"It's too late to back down now," I stated. "Come on, William, you already confessed that much, I'm sure there's nothing embarrassing about it. I promise not to laugh."

He bit his lips and lifted his head from his hiding place behind his arms. "The aquarium."

"You mean their first meeting?" I asked. "When they see each other through the aquarium with all of the blue and yellow fish?"

"Yeah," he said, and still sounded a bit nervous.

My lips curled and a small giggle burst between my lips.

"You promised not to laugh," he mumbled and gave my arm a gentle squeeze.

"I'm not laughing at you, I'm laughing at myself," I explained. I didn't want him to ever feel embarrassed with me. "I just can't believe I didn't see it before."

"See what?" he asked, confused.

"The National Tulip Day, when we talked about our view on love, you said that it was different than your grandma's, but not that different," I said softly, not wanting him to ever think he had a reason to be embarrassed about what I was about to say. "Your grandparents are romantic and loved each other in many ways, but you're way more hopeless romantic then they ever were."

"What made you think that?" he asked, and by his voice, I could tell I wasn't wrong.

"When we talked about Troy Bolton you said that he and Gabriella belonged together since that one random night they met, and your favorite scene from Romeo and Juliet is their first time meeting, where they didn't even say a single word to each other and already were infatuated with each other," I said as I studied his face, "you believe in love at first sight."

He squirmed under my gaze. "You think it's stupid."

"I think it's beautiful," I said in full honesty. I didn't meet many people in my life who believed in love at first sight. Maybe Luuk believed in twin flames and the existence of soulmates, but it wasn't like being infatuated with a person when you first lock eyes with one another. It was beautiful, believing in such a pure encounter.

We kept on looking at each other silently as the movie was playing in the background, none of us wanted to break the comfortable silence between us.

"You do?" he asked, there was still some uncertainty in his voice.

"I do," I said, and when I watched his shoulders relax, a new thought came to mind.

"What is it?" he asked. "What are you thinking?"

I smiled at him. "Nothing, it's just…We haven't had a chance to talk lately, so I forgot to tell you something, but it's about your mom."

He nodded. "My mom told me I'm invited for dinner at your house tomorrow."

"That would be true," I confirmed. I should've expected her to tell him, she seemed pretty pleasant of the idea.

"Did she pressure you to do it?" he asked. "Because my mom can be like this sometimes, she can—"

"I suggested the idea," I said immediately before he could go any farther with his worries. "I thought that after I met your parents, it's only fair you'd get to meet mine. Besides, you won't have to deal with them alone, Luuk would be there and Xander…Well, I need to see about Xander, but the point is that it's going to be a normal dinner."

"Yeah, normal dinner," he said, and from knowing him, I already knew where his thoughts were going.

"They're going to love you William," I reassured him.

"You sound confident."

"Well, luckily for you, I usually know what I'm talking about." I put my hand on his arm.

That made him smile.

"Now, what do you say that we try and enjoy the rest of the movie?" I asked. "I know we missed the first meeting, but there's still some more love confessions in the way, a sleep position and some more interesting parts."

He lifted his head and put my hand back down gently. "Yeah, we do have all this parts. But before that, there's something I need to give you first."

He got up from the chair and went towards the kitchen.

"If it's more of your coffee, than you should know I'm more than fine with it," I said as I watched him walk away.

I pouted when I saw the chair beside me become empty again, and turned my attention back to the movie. I chuckled when I thought of other movies that I might find on William's "favorite movies list" and I wondered how many more "love at first sight" couples I was about to meet.

"Here." William returned, and when I turned to him, my eyes widened as I stared the bouquet of pink tulips that were wrapped in paper.

There was a hopeful spark in his eyes as he waited for me to take the bouquet.

"William...You bought me tulips?" I whispered, speechless.

"I know we've both been busy this week, but I wanted to give this to you, to show you how proud I am."

"It's just a movie night, anyone could pull it off," I mumbled as I took the tulips and brought them closer to me, breathing in the fresh scent.

"Yeah, but you're not just anyone. It's not *just* a movie night, it's your first official event, and whether it's big or small, it's your first step to completing your dream, and I believe first steps should be celebrated," he admitted.

Then when I hugged him, it hit me.

I wanted more tulips, whether they were pink or white.

I wanted more coffee and walks on rainy days.

I wanted to know his love language, his zodiac sign and every other significant or not detail about him.

I wanted *him*.

CHAPTER 21
Nora

I walked slowly through Xander's quiet neighborhood as I was looking at my phone at the new song that was playing through my earbuds: "Summer Child" by Conan Gray.

I knew it was ironic to listen to this while the sky was grey and there was a glow on the pavement from the rain, but I couldn't just *walk*, I needed to have music on. I had a terrible habit of overthinking when it got quiet, it's gotten to the point where my thoughts would consume me. *I hated that habit.*

"Nora, how lovely seeing you here," Xander's mom hugged my body tightly the moment she opened the door for me.

His mom was one of the loveliest ladies I knew, and thankfully she always let me right in without any questions asked. Which was good, because I had the feeling I was on my way to ruin Xander's beauty sleep.

"You sure he didn't go on his morning run yet?" I asked and glanced at the clock again. "He never misses his workouts."

"He's been acting weird lately, he is reading most days, locking himself in his room. He still keeps eating according to his diet, he takes his meds and everything but he doesn't feel like himself, you know?" she frowned and crossed her arms. "Did he tell you anything?"

She knew the answer once she looked in my eyes, though if she knew the way our friendship worked on the inside, she would know that Xander, most of the time, turned to Luuk when he was in trouble or needed some advice. I was the big gun; I would show up when even Luuk couldn't reach him. Maybe this conversation would've been more awkward if we weren't such close friends. I already spent enough time here trying to get Xander from bed along with Luuk. Those were some dark and complicated times. I had hoped it would take a while before I needed to do it again.

"I'm sure it's only because of all of his assignments and courses; the first year is always the hardest, or so I've heard." I rubbed her shoulder. "I'll talk to him."

I left her after we had our small chat and knocked on Xander's door, and when he didn't answer I knocked again. "Xander, you'll miss your morning run."

I waited a bit longer when I heard steps from behind the door, and moments later, a blond girl opened the door. She carried high heels in her hand and tried to fix her hair as she nodded at me in passing and went downstairs quickly, trying not to make any noise.

God, she was lucky that his mom was back in her room.

"You should try the orange juice before you—" I started but she already closed the door after her. "Nevermind," I mumbled and walked inside the room, not at all surprised to see Xander laying in his bed, his blond hair was messy on the pillow as he covered himself with the blanket.

He didn't even move or flinch when he noticed me but groaned. "Nor, why the hell are you here?"

"You'll miss your morning run, remember? You gotta work out…the doctor said it's important to stay active when you have diabetes." I crossed my arms and rested my back against the wall. His room was an entire mess, books were scattered on the table and clothes on the floor. "But apparently you were working out another way. You know, I never took you as a one-night stand kind of guy."

"Who said it was a one-night stand? Maybe she's my new girlfriend, maybe I met her in English class, and she told me her name, and that's it, I was done for?" he mumbled against the pillow.

"It must be one hell of a name," I replied. "Maybe it was a name you can see in a book. You know, something like Elizabeth, or Jane, or-"

"Her name was Sofie, but I didn't meet her in English class, it was the library, she was reading a book about Van Gogh."

When he realized I wasn't going to disappear, he sat up in his bed and put on his T-shirt from the floor.

"How lovely," I said, and when I made sure he was awake, or as awake as he was capable off, I opened the door again. "Okay, so that's the plan. I'll wait for you downstairs; you do whatever you need to do and will go on a nice walk."

"Why are you doing this Nor, you got a free day from your new work on something and you try to find something or someone to walk around with? Because I should warn you, I'm not the best company."

"No, I always have work, and if I don't have anything, I can just add more stuff to my to do list, it's pretty simple actually." I gave him another gaze, and gladly he was fully clothed and outside the bed, picking up what was left on his floor. "From what it seems, you could use someone to talk with."

He looked down at books on his desk but didn't say anything else. He nodded for me to close the door and I took it as my sign to wait for him, he was grumpy while he got ready but eventually he walked out of his room with a frown on our way out.

Twenty minutes later, we were walking in the park. I knew

Xander preferred running in the city as he passed the people and the architecture of the buildings, but it seemed like this morning he didn't feel like arguing about the scenery, and he accepted my desire to be in nature.

"So, read anything interesting lately?" I asked after a long silence.

"Really, Nor?" He lifted a brow as he looked up at the trees. "That's how you chose to go with this?"

"It's a better way than asking you directly about your dad, or about *her*," I emphasize. "I don't know what to do with you, Xander, honestly. I want to be there for you, Luuk and I want that, but at the same time we don't want to push your limits or meddle with things that are none of our business. I hate not seeing you at our usual spot, and I hated not seeing you there yesterday at the movie night. It could help if I had a Shakespeare expert by my side. " I bumped my shoulder into his in a friendly manner.

"I'm sorry I wasn't there for you, it was supposed to be your big night," he said quietly as he put his hands in his jeans' pockets.

"I wouldn't call it *my big night*, and you don't need to apologize, I'm just worried about you," I said, and bit my lips. "Your mom is worried, too."

He sighed. "My mom was born worried, all she does these days is worry."

My heart ached when I saw the miserable expression on his face, like he was lost more than he admitted to being.

"And it is about *her*, it's always ends up being about *her*," he said in a pained voice. "I know what you're thinking Nor. You think that I'm an idiot for letting her go. I mean, no one would cut connections with his childhood best friend out of nowhere, with one cruel text message. No one would do such a thing. But I did. I cut her out of my life in one moment I would regret forever."

He pressed his lips together and took a dip breath. "When I studied English in high school, I always thought I would learn how to be good with words. I never thought I would use them to hurt someone I care so much about."

I didn't know what to say to make him feel better. From the stories I heard, before I met Xander and Luuk, he had a childhood best friend named Delilah. Long story short, when his father cheated on his mom, he wrote her a message that pushed her away from him. But even if I never met the girl, I saw pictures of them together, I heard about their magical summers and saw all the books she gave him. Even if he didn't see it that way, it wasn't too late to change his story.

"You can still fix it," I advised. "All you need to do is apologize."

He shook his head and went to look at me, the pain in his voice was seen in his blue eyes too. "No, Nor. I can't."

"I get that it can be scary, but—"

"It has nothing to do with fear, well, not this kind of fear. "He ran a hand through his thick hair. "Delilah knows the teenage me, the one who played chess with her, and showed her around the city on the most perfect summer days. But she doesn't know the guy that got diabetes all of a sudden who locked himself in his room for months, the guy whose dad cheated on his mom. My life is one big mess, Nor."

"You can always fix the mess," I said, though I didn't feel like my words cheered him up, he only got more and more frustrated the longer he talked about it.

"Not this mess." He shook his head. "When my dad cheated on my mom, I promised myself I'll never be that guy, I'll never hurt someone in my life that much. I'm going to be selfless, and be good... I want to be the good guy in the story."

"So you think the selfless decision is to leave her behind, Xander?" I stopped walking. "Your dad maybe cheated, but it's not who he is, people should be given second chances, he might change. I mean you parents are working on their marriage, and-"

"My mom would be even more heartbroken when he inevitably disappoints her once again and shows her who he really is," he said bitterly.

He sounded so sure of himself that I almost feared he was right, that he was going to be even more disappointed by his dad in the future.

"It's just a matter of time, Nor," he said with a sigh. "Anyway, now that we finished this short life update, maybe you can finally tell me what you came here for?"

I shrugged. "I came here to check on you."

He let out a chuckle, like he expected that much from me. "I didn't say you didn't, and you're a great friend for coming all the way here, but in any book I've read, when the characters having a dialogue, it's never one-sided, even if it doesn't seem that way, each character hides something or has something to say. And you Nor, you have something to say."

I played with the sleeve of my sweater and looked around at the trees who looked lively, more than expected in the colder weather. "I wanted to ask if you might want to come for a dinner at my house today?"

"Today?" he asked as we kept walking again.

"Yeah, I know you've got things on your mind, but William is coming to eat dinner at my house, and I want it to be perfect for him. Knowing him, he would get in his head if it was just me and my parents, he would stress out and think he needs to impress them, or I don't know what. But with you and Luuk, he would feel more comfortable," I said, hoping he would say yes.

"William," he narrowed his eyes.

"Come on, Xander. I know that you're not his biggest fan because you want to protect me from getting hurt again, but if you get to know him a little bit better, you'll see what an amazing, genuine and a kind human being he is," I said as I clasped my hands together. "Please?"

"Why is it so important for us all to get along? I mean just because I'm your friend, and Luuk is your friend, it doesn't mean that..." He stopped when he looked at me. "Unless..."

"Unless?" I asked, confused by his sudden pause.

"Unless, you know, you want him to play a bigger role in your life," he said slowly. "Unless you like him."

My heart thundered in my chest, Xander wasn't as tired as I thought if he managed to be this observant. Why on earth did he have to say it? I was already conflicted and confused with my own emotions since watching that tragic Shakespearean movie. If Xander, who got dragged from his bed, bitter and tired, could read my feelings so easily, then it meant they were deeper than I thought, and I made a miserable job at trying to deal with them on my own.

"When did it happen?" he asked.

I eyed him. "It hit me yesterday like a ton of bricks, right before, or maybe between, you were having a fun time with Sofie from the library."

"Funny," he commented. "So, when are you going to tell him you feel something for him?"

"I don't know, Xander," I crossed my arms, suddenly I felt a bit regretful for letting him know my feeling at such an early stage. "Besides, you're not supposed to support this, you're not his biggest fan."

"If you met a good guy that treats you right and makes your heart flutter, then I will never get in the way of that, Nor," he said and stepped closer to me when a few people passed by us.

"He's more than a good guy, and he treats me more than right, but—"

"Don't tell me you think of not going for it because you kind of work together," he said, "because believe me, when you save that restaurant and make more hundredth events, you'll move up to a new and better jobs until you're a professional."

"It's not because we work together. I know I said at the beginning that I would be a professional and treat him as a friend, but it's not what's stopping me, not really," I sighed, almost regretting talking about William. Talking about my feelings made them real, but it also made my demons and fears real. After everything that happened in the past, after all the things my pressure, and anxiety and stress led to, I didn't want anyone I cared about to see me *that* way. The tears, and lack of sleep, and bad sides of my life.

"So, what are you afraid of?" he asked, and when I kept looking around, he put his arms on my shoulders to bring me back to him. "Nor, come on, I'm like a brother to you, right? So let me give you a brotherly advice. You didn't get me out of bed and made me walk in the park just to talk about my messy life."

"Brotherly advice?" I asked him.

"Just roll with it," he sighed.

I bit the inside of my cheek and looked down at my white nails. I could've changed their color, but I found myself choosing white again. "It's Aart."

"Nor, it's been almost two years, you need to move on."

"He broke up with me for a reason," I insisted.

It didn't matter how much time has passed, or how many pep talks I got from Xander, or Luuk, or even messages that were written in a horoscope, a part of me couldn't move on.

"He just didn't know how to handle what you've been through. If he was more patient, or more open minded, then-"

"Then I would still have collapsed on the floor that day, I would still have to go to a therapist and learn how to deal with all the pressure and stress I've put myself through," I said the harsh truth that was hard to admit.

"Again, I'm not his biggest fan, but from what I've seen, William doesn't seem like the guy to judge you. He probably knows what pressure and stress can do to a person with all the responsibility he deals with in his family business, correct me if I'm wrong."

"You're not wrong," I said.

"Then what is it?" he asked. "If it's me, I promise to be nicer. I'll even lend him a book, okay? And you know how cautious I am with who I give my books too."

That made me smile, but only slightly. I sighed. "I don't want him to see my dark side."

"I don't understand. "He blinked as we started walking again.

I wondered how long it takes him to run around the city, it probably took less time than having this walk.

"When we first met, he told me I radiated like the sun. I want to stay like the sun. I want him to keep seeing me as this light, and fun person. I want to be the girl who wakes up with energy and drinks crazy amount of coffee every day."

"Nor…"

"If we get into relationship, he'll see all my sides. He would see how exhausted I can get from my own thoughts, or how much I actually write down in my sweet and innocent looking notebook, or how many times I can't fall asleep because of the stress," I said. "I just want to stay like the sun forever."

There was a short pause before Xander opened his mouth. "Can I give you my brotherly advice now?"

"Sure," I giggled. "Go ahead."

"If he likes you back, and genuinely likes you, then he would always see you as the sun. Whether it would be on your bad days or good days, when you can't sleep or when you're high on caffeine. He just would." He brushed my shoulder lightly. "Don't be a chicken Nor, just tell him how you feel."

That made my whole mood to shift. "I'm the chicken? What about your childhood friend, when are you going to fix things up with her?"

He started to run away from me. "I can't hear you, Nor."

I walked faster, though it was hard to keep up with him with my tight short skirt and high heels of the boots. "I don't stand a chance when I'm dressed like this and you know it!"

"Don't hate the player, Nor, hate the game," he said loud enough for me to hear. Apparently Xander was full of brotherly advice this morning.

"One hell of a game." I mumbled as I watched him run between the trees.

CHAPTER 22
William

I was standing outside of Nora's house as I was running my hand in my hair one last time. I tried not to make a big deal out of this dinner, I mean I met Ethan's parents in the past and it was the most natural thing in the world. He met my parents and sometimes it feels like they love him more than me.

"You know it's not the same thing," the small voice in my head reminded me. "You like her, you want her, and you want her family to like you too."

I wanted to laugh at myself for getting to this type of situation. I needed to stay away from her, I needed to treat her as just my friend, she deserves normal and uncomplicated people in her life, but no matter what I promised myself every single day before I met her, every plan or promise disappeared when I saw her.

All I could think about was her beautiful green eyes, her brown hair that was tied in a braid every time I saw her, and I wondered if would look like falling on her shoulder in the most natural way.

I tried to remind myself that would never happen, but my thoughts were always on the move, no matter what I told myself, I still was going crazy watching her walk around in a short skirt and long boots, with nails painted in white and pink lipstick.

I looked up at the gray sky and sighed. "I wish you were here, Grandma; I could really use your advice."

Nora was right, I was a hopeless romantic, more than my grandma, more than anyone in my family. But that also meant that I was vulnerable, and scared. So scared of not being enough for the person I'm falling for.

I kept looking up, hoping to get a sign in the shape of an animal or other force of nature.

I closed my eyes as I tried to think of any of my grandma's past advice.

I could picture myself as a little boy in the garden, looking at the tulips grow on a sunny day, with blue sky above our head.

"But how will I know when someone is the one for me, Grandma?" I asked, as I watched her take care of the tulip, treating it with care and love.

"William, what did I tell you?" she smiled brightly. "You'll know, and who knows, it might happen at first sight, like in the movies."

"First sight?" I mumbled.

"Yes, love at first sight is when you see someone for the first time, and you immediately know you feel something romantic towards that one person, it happens in an instant," she said.

"And if I'd be scared to tell her? Girls at school don't like me, they just like the boys who play sports and make jokes in class," I asked timidly. "They don't like when I talk about flowers, or tulips, or—"

"That one person will love you as you are, she just will." She caressed my face. "Look at that tulip, if I didn't plant a seed in the ground months ago, we wouldn't be looking at any tulip right now. Love is like that, you need to make the first step, even if it's scary."

"I don't know how to talk to girls, Grandma," I sighed. "I'm too embarrassed."

"You don't have to talk. If you like someone, you can always give her a tulip, like your grandpa did with me." She winked. "That worked."

I looked up at the white tulip quietly, I frowned when I thought of love.

"What is it, my sweet boy?"

"Nothing, I just...I can't talk with anyone about stuff like this, I can't talk with Mom or Dad about ...this stuff, sometimes I can talk with grandpa, but I always love coming to you."

"I don't see what the problem is," she said. "I'm always here to talk and give you advice, about whatever you want, as long as you'll help me with the garden every once in a while."

She was in a good mood today if she had the energy to joke around, but my mind reminded me that when I'd leave back home, she would go back to her bed, she would get tired again.

"Not always..." I muttered; I wasn't able to say it.

She sighed when she understood the reason for the sadness in my voice.

"Yes, always," she insisted. "It would just be different, but very simple."

"Simple?"

"Yes." She looked up at the blue sky and I followed. "When you feel troubled, or want some advice, just look up, even if the sky is gray, or black, I promise I'll be there to listen to you."

"How would I know you really there?" I asked, still feeling conflicted.

"You'll know." She brushed my cheek as if she tried to memorize my face in the sun.

My body froze when she coughed again and dropped her glass of water on the ground.

"We should go inside," I muttered. I stood and helped her get up.

"Okay, but only because I want you to eat lunch, you helped me a lot with the garden today," she smiled down at me. "Can you promise me something?" she asked me when we got closer to the door.

I nodded quickly, like a good boy would do.

"Promise me that when you know you found the one, you'll let me know," she said.

I smiled widely at her. "I'll tell you everything. Her name, the color of her eyes, what she's like, and if I'm unable to tell her how I feel, then I'll give her tulips, like you suggested."

"That's my boy." She patted my messy brown hair before we entered the house.

I looked up at the sky again, and to my surprise, it wasn't that sad gray shade anymore, some of the clouds cleared and revealed the sun that was hiding behind them all along.

A small smile found its way to my lips.

"You must be William." I jumped in place when I heard a woman's voice behind me.

"Yes, that's me. I mean, I'm William, and you must be Nora's mother," I said while my hand was still on my chest, my heart was beating quickly. "I'm sorry for getting here so early, it's a habit I'm afraid of, getting to places much earlier than I'm supposed to."

God, I hope in some magical way she couldn't tell how nervous I was.

"That's okay," she laughed it out and then stepped closer and lowered her voice. "It's actually good that you're early, because maybe now Nora would stop walking around the house nonstop and making sure everything is perfect. I swear, that girl will burn a hole in the floor from pacing around so fast."

"She… Has she really done that?" I asked as she let me walk inside.

"After all the things Nora told us, I wouldn't be that

surprised." She smiled at me as I took off my coat and put it on the hanger near the door.

I could feel my cheeks heat up. "What did she tell you about me?"

She opened her mouth, but just when she was about to answer, we both heard a noise of a plate falling to the floor.

She looked at me once again, and walked quickly to the living room and kitchen area. I didn't spend too long checking out the furniture or books at the library, because my gaze was immediately fixated on Nora who was running around the kitchen.

I roamed my eyes over her body. She wasn't wearing a skirt or boots with a sweater as usual, but a pair of jeans, slippers and a yellow sweater that was much bigger on her than her other ones. It was the same sweater I lent her the night we met.

But it wasn't just her clothes that made me stare at her shamelessly, it was her hair that fell loosely over her shoulders. It looked nice and soft as I imagined it to be, and her face, even from the place I was standing, I could tell she didn't have much makeup on her face.

"Mom, where is the broom?" she asked as she was looking around for something to pick up the broken pieces of the plate from the floor.

"Here, let me help." I walked towards her and bent down to carefully pick up the pieces so she wouldn't accidentally get cut in the process.

"William." She let out a breath, and when I lifted my head to smile at her, she covered her face. "Don't look at me."

"Why?" I laughed, and moved her hands slowly from her face, until I got to meet her green eyes once again.

"There's another half an hour, I'm not dressed yet, and I didn't have time to braid my hair. And the pasta, I just put it in the water because it took forever to boil and..." she sighed when she looked at me again. "I have so much more to do! You weren't supposed to see all the mess before you came here, you were supposed to enter when everything was ready, and when the food was on the table, and when Luuk and Xander could keep you company until I showed up. I had a plan, a checklist, everything." She frowned and got up the moment I did.

"A whole plan, huh?" I chuckled and threw the pieces I was holding in the trash can closest to us. "Me showing up early wasn't part of your plan, was it?"

She bit her lips. "I know you like coming early, but part of me hoped I would have more time to prepare everything."

I smiled at her. I wanted to tell her she looked perfect just like that, even when her mind was all over the place and when she wore clothes she didn't usually wear outside. But I've known her long enough to realize that it didn't matter what I was going to say, she was going to look for a way to stick to her plans as much as possible.

"I'll help you. What else do you have on that check list of yours?" I folded the sleeves of my sweater and leaned over her shoulder to look at the pasta in the pot. On the counter, I saw a few vegetables that needed to be cut into a bowl, and then when I looked down at the stove I recognized the smell of the pizza that was heating up.

"No, you can't help, you're the guest, it doesn't work that way." She shook her head and put her hands on my chest to push me away, but I put my hands gently on hers.

"Nora, you remember that day when you helped me with Oasis, and we promised that we were going to look after each other and tell the other person when they needed a break?" I asked. "This is me saying you need a break. I'll take care of everything, and I'll finish the cooking. Before you even try to argue, let me remind you how much I enjoy being around the kitchen. I don't mind it at all, especially when it comes to pasta."

She pouted, clearly not happy with me. "But—"

I tried to fight my smile as I looked at her pouty lips. "Turn around." I motioned to her with my finger to spin, and after she rolled her eyes, she did as I told. I ran my hand through her hair and divided it into three parts, and then started to braid her hair.

"You know how to braid?" She mumbled her words, and whether she intended to or not, she leaned her body into mine. My body shivered at her closeness.

"I have little cousins," I explained, and after a slight hesitation continued. "My grandma taught me how to braid. When I was a kid, I told her that if in the future I'd meet a girl with braids, I would like to know how to do it too, just in case."

"So, you were always like this." When I leaned my head forward to check on her, I saw her closing her eyes with a smile on her face as I messed with her hair.

"Like this?"

"Romantic at heart," she said.

I let her words sink in when I finished her braid. She handed me her hair tie, and when her braid fell over her shoulder, she turned back to me.

"So, you know how to braid. What else should I know about you?" she asked jokingly as she put her hands on her hips.

That I'm dying to kiss your lips and wrap my arms around you.

That I want to see you wear my sweater every single day.

That if I lose control for once, I want it to be with you.

"I don't know." I shrugged my shoulders. "I can't think of anything in particular."

"You can't think of anything?" She tilted her head.

My eyes immediately landed on her lips when she bit them. I was happy she forgot all about her plans when she was with me, when our talk flowed like it always did, but there was nothing innocent in the way she bit her lips, or the way my eyes looked at her.

I wanted to do much more than talk, or eat dinner, and

standing alone in the same space with her started to feel like an impossible task.

I took a step back and cleared my throat. "You... You should go and take care of everything before your friends get here, I'll take care of the food for now."

I could see the wheels turn in her head, like she was trying to think how much she would be able to check off her list if she'd just accept my help.

"Come on, Nora." I encouraged her by brushing her arm lightly. "Let me help you."

"Fine," she sighed. "I'll go do everything I need to, but only for a couple of minutes. I don't want to leave you alone in the kitchen, and I still want to show you the house, and—"

Then, we heard a knock on the front door.

"Or I won't be alone after all." I smiled at her." Take your time, I'll open it."

She looked at the dining table to make sure all the plates and glasses were in place, and then turned to look at the hallway that led to the door before she turned back to me and nodded. "Okay."

When she was about to walk upstairs, I let out a breath, taking in her outfit as long as I had the chance. "Nora."

"Yeah?"

"I know you said you need to get dressed, but you should know I like seeing you like that, too," I said until my eyes landed on the sweater once again. "With that sweater."

She laughed, "You mean *your* sweater."

I put my hands back in the pocket of my jeans, trying to hold back from coming any closer to her. "Yeah."

She was playing with the hem of it. "Just so you know, I'm not some weirdo that walks around the house in your sweater, or sniffs it before I go to bed, or anything like that. It's just the most comfortable thing I have in my closet for now, so..."

"Even if you did all those things, I wouldn't mind, Nora," I said. My words make her eyes widen slightly. "I wouldn't mind at all."

"You wouldn't?" she asked, her eyes turned to a darker shade of green.

I shook my head. "I would take it as a compliment."

We looked at each other for a moment, none of us said anything, but I could feel the tension, and I had hoped that just maybe, she had thoughts similar to the ones I had.

Then there was another knock on the door, louder this time.

I swallowed and turned to the hallway. "I should probably get the door."

"And I should get ready." She smiled at me one more time and walked up the stairs.

I opened the door quickly to see Luuk standing there, who didn't seem all too happy we left him outside all this time.

"Should I even ask why it took you so long to open the door?" he asked.

Because I was standing in place like an idiot, looked at your best friend and imagined how Nora would look wearing only my sweater, with nothing else on.

I thought of what I would've done in that kind of scenario.

I settled for the easiest answer I could find. "Check list stuff."

"Check lists?" he laughed as he walked inside. "Sounds like Nor."

CHAPTER 23
William

When the pasta was ready, I tended to the vegetables. While I was doing that, I could feel Luuk looking at me as he sat on the counter, moving his legs in a rhythm. I don't know how I ended up being alone in the kitchen with Luuk. For some reason, Nora's parents were out of sight, and Alexander was off somewhere reading, or so I've heard. Luuk didn't seem to be bothered about it, he ate a few cubes of chocolate and used our time to ask me more questions about myself.

"So, are you a morning person or a night owl?" he asked as he watched me putting more tomatoes into the big bowl.

"Umm, night owl, I guess?" I cleaned my hands with a towel nearby, it was getting hard focusing on two things at once with all his questions. "Though, I usually wake up early because of certain classes, or if my parents need help around the restaurant."

"You study business, right?" he narrowed his eyes. "I remember Nora saying something about it."

"Yeah."

"Your parents must be proud," he commented.

"They were proud, they still are, but they always remind me how hard it is to run a business. They know I'm studying it because I want to run the restaurant someday," I sighed. "They just don't want me to get disappointed."

"But Nora is helping you. I mean, I saw how many customers you have," he offered me some of the chocolate, but I shook my head.

"They're pretty strong minded when it comes to the future of the place, and at this point, it would take more than customers to convince them."

I started to clean up the counter, because I knew it'd be on Nora's checklist at some point if it wasn't already.

"Can I maybe ask you something?" I asked. "I know I told you I don't believe in zodiac signs, but—"

His eyes lit up when I mentioned the word *zodiac*. "But you want to know more now, don't you?"

"You said that Nora is a Virgo, and I'm a cancer. Do the stars, or planets, or I have no idea how exactly it works, but is there any compatibility between people with those signs?" I asked.

I heard Nora and Luuk talk about horoscopes once when they ate lunch one of the days they hung out while I was working, I was almost sure they said something about compatibility between people somewhere in their conversation.

"Like, a romantic compatibility?" He sent me a crooked smile.

"Forget I asked anything," I muttered under my breath, feeling my skin heat up.

"A Cancer and a Virgo have strong potential, in terms of dating," he said quietly, bringing my attention back to him. "I mean, both of your signs are leaning towards more of a serious relationship than flings, and the Virgo is drawn to the kindness and dedication of the Cancer, and the Cancer is attracted to the intelligence and the way a Virgo can understand him. If I didn't know you two, and you asked for an objective opinion about this match, I would say it's a pretty good one."

"And if you needed to say it based on knowing Nora?" I asked after I looked around me to check no one was around. "What then would you say?"

"I would say that you should stop wasting your time asking for answers from me, or the stars, or god knows from who else."

I opened and closed my eyes as I watched him. "You don't seem surprised at all."

"I'm a hard person to surprise."

"No, that's not it." I went to put the pasta bowl on the dining table and came back to him. "When we played monopoly, and the two of us talked, you told me I shouldn't fight it when it came to Nora. I thought you meant only the game, but...but you meant my feelings. You knew I was developing feelings towards her, didn't you?"

He pressed his lips together, and crossed his arms, like he preferred to keep quiet and let me adjust all this new information by myself.

"And we had that talk in the restaurant, when you asked me to look after her, it wasn't just a friendly request," I mumbled.

When I looked around me now, the house didn't feel as big as it did when I just walked in, the walls felt close, the dining room felt much closer than it actually was, and the smells, and noises in the house all mixed up together.

"The last person who was with her, Aart, he seemed like a good guy at first, but he didn't look after her as I would've hoped a boyfriend would. It's not my right to tell you the details, because it's her business whether to tell you, and if so how much."

"He didn't?" I whispered.

I knew that already from our talk, but it was still sad to hear. Nora deserved to be treated right, to be looked after, to feel comfortable, and happy.

"When we met, I needed to make sure you would be different. That when you'd be together, things would be different for her. Better."

My pulse was racing. "Wait, did you just say *when*?"

"I didn't say when exactly, I don't know the date and time, I mean *when* in a general sense, somewhere in the future. Near, or far, it's up to you, I'm not judging." He kept looking at me when I went to sit down on the chair. "Though, I do hope it's more near than far."

I was astonished by how sure he sounded. "How can you possibly know all of this?"

"Let's just say people in my family have gifts, and that's my gift. I just know stuff."

"Stuff?" I lifted my eyebrows.

He slowly moved towards the table and sat down on the chair. "I also know Nor. I've seen her go through dark times in her life, and bright ones. She might convince herself that love isn't in her cards and that she's this goal-oriented person, but she wants it, and she deserves it. She deserves to be loved. She just needs to lift up her head from her notebook to figure that out."

"She really does love writing in that notebook," I mumbled.

I hoped the day would come where she'd let me in, when she'd show me more of her, more of her struggles, more of what she wrote down, just so I could hug her once again, comfort her in any way she needed.

"Will?"

"Yeah?"

"When the time comes, and you want to tell Nora how you feel, you'll have to make the first step. You do know that, right?"

The first step.

My grandma's voice echoed in my head again.

Love is like that, you need to make the first step, even if it's scary.

"What have the two of you been up to?" Nora's mom walked in and joined us at the table.

"Just chatting a bit, Miss T. William here wanted to show off his cooking skills."

I scratched the back of my neck. "I don't really have cooking skills, I just wanted to help Nora out."

"Aren't you a good friend?" She smiled to me kindly as she called her husband, Nora, and Alexander in. "You have no idea how excited she was about you coming here. She's been going through recipes for days, and she made me go with her in that weather to get advice for the specific napkins she wanted to match the plates. She wanted everything to be…"

"Perfect," I smirked.

I thought it would be more nerve-wracking meeting Nora's parents, but it wasn't. I felt pretty comfortable and at ease chatting with her mom. She was likable, chatty like Nora, and she seemed to know exactly who her daughter was. She just accepted Nora's perfectionist side as it was. Being in Nora's world, though, there was nothing stressful about that. I couldn't wait till the dinner was over and I could see more corners of the house, learn and hear more stories about the place.

Though I knew who Nora was when it came to organizing and planning, whether it was family dinner or an entire party, I felt flattered that she did all this effort for me. That it had nothing to do with business.

Then after a while, Alexander and Nora's dad entered the room while they were talking about a certain book Alexander took from his library. But I didn't look at them for long, because Nora entered the room, still wearing my yellow sweater.

I watched her closely as she sat next to me, and looked over at the food Luuk and I were working on.

"What is it?" she asked as she felt my eyes on her. "Did I disappear for too long?"

"No, it's not that," I said, and leaned a bit closer so her

parents or friends couldn't hear me. "You're still wearing the sweater."

"Oh," she played with one of the sleeves. "Well, I gave it more thought. It matched the skirt I wanted to wear, and as I said, I feel comfortable in it."

"So, you did," I muttered, and after gazing at her one more time, I went back to talk with the rest of the table.

During the dinner, I tried to observe more of Nora's interactions with her friends and parents. Something I learned while being a more introverted person and working in a restaurant on a daily basis is how much you could learn by watching people—and I wanted to learn more about Nora. In one simple dinner, I learned that she got her confidence from her mom, the both of them were quite the duo. I could tell her dad was used to being the quieter and more reserved person in the family as he focused on his meal and smiled when his wife made jokes and told stories about work.

"I told Nora that when she finishes her degree, I would help her find her way as an event planner," her mom said while giving her more of the pasta. "But there's no pressure, no rush, she should focus on her studies for now, nothing more. Right, sweetheart?"

I watched Nora as she swallowed her food slowly as her mom kept on talking.

"Mom, can we please talk about anything else?" she asked as she moved a bit in her chair.

"I'm just glad you gave up that ridiculous idea of working right now. I'm sure your friends would agree that studies can be more than stressful."

"Mom," she hissed.

"Look at William, he is studying business, I'm sure he's wise enough to know he needs to give all his attention and focus to his classes. Wouldn't you agree, William?" She made the rest of the table look my way. "You've known my daughter for a while now, wouldn't you agree that it's wiser to take things easy?"

I watched Nora again, she stopped moving her fork over the pasta. "Mom, don't involve him in this."

"Did you guys know that Xander just finished reading this fascinating book?" Luuk touched his friend's shoulder to get him to join him on his mission to change the subject. "Tell them Xander."

"Right, the book," Alexander cleaned his mouth with a napkin.

He talked about this book he recently read, some romance in an historical period, but I wasn't focused on the story, my eyes were stuck on Nora who's gone quiet as she stared at her food. She was joking just minutes ago with her friends before mom made that comment about her. My heart ached for her, because I was in similar situations more often than I wished to be. I knew what it was like when parents didn't listen.

"I'm sorry to interrupt your story," I motioned to Alexander. "But I have to say something."

"Are you finally going to tell us the secrets of working in a family business?" Luuk offered and leaned back on his chair. "Because I've been waiting for this moment for a while now."

"Maybe another time," I mumbled, as I gently covered Nora's hand under the table. "I just wanted to say that I know everyone here has known Nora way longer than I have, and you might know things that I still have to learn, but I do know that I don't agree with you about Nora having to take things easy."

"Will," Luuk tried to warn me with his eyes not to go there, not now at dinner, but I had to go there.

"I know she needs to take into consideration what happened in her past, and she obviously can't put herself through the same pressure, I know that. I get your worries; I worry about her well-being all the time." I said as I squeezed her hand. "But asking her to stop herself and not do everything her heart desires is insane.

You don't need me to tell you what intelligent and creative ideas she has, or how much passion she puts in everything she does. She's a force to be reckoned with, and I think the best thing you can do for her and yourselves is to support her decisions and listen to what she has to say. But really listen." I gazed at Nora and put on a smile when our eyes met. "At least, that's what I'm trying to do."

If no one could feel the tension in the air, it was obvious now. Her parents were looking at me, and I could already imagine in my head how they were going to talk about me later, about the rude boy who made a whole speech over dinner, the boy who couldn't just agree with their educational approach and eat quietly.

I lifted my head towards her friends, because it got too intimidating to watch her parents send intense looks my way. Luuk lips curled up, and after looking sideways, he put his thumb up to show me I had his full support on this.

Then my head moved slightly to Alexander. I expected him to sigh or roll his eyes at me because I interrupted his story and ruined dinner, but there was no sign of annoyance on his face, he just looked at me and nodded. He seemed…impressed.

We quickly went back to talk about Alexander's book again and the conversation shifted to a lighter topic, like nostalgic memories and experiences from university life.

When we finished dinner, Luuk went to help Nora's mom with the dishes, as her dad and Alexander returned to the talk they had before dinner. As I watched them, my mind was already overthinking how I ruined this whole dinner for Nora. She wanted the perfect night, and I gave her the entire opposite of that.

Nora touched the sleeve of my own sweater to grab my attention before she went to hold my hand. Her hands were small and warm, but they fit right into mine. "Come with me."

I followed her with hesitant and slow steps upstairs until she opened the door to what I guessed was her room. She closed the door behind us and crossed her arms as I was examining her room.

Learning her favorite color or movie was nothing compared to looking in her room and learning that she decided to paint the wall in a pink shade, or that her room was as organized as her notes. At her desk, beside a computer and her notebook, there was also a vase with the pink tulips I gave her yesterday.

"You kept them in your room," I mumbled and went back to look at her, hoping she couldn't tell how that affected my entire body.

"I keep all the tulips you give me," she said. "Whether it's one or a dozen, it makes me feel special in a way. You're actually the first guy who has ever given me flowers."

My eyes widened at that confession. "So, your ex- boyfriend, he never…"

"Never," she said. She laughed as she was looking at me looking at the tulips. "You look surprised."

"How wouldn't I be surprised?" I asked. "I mean, you're… you."

Her smile grew bigger. "I'm *me*?"

"I'm not explaining myself right." I chuckled and looked aside so she wouldn't see my rosy cheeks. "What I'm trying to say is that if I was your boyfriend, I would give you a tulip every single day. I wouldn't wait for special occasions to let you know how I feel about you."

"Every single day?" She took a step closer to me. "That's a lot of tulips."

I smiled at that. "There's no such a thing as too many tulips. Look at my grandparents for example, they gave one to each other until they grew an entire garden of tulips in their house. There's never such a thing *too many* when it comes to flowers."

"Wise words from a wise guy." Her lips crooked. "What else would you do if you were my boyfriend?"

My body turned stiff as my eyes moved to look at her pink lips. Nora and I got a lot of back-and-forth questions at the time we got to know each other, but that was probably the easiest, yet the toughest one to answer.

Because right now, at this moment, standing with her in her room, I could only think of kissing her.

"Would you really want a boyfriend that ruins your family dinner you worked so hard on?" I asked her genuinely. "You deserve a boyfriend that makes a good impression with your parents, someone that doesn't make you work as hard as you do, someone you can hang with in any restaurant in the city instead of the same one over and over again."

"Wait, you think you ruined dinner?" Her voice turned softer. "William."

"You ordered special napkins, looked for recipes, made a whole checklist, and—" My voice went quiet when I felt her wrap her arms around me, bringing me closer to her body.

"You didn't ruin dinner; it was the perfect dinner," she whispered to my ear.

"But..." I pulled away to look at her. "But I went against your parents."

"You stood up for me," she corrected.

"I'm the worst guest of honor in history."

"I would say that's a slight exaggeration."

"So, you're not upset, mad or disappointed about how that night turned out?"

"William." She cupped my face between her hands. "You looked after me, like you always do."

My heart was beating loud as she kept looking at me with those beautiful green eyes. "You have to stop doing that, Nora."

"Doing what?" she said. "I'm only telling you the truth as I always do."

"No, you're making it harder for me to hold back from you," I said in a low voice and covered the palms of her hands that cupped my face with my own hands. "If I'm being completely honest, you don't even need to utter a word or say something nice to me to make it harder. All I need is to take one look into your green eyes, or at your pink lips. It's enough to make me want to…"

I stopped when I looked back at her slightly parted lips.

"William?" she whispered.

I could see the clarity in her eyes, she didn't need more to figure out why my breathing was heavy, or why my chest was rising up and down, or why I kept staring at her lips.

Before I could convince myself it was wrong, or count all the reasons I shouldn't do it, I lowered my head and pressed our lips together.

My hands were slightly shaking when I closed my eyes and felt my lips on hers. I didn't expect to lose shreds of my self-control, I didn't think I'd ever cross that line, I didn't think I'd ever make that first step, but I realized that with Nora it was impossible to keep denying it.

Luuk was right, it wasn't a matter of *if,* when it came to Nora and me, it was a matter of *when.*

My lips were desperate. I wanted to feel more of her soft and warm lips, to feel more of the girl I wanted since the first night she entered my family's restaurant and demanded that I make her coffee.

A part of me was terrified that she didn't want any of this, but she responded to me immediately, like her words and attitude, I could feel the same confidence in the way she kissed me. She didn't hold back as our lips were moving against each other, and she didn't give it a second thought when her tongue parted my lips and glided over mine, making me groan.

Like everything that involved Nora Tuinstra, that kiss was perfection.

When we pulled away, I kept my eyes closed for a few more

seconds, just to savor the touch of her soft lips, before I opened my eyes and looked at her through my lashes.

"I like you, Nora," I blurted out before I lost the guts to say it.

I didn't feel like a grown man when I said it, I felt like a shy kid who just wanted the girl he liked to like him back.

She giggled. "I like you, too."

"What's so funny?" I scratched the back of my neck, feeling shy all over again.

"Nothing. It's just…I always thought you looked beautiful every time you blushed and your cheeks were covered in pink, but now that I look at the way your lips turned puffy and pink after I kissed you, I'm not sure which one I prefer."

My voice was raw when I looked at her eyes once again. "You did not just say that."

"Oh, but I did." She laughed.

She knew exactly what she was doing to me, wasn't she?

"Come on, I don't want you to skip dessert. My cake is nothing like Ethan's cheesecake, but no meal is complete without a desert." She held my hand and led me out the door.

I didn't mind skipping dessert, I didn't mind staying the entire night in her room, just to get the chance to kiss her again. But I wasn't going to say it, I already confessed enough for one evening, and I didn't think that staying in the same space alone while her parents and two best friends were downstairs was such a good idea.

She stopped near her door. "William?"

"Yeah?"

"Remember when I told you that some compliments are just compliments?"

How could I forget, her compliments made me lose my goddamn mind.

"Well, when it comes to you, my compliments were always more than just compliments. My love language was never words of affirmation, but looking back, I think it was the easiest way for me to express my feelings to you, even when I wasn't sure about them or could understand them fully."

I let out a shaky breath. "Are you sure about your feelings now?"

Her lips curled up, like she expected me to overthink this, even after the kiss, even after what she just said.

"I wouldn't have kissed you back if I wasn't."

CHAPTER 24
Nora

It's been only a couple of days since William kissed me, and yet, I couldn't stop thinking about it. I was supposed to be focusing on my studies, and the next posts or plans that'll help the restaurant, but when I closed my eyes all I imagined was his lips, and the way they felt on mine. When I opened them and looked down at my notebook, all I could see was his name that I wrote in cursive letters.

I wasn't a hopeless romantic, I didn't think I'd find myself in love so soon after my last relationship, but here I was. Sitting in my room and playing the same scene in my head like it was taken right out of a movie.

"You're smitten," I heard Luuk's voice. "Thinking about that kiss again?"

I sighed, took a pencil that was nearby and threw it towards Luuk, who tried to catch it, but ended up sitting on the bed and picking it out of the floor.

Xander was laughing and moved aside so Luuk could get comfortable on the sheets of my bed.

These two were something else...

When I just became friends with them, I didn't mind their

annoying comments or times where they acted like typical boys, but sometimes, just sometimes, I regretted telling them stuff like that.

When you tell normal friends your age you kissed a guy you like, they become supportive, maybe even ask for some details. But when you tell it to guys like Luuk and Xander, you need to prepare yourself for follow up questions, and nonstop comments.

"You know, sometimes I wish you were normal," I said, though they knew I didn't seriously mean it.

"And I wished you said yes when he asked you to meet him on Valentines Day," Luuk mentioned. "What girl says no to a date on Valentine's Day? You know how hard it was for me to get one?!"

"A girl who wants his restaurant to succeed. You know how many couples celebrate their love and go to eat a nice lunch or dinner at this time? I didn't want him to have to choose between me and his family, I know they need him there more than they let on." I kept scribbling down my notebook. "Besides, he didn't ask me out on a date, he asked me if I wanted to hang out together, nothing formal, or official. He sounded super chill when I said I was busy with work and classes."

"Super chill?" Luuk asked. "From my conversations with him, he's totally one of those people who cares about special dates, and from the way he talks about you…"

"What way?" I asked quickly.

"Like he wants you," he answered in the simplest way, but it was enough to make my body shiver.

"Like he wants to look after you like you deserve," he continued. "I believe him Nor, he's not just a good guy, but genuine too."

His gaze was fixated on the tulips in the vase behind me. These were new ones that I got on Valentines when I came to help him wait on tables a bit. It wasn't like the red roses I saw girls walk with; it was better than any rose. I wasn't a bouquet, I wasn't a florist, but I knew that the tulips I got from William time after time, whether it was day or night, pink or white, they showed his love for me, that he cared. William once told me that tulip blooms last only a week or two, but we bloomed from much longer than that, we still do.

I wouldn't say I didn't want to spend time alone with William, after that kiss I could only imagine how that experience would go. I already knew I liked him too; I already wanted him; it was easy to understand my feelings the moment I let them in. But at the same time, I was scared, and just because we made it one step forward, it didn't mean all my inhibitions were gone. He still looked at me like I was the sun, and I wished I could be that, forever.

But right now, I was trying to be that when I was in his company. I was trying to bring that bright, optimistic, outstanding light into his world.

"Nor, you have to stop being so scared," Xander said after a short silence in the room. "That's why you told him that excuse about being busy, isn't it? So, he wouldn't get to see more of that *darker* side of you?"

"You don't get it, Xander. That kiss, it was…" I leaned back in my chair and looked up at the ceiling. "It was perfect, absolutely perfect."

"Yeah, you told us that already. In the morning after dinner, yesterday over coffee, now in your room…ouch." Luuk mumbled and then glared at Xander that hit his arm.

"You should tell him," Xander continued when he made sure Luuk wouldn't interrupt him again. "About Aart," he clarified.

"Yeah, that's not going to happen." I shook my head. "If the exes talk would come up, it would happen later on, far into the future."

"I hate the exes' talk." Luuk hugged a pillow to his body.

"Well, I think you should talk to him about it, he should know what it's been like for you. How else do you want him to understand what you're going through?" Xander asked as he tried to look at me while I was going through the pages in my notebook. "I know it's scary, but I also know you, Nor. You're the girl who goes after what she wants, you always have been."

"In life maybe, in career maybe, but I don't know how to do it when it comes to love anymore." I brushed my fingers over the petals of the tulips. "It's like I'm in a conflict with myself. I want to show him everything that I am, but at the same time I don't want him to see it all. I can't risk getting hurt again because of my…"

I felt myself choke up when I thought of everything Aart used to tell me.

"I don't get you, Nora," Aart kept walking back and forth in my room.

"You never do," I sighed. I was so exhausted from trying to explain it, of feeling like I was doing something wrong, but I didn't know how to make it right either.

If he only tried to listen, if he only tried to hear me out.

"What do you want from me Nora?" He ran his hand through his blond hair. "I just want my girlfriend back, the fun and outgoing Nora who likes to go to parties on Friday night and doesn't lock herself up in her room. I'm so done with canceling plans with people because of your…"

"Say it," I said in a shaky voice.

"Everyone gets stressed out, Nora. It doesn't make you that special, no need to be dramatic over this. I also get stressed after an exam, and then I go to sleep at night and I feel all better in the morning."

I looked down in my hands. "I wish it was that simple, but it's not."

"Maybe you'll get some sleep if you stop overthinking everything all the damn time," he sighed.

I tried to look him in his eyes, though he didn't try to do the same. "It doesn't work like that; I can't just decide to stop feeling pressured or burned out. I can't just do what you ask for me, it's going to take me time. I know it's hard to understand but-"

"No, Nora, it's more than that, much more than that," he said in a cold voice as he pointed his finger at me. "You have a beautiful life, amazing parents, great friends, what do you have to be so stressed about?"

"Aart—"

"You know what, I don't need this." He put his hands in the air. "I don't need to stay here and listen to this nonsense about burning out, or having headaches or whatever it is you feel. I'm going to meet some friends, have a nice drink, if you want to come then great, if not then don't expect me to wait for you to feel better."

"Nor?" Luuk asked.

My attention is brought back to them. "I...umm...I think you should go to eat lunch without me today, I just have a lot on my mind, and I didn't get much sleep last night, I..."

"Nor," Xander said, his voice was much harsher than Luuk's. "You should go to him."

"What?" I asked and watched him as he got up off the bed and closed my notebook gently and put it on my shelf. "Didn't you just hear what I said?"

"I did, and as your friend I see it as my responsibility to tell you to go out and get some fresh air. You just had your first kiss with the guy you like and instead of going on dates and experiencing some romance you look for ways to stay inside and write in your notebook about him."

"I like writing about him," I said. "It's a nice way to express myself."

"Another good way to express yourself would be to go to Oasis, have a hot make out session with him, and say yes when he asks you on a date," Luuk mentioned, still sitting on my bed with crossed legs.

I rolled my eyes at him, though deep inside I would love nothing more than see William and get to kiss his soft lips again.

And that was just the beginning of my fantasies about William and me.

"What is it?" Xander asked when he looked over me with concern when I kept quiet.

"My overthinking took control over me again." I blinked my eyes to not cry. "I hate when it happens."

I was frustrated, and tired, so tired.

"Look, I appreciate you two for coming here and trying to keep me company, I really do, but I think I'm going to try and take a nap. When I'll wake up I'll decide what to do and if I feel like seeing William today. Okay?"

Xander and Luuk switched glances. Xander hugged me goodbye and waited for Luuk to get up from my bed and hug me as well before he followed Xander.

"If you need to talk, and you're not ready to talk with William, then you have our number." Luuk lifted his phone.

I nodded. "Have a nice lunch, I'll have one with you tomorrow."

Luuk smiled at me and closed the door behind the both of them.

I stayed near my desk for a few more moments, and when I heard them walking out the house I went to my bed and covered my body in a warm blanket. I closed my eyes and prayed that the sleep would come easily to me, and thankfully it did.

When I woke up from my sleep and opened my eyes again, the first thing I saw was the sky through my window that changed its color into a darker shade of blue. I looked blindly for my phone near my bed and when I found it and it lit up, I saw William's text he probably sent while I was sleeping.

WILLIAM

I know you're busy, but if you have some time, I would love to see you. Maybe we can go on a nice walk after my shift?

I bit my lips as I stared at the screen, my hands paused when I tried to think what to write back. My head was a bit clearer now, I didn't have a headache, or tiredness surrounding my body, a nice walk could be nice.

ME

You are aware that it's raining outside, right?

WILLIAM

Says the girl that walks in the rain without an umbrella.

Oh, I'm not talking about myself, I can survive the rain. Can you?

With you I can.

How romantic.

I'm romantic at heart, you said it yourself.

So I did.

Meet me at the restaurant in about an hour?

See you there.

It didn't take too long to get out of bed and get ready with his text in mind. I walked outside in the cold weather, feeling the rain drops fall quickly down my face, hair, and warm clothes as I was on my way to Oasis. When I got there I checked there was no sign of lack of sleep on my face in the glass reflection and then opened the door.

The place was empty, though this time my heart beat was rapid at the thought of William waiting for me.

His bag was all packed on the stool near the bar, where he was busy cleaning the counter, careful not to touch the cup of coffee he put there.

It was funny thinking that not so long ago we were in the same position, only I was a stranger who looked for a coffee and he was the guy who helped me feel that desire. Now he wasn't some stranger, we were far past it. He wasn't some nice-looking guy at the bar, he was the guy that filled my thoughts, that I desired to walk with in the rain, that I desired to do so much more with.

He must've felt my gaze on him, because then he lifted his head. "Nora."

"Hey, you." I smiled at him.

He left his cleaning cloth behind and walked quickly toward me for a hug. "I missed you."

"We saw each other on Valentines' Day." I giggled as he wrapped his arms tighter around my body. "You gave me beautiful tulips," I reminded him.

"I wished it could be more romantic for you, we barely got the chance to talk after our..." he stopped as he pulled away enough to look at my face again.

"Kiss?" I asked.

He grinned as his eyes wandered down, like he was repeating it in his head as much as I did.

"It was a perfect kiss," I admitted.

"Yeah it was, it was just—" His grin disappeared when he met with my eyes.

"What?" I asked. "Is it the rain? Because I was sure I wiped away my cheeks and everything."

I lifted my hand to touch my cheek, but he took it and covered it with his. "It's not your cheeks, it's your eyes."

"Is my makeup smeared, or something?"

"No," he whispered as his gaze just turned more intense. "They look sad. They're beautiful as always, but it's almost like there's a sadness behind them. I don't know how to explain it." I tried to look away from him, but he was fast. He put his hand under my chin and made me look at him. "Nora?"

I wanted to crawl up and hide when he looked at me this way, in an intense and genuine way. "It's nothing, we should go outside, have that walk in the rain you talked about."

He took a look at the rain that got stronger outside, rain drops dripped down the glass windows as we were inside. "The rain can wait for us."

He was silent as he patiently waited for me to talk. He walked back to give me some space but held my hand and ran his thumb over the palm of my hand to keep a physical contact.

"I lied to you," I said, but couldn't look him in his eyes when I did. I felt like my pride was wounded. "I wasn't busy the last couple of days. Well, I was, but not as much as I claimed to be."

"Was it because of me?" He looked at me with hurt. "Did I take it too far between us? Did you think it over and decide you don't want me that way? Because it's okay, Nora. You can always talk to me, even if you think it will hurt my feelings. I want us to be honest with each other."

He was about to leave my hand, but I only pulled it to my body and held it close. "William, this kiss was perfect, you were perfect, you're the one who made that all dinner perfect for me."

His lips curled up, but just a little.

"I didn't want you to see me, because I knew it would take one look for you to know something was wrong with me. Since that kiss all I've been doing was overthinking this entire thing. I just let my worries get the best of me. You might not get it, but all I thought about was how scared I am of it not working, that in the future you'll see a side of me you won't like and it would be over," I explained everything fast that I wasn't sure if he heard it all that clearly.

I let out a breath as my heart tightened.

"I'm not a sunshine person all the time, I might seem like I am, but I'm not. I wish I could be like the sun you love to talk about, but sometimes I'm like this rain outside. I can get messy, and dark, and sad." My hand was shaking slightly as it held his warm hand. "I was thinking about my ex today, and how he treated me when I was trying to deal with everything back in high school, and then I got scared."

He took a deep breath and pulled his hand away from my chest. While he was doing that, he took my shaky hand and brought it to his lips, kissing each finger as he looked at me through his thick eyelashes.

"You can be the sun, you can be the rain, you can be whoever you want to be when you're with me, Nora. Okay?" he asked softly.

My lips parted as I looked at him.

He wiped the tears that fell on my already wet cheeks. "I'm scared, too, you know?" When I didn't answer he tucked a strand of hair behind my ear. "I'm an overthinker, too."

"If that's your way of trying to make me feel better, then it isn't working," I mumbled under his gaze. My face felt warm after all the tears, and emotional confession and then having him looking at me like that after it.

"Are you sure? I think I've noticed a smile there," he looked at my lips.

He put his hands at the side of my face and pressed his lips to mine, in a gentle peck. And then another one, and another, until I giggled.

"Yep, there it is," he said against my lips.

He let go when he saw I wanted to wipe my cheeks some more.

"Sorry about that," I said through puffy eyes. "It's been an emotionally exhausting couple of days."

"Don't apologize." He handed me a coffee and pecked my

lips once more before he let me go completely so I could drink peacefully.

Usually when I cried, or felt emotionally burned out or tired, I didn't get this kind of reaction, never had anyone this kind and understanding. I always needed to find reasons behind my tears, for explanations and different ways of saying "I'm sorry, I promise I'm trying." It was never sweet, no one ever wiped the tears, not like William did.

"I know it might be a bad time to ask, but if I don't do this now, I don't know when I'll master up the courage to ask," he said as he watched me drink the coffee he made me. "Will you go on a date with me, Nora?"

I blinked my eyes at him, wondering if I just imagined him saying it. Maybe it was part of the dream I had in bed earlier that found its way to creep into my reality.

"I actually planned to ask you by giving you tulips from the market, a combination of pink and white, but I didn't know if we'd see each other today, and I wanted to give you beautiful tulips, with that fresh, sweet scent, and...." He chuckled as he looked at me again. "Yeah, that's definitely not how I planned this."

I tried to hold myself back, but after crying I felt so much relief that I laughed.

He narrowed his eyes. "And now you're laughing."

I put down the cup and turned to him fully. "No, it's not what you think. I didn't plan to be asked out on a date after crying, with puffy eyes and wet hair from the rain, that's all."

It made both of us laugh.

I tilted my head. "Will I get tulips on our date?"

"In any color you want, though I know you prefer pink."

"Will there be coffee?"

"That can be arranged."

"And will you kiss me?"

His blue eyes darkened. "I hope so. I definitely hope so."

By the way he looked at me, I knew he hoped for more than a kiss, just like I did, but he wasn't going to say it out loud yet.

"Then it's a yes from me."

CHAPTER 25
William

I tried to keep my calm when I looked at Nora holding the tulips I gave her, but it was hard to stay calm when I saw the white sweater dress she wore under her coat, or when I noticed that her nails were still colored in white. I wanted to take her hand, bring them closer to my lips and kiss it.

It was hard to not overthink on our way to the Italian restaurant I picked for tonight. It wasn't a fancy one, fancier than the one we went to the other day. From their site, it seemed like the kind of place Nora might like. It had delicious food, nice music in the background and decorations like a piano and the right lights that brought a certain energy, a peaceful one. We've had so many lunches and dinners together she loved basically any kind of food she was offered; she tried the entire dishes on our menu, but I was still worried I should've let her pick the place. I wanted this to be perfect, everything that she loved.

Then I felt her wrap her hand around mine and pull me closer to her body, so our shoulders brushed against each other. Luckily my hand wasn't sweating, instead, I felt chills down my spine when she was this close. I should've relaxed and enjoyed the moment, but no matter how hard I tried, I couldn't. I remembered how things were in my past relationship for me, how quickly the ship can sink, I didn't want to ruin anything this time.

"Don't overthink it, William. Out of all the things you could overthink, don't waste your time on this," she said as she looked at the rest of the path ahead of us. "I love walking in the city more than driving or riding my bike, I love Italian food as much as I love any other dishes, and I love the tulips you gave me. So please don't overthink this."

I sighed and looked up at the starry night. If I was with Ethan, he would probably mumble something about them, find something to say about stars dying, or their distance from the earth—but I was with Nora. She didn't talk about the stars, she looked up at them, enjoyed their beauty, like she did when a rain started to fall, or the sun showed up in the sky after a cloudy day.

She was starting to look at me in the same way, which made my heart flutter. I wanted to be deserving of that look, I wanted to deserve *her*.

"I wish I could Nora. It's our first date, and all I want is to be able to enjoy it and tell you how stunning you look tonight," I let out a breath when I looked at her once more, at her perfect lips who were covered with pink lipstick, at the way the green in her eyes was even more bright at night. "I want to be deserving of you."

She pressed her lips together as she looked up at me, until eventually she nodded to herself. "Then tell me."

"Huh?"

"If you want tonight to go perfect, and that means you tell me how stunning I look, then tell me."

My lips turned into a smile, though my cheeks hit up, I lingered my gaze over her, taking in her look. "You look stunning."

She giggled, content with the compliment, but then stopped when a more serious thought flashed through her mind. "At the market, you told me that there must be other people who could take better care of me than you can," she said slowly, her eyes not leaving mine. "Why is that?"

"We shouldn't go there, Nora, not tonight," I shook my head. "That's not how dates go."

"Oh, really?" she laughed lightly. "So, how are dates supposed to go?"

"Nora," I chuckled as I tried to gain some of my seriousness back.

"No, I mean it, do tell," she motioned for me with her hand to keep talking.

"I had a plan, okay?" I told her. "I planned for us to get to know each other a bit more, ask more questions, have a nice dinner that I'd pay for at the end, because I want to, even if you'd try to fight me on this, and knowing you, I'm sure you will. Then I'll walk your home and kiss you goodnight. Because even if you don't deserve me, you can still have a perfect date with me, because you deserve that much."

She stopped walking, and I did the same when she stepped in front of me. "William, can we make a deal?"

I looked sideways at the street we were walking and then narrowed my eyes at her, a bit confused by her sudden stop. "Okay."

"How about I take over the planning?" she asked gently. "Besides, you have a way of wrecking my plans anyway." She probably felt my nerves, because then she squeezed my hand. "Don't get me wrong, I love all the efforts you put into this date, and how closely you thought of the details, but I don't want this to distract you from living in the moment with me. The date would be perfect whether you pay for the meal or not, and it would be perfect whether we kiss at the end of the night or not, so please don't get too caught up into that."

I opened and closed my mouth. I wanted to let go of my worries, but my brain, as always, got caught up to specific words. "I wreck your plans?"

"William," her voice was softer when she heard the worry in my voice. "I didn't mean it in a bad way. I was focused on dealing with every day at a time, hoping I wouldn't feel too stressed out again if I do things right, but then you showed up," that made her smile. "Or more correctly, I barged into your family's restaurant."

"Yeah, you do have this kind of a habit," I smiled back. "Showing up in a guy's life and not letting go."

She went to look at me, like she tried to tell me with her eyes that she wasn't planning on letting me go anytime soon.

"You wrecked my plans, but I think I needed someone to do that for me for a long time." She watched me closely under the street light. "I think I needed someone like you in my life for a long time, William."

I barely heard her, because my heart was beating hard against my ribcage. That was more than I expected to hear from her. On the other hand, Nora wasn't the kind of person you could easily predict her next actions.

I could only guess how hard it was for her to say these words. Sure, she was confident, she said her opinion every time I asked for it, or didn't, but it had nothing to do with her confidence, it had everything to do with her daring heart.

I cleared my throat. "These are big words for someone who claims not to be a hopeless romantic."

"You said it yourself... I'm more of a hopeless romantic than I let on," she replied, and then took a step closer and brushed her nose against mine in a childish manner. "Now, what is it that makes you believe that anyone else could look after me better than you can?"

I looked down at my shoes and sighed. It was silly thinking I could brush it off like nothing and she would let me do it.

"Because I wasn't the best boyfriend in the past, and I don't want to be a bad boyfriend to you," I said, my cheeks heated up from embarrassment and shame of who I used to be.

"I find that hard to believe," she whispered.

"No, Nora, you say it now, but you didn't see how I was in my last relationship. I was so caught up with grief and trying to help my parents with Oasis that I couldn't give my ex-girlfriend what she needed, I couldn't be the boyfriend she wanted me to be," I sighed and put my hands back in my jean pockets. I closed my eyes when flashbacks started flooding my brain like a short movie in my head with all the mistakes I made in the past. "She wanted a boyfriend she could go on dates with, and spend time after school at each other's house, not in some restaurant. I think she got sick of it at some point, and I can't blame her for that. She didn't sign up for this."

"You didn't sign up for this either," Nora said immediately. "No one signs up to see someone in their family pass, unfortunately it's just something that happens in life."

"I know you want to defend me Nora, but—"

"William," she said my name out loud in a way that made my entire body shiver. "The way I see it, you could've run away from your responsibilities, from your family, from everyone and everything. Yes, you could've spent more time with your girlfriend, that could be a nice distraction from all you've been through, but you chose your family, you chose to look after the people you care about while still dealing with something as hard as losing someone at a young age."

Her sweet words would kill me one day, if I wasn't sure of that in the past, I was sure of this now.

I blinked my eyes. "That might make me sound like a good person, but it also only proves how bad I am at being someone's romantic partner. That's why I wasn't planning on telling you how I feel, I wasn't planning on kissing you, I…"

"Didn't we just say you should leave the planning to me?" She tilted her head to the side.

"I'm being serious, Nora."

"So am I."

"Nora—"

"You want us to work, right, William?"

I swallowed. "Of course, I do."

I was a bit fearful she couldn't see it, but by the way she smiled at me I knew she already did.

"I know you fear being a bad boyfriend, but I don't think you have it in you," she calmed me with the touch of her hand on my shoulder. "A guy that watches movies like the Notebook, talks about love the way you do, or grew up with such an amazing example of love like your grandparents couldn't be a bad boyfriend."

Then, there was a gleam in her eyes as she brushed my lips for an instant. "Tulip field or a battlefield, William?"

"What?" I closed my eyes and tried to close the gap between us, but she didn't let me.

Nora pulled away from me with a smirk. "Pick one."

"You already know what I would pick."

"That's not an answer, William." She giggled when I lowered my head more, but my lips only reached her forehead.

I groaned in frustration. "Tulip field, *always*."

With you, always.

"Now you see what I mean when I say that you don't have it in you to be a bad boyfriend?" She caressed my cheek. "As long as we both put effort and work into this relationship, and work as a team like we have with the restaurant, we are going to be just fine."

"You sound confident," I chuckled, but couldn't ignore the relief I felt in my chest.

"No one looks after me better than you." She laughed at my pouty lips. "Did you forget already? You look after me, and I look after you."

"I guess I needed a reminder."

Her eyes flickered back to my lips, and like she wanted to give me more than a reminder, she put her hand holding the bouquet on my other shoulder and then our lips touched. When she stroked my bottom lip with her tongue and ran her nails in my hair, it was her way of emphasizing her words.

She didn't hesitate, or think it over, she did more than I planned on doing by the time the night was over. I hummed as she twisted her tongue with mine and started to drag my hands down her body, first her back and then her waist, until my hand found a way under her coat and wrapped around her hips that were covered in a sweater dress.

I could feel my body burn for her.

I trailed kisses to her neck as she tightened her grip around my shoulders, till she wrapped her hand around my neck to pull me closer to her skin.

My body stiffened when I heard her whimper and say my name.

"William," she said once again, her voice more urgent.

My lips stopped at her collarbone and I pressed one last kiss there and withdrew from her.

I was an aware person. I was aware of my own faults, and my own desires. I was aware of the effect Nora had on me, and I was aware that if I didn't stop now as I still held her in my arms, I wouldn't stop at all.

"Was that the goodnight kiss you planned on giving me?" she asked.

She made it sound like an innocent question, but there was nothing innocent in her intentions.

I tried to bring my breath back to normal as she gazed at me.

"No, it wasn't," I shrugged my shoulders. "You were right, Nora."

"About?" she asked, and I felt a weird sense of pride when I saw how her pink lipstick smeared and needed a short fix.

I lifted my hand to her face, and touched her lips gently as I tried to fix her lipstick. My fingers paused on her bottom lip. "From now on, I'm leaving the planning part to you."

CHAPTER 26
Nora

We left the restaurant hand in hand. For a moment, I wished I could bring my notebook, just so I could write down everything about this night. It wasn't like I didn't go on dates before, or didn't eat dinner with a guy, but when it came to William, I felt the need to remember the details, to write down everything I learned about him. Like the way he smiled when he hummed in content every time he ate pasta, or how his blue eyes shined every time he mentioned his family, or the way he was so sweet to me.

My heart ached when I thought of what he said before we went to the restaurant. How could a guy like him ever think he wasn't deserving of this, of me, of experiencing what we have? How could such a sweet guy have such bitter and sad thoughts hunting his mind?

Though, he could say the same about me. How could a girl that reminded him of the sun could be as dark as the rain?

But before I let myself go down that road, I heard his voice, and just by how raw it was, I could tell it was serious. "Nora, can I take you somewhere?"

Maybe for the first time tonight I felt actual nerves running through my body, the thought of saying goodbye and kissing at my doorstep already left my heart feeling empty and the night wasn't even over yet. It took both of us a lot of guts and effort to get here. It took guts of him to kiss me, it took a lot of guts from me to kiss him back, it took a lot of courage from the both of us to go on this date together.

The last thing I wanted to hear him say was that he wanted to walk me home.

He could act like a gentleman for as long as he wanted, but I could see in his eyes he didn't want it to be over yet too.

"Follow me," he whispered in my ear, and soon enough, he led me through the streets of the city.

It was the start of a new week; the bars and restaurants were filled with people who wanted to spend the night outside. The canals looked beautiful in the nighttime even more than they looked during the day.

If I wasn't as curious as I was to see where he wanted to take me, I would've dragged him to one of the bridges between the canals and made him take a picture. It was a shame that a gorgeous guy like him barely had pictures, hopefully with time I could make him open up to the idea.

He slowed down his steps when we reached a small neighborhood. It was the kind of neighborhood where people decorated their windows with different objects or flowers that could tell more about the character of the people who lived inside. As we were walking, I checked the windows, until we stopped near a house with nothing at the windows. It had a glimpse into a dark living room instead.

"There used to be tulips in a vase there, they looked beautiful on sunny days." William looked at me like he knew exactly what I wanted to ask. "There were also some pictures from romance movies from the 80's, too. My parents took everything down after..." He cleared his throat. "After my grandpa passed away, they didn't see a point in keeping it all there. They packed everything up, they said it was a necessary step to move on with our lives."

"It's your grandparents house," I whispered.

After everything I heard of them, I wished I could see the house as it was when he was a kid, with pictures, and tulips along the window, with color, and life, not this sad house with no one inside.

"My parents put all of the photos and the rest of their stuff in boxes, but the magic of the place isn't all gone." He squeezed my hand, and motioned for me to follow him inside.

My eyes widened when I watched him take out the key chain from his pocket and open the door of the house.

He led me through the darkness as he kept on telling me the story. "There was no one to live in here after they were gone, my grandparents don't have any close relatives. My dad thought of selling it, but even after he found buyers, he didn't have the heart to go through with it. I think part of him knew my grandma wouldn't have wanted that, this house held too many memories to be sold."

He stopped to put his arm around my waist and pulled me to his body when we passed the kitchen and I almost tripped over one of the chairs. My heart was beating fast when I felt the warm touch of his hand through the thin fabric of my dress.

"Sorry about that. I would've turned on the lights, but knowing my grandma, she would want me to show you the garden before you see anything else. My grandparents joked that the heart of the house was the garden, and I have to agree with that."

Even if I couldn't see his face clearly under the lights, I glanced up, just to get a small peek of the way they probably lit up when he walked me through a place that meant this much to him.

He opened the door to the garden and waited for me to go outside before he did the same.

My eyes widened as I stared at the garden that was filled with tulips. They weren't only white, or pink, but they were in every color; they blended together in a way that made my eyes jump from one to the other, wanting to soak up everything in.

William hugged me from behind and my back was pressed to his chest as I put my hands on his arms that wrapped around my stomach. His head leaned on my shoulder, near my head, and I could feel him smile against my skin. Like he knew exactly what I felt as I looked at the heart of the house.

"My dad had a dilemma, he didn't want to sell, but didn't want to leave the place empty, so we use it as an Airbnb. People come here at times when they're on vacation. Some are older like my grandparents; some are young couples that are looking for a nice and clean house with a garden."

"How does that make you feel?" I asked him as he tightened his grip on me, like he needed to hold on to something, someone, when he talked about them.

"Like it's another reminder that I need to move on, too," he laughed bitterly. "Enough time has passed, people come and go into this house, and still, I keep on coming here to plant tulips each winter, acting like the same child I was, trying desperately to feel their presence."

"William..." I moved his arms off my body slowly and turned to look at his face. Unlike the inside of the house, the garden was lit up, and I could see every bit of pain behind his beautiful eyes. "You're the one who planted all of these tulips?"

I looked down at the tulips he gave me earlier this evening that rested on the chair. It made sense, his dad's way of moving on was packing everything and keep on moving, and Willaim's way was planting tulips, not letting them die, not like his grandparents did.

I could feel how my whole heart felt his pain, wanting to comfort him.

"My dad doesn't know I do that, or he does, but he doesn't

say anything about it. I mean, the last time I checked the reviews, they took pictures of the garden in the summer, so I'm sure he has some sort of idea of what I'm doing in the place," he muttered. "I know he'll never understand, but I couldn't let the tulips die. I couldn't let everything my grandparents built, all the hours my grandma spend in this garden, even when she...even when she got sick, she stayed here, I owe it to her, to my grandpa, they didn't teach me everything I know about flowers just so I'll sit with crossed arms from the side and do nothing."

I took in a deep breath as I looked around us. "Even if he never understands you, then you should know that I do. Since the day you told me about your grandparents' history, I could tell it was a big part of who you are."

"You're the first person I told this story to," he said quietly as he watched me carefully. "Besides Ethan, I never told anyone about the tulips, or talked about my grandparents in general. Not even my ex-girlfriend."

I tried to hide my surprise by playing with my braid. "Why not?"

"I would say it was too painful at the time, but that would be just another excuse. I didn't feel like I could open up to her about this stuff, I couldn't bring myself to do that with her," he explained.

I knew he was too good of a guy to compare between her and I, but I could tell what he tried to say between the lines. He didn't just tell me about his grandparents' love story, but he did it early on.

He ran a hand through his hair with blushing cheeks. "I didn't plan on bringing you here tonight, I feel like I keep dropping heavy stuff like this on you. Ever since we met, I keep doing that. I know I shouldn't do this on a first date, but it felt right bringing you here. You've heard so many stories, you deserve to see where all these stories came from."

"Is that why you brought me here?" I asked as I walked between the tulips. "To see where all these stories happened?"

"Yes and no," he followed me and bent down to smell one of the tulips. "Since they passed away, I couldn't bring myself to talk about them, to open up about them, to tell stories. I tried to keep them alive in my way, by working at the restaurant, or growing tulips, but I never actually voiced how much I missed them, I didn't let myself think of them or go back to old memories. I was scared I wouldn't be able to handle it, I'm maybe a nineteen-year-old guy, but when it comes to my family, to *them*, I go back to being a child."

I froze in place near a white tulip as I felt him looking at me. "What changed?"

"On January 6th I was about to close the restaurant, and then a girl came in, demanding me to make her coffee. Minutes later, I found myself telling her my life story like it was the easiest thing I've done."

I blinked my eyes. "You remember the date we met?"

His cheeks burned a deep shade of red and he looked down at the tulip. I shouldn't know he was the kind of guy to remember dates, he believed in love at first sight, of course he remembered the day we first met.

"Don't be embarrassed, I wrote it down, too," I laughed at myself. "I couldn't even wait to get home to open my notebook. I was on the metro and had to write your name down. It was something like: *I met a guy, his name is Will, but I'm going to call him William. He has beautiful blue eyes, and he makes the best coffee I ever tasted. We're friends now. I hope it's going to be a long friendship, the kind that can last forever.*"

Usually my notebook was that secret escape I could run to. It wasn't meant for sharing, or for anyone else to read or know what was written in there. But it was easy sharing it with William, it was easy telling him what our first meeting meant to me. It wasn't a love at first sight on my part, but it was *something*.

He sucked in a breath. "You wrote all of that?"

That made me laugh even harder. If he only knew it was one of the least personal and intimate things I wrote about him in my notebook.

"Yes, I wrote all of that."

He nodded, taking the information in. "Umm, anyway, I was used to pushing all the memories I had from my grandparents aside, looking at it now, I think it was a coping mechanism, like a way to protect myself from dealing with the loss, but since we met I started to get some of these memories back."

I couldn't recognize my own voice when I turned to him. "Really?"

"I even talked with my grandma for the first time," he laughed when he sat down and looked up at the dark sky. "When I was a kid, she said that if I ever needed her, all I needed was to look up. When I came over to dinner at your house, it was the first time I actually did that."

I walked between the tulips till I reached him and sat down beside him. "Did you get the advice you needed?"

His eyes found their way to my lips. "I did."

I smiled when I realized he didn't get *some* advice, but a relationship advice. He didn't need to say more, it just made sense. He talked about how planned all his moves towards me, kissing me wasn't supposed to happen like it did, *when* it did.

I hugged his arm and leaned my head on his shoulder. "I bet you were the cutest kid ever when you were planting tulips in the garden with your grandma."

"I don't know if 'cute' is the right word. My hands were covered with dirt and my mom got mad that instead of doing my homework, I was spending so much time in the garden. I always came home tired and went straight to bed, it wasn't a cute look."

"I beg to differ."

His shoulders were shaking from laughter. "Well, I bet that even as a child you forgot to take an umbrella, but still radiated as the sun on rainy days, and god knows we have a lot of those."

My body stiffened when he mentioned that.

Radiant like the sun.

I remembered a lot of my childhood, my mom dressed me in the best dresses, I felt like a fashionista even in kindergarten. I was happy, relaxed, and easy going. That was how the sun was like, wasn't it? It was meant to be something beautiful to look at and seek comfort from, something with no dark side.

But I didn't feel like one now. William said I could be whatever I wanted to be, but it didn't make me feel any better. I wanted to shine as bright as I did before all the stress, and pressure and the consequences of it came into my life.

He wasn't Aart.

I needed to keep reminding myself that.

It wasn't going to end like the last time.

"Hey, are you alright?" William's voice woke me up. He looked down at me and moved a few strands of hair. "I'm ruining your clothes by making you sit on the ground with me, am I?"

"It's not that, I couldn't care less about my clothes right now."

"Then what is it?"

I sighed, because I didn't want to talk about my last relationship while we had such a beautiful moment, after he took me to a garden filled with tulips he planted by himself for god knows how long.

"I'm grateful you brought me here, and told me everything you did. You are, without a doubt, the most genuine guy I ever met."

He didn't need to tell me how my words affected him, I could see it, I could feel it in the way his muscles tightened under my touch.

I wondered how he would react if he saw the list of characteristics I wrote about him in my notebook. Not just the ones I already told him, like him being a gentleman, and genuine, and sweet. But the more specific ones.

He is the perfect partner to have walks on rainy days with.

He is the best at accepting my tears.

He is the only one I want to listen to Noah Kahan's songs with.

He might have one favorite love language, but he's good at it all.

He is the first guy who has ever brought me flowers, and I put them all in the vase on my desk.

He is an overthinking Cancer, the undeniable fit for a perfectionist Virgo.

Would that make him lose control around me completely?

Would that make him understand he was the opposite of a bad boyfriend?

I lifted my head from his shoulder. "Can you show me the inside of the house?"

"You can't sit still for five minutes, can't you?" he laughed but didn't argue and helped me get up from the ground.

"No, I can't."

CHAPTER 27
William

Holding Nora's hand and showing her my grandparents' house felt natural. Somewhere at the beginning of our friendship, after I told her about them, I knew I would take her here someday, like I knew I fell in love with her at first sight, or like I knew I was going to take her to a *real* tulip field someday.

I glanced at Nora and smiled when she scanned the walls like she hoped to find a picture, or any clue to how things looked like in this house when I was a kid. It was almost surreal looking at her, knowing that after everything I told her about myself, and my own grief, and everything involved my family, she chose to stay every single time, eager to hear more stories and learn about me.

I leaned against the door frame when we reached the guest room. I turned on the lights and let go of her hand to let her look around inside. "It's supposed to be the guest room, but I was the only guest who got to sleep here, so technically it was my room. It used to have more posters on the walls back then, and the bed was smaller too, but since my parents did a small renovation, they took everything down and switched my bed with a larger one."

My body was uneasy every time I came back here and walked these halls. I couldn't bring myself to walk inside the room, and definitely couldn't imagine going to what used to be my grandparents' room.

I put my hands in my pockets as I watched her walk in the space, looking up at the new furniture until her eyes landed on me.

"You used to spend a lot of time here, didn't you?"

"I did," I nodded. "But I stopped coming here when my grandma's sickness got worse. I regret many of the decisions I made back then."

"You were just a kid William." She stepped closer, but still gave me the space I needed.

"It's not just this place, this house—I didn't stay for my grandma when she needed me most. When we went to the hospital, and it was our time to say our goodbyes, I ran away from the waiting room when my parents weren't looking. I ran so fast, for what felt like hours, until I got to a tall enough tree to climb up." I leaned my hand against the wall and looked at the view through the window of the room. "If not Ethan, I would've probably stayed there for the entire night, too."

"How did he convince you to come down?"

My lips curled up despite the tragedy behind the story. "He came with a cheesecake, that was about it."

"A cheesecake?" she asked in misbelief.

"I ran for a long time, okay?" I laughed. "I was upset, but at the end of the day I was just a kid, I needed to gain my energy back somehow and I guess the sugar helped take the pain away temporarily."

"So, what you're saying is that I should maintain a good relationship with Ethan just in case you decide to climb up a tree again?" she asked.

"Even if I ever go to that tree again, you wouldn't need to bring a cheesecake or say anything to convince me to come down. I would go to you the moment you said my name," I promised.

It was supposed to be scary, knowing how much power she had over me, but it wasn't, it wasn't scary at all.

"What more do you regret?" she asked.

I bit the inside of my cheek as I watched her coming closer, and by doing that she only made the air ticker, and it made me want to cross the doorstep and enter the room just so I could reach her.

"I can tell you what I don't regret instead," I blurted out. "I don't regret taking you here."

"You don't?" she stuttered.

Despite all her confidence, she sounded uncertain, like she needed reassurance when it came to a serious matter like this.

"It feels right having you here," I admitted.

When she was close enough to me I put my hand under her chin. "I don't regret kissing you either, I waited a long time to do that."

I could see her mind lingering on my words, like she just realized something, and as I guessed, she wasn't going to leave me questioning her thoughts for long.

"Wait," she hesitated. "Did you fall in love at first sight with me?"

I shrugged, because I didn't want to lie, but I didn't want to freak her out either. I decided to be honest, only because Nora wasn't one to freak out easily. "I wanted to ask you out the night we met, but I didn't know how to do it. I never asked a girl properly to go out with me, and then you proposed for us to be friends, and…and it's really hard saying no to you, Nora."

I moved my hand to scratch the back of my neck that felt way too hot right now. "When I say long time, I don't mean that long, it's been only a few months…ouch."

I put my hand on my chest after she hit it softly.

"I can't believe that you waited that long for me."

"Again, Nora, it wasn't that long, and I didn't mind waiting. I didn't even know I had it in me to make that first step with you," I commented.

"But eventually you made that step." She smiled as she took my hand and walked backwards, trying to pull me inside the room with her.

"No, Nora, I can't," I swallowed as I held onto the wall desperately. "I haven't been inside since…since…"

"Yes, you can, William. You're better at taking first steps than you think you are." She encouraged me and waited patiently for me to let go of the wall and walk inside till we stood in front one another.

"See," she whispered to my ear. "You have it in you more than you think."

My heart kept on beating fast as she led me into the room, deeper and deeper, as we were surrounded by all the new furniture my parents brought.

She was patient with me, more patient than I ever pictured anyone being. She raised one of her hands and moved a few strands of hair from my face, calming me with her smile until my body relaxed under her touch.

I studied her beautiful face, and instead of overthinking everything about this place, or letting the bad memories come back, all I thought about was Nora. I thought of her daring heart, and how it might've been contagious, because all that ran through my head were things that my shy self could never picture doing so soon.

"I should…I should take you home, it's getting late," I muttered, but still couldn't stop looking down at her parted lips. It was happening again; I was reaching the surface of my self-control again.

She didn't move an inch. "You have to stop doing that, William."

"Doing what?"

"Saying the opposite of what you truly want," she stated. "Do us both a favor and for one night don't act like the perfect gentleman."

I took a deep breath as I considered my next move, my hands were shaking from holding myself back from her, my breathing was uneven, my entire body wanted to close the gap between us for once and for all, and give her a goodnight kiss she wouldn't forget. When our eyes met once again, it took us less than a second until our lips collided. Her lips were soft, and as they moved against mine, her hands were moving down my chest and reached down my sweater to explore my bare skin.

"Nora," I moaned when I felt her hands touch me.

I could picture her hands moving under the fabric, nails colored in white, contacting my skin, just picturing her hands making their path over my body made me go crazy.

I wasn't good at writing down my thoughts, or making checklists like she did, but my imagination was going wild when it came to Nora. I never gave in to my thoughts, but when she took off her coat and helped me take off my sweater, they were running wild in my head.

"Tell me what you want, William," she whispered in my ear as her nails grazed my bare chest, making their way slowly to the sensitive skin of my stomach, and stopped at the waistband of my jeans.

I opened my eyes and looked deeply into her green ones. Her pupils were dilated as she waited for me to tell her all about what I wanted. I rested my hands on hers and started to move her backwards towards the bed.

I put my hand carefully under her head when her knees buckled at the side of the bed and she fell on the mattress. When her head rested on the pillow, I went to lay on top of her, both my legs between hers.

"I know you said I shouldn't act like a gentleman tonight, but for our first time I want to be like that for you." I kissed her mouth in a quick peck and then wrapped each of her legs around my hips, I felt hard already by having her body this close to mine.

"I want to take care of you, Nora." I kissed her neck next, and nipped the sensitive skin till I heard her whimper my name.

She wrapped her arms around me and moved her hips so I could meet with her aching core, which in Nora's language meant she didn't like the idea of me taking it slow.

"I want to look after you."

My hands skimmed under the fabric of her dress as I slowly lifted it up her body, revealing more of her soft skin.

She left my shoulders and lifted her arms. I laughed but didn't fight her on this and kept moving up the fabric until her dress was on the floor.

"I promised to look after you."

I kissed the valley between her breasts that were still covered in her white bra. She had to go and wear a matching white bra and panties, didn't she? Her true plan was to ruin me completely, I was sure of this now.

"Let me keep my promise."

I placed a trail of kisses down her stomach, and hummed against her skin as she kept on calling my name in the sweetest way possible.

"Okay, Nora?" I whispered as my thumbs traced the inside of her thigh.

I could hear her suck in a breath when I moved her legs away from my body to slip down her panties. The moment they were on the floor, I wrapped her legs around my shoulders and dipped my head lower to her center.

"William." She gripped my strands of hair. "You...you didn't say what you wanted me to do."

"What *I* want?" I lifted my head barely just so I could look at her eyes. "I want to eat you out until you come first, then I want to touch every inch of your body, and lastly, I want to make love to you. I don't want you to do anything, I just want you to enjoy it, okay? Not overthinking it or giving any of this a second thought, no pressure or stress, just us."

I didn't even know what came over me. I was never this blunt with a girl, this honest and true about what I wanted, but with Nora it came so easy to me.

Her eyes warmed up to me, her shoulders and muscles completely relaxed. "The same goes to you. Just us."

My lips curled. "Okay."

"Okay, then." She pressed her lips against mine one more time for a long kiss before she laid back and let me wrap my mouth around her clit, though this time I didn't hold back.

I sucked, licked, and circled my fingers to add pressure until her legs were shaking around my shoulders as she came. I lingered there for a few more moments, just to savor her taste before I faced her again.

My lips made their way up her stomach as my hands were tracing the sides of her body. I was grazing the fabric of her bra before I kissed her collarbone, then her neck and finally pressed a kiss to the corner of her lips. I used to be the one who blushed easily around her, but here she was laying in bed with rosy cheeks and it was all because of me.

"It's nice to know I affect you, too." I caressed her cheeks while I looked down at her.

She laughed. "You needed us to get to that point to find that out? Wasn't it obvious before?"

"I think I was too busy overthinking all of this to notice." I traced the side of her body again and stopped at the underside of her breast. "You do know we don't have to do anything, right?"

She cupped my face and pressed her lips to mine. The kiss was intense, strong, full of emotion. Her lips moved against mine till she left me panting from need for her.

I groaned when she pulled away, her voice was reassuring. "I want this, William, and I also really want you to keep your promise and touch every inch of my body, so…"

She didn't need to say more. My hands reached her back and I unclasped her bra quickly.

I admit, she was beautiful in white, but she was more beautiful laying under me, begging me to touch her.

I leaned down and wrapped my mouth around her nipple while cupping her other breast. She closed her eyes, arched her back, and sank her fingers deeper into my skin, bringing me impossibly closer to her chest.

"That's it." I grazed her nipple with my teeth. "Let me look after you."

"I want to look after you, too." She whimpered when I sucked her other nipple. "Take off your jeans."

I tugged her nipple one last time and drew up her body. My face hovered over her and I groaned when I noticed swollen lips and wide eyes. I kissed them once again and my lips curved into a smile when it hit me. "Nora, you smell like tulips."

"I do?" She sounded surprised but she didn't stop me from burying my head in her neck to get a better sense of it.

I nipped her neck and sucked her sensitive spot till my lips made a mark there, and then I pulled away from her and got off the bed. My cheeks heated up when I felt her watching me take off my jeans and boxers. Her eyes were roaming my figure shamelessly, and I knew I wasn't going to forget the way she was looking at me for a long time.

I was ready and hard for her, and she knew it.

She didn't waste any time, she brought me back to the bed with her.

I chuckled when she peppered my chest with kisses and left a mark of what was left of her lipstick on my skin. "Wait, Nora, you have to let me grab the condom if you want us to go further with this."

"You don't need to go anywhere, I'm on the pill," she mumbled as she wrapped her hands around my neck and brought my body to hers, till I felt her nipples grazing my chest. "I'm clean, and you're clean, right?"

"Right," I said but still hadn't moved as my eyes trailed her face. When she tried to wrap her legs around my hips I rested my hand gently on her ankle to stop her. "Wait, before we do this…"

I pulled the rubber band that held her braid in place and ran my hand through her hair, letting it come undone and frame her face on the pillow. I grinned and pulled a few strands of hair from her face and kissed her.

I helped her wrap her legs around my hips and deepened our kiss when I felt her legs spreading farther apart and my cock at her entrance. The heat of her skin, the softness of her body, the way she kissed me back with such passion and need made it impossible to not lose any shred of control I had. I started to learn that my self-control was out of the picture when it came to Nora.

I barely pulled away from her, just enough to meet with her eyes, asking her for permission without words.

"Yes, William," she pleaded and pecked my lips once more. "No one could take care of me better than you can."

My heart soared from her words, and at the next time our lips met, I pushed my hips to hers and slid inside her.

Despite her needy hands that dug into my shoulders and her trying to pull me in one quick thrust, I did my best to take it slow. I traced her knees, then her thighs, and stopped at her ass. I squeezed it lightly to get out another moan from her and she arched her back away from the mattress.

"William," she gasped.

That sound. I hummed in response, wondering how many more times I'd get her to call my name that way.

I liked observing her when she was sitting at the restaurant, writing in her notebook, talking about all the ideas in her head, but that was a different kind of observation. Her sounds, the way she said my name when we were in a room alone, the fact I would always prefer to be called *William* than *Will* just because of her.

I pulled away just to slam back inside her with more force as our tongues danced together.

My body was shaking with desire when I kept rolling my hips forward, our sweaty bodies met with each movement. Shivers ran down her legs as I touched her and roamed my hands over her skin like I couldn't get enough of her.

I *really* couldn't. Her body, her smell, her tender touch over my chest, it made me want her even more than I already did.

"Nora," I told her through hooded eyes. "Tell me what more you want."

She ran her hand through my hair and spoke right against the shell of my ear. "I want to see you lose control."

My Adam's apple bobbed.

"Nora," I warned.

"I know you're holding back," she whispered. "*Don't.*"

"I want this to be good for you," I said against her lips.

"It's more than good for me already," she replied. "It's perfect."

Perfect.

My eyes got lost in hers, and when she roamed her hand over my arm and stopped at my biceps, I granted her wish.

I plunged into her harder, faster, tighter.

I took her hands and put them over her head and laced our fingers together when I slammed into her over and over again. I growled when my mouth found its way down her neck and then back to her breasts.

I wrapped my mouth around her rosy peaks. I dedicated my full attention to each one of them as we rolled our hips to meet one another, each time the waves of pleasure became more intense than the ones before.

Her walls clenched tighter around me. "William, I'm close."

"I know, Nora, I know." I kissed her breast. "I'm close, too."

I let go of her hands and rested one of mine on her waist to hold her in place as I lowered the other one to the spot where we were connected. I was watching her closely as I rubbed her. Her eyes closed and she leaned her head back when the orgasm took over her, and when she clenched around my cock I came too.

I didn't recognize my own voice, that sounded almost animalistic when I called out her name and dug my hands into her waist.

"God, Nora," I muttered into the crook of her neck and hugged her tightly.

I moved to the side and nestled her into my chest, still wrapping my arms around her. I knew she wasn't going to leave me, but just in case.

She smiled when she watched me kiss her hand. "I hope that after tonight, you don't have any more doubts about me wanting you."

I grinned. "You smell like the tulips I planted in the garden while laying naked in bed with me, I don't think I could have doubts anymore."

She smiled, and after I peppered kisses over her face and chest some more, she turned to me. "William, can I say something?"

"Yes, I can keep the window open so you can hear the rain outside at night, but you would have to sleep close to me so I could keep you warm," I said, and to prove a point, I embraced her and put the blanket over us.

"It's good to know we can find a common ground on this matter, but that wasn't what I was going to say," she said. "I wanted to say that I like seeing you lose control, it's a good look on you."

My heart fluttered, because God knows that with her around me, it wasn't going to be the last time.

I brushed a kiss against her hair. "It's a good look on you, too."

I watched her smile, and I watched the way that smile stayed on her face even when she fell asleep by my side.

Before I went to sleep too, I took the time to look over at her as it started to rain outside over the garden we were sitting in not that long ago.

"One day, Nora, when I'm ready, I'll take you to a *real* tulip field." I whispered and pressed a kiss to her forehead. "I promise."

CHAPTER 28
Nora

The side of the bed was empty when I woke up, but I could hear William downstairs. While I waited for him, I pulled his sweater over my naked body. Last night he told me I smelled like tulips, but so did his sweater.

Then I ran my hand through my hair and smiled when I remembered how his fingers slipped through my hair to break apart my braid. No one has ever done that before.

I stood by the window to look at the garden while I went through my phone to work on a new post for the social account of the restaurant. I know, I was supposed to stay in bed, and think of everything that took place last night and the best sex I had in my life, but William was right, I couldn't stay still, not even now. Besides, my brain kept going back and forth with ideas when he took me on the date. There were so many events I wanted to plan out, so much that needed to be done.

The garden was more beautiful in daylight than it was last night. I could see why William spent so much from his childhood in this place. Even without family pictures on the wall or having any personal objects, I could imagine what it was like all those years ago. There was something nice about waking up in the morning to a view of a tulip garden in the middle of the city.

Then I heard William's voice. "You're awake."

I looked up from my phone and stared at his bare chest and pair of jeans. He looked even more beautiful than he did last night, his hair was messy and the marks I left with my lipstick were vivid on his chest. I didn't mind the darkness of the night, but it felt nice to be able to see him, and the room in the daylight. He was toned, and it took all the power in me to hold onto my phone and not trace my finger along his defined muscles as I wished. I could get used to it. Waking up in the morning, wearing William's clothes as he brings me coffee in bed. There was no awkwardness or weirdness to the idea of seeing each other in a more vulnerable way. Even William, who seemed a bit more conscious of his actions than I was, seemed to feel the same.

His eyes burned into me when he roamed my body slowly, as he tightened his grip on the mug he was holding. He was thinking something, something *dirty*, I knew him well enough to recognize when that switch happened behind his eyes.

"I made you coffee." He mumbled and didn't tear his eyes away from me as he stepped closer.

"You're so sweet, thank you," I said when he handed me the mug and kissed his cheek before sipping from the warm drink.

"What are you doing?" he gazed at my phone. "I thought you would be sound asleep when I get back to bed and wake you up with coffee."

"You know me, I couldn't stay still and wait around, and I didn't want to ruin your sweet gesture either, so I decided to kill some time by working on some more stuff for the restaurant. I got ideas last night after we tasted that Italian menu, and-"

He pressed his lips to mine and then took my phone gently from my hand and put it aside on the desk nearby.

"We have all day to talk business, I promise I will listen to all of your ideas later, but right now I want to focus just on us, okay?" He rested his hands on my hips, dangerously close to the hem of his sweater.

I would lie if I said I wasn't a little turned on by it.

Okay, more than a little.

"How did you sleep?" he asked. "I didn't wake you up, did I?"

"I slept well, really well actually. I woke up to a view of a garden and now I'm standing with a handsome guy in front of me." I tilted my head up to brush his lips. "I have energy for whatever it is you're thinking about."

He held tighter unto my hips, his cheeks covered in red. "What do you mean?"

"I mean that I noticed how you looked at me when you walked in," I said. "You don't need to hold back your thoughts from me, William, not anymore."

His hands froze when he watched me through his eyelashes. "I...it's my sweater."

"Your sweater?" I smirked when he held onto the fabric of it. "What about it?"

"It might sound stupid, but when I came over to your house for dinner, and you wore my sweater back then too, I imagined you wearing nothing underneath with only my sweater on. I was thinking what I would've done if that ever were to happen." He gazed down at my body. "I went to prepare breakfast and bring you coffee, and then I saw you dressed like that."

His voice was unstable, like he tried his hardest to think of anything else.

"It's not stupid, William." I caressed his face slowly and then rested my hand on his chest to feel his beating heart before I put my hand on one of his and guided it under the sweater, making our way slowly over the inside of my upper thigh and let go of his hand on the skin of my hip.

"Fuck, Nora," he hissed against my mouth. "You're not wearing panties."

I stepped on my tiptoes until my lips brushed his earlobe. "I'm not wearing a bra either."

He made a noise in the back of his throat.

"You promised me a tulip field, William, and it means you start to communicate with me about what you want too," I kissed his cheek and then trailed my kisses down to his jaw. "Whether it's round two, or anything else, you should know I'm down for it. I don't have any classes today anyway, so take as much time as you need to do *exactly* what you have in mind."

He shattered. "You always have a way with words, don't you?"

"Well, it is your love language, after all." I mumbled when I pressed a soft kiss to his chest.

For the longest time, I tried to figure William out, but when I saw the twinkle in his eyes appear once again, I realized I figured another part of him he tried to hold back.

For the longest time, I was confused by him. I thought his love language might be physical touch, or acts of service such as giving tulips, but it was never just the tulips, he always looked for words of affirmation, for *my* words.

If he needed more of my compliments, more appreciative gestures, and sweet words to feel more comfortable and open up to me about his desires and wants, I was going to give it to him. If it was going to make it any easier for him, I was going to say what he needed to hear.

I took his other hand that clung to the fabric at this point, and moved it towards my core, where I was aching for him most, all while our eyes were linked.

I gasped when he finally touched me. He slipped one of his fingers inside and I clenched around him. Pictures from last night appeared in my head, and I hummed when I pictured his lips taking over instead of his fingers. I wasn't just wet, I was drenching because of his touch.

"God, Nora, you're so wet."

"I hope you're planning on doing something about it."

"Oh, you bet," he murmured.

He leaned down and kissed me. His lips were soft as always, beautiful as always, but there was something more needy in that kiss. He slipped his finger out and patted my hips. I took in the sign and wrapped my legs around him. He moved his hands up towards my butt to safely keep me from falling down as he walked us to the bed.

The moment my back met the mattress, he pressed his lips to my hot skin. He didn't stop just in my thigh or hips, but lifted the sweater higher, and higher, and higher until his lips covered my breasts. He slipped his finger inside me again while his tongue swirled around my nipples. He sucked them roughly and then my breasts until he left marks on my skin. Then nipped my skin and kissed down my stomach, and down back to my inner thigh.

"Spread your legs more for me, Nora." He kissed my warm thigh. "Please."

And he said I had a way with words.

He glanced up at me when I did as he asked and opened up for him. "You have no idea how hard it was not to lose control around you."

My chest heaved when I watched his head between my legs when he wrapped his mouth around me again. He grabbed my hips to tug me closer and twirled his tongue inside me. His mouth, his tongue, his movements were eager, desperate, like he missed it, like he couldn't get enough.

I wondered what more he imagined, what more he wanted to do with me. Even when he was a bit rougher, I felt his eyes on me. He was attentive to my reactions. He glanced at me every time I moaned, or lifted my hips up to meet with him or pressed his head into me harder.

Like last night, and like any time we were together, he looked after me, he made sure I enjoyed every second of it before he went any further.

My hips rocked into him once more, and my hips trembled when I chased the high and came against his lips. He gave me a few gentler strokes before he lifted his head. He licked his lips and then pressed kisses along my inner thigh, up to my stomach and tugged my nipples gently before he looked for my lips.

He gave me a short kiss and pulled down the sweater to cover my body.

"Was that too much?" he asked when we faced each other on the bed.

"No," I giggled. "Maybe I should wear your clothes more often."

He rested his hand on my ass and pulled me to him till he pressed another kiss to my lips. "Only if you're okay with the idea of staying in bed the entire day."

"I can be okay with that. Will you be okay with leaving the restaurant for that long?"

He raised a brow. "Will you be okay with 'no business talk' for that long?"

I grinned and pulled my hand forward between the two of us so he could shake it. "When you give me a private tour at your house, don't forget to dedicate a good amount of the time to your closet."

He shook my hand and brought it for his lips to kiss. "Consider it done."

I could picture it in my head, so easily. I could picture us having more mornings like this, cuddling under the sheets, more tulips, more sweet smiles, and dirty thoughts, just more than we already had. I didn't want to admit it, but Luuk was right. After all the mornings we spent reading horoscopes, not everything written there was completely wrong.

My Venus house didn't point at all the opportunities I had, it pointed at *one*. My heart wasn't directed in many directions, but it was directed to William. I didn't believe it back then, but I believe it now, as I was laying in bed with the guy I liked.

"Why are you looking at me like that?" William smiled as he played with my hair.

"I'm thinking of my Venus house." I wrapped my leg around his knee, because even if he touched my hair or face, it wasn't enough, I needed more of his touch.

"Your Venus house?" He chuckled but seemed intrigued to learn more.

"Luuk said I had opportunities to meet someone, that I had an opportunity to fall for someone, but I didn't see it," I explained. "After everything that happened in high school, and with my ex-boyfriend, all I wanted was to focus on event planning, and finding a job. I turned into an even more practical person than I already was."

He narrowed his eyes, but didn't say anything, he was just there to let me process all my emotions. "I didn't realize how much everything that happened affected me until I met you."

"Do you want to tell me more about it?" His voice softened. "About what happened with you and your ex-boyfriend? The full story?"

His eyes looked at me with such warmth that I almost blurted the entire story of my life to him, too.

But I couldn't, because if I talked about it now, then I would have to go back to my high school days. When I felt hopeless every time I spent time with Aart. When I needed to go to therapy to learn how to take care of myself again. When I felt like no guy could accept me as I was.

I wrapped my arms around my body and shook my head quickly. "I'm not ready for that yet."

He must've noticed my panicked state, because he pulled my arms slowly away from my body and wrapped his arms around me instead. His touch comforted me in an instant.

"You don't have to," he whispered. "We have all the time in the world."

It was supposed to reassure me, but I only felt more guilty.

"I'm sorry," I looked at his bare chest. "It's not fair to you."

"Don't be sorry."

"You told me your life story, William. You told me about your last relationship, and your grandparents, and family complications. You were always so open with me, and I can't give that to you, not yet," I said with a shaky voice. "It's not fair to you."

It wasn't fair, and even if he didn't think that way, I did. He shared so much with me, his heart was wide open just for me, which I knew how hard it was for him. He could say we had time, but I was the practical one out of the two of us, I didn't know how to give myself the time, how to not feel guilty for holding back still. It wasn't fair, and saying it out loud made me feel worse.

He sighed, and after what felt like forever, he spoke again. "Tulip field or a battlefield?"

"What?" I lifted my head to him.

"Pick one," he asked.

My lips curled when I realized what he was doing. "You already know what I would pick."

He peppered my face with kisses until he heard me laugh. "That's not an answer, Nora."

"Tulip field, *always*."

He hummed in content at the words and brushed my lips. "We have all the time in the world, Okay?"

"Okay."

CHAPTER 29
William

I leaned against the wall as I waited for Nora. Since our date, it was getting harder to stay at the restaurant when I knew she came to see me. The last two weeks, we spent as much time as we could trying out new restaurants and menus, buying more books and groceries at the market, and giving each other tulips. Even now getting off the metro to come see me, she had tulips in her hand.

I leaned down to kiss her, but she shook her head and pointed at the note she attached to the bouquet.

I want to kiss your two lips.

I looked up at her hopeful gaze and laughed when I accepted her gesture.

"Get it?" she asked in a childish manner. "Two lips?"

"Come here." I wrapped my arms around her back and pulled her into my body. Our lips met, and I moved my lips against hers as I trailed my hands down and gently rested them at the end of her back. She let my tongue in, and when it slipped against hers she let out a sigh, that made my entire body shiver.

I traced my hand on her pink lips when she pulled away.

"Was that enough kissing, or do you think I should kiss your *two lips* again?"

She laughed. "I...I didn't think you were going for *that* kind of a kiss. I never took you as a PDA kind of guy. Not that I'm complaining."

"But you like PDA," I noted.

I chuckled when she kept staring at me, and I leaned down so I could speak against the shell of her ear. "It's your love language after all, touching, kissing, PDA is a part of that."

She blinked her eyes. "How did you know?"

I lowered my voice when I saw people pass by us. "Nora, you're my girlfriend, I think it's something I should know if I want to make you feel good."

It felt nice calling her my girlfriend. After that morning in my grandparent's house, it was pretty clear to the both of us that's what we were. We didn't need time to talk about it, or ask ourselves if we should be official or not if we should be a couple or not. Calling her my girlfriend felt natural as hearing her calling me her boyfriend.

For the first time, I wasn't the only one blushing. I knew that if I told her we could ditch from our responsibilities and go to my place, she would say yes. Then we would go further than just kissing.

"So, what is the bouquet for?" I tried to change the subject when pictures of us in my bed invaded my head.

I knew something was up with Nora. We never used bouquets, unless there was a big occasion or event coming, like her first event or our date.

"I just woke up this morning, and realized it's March," she said. "It made me sad because it meant there wasn't going to be much rain the next couple of months, but then I realized something. It also means we're getting closer to spring, and you told me once that spring is tulip season."

My lips curled when I looked down at the bouquet. "You wanted to give me that reminder that spring is approaching."

"I know that after what happened with your grandparents, you might not feel like celebrating spring, or enjoy it fully, but I hope that this year you'll feel differently about it," she concluded.

When I told Nora about my grandparents, she was understanding, and compassionate, but this was another level of that. Spring was never just spring to me; it was the season where I watched what my grandma and I planted together in the colder seasons bloom and come alive. And here I was, coming alive again because of Nora.

"Thank you." I pressed my lips first to her upper lip and then to the bottom one, and then backed away. "Are you ready to go?"

"I still can't believe you waited just for me before going to work." She laughed as we walked hand in hand to the street. "What happened to the hard-working guy that stayed late to work even with one customer?"

"He met you," I answered simply. "I realized that nothing would happen if I took a day off once in a while or spent some more time with people I care about."

"I'm sure your dad is happy about that."

"I hope he doesn't get the wrong message," I sighed. "I don't want him to think I gave up on the restaurant because I'm working less. I don't need him to have more reasons to sell it to someone."

We didn't have a long walk from the metro to the restaurant, it was a matter of minutes. I preferred to look at all the streets that led to the restaurants, or people riding a bike and sitting on a bench to observe the view instead of thinking of my dad.

She squeezed my hand. "I think he's just happy to see you doing things besides work. I think you look happier, too, you know? I hated seeing you so stressed, trying to balance everything out. You have to admit it's kind of nice to let go of control sometimes, even a little bit."

I wanted to fight her on this, but she did have a point. I mean, if I didn't let go we wouldn't be together, and I wouldn't have more time to spend with Ethan, and I got used to having walks with Nora, even when it was raining. A part of me waited for that moment of the day, where each one of us could tell the other about classes and normal things that didn't involve just business, and marketing or anything too serious.

"Admit it," she poked my arm.

"If I admit it, will you admit it, too?" I asked.

"That it's nice seeing you that way?" she questioned. "I thought I already told you I like it when you enjoy the moment. If you really want me to go into details, then I admit I loved the time we spent together at your grandparents' house, especially that morning when I wore your sweater, and you—"

I put my hand on her mouth and looked around nervously.

That morning when I ate her out, sucked her nipples and kissed her body like I couldn't get enough of her. I didn't know which part she was going to refer to, but it was better I wouldn't hear her say it right before I needed to start my shift.

She pulled my hand down gently. "What I was going to say was when I wore your sweater that morning and you made me coffee."

There was a flicker in her green eyes that I knew way too well.

"Yeah, right." I lowered my voice and breathed heavily as I looked down at her. "It isn't even close to what you planned to say."

She rolled her eyes. "Okay, you caught me, it wasn't."

"Don't pout at me." I chuckled and played with the end of her braid. "You can finish that sentence later, when we're in a less... public place, *alone*."

I pulled the tulips closer to my nose and smiled. "It wasn't what I meant, though. I wanted to hear you admit it, that you like not writing in your notebook as often as you used to, that you like not planning every element of your day and stay in bed an entire day without doing anything if you feel like it."

"Hey, that's not fair, the only reason I stayed in bed for that long was because of you," she said, pointing at me. "If it wasn't for your ocean blue eyes, and those soft lips of yours, and your hands and..." She stopped to study me. "And your gorgeous body, I wouldn't have stayed in bed for that long."

She talked about my entire body, but I was getting hot and bothered already and it was all because of just her mouth.

"I admit, it's kind of nice for me, too." she said eventually, but before I could say the same, she stopped walking. "Why is Oasis closed, are you opening late today or something?"

"What?" I asked and followed her gaze to the front door with a *closed* sign.

I left her hand and walked to the door. I was about to take out my keys, but when I turned my hand around the handle, the door opened easily. I peeked inside into the empty restaurant, until I found my dad sitting at one of the tables with another man, both wearing suits with a bunch of papers scattered on the table.

"I can trust you, right?" my dad asked him as he played with the pen in his hand. "You'll take care of this place?"

"You can count on me; you'll leave your restaurant in good hands." The man, who I could only see from the back, shook my dad's hand. Then he picked up the papers and put them in his black bag.

"I'll be in touch with you towards the end of the month after we finish packing everything we need." My dad picked up his stuff as well.

"Sounds good to me." The man shook his hand once again and waved goodbye to my dad as he walked to the door.

"Hello." He smiled when he noticed me standing there, with my hand resting on the handle. He was in his forties, black hair, brown eyes, but didn't seem familiar in any way.

He walked past me and nodded towards Nora before he

walked across the street. My heart was beating loud, and my mind already started to spiral and get into full on stress mode. I watched my dad in disbelief and shook my head. He did it, he sold it.

"William," my dad said when he noticed me near the door. "What are you doing here, I thought you went to the metro to..." He stopped his gaze at Nora who walked to us.

"You sold the restaurant," I stated.

I hoped my dad would deny it, or tell me I didn't understand the situation right, but he only looked at me.

"You sold the restaurant," I said. "After everything we've done, after all the work, after Grandma and Grandpa put their heart and soul into this place, you sold it without blinking."

He sighed and sat back on his chair. "I'll talk with you about everything, but can you sit down first?"

"Sorry, Pa, but I don't feel like sitting down." I looked around at the empty place, almost like it looked about two months ago.

"William, I know how much you care about this place, it's admirable seeing you work so hard to make us proud and help the family. I'm glad your mom and I got to raise such a hard-working young man, but you know just like us that this place wasn't going to make it for much longer."

I put the bouquet down on the counter and turned back to him. "No, you're wrong, Dad. We had a shot at making it work. If you only knew what Nora and I were doing, then you would know that—"

"That you opened an Instagram account for the restaurant? And a few other accounts?" He clasped his hands together. "That you opened a site and organized a movie night to attract more customers?"

Nora and I switched glances.

"You might think I'm old, William, but I still know my son pretty well," he said slowly. "I knew how special your connection was with your grandma, how much you wanted to make her proud and keep this restaurant alive, I knew you weren't going to give up, even after all our talks. You turned out even more determined than your grandma ever was. I knew that with such determination, you weren't going to listen, so I watched you closely instead, from the sidelines, hoping that eventually you'll be ready to say goodbye to this place."

He motioned to me to sit on the chair next to him, but I didn't move from the bar.

"William," Nora touched my arm with the briefest of touch. "I think I'll go, give the two of you some privacy to talk."

"Don't go," I blurted, and held her hand to stop her from leaving.

"I'll talk to you later as much as you want, but right now it's more important that you talk to your dad," she whispered and kissed my cheek.

I watched her close the door after she walked out.

"I planned on telling you," I said quietly and sat on the stool near the bar. "I didn't mean to lie for that long, but I thought it wouldn't matter anymore if I'll make you and mom see this place can work with the right marketing, and right approach, I..."

I covered my face with both of my hands when I felt tears coming, I didn't want my dad to see me cry, I didn't want to cry and admit that I failed, that everything I tried to do to change the situation wasn't enough.

"William, come on, look at me." I felt my dad's hand on my shoulder.

I pulled my hands away but kept my eyes on my knees.

"I know it's hard to see it now, but it's for the best. Don't think I didn't see how you've been acting lately; you have no idea how much joy it brought me to see you hang out with Ethan, the guy barely got to see you anymore because of all the work you put over your shoulders."

He sighed when I didn't answer him.

"And this girl, Nora, she makes you happy, doesn't she?" he asked as he wrapped his arm around me.

I wanted to laugh at that because *happy* sounded like such a small word in comparison to how she made me feel. She didn't just make me happy, she made me want to ditch all my plans, she stopped me before I completely burnt out, and she made me want to overthink less and live more.

"Move on, William."

Move on.

My heart ached, my entire body ached when he said those two words, like it was so simple to do. The words rang like an alarm in my head.

"You can't see it, Dad, can you?" I lifted my head and wiped away the tears from my cheeks. "I can't move on like you did, I can't give up on one dream and switch it to another in a blink of a night. *I can't.*"

"William."

"No, I can't do this, not right now."

I got up from the chair and took a deep breath as I walked to the front door.

"William, I know about the tulips, I know you still plant them in the garden every winter."

I stopped in my place.

"Your grandma wouldn't want you to go through this."

I laughed bitterly. "With all due respect, Dad, you don't know what Grandma would want, or what Grandpa would want. You didn't spend days with them at the garden, you didn't see how they talked about their love story over and over again. You and Mom were so quick on packing up everything they owned, and now you're doing the same thing with Oasis. So don't talk to me about what they would want."

Then I walked through the door and closed it behind me. With shattered dreams, a sad heart, and the urge to run away as far as I could.

CHAPTER 30
Nora

I was looking down at my mug and turned back to the book William bought me at the market. The pages told me everything I needed to know about flowers, and how to show love, or warn an enemy, but it didn't tell me how to comfort a friend. I've been watching the clock on the wall every few pages, then I stare at the mugs on the Metropolitan Mugs' walls, like I expected them all to fall one by one. I wanted to be there with William because I hated leaving him alone with his dad like this, but at the same time I knew he needed space to figure things out and take in the news. So, I was sat down, drank mugs of coffee and flipped through the pages of a book, waiting for him to call and tell me how things went down.

"So, that's where you've been hiding." Luuk approached my table with his own mug. "I thought you were going to spend the day in the restaurant with your boyfriend. Don't tell me you lovebirds had your first fight already?"

I put my bookmark between the pages and closed the book. "I wish I was the one he was fighting with, instead of his—"

"Who was he fighting with?" Luuk narrowed his eyes.

I took another sip of my drink that got cold already and put the mug aside.

"Nor, in case you forgot, it's Xander's thing to read a book and keep quiet about stuff. You're starting to scare me with that silence," he said and when he noticed me checking my phone for new messages, for the thousandth time in the last couple of hours, he sighed. "What is it, Nor?"

"It's complicated, that's what it is."

"Complicated," he repeated and crossed his arms. "How complicated?"

"Luuk, aren't you supposed to go and have your daily talk with your sister over the phone? Jupiter hates it when you're late, you know her," I commented, but he didn't even budge.

"We talked already. I told her I need to look for you because I didn't hear from you the entire day," he said back. "What are you doing here, Nor? Didn't you say you don't want to drink their coffee anymore because William's is much better?"

I sighed. "Well, William isn't exactly available to make me coffee right now, he has bigger things to deal with."

"Nor, I'm not a fool, I can see something is going on with you." He reached out to hold my hand. "Whatever it is, whether it's a romantic problem, or something else, I can help, I wouldn't tell anyone."

"Says the guy who told William my sun sign, and God knows what else."

He studied my face. "Don't act like you're mad at me for it, someone needed to help the poor guy reach your heart, you're more practical than most Virgo's I know."

"William didn't fight with me, he had a fight with his dad. Well, not exactly a fight, more of an intense kind of talk." I played with my fingers.

It didn't feel right sharing Willaims' problems with someone else who wasn't involved, but I didn't hear from him for hours, and I started to get too worried to think rationally. "His dad sold the restaurant."

He put down his mug slowly. "His dad did what?"

I looked around at the almost empty place. I knew none of the few students who sat around to drink coffee or eat something to take a break from their assignments and studies knew me or William, but it felt wrong talking about the topic without him around.

"They can't keep the place, his dad sold it to someone who clearly can. William tried to talk to his dad, but I have no idea what happened there because I left pretty early on," I explained to Luuk who listened to me patiently to take in everything. "He didn't answer me since I left the place, it's been hours Luuk, I'm worried something bad happened."

"Wow, that's heavy," he muttered. "Do you think his dad is a Scorpio? That would explain the decision. It's a good month for financial decisions."

"Luuk!"

"Hey, don't look at me like that. When I run into a problem, I try to find an explanation. Excuse me if my solution is usually found in the stars," he sighed. "You're his girlfriend, Nor, it's natural for you to be worried about him, but I'm sure he just needs some time alone. You know he's not much of a talker, so he probably went back home after talking to his dad and he takes the time to process everything."

Luuk's intentions were good, but he was wrong about one thing.

"That's what you don't get Luuk. William was never much of a talker, I'm sure that the day I take him to a party, I will be the one to pull him into the dance floor or have to introduce him to people. But I promise that he is a talker with *me*." I sighed in frustration when I looked at my phone once again. "He wouldn't keep me hanging like that, he would at least text me if the conversation with his dad went well or not."

"I see," he mumbled.

"I don't even know how to explain it to you, Luuk. I have no idea where he is, or why he doesn't answer the phone, but I know I can't let him be alone. He told me what happened when he was in the waiting room as a kid, not wanting to deal with his grandma passing and I don't want this to happen again, I don't—" I grabbed my phone and looked in the list of contacts after Ethan's name.

"Nor, what waiting room?"

I pressed the phone to my ear and waited for Ethan to pick up.

"Nora?"

"Hi, Ethan, sorry for calling at this hour. I know you're busy with all your assignments lately, but I wouldn't have called if it wasn't important."

"Nora, is there something wrong?"

I took in a deep breath and tried to sound calm. I didn't want to make his best friend worried for no reason.

"It's William, I haven't seen him since the afternoon after he talked with his dad. I can't explain everything now, but I need to ask you something." I paused. "Can you tell me where the tree he ran to when he was a kid is? It only makes sense that he would go there."

"He told you about that?" he whispered through the other line. "Wait, why do you think he went to that damn tree again? What happened?"

I put the book in my bag and made sure all my things were packed. "I'll explain everything tomorrow, okay? I just need you to send me the location of the place so I can go there."

There was a long pause that followed a deep sigh. "I'll send it to you now."

"Thank you, Ethan," I said before hanging up the phone.

When I got up from my chair, Luuk wrapped his hand around

my wrist. "Nor, where are you going? What tree are you talking about?"

"It's a long story, Luuk. What matters is that I promised to look after him exactly like he has for me, if I'm right and he went there, then I should be there too."

I gave Luuk a quick hug and left the place. When I got the address from Ethan, I got into my car and followed the directions. I could've taken the metro, but I had a feeling that if we were going back together, we should be just the two of us, with no other people around.

When I got out of the car, I walked through the open area.

I didn't need to look much for a tree, there was only one standing there. The lack of leaves and the small number of branches made it easy to see someone hidden between them, to see *William*.

I moved quietly towards the tree until I stopped in front of it. I lifted my head and smiled when I saw him there. His eyes were puffy, like he had been crying for a while, and his body was hanging onto the branches like his life depended on it. But he was there, I found him.

I could only imagine how he ran here as a young and scared little kid who wanted to run away from all his problems. I could understand it, that need to run.

I kept my voice quiet so I wouldn't scare him with my presence. "William?"

He blinked his eyes and wiped his tears away but he still didn't look at me, his eyes fixated on his legs that were hanging in the air. "Nora."

"I was worried about you," I said gently and stepped closer to the tree. "What do you think about coming down so I could see you?"

"I don't want you to see me like this," he answered and turned to look the other way when our eyes met.

"William, you have nothing to be ashamed about. So, you

cried, it's good to cry once in a while to deal with your emotions. I felt embarrassed when I cried in front of you, but you made me realize I did nothing wrong, it's normal, especially in these circumstances." I searched for his eyes again when I heard him sniff his nose. "You look beautiful when you cry, William. Did anyone ever tell you that?"

He chuckled. "You, and your compliments again."

"Me, and my compliments again." I smiled at him. "You will get more of them if you come down, what do you say?"

"Are you trying to bribe me?" he asked, but he didn't sound surprised by it, but amused.

"Are you going to let me?"

He studied me from where he was sitting, and then stood up and in a few quick movements he held onto the branches of the tree and found his way down to me.

"Hey," I whispered when he was on the ground.

"Hey," he whispered and fell into my arms. His head rested at the crook of my back as his arms wrapped around me. I felt one of his tears fall into my skin, and then another one, and another. His shoulders were shaking and he held on tight to me.

"It's okay, let it all out," I rubbed his back gently.

I didn't know what to say, because even if I went through my own darker times, I didn't know what it felt like losing another part of his memory from his grandparents, or how it felt to lose something you put so much energy and work into, but I did know what it felt like to breath after stressing about something for so long.

When he pulled away from me, I cupped his face and looked in his eyes, which were still beautiful, despite all the tears. "I know you're spiraling right now; I know because I've been there, but I'm also here to tell you it will get better, we'll work things out."

"How?" he said, choked up.

"Well, first we'll get you into a warm shower, and after that, we'll get you clean clothes and a good night's sleep." I wiped his wet cheeks again. "How does that sound to you?"

"I don't want to sound dramatic here, but I don't feel like going home tonight. I need space to process everything before I talk to any of my parents again. You didn't see me back at the restaurant, after you left I said some things...I think I really hurt my dad's feelings."

"You do know I'm the dramatic one between the two of us, right?" I caressed his cheek. "I didn't say anything about going to your house, we can go to mine. My mom is busy with an event, and my dad is probably working in his office."

He nodded, but when I held his hand to walk with him to my car, he didn't move. "Nora, I'm sorry."

"For crying?"

"For running away. I didn't mean to worry you, I wanted to write you, but my battery died and I didn't want to walk back home, and-"

"Don't apologize, I'm just glad to see that you're okay, and that I didn't need to bring a cheesecake, because I don't know where I would've found one at this hour," I said and when I heard him laugh again, my heart warmed up, his laugh was always a good sign.

"Before I get in the car with you, can I ask you for a favor?" He looked down at our hands.

I pressed a kiss to his cheek. "I'll call your mom."

This time when we headed to my car, he followed. He was quiet the entire drive to my house, but I expected that much. After taking one look at him, I could tell he was exhausted. Not just emotionally, but physically too.

I remembered how I felt after I collapsed in class from exhaustion. I didn't want to talk to anyone either, not even with my best friends or my parents, I just wanted to get home to my bed and sleep.

When we entered the house and went up to my room, he

didn't look around much, but focused on the vase on my desk with a tulip he got me a few days ago. I knew it wasn't going to survive for much longer there, but I liked looking at it and thinking of William when I wrote in my notebook or had to study.

He must have realized he looked at the tulip for a long moment, because he rubbed the back of his neck and turned back to me. "Sorry, I know I've been in your room before, but every time I look at your desk, I think of the first night I've been here and saw that you kept my tulips."

"You mean you remember the first time you realized I have feelings for you too," I tilted my head as I looked over his face. "The first time we kissed."

"Yeah, that too," he admitted and looked down at his shoes. "I was so nervous back then."

"You were so nervous about my parents not liking you, but now you're on good terms, as I told you you'd be." I went to my closet and looked for the sweater and pair of sweatpants he left here the last time he slept over. I walked back to him and put the clothes between his hands. "I knew from the beginning they were going to love you."

Like I did.

"You always know everything, don't you?" he chuckled.

"Not everything, but I know a lot when it comes to you, like I know you will feel better after a long shower or bath, depending on your preference," I said and went to the attached door to my bathroom and bent down to take out one of the folded towels there.

"Can you join me?" he asked when I handed him the towel.

"Don't you want to be alone?" I asked.

He wrapped his hand around my wrist and looked down at me with parted lips.

I knew him enough to read what he wanted to say with his mouth but settled for his eyes.

Don't go.
Don't leave me alone.

"Well, okay. I guess I didn't get the chance to take a shower today, and being in one with an attractive guy doesn't sound like a terrible idea," I said with a wink.

When he let go of my hand, I pulled my sweater off my body and threw it to the floor. My skirt came right after it and found its way on the floor while I waited for the warm water to fill the bath. I used the time to throw in a water bomb that colored the water in pink.

When I put my hand in the water to make sure it wasn't too hot, I was about to go inside, but William was quick to pass me. He entered the bath, and reached towards me to help me get in. When he saw I was comfortable in the bath, he went to sit on the other side and faced me as the water and bubbles covered most of our bodies.

"You always have to act like a gentleman, even when I try to do something nice for you." I giggled and played with the foam to create a shape in the water.

He wrapped his arms around his legs. "That's the least I could do after bothering you, especially at such a late hour."

"It's 8 PM, I wouldn't call it late. You know I usually go to sleep at like…2 AM, though on a good day, it can be earlier than that," I shrugged. "You're not a bother, I like having you here, and taking care of you for once. You do so much for me. You help me with my career path, but you also know when to help me take a break to deal with my stress. You give me tulips and always take care of me. Preparing you a bath or calling your mom is nothing."

He nodded, and after a short silence, he reached out his hands for me to take. I didn't know what he had in mind, but I moved closer till I could touch him.

He motioned for me to turn around and then I felt him pushing down the rubber band that held my braid in place. Then when he finished running his hands through my hair, he grabbed the shampoo bottle and massaged it through my scalp. I closed my eyes and melted into his body, letting my back brush against his chest.

"So, why are you going to sleep so late?" he asked with a little hesitation.

"Because of stress, there's so much to do and not enough time for everything I want to do." I hummed when his hands moved delicately in my hair. "But I fall asleep quicker when you're near me. The first time I fell asleep that quickly was the first time we spent the night together."

He kissed my temple and moved to my shoulders when he found the body wash.

"Wait, William, it's not fair, I made this bath for *you*, so *you* could feel better, you're not supposed to do all of this for me right now." I tried to move away, though I wanted to stay exactly where I was with his hands massaging my shoulders.

"Taking care of you makes me feel better," he said. "If I stayed here by myself with my own thoughts, I wouldn't be able to enjoy it, not really."

He grabbed me gently and pulled me back to where I was as he continued his work with his hands.

"William, I know you feel a lot at the moment, but you don't have to figure out everything right now. All you need to know right now is that I'll help you with whatever you need. If you'll open a new restaurant in the future, I'll help you. If you decide to do something completely new in life, I'll be there. And—" I stopped myself, hoping I wasn't crossing any line. "If you want someone to help you plant tulips next winter, I'd love to learn how."

His hands stopped moving on my warm skin. "Let me get this straight... Nora Tuinstra, planting tulips?"

"I can add it to my checklist quicker than you can imagine."

"I'd love to teach you." He kissed my cheek and continued from where he stopped.

"Will your grandma be okay with this?" I asked carefully. "Isn't it like your kitchen, or secret recipes? There must be some family unwritten rules, or gardening secrets I'm not supposed to know because I'm not family."

"My grandma, my grandpa, they would be more than okay with this." He wrapped his arms that were covered with foam and soap. "That's what they would want me to do after teaching me all those years, that I'll teach someone else, that I'll do this with you. I just know it."

I held onto his arms and smiled. "Next winter then, me and you in your grandparents' garden?"

Instead of answering, he kissed my lips, and I could feel his smile against them. I could tell he liked that idea; he liked it a lot.

CHAPTER 31
Nora

Waking up in bed with William was always an experience I wanted to capture in my mind. Whether it was after a pleasurable night, an unforgettable one, or a heavy emotional one, I liked to meet with his blue eyes when I opened mine. Yesterday was the emotional kind, but it didn't matter, all that mattered was that Willaim got a goodnight sleep. The sun came through the window, covering my room in a warm morning light. I gazed at William. His hair was messy and his eyes closed, so I ran my hands slowly over his cheek, knowing that it was one of those rare moments where he was peaceful.

"Nora," he rasped and curled closer to me until he brought his leg above mine, like he needed to be certain I wasn't going to leave this bed.

"How did you sleep last night?" I ran my hands in his messy hair.

"Good," he mumbled. "My eyes don't burn anymore."

"They're not red anymore, either," I said quietly. "You fell asleep the moment we got to bed, you must've felt really tired after yesterday, you slept for twelve hours."

"Twelve hours?" He muttered and wrapped his arm tighter to pull me to him. "I never slept for that long. Wait, what time is it?" his voice was still raspy from his long sleep and he turned his head to look for his phone. "My dad will kill me, I was supposed to go there this morning, and—"

"I already talked to your dad, I told him you needed more sleep after everything..." I caressed his cheek. "I know you don't want to think about it yet, but maybe it will be better if you don't wait it out and talk to him today. He sounded worried, and I know you said some things you didn't mean, it's better to resolve things now than keep it in."

"I know I should do that, but I don't even know what I'm supposed to say," he shrugged and rested his head back on the pillow. "I don't even know what I'm supposed to do now. When I woke up this morning, I hoped it would all turn out to be a bad dream, but it's real. I heard my dad and that man talk; they mentioned us packing everything up until the end of the month." He buried his head in the soft pillow and groaned. "It's real, but I can't actually believe it is. I mean, how can I move on with my life without working there anymore, or going there every single day? Just thinking about it feels like some bad joke."

"Don't think about the future right now, it's easy stressing out about it, believe me, I'm talking from experience. Focus on right now." I rubbed his back in comfort and he leaned further into my touch. "Go to the restaurant, talk to your dad, you'll feel better after that, you'll see."

"I guess it was bound to happen eventually, I can't hide in your room forever." He looked around at my pink walls. "Though I do hope we get to experience more showers and warm baths again soon."

I chuckled and pressed a kiss to his neck before I lifted up my lips to tease his ear. "Or maybe you hope you'll get to finally kiss and touch me against the wall under the steam while we're both wet and naked, because I'm fine with that option, too."

My lips curled when I felt his body stiffened under the touch of my hand and his arms froze. "First, talk to your dad and solve things, then we can have as many showers as you want."

"So, my plans today include more serious talks with my family. What are your plans for the day?" he asked me. "I'm sure you have a checklist prepared somewhere in your notebook, ready to be fulfilled."

"I'm going to talk with my mom today," I breathed out. "Since that dinner, the topic of me working didn't come up again, and after I saw you talk with your dad, I realized it's time for me to talk about what I want with my family, too. I'm going to make them see that I'm a grown adult, and that they can count on me and my decisions."

"Wow, Nora, that's huge…" he said, his eyes wide open. "How are you planning on doing that?"

"I didn't plan that far; I think I'll just crash one of the events she has today and find the time to talk to her. Yesterday made me realize it's not worth waiting out on these kinds of things. I need to just talk, say whatever is on my heart like I always do and not stress about what would happen after that. I mean, the last part is a bit more challenging than the others but if it goes badly, I can always write about it in my notebook and let all my frustration out."

"Or you can come to me instead," he whispered and moved a strand of hair from my face.

"Or I can come to you," I smiled and he pressed a kiss on my forehead.

When William left my house, I went back to my room and put on one of my more expensive and glamorous dresses from my closet and headed outside. I followed the address and reached a big studio filled with artworks that were up for auction. My mom was sipping from her wine as she talked with one of the customers. She looked calm, like she knew that once again she had everything under control, she planned her goals, budget, and everything else was wrapped up together perfectly.

"Nora?" my mom asked as I walked to her. "What are you doing here?"

"Hey, Mom," I mumbled when she kissed my cheek and hugged me, asking from the woman she was talking with to continue that conversation later.

"Is everything okay, you look like you ran over here." She studied my body and stopped at my heels.

"Yeah, no, I didn't run, because I tried but it's nearly impossible with these shoes. I just needed us to talk, because I don't want to be a chicken, not with William, and not with you. I want to be honest with you, because I want you to understand, and even if you don't understand now, I hope you'll understand in the future," I said.

When one of the waiters passed by me, I grabbed one of the glasses and drank the entire glass of wine in one sip. It wasn't as good as coffee, but it was something. My pulse was racing, and I swear I could feel my hands sweating a bit. On my way here I was thinking of everything I wanted to say, I pictured exactly how I was going to enter the place, stand and stare at my mother's eyes and say it all, no looking back. But no mental preparation could erase my fears completely.

"Nora, what are you talking about?" she asked me. "Did something happen with your boyfriend?"

"Yeah, something happened with William. I saw him talk with his dad yesterday, and when I saw them talk about something as hard as selling one of the last thing they have left from his grandparents, I realized I can talk with you too about something as complicated as my dreams, because if not now, then who knows when we will be able to talk about it. I don't want to wait till I'm twenty-one to have the guts to talk to you and Dad." I swallowed. "I don't want us to have this kind of relationship, I don't want to have to wait and hide things from you."

"Nora, I already know your dreams, and we already said that you need to focus on other things now."

"I didn't say it, or agree to it, *you did*," I clarified. "Look, Mom, I don't blame any of you, I know you're worried about me, I know you're scared I won't be able to handle it, I know that you just want me to focus on my studies and nothing else, but the thing is that I can't."

"Nora, maybe we should talk about this at home?" She looked sideways at the people around.

I would lie if I'd said I didn't come here for strategic reasons, my mom wasn't able to yell or raise her voice when there were people drinking wine and looking at paintings in the background, and if it wasn't enough they put some classical music there too.

"Mom, I lied to you, and I lied to Dad for some time now. All these months I was busy helping William with his family business. I went there every day, I posted about it on social media, I even planned my first event. I did everything you taught me, including the logistics and tying up loose strings in case something went wrong. *I did everything*." I took another deep breath. "I was happy doing that, and even though we didn't manage to save the restaurant, I'm still happy, I just want you to see that, too."

"You lied to us?" she asked, and I wanted to shrink from hearing the pain in her voice. "You planned your own event and I didn't even know about it?"

"Mom," I sighed. I didn't want to hurt her more, but I didn't want to keep up with my lies either. "You and Dad both have been so careful with me since what happened in high school. I don't want you to think I don't appreciate it, I do, I really do."

"But?" she smiled weakly, expecting more to come.

"But I'm not that kind of person. I can't focus on my degree and abandon my dreams because of past experience. I can't let it change who I am as a person, even if it's scary. Believe me, I'm scared. I still have bad days, but I don't want to let it control the way I'm living, or how I choose to love and be loved."

I knew it was hard to understand, it would take her time to understand. She would probably want us to talk as family and hear about everything I hid from her and my dad. It wasn't going to end quickly, their worry about my mental situation wasn't going to fade in a day, or a week or even a month. But it was a start, and when I looked in her eyes, I could see something click behind them.

"So, all this time, you weren't smiling so much because you had a new boyfriend?" she asked and asked from the waiter another glass.

"I mean many of my smiles are because of William, but they come from working alongside him too. We're a good team."

"I should've known something was going on when he defended you at dinner."

"So, you're not mad?" I asked carefully. "You're not going to give me some life lessons or send me to my old therapist again?"

"Nora, you're not seventeen anymore, and I guess I should've realized it sooner. If you managed to work on a project for that long and handled all that pressure without collapsing or feeling bad again, it's a true sign that you changed your approach with work." She smiled at me with eyes filled with pride. "I guess the apple doesn't fall far from the tree after all, you do have a bright future as an event planner. Even when I didn't want you to work yet, I could still see that potential in you."

"Thanks, Mom," I said and looked around. "I'm sorry for crashing your event, next time I'll give you heads up."

"If you're already here, maybe you can let me introduce you to some people?" she offered, and I quickly accepted her offer and let her walk me around in the gallery. I shook some hands and talked about myself with strangers dressed in suits or expensive long dresses, but when the auction was about to start, I told my mom it was time for me to go.

As I was walking down the stairs, I heard a voice I haven't heard for a long time call out my name.

"Nora Tuinstra, I didn't expect to see you here." Aart sat on one of the stairs with a cigarette between his fingers, the smoke that came out of his mouth made the space between us fill with blurry haze.

"Aart," I gritted between my teeth.

"Since when are you so interested in art auctions?" he asked. "Or maybe I should ask since when you're interested in walking outside? The last time we saw each other you weren't so eager to get out of your house, or even your own room."

I pressed my lips together, I wished he didn't have that effect on me, I wish his presence didn't take me back, I wish I could slap him in the face or walk away like I didn't see him, but my body forgot how to move.

The last time you saw me, you dumped me right before I had one of my biggest exams.

The last time we talked, you were as condescending and mean as you are now.

The last time, you didn't take how I felt seriously.

The last time was more than enough.

"Since when are *you* so interested in art auctions?"

"Since it's my parents' friend's artwork," he commented, and when he took another look at me, he chuckled. "Pink isn't your color, Nora, I thought you knew that."

"I need to leave, so if you'll excuse me." I tried to walk down the rest of the stairs but he put his hand forward and blocked my way. "What do you want, Aart?" I asked. "We both know you want to say something, probably idiotic, so let's hear it and get it over with."

"Hey, I just want to have a friendly chat." He put his hand in the air. "I hope you don't talk that way to your new boyfriend."

My heart skipped a beat. "How do you know about William?"

"I'm on social media, Nora, it's hard not to see all your posts about the guy's working place. I've been there once, he was my waiter, such a nice guy. He explained to me the entire menu and recommended some of the meals, the pasta there is chef's kiss, did you try it?"

"Yes, I've tried it, *multiple times*."

"He really is such a *nice* guy."

"You said that already."

"I just wanted to make sure you're aware of that," he muttered. "You think you two are meant to be?"

My hand clenched. I should've felt the need to defend myself to him, or justify my actions at all, but somehow with Aart it always ended that way. His questions always made that defensive mechanism in my body to work extra hours.

"What kind of question is that?"

"Do you think he's going to stay with you when he finds out how hard it is to be your boyfriend?" he asked, then the air was filled with smoke again. "What do you think will happen when you get another panic attack like you did in class that day?"

He had to bring that up, didn't he? Every time I thought I managed to move on with my life Aart had to show up and remind me of how I used to be, though now it was a few times worse. He wasn't just in my brain, but he was sitting on the stairs, wearing a suit as he was smoking a cigarette.

"I learned to control it."

"No, Nora, you haven't. Even I know a control freak like you can't control something like this, it's bigger than you," he laughed when he looked up at me. "Do you really think he's going to stay home with you instead of going out with friends? Do you think he'll wait for you to fall asleep when you have bad dreams? You're many things Nora, but I didn't know you were that naïve."

I blinked my eyes, but I didn't let the tears fall, he wasn't worth my tears. "Why are you doing this?"

"I'm doing this because I don't want this William, who seems like a nice guy, to go through what I had to go through."

"Wait, what *you* had to go through?" I asked to make sure I heard him correctly.

"Yes, what I had to go through, Nora. You know, it's been a long time since we dated, we both clearly moved on with our life, I'm going to art auctions, you're…trying to do something with your life, which is great, but don't you feel bad for deceiving this guy?"

I pressed my lips together. Every part of me who was afraid and hesitant because of Aart, disappeared. Suddenly it was like I saw him in a whole different light. Maybe it was because of the time that passed by, maybe it was all the therapy sessions I've gone through, and maybe it was William who opened my eyes since I met him. Whatever it was, I couldn't believe I hadn't seen it before.

"You think I'm deceiving him?"

"Yes, Nora. I get it, you want love in your life, but you can't use other people's kindness like this. He'll just suffer near you, at the beginning it's nice dating you, but then it becomes exhausting. You should let him date someone normal."

"Normal?" I repeated. "Like you?"

"Don't take it personally, Nora. You want to be an influencer, or social media person, or something like this, right? You should know how to accept some healthy criticism."

I walked down the last stairs and stood in front of him, I hoped I managed to block most of his view. "Here's some *healthy criticism,* Aart. You're right, it's been exhausting. I tried to be the perfect girlfriend, I tried to deal with my stress, my bad dreams, my bad days. And all by myself, *that's* the exhausting part. Every time you made a comment or blamed me for wanting to stay home or cancel plans with people you made me feel like shit. After you broke up with me I couldn't even put myself out there. I thought that no guy deserved to deal with all of me, that the wise thing to do is focus on myself and my healing process."

"From what it looks like you have a whole lot of healing to do," he said. "Maybe you should try a new therapist."

I gritted my teeth. I hated when people tried to tell me what to do and put a label on me or what I was going through. It wasn't their place; it wasn't his place.

I shook my head. "I was never the problem, Aart. Sure, I have bad days, I can't be the bright light in people's life all the time, but at least I'm not as cruel as you. I would never treat someone like you treated me, I would never make someone think he's a bad boyfriend because he has to deal with anxiety, or stress or anything like that."

"Well, good luck finding someone who can deal with *all of you*, as you mentioned?"

"Oh, I don't need you to wish me anything, I already found him, his name is William, and he's a better man than you will ever be. He knows how to treat me right, and he's the perfect gentleman, and believe me that the day I wouldn't be able to sleep at night, he would stay up with me until the morning and talk to me until I'm alright. That's *real* love."

"Well." He looked down at his watch. "That was a nice chat and all, but I need to go to the auction, I'm sure you can understand that some of us have important things to do."

"Oh, of course, I wouldn't want to ruin that auction for you, I'm sure you have a great eye for the things that are worth a lot." I crossed my arms. "Like this suit, very chic, though I hope for you that you rented it and didn't plan on adding it to your closet."

"Why?" he asked as he looked down at the black sleeves in panic. "Do I have a stain or something?"

"No stain, but you already ruined it with your ugly character," I muttered. I took another look at his face, but despite the pain and hurt I felt all these times when I thought of him and what we had, I felt only pity for him. "Goodbye, Aart."

CHAPTER 32
William

A few hours passed since waking up in Nora's bed and I already found myself sitting near Ethan at one of the newest bars in our neighborhood. I didn't feel like being in the restaurant. Even though my dad and I found our common ground, I didn't want to be there and help him pack, or work while knowing it wasn't going to last for much longer.

Ethan drank from his beer and looked at me. "I knew something was up when you asked if we could go to a bar, but I didn't imagine that's the reason why."

"I didn't plan on any of it happening either. I feel like an idiot for running away to the tree and not talking to anyone about it. When Nora and I started this whole thing, our work together and all the brainstorming and planning, I didn't think of what would happen if we didn't succeed. I couldn't imagine my parents selling the place, so I never thought what would happen to me if it were to happen," I explained as I held onto my beer. "I ran right over to that damn tree without thinking twice, Ethan."

"I'm glad Nora was wise enough when she thought to look out for you there," he mentioned. "I know things are crazy in your life right now, but *she loves you*, I hope you know that."

I rubbed the back of my neck. We never said those three words to each other, but just imagining the moment she would say it made me fluster.

I fought the urge to hide my face in my hands. "I feel so bad about yesterday, Ethan. I feel like she has to deal with so much because of me, she had to drive to that tree and convince me to get down. It was so embarrassing that she had to see me that way."

"Well, I guess at some point, when you date someone, it means you're going to have to allow that person to see you in all kinds of situations," he shrugged, like it wasn't such a big deal. "Take our friendship for example, we've known each other since we're kids, I saw you in all kinds of moods. I saw you laughing while playing soccer, but I also saw you grieving your grandma. I saw you working hard at the restaurant, but I also see you right now sitting in a bar and having a drink with me. It doesn't make me want to be less of a friend to you, and it wouldn't make Nora want to be less of a girlfriend to you either."

My lips curved but only slightly. "Did you hear from her today?"

"From Nora?"

I nodded.

He laughed, and after he asked the bartender for another drink, he turned back to me on his stool. "Don't tell me after she found you, then you managed to lose her."

"I didn't *lose* her, she told me she planned on talking with her mom, I want to know how it went down. See if she needs me."

"Don't worry," he put his hand on my shoulder. "I think that even if it went badly, she wouldn't run to a tree and wait for your rescue, if that's what you're afraid of."

I rolled my eyes.

"Too soon?" he asked slowly, but I shook my head.

"I also made a deal with my dad," I added nervously.

"Look at you, acting like a true businessman," he said proudly. "What kind of deal?"

I took a deep breath. "After our talk yesterday, I went to him today, we talked about everything over breakfast. I told him that I may not understand him now, and I don't see eye to eye when it comes to selling the restaurant, it's going to take me time. But... but if I have to say goodbye to the place, then I want to do it right. I told my dad I wasn't going to argue about the matter anymore so we could all move on as he and my mom wish. And in return, he's going to let me organize a goodbye party, or event, however you want to call it."

"You want to let Nora plan the event, don't you?" he asked and put down his drink slowly.

"You know, I've only started my degree, I have a lot to learn about business, but I managed to learn that in every deal you give up on something in return for something else. This time I lost, I have no idea what I'm going to do with my life right now, it's all one big blur of smoke. But Nora, she can win from it. She can plan an event, something bigger than a movie night or updating stuff on social media. After everything she did for me, I want to give her that opportunity."

"Would you look at that?" He crossed his arms and watched me. "You're completely in love."

I chuckled, and at that moment my phone rang with the song "Here Comes The Sun" by the Beatles, I smiled at the screen. I lifted my head and Ethan had already been staring at me with a knowing smile, his eyes said it all.

Your girl is looking for you.

I answered immediately and pressed the phone to my ear. "Hi, Nora."

I heard her take a long sigh from the other side of the line. "Hi."

Her voice didn't sound as full of energy like always, like it was this morning. She sounded tired. I never heard her sound this way, not even when we met in an early hour before she got to drink her coffee.

"What's wrong? What happened? Is it your mom, did she—"

"William, I'm okay."

"You don't sound like everything is okay," I murmured and took out my wallet from my pocket to pay for my drink. "I'll talk to you later," I said to Ethan, still with my phone pressed to my ear and went to the front door.

I glanced up at the gray sky and when I felt the raindrops fall down on my face, I opened my umbrella and started walking. "Where are you Nora?"

"I'll tell you if you'll stop sounding so worried about me. I'm okay, I didn't mean to scare you, I just needed to hear your voice."

"What happened, Nora?" I asked again.

It was getting harder to act like I wasn't worried and wanted to run right to where she was.

"I went to my mom's event, an art auction, I drank some wine, the wine was really nice. I don't understand anything about art, but the paintings looked very modern, I guess. Is that even a way to describe art, modern?"

I pressed my lips together, and looked up at the rain through my umbrella. I knew something was off, I knew she wanted to tell me something important, but she needed a second to organize her thoughts, and I wanted to wait for the moment she felt ready to tell me why she wasn't okay, why her voice sounded off.

So I listened to her patiently as she told me about the auction, and the pink dress she picked out, which apparently was an expensive long satin one she bought not a long time ago. Then she told me about her talk with her mom, until she got to the last part of her little story.

"When I went outside, I saw him. He looked exactly as I remembered, still smoking, the only difference was seeing him wearing a suit." She sighed, and by the noise in her background, I could imagine her standing outside, looking up in the rain too, only without an umbrella, or a coat, but only a dress. Then she said the words that could make any man's heart drop. "We need to talk, William."

I nodded. "Then we'll talk. Where are you?"

"Near your house," she whispered.

I let out a deep breath. "I'll be there in a few minutes."

"Okay."

Before she could hang up the phone, I said her name once again, softer this time. "Nora?"

"Yeah?"

"Thank you for calling me."

Then I ended the call. I wanted to say I walked slowly with my umbrella, maybe even took the time to admire the way the rain fell from the sky until it touched the pavement, but the moment I put the phone back in my pocket, I ran to my house like my life depended on it. Every thought that was running through my head was worse than the one before. After everything that she told me about her ex, I had a bad feeling he did something to her, said something that made her want to talk. I hoped that he didn't try to put her down again, talk badly about her and her character. I really hope that wasn't what she needed to talk about, I didn't want to find her crying or upset because of his words.

Just when I thought of all the things I would do to the guy if he ever dared to hurt her in any way, I saw her standing in a dress in the middle of the rain. Her hair fell to her shoulders as some strands stuck to her face, and her wet dress clung to her body.

"Nora," I said through my quickened breath and hugged her body.

I wrapped my arm around her as I tried to keep the umbrella above her so the rain couldn't get to her any longer. "Come on, let's get you inside. I'll give you some of my clothes, make you coffee and-"

She put her finger on my lips and shook her head. "Can we stay here a little longer instead?"

"But—"

"I'm not cold, not anymore. I want to stay outside, in the fresh air, it helps me think, it helps me process, it just...*helps*."

All my instincts told me to pull her out of the rain into a warm place, but in her case, the rain did help her think better than it did to other people.

"What happened, Nora?" I asked quietly. "What did he do?"

"What did he do?" she laughed bitterly. "He told me he met you. Apparently he went to the Oasis to eat one day and you were waiting on him. He went on and on about how you are being such a great guy and that I needed to break up with you, because you deserve someone better, you deserve someone that doesn't deal with the same things I do. He said he didn't want you to go through what he's gone through when he dated me."

I held on tighter to the umbrella. I never punched anyone in my life, but if I wanted to try, her ex could be a good first choice.

"What he's gone through?" I whispered.

"You should've seen him, William. He talked with no remorse, so sure of the things he said like he couldn't see me at all." She rested her hand on my arm and touched the soft fabric of my sweater. "He was mean, so mean. I never saw him as a cruel person, I always justified his behavior, but all the time when we were talking all I could think about was how cruel he was towards me, he didn't hold back."

Her last words came as a whisper as she grabbed my sweater tighter, like she needed to make sure I was there with her, that she wasn't standing alone in the rain.

"Hey, Nora." I caressed her wet cheek. "Look at me."

She raised her head, and after all this time I searched for her eyes, I found them; green, wild, and tired.

And yet, they were beautiful, and so did she. The longer I held her close to me in the middle of the rain, the more I felt the need to tell her how I felt for her. I couldn't keep it in anymore, not when she looked at me that way, not when she was wearing that dress, not when my heart was exploding, but because of all the right reasons.

"Remember that day when I kissed you?" I moved a wet strand of hair off her face. "When I came to a decision that I wanted you to know how I felt, I realized I also needed to make the first step. When I was a kid, I never dared to be the first to act. There was this girl I liked in my class. I wanted to give her flowers, but I never went through with it. But when it comes to you, Nora. I'll make as many first steps as it takes. I'll be the first one to tell you that you're radiant, even now under the rain. I'll take the first step and kiss you, and admit how I feel, and the first to say *I love you*."

She gasped. "You…you what?"

I laughed, it was such a relief saying it, even if it wasn't the perfect moment I planned on. "I love you, and I'll keep on loving you no matter what you have to deal with. You've been such a breath of fresh air in my life. You helped me when I didn't let anyone else do so, and I love you, I do. Whether you have a bad night, or a bad day, or a bad year, I'll be there by your side until the sun comes back again, so don't listen to whatever nonsense he said to you, because it's not true."

My heart was beating loud in my chest. The rain kept pouring as I waited for Nora to say something, but she didn't talk. For the first time since I met her, she didn't say a thing, she was standing there and staring at me.

"I wanted to say it to you for so long, but I was scared, and then when I got the courage I was embarrassed, and then I wanted to find the perfect timing, but it never came," I whispered as my eyes wandered to her lips. "Can you please say something? I love your eyes, and these lips, and your face. I could stare at them an entire day, but right now it would be a great moment for you to tell me what you're thinking."

"You're not as bad with words as you think, William." Her lips curled up. "I love you, and not just because you make the best coffee I've ever tasted or own the comfiest sweaters I've ever worn."

"That's...good to know," I whispered and sealed our lips into a kiss.

Her wet lips felt amazing against my warm ones. Her dress was drenched, and my needy hands looked for ways to touch more of her, to cover her entirely with my warmth. I dipped my head lower to meet her lips as my hands rested on her bare back because of the low cut of the dress at her back.

"Nora," I breathed out when I left her lips. "Dance in the rain with me."

She laughed. "You can't dance with an umbrella."

"Who said anything about an umbrella?" I smirked, and in one swift movement threw my umbrella to the ground and let the rain pour over me. "You got soaking wet already, it's too late to stop you from the rain. The least I could do is join you."

I took her hand and intertwined our fingers together. I pulled her closer to me, and when our chests touched, I hummed at the warm touch of her skin. I never could figure out why she loved the rain that much, but when we moved as we held each other, with the rain pouring, and only our warm skin touched briefly with each step, I could see it; I could see why she found the rain so thrilling.

We're clearly both soaked to the bone. I twirled her around before I lifted her up, my fingers dipped into her wet skin. She squealed and held onto me when her fit was in the air.

I spun her around in circles, my shoulders were shaking from laughter until my cheeks hurt. There was something freeing about dancing in the rain with Nora, about letting the rain fall down slowly but not trying to escape to find shelter or find a place to hide. We accepted the rain; we embraced it as a part of us like we embraced each other.

I licked my lips as I looked at her face, and then she kissed me. It was a different kind of kiss, the cold of the rain and the warmth of our bodies mixed together into a feeling of bliss. And when she ran her hands through the locks of my hair, I groaned and pulled her to me. I was trying desperately to get more grip of her body that was covered in the most gorgeous dress I've seen her wear.

"Nora," I swallowed when I barely managed to open my eyes and look at her. "You haven't braided your hair today."

"No, I haven't." She kissed my neck slowly. "Do you like it?"

"I freaking love it," I said in a husky voice. "And that dress…"

"What about it?" she teased, and maybe just because she wanted to drive me completely crazy, but she pressed her body closer to mine as I held her up.

Her chest was rising up and down as it grazed mine through our drenched clothes and I could see her nipples through the thin fabric. I could see the goosebumps that appeared over her skin when I lifted my hands higher on her hips and lowered her down until her feet touched the ground.

"You look stunning in it," I barely managed to let the words out.

"William?"

"Yes?" I roamed my eyes over her, at her heels, her short legs, and her curvy hips. I lingered on her chest a bit longer than the rest of her body, and she noticed that.

"You've made so many first moves, don't be afraid to make another one," she said, her voice was encouraging.

"Can I do for you that private tour in my room we talked about?"

"Lead the way, William," she whispered to my ear. "I'll follow right after you."

CHAPTER 33
Nora

I love you.

The moment those three words left William's mouth, I knew I wanted nothing more than to kiss him again, and again, and again. I always had this fantasy of dancing with a lover in the rain, the kind of dance that could melt a heart, and the kind of rain that could leave you soaked, but I would be so in love and caught up in the moment that I wouldn't care how my dress would look like in the next day or if I would need a long shower afterwards.

I was so in love that all I cared about after dancing in the rain was getting to his room to take off all of our wet clothes. I felt the same desperation in his lips when they covered mine. He was getting better at this—not the kissing thing, he always knew what he was doing at that department, but at showing me what he wanted.

He kept devouring my lips, while his fingers fumbled with the keys. The moment he managed to open the door, he walked me backwards in his house. I didn't pay much attention to the kitchen or how big the living room was; my eyes were closed while I cupped his face and deepened our kiss.

A deep groan came from the back of his throat when he pulled away from me, enough to open the door of his room and walk me inside. The room looked as I imagined, *sort of.* White walls, a desk with a computer he probably worked at every time he returned from work, a bed and a closet that probably contained many more comfy clothes I could steal on another time.

"Nice room," I mumbled.

"Thank you," he said and pressed our lips together again.

My hands took the time to explore his chest, which was hard and solid even through his sweater. I wandered down and gripped the bottom of the sweater. I pulled it up and over his head and threw them until they hit the floor. His breath turned shaky when my fingers trailed down his chest to his jeans that were hanging low on his hips.

"Nora," he groaned like he was in pain when my hands slid under the fabric of his jeans and cupped him in my hand.

"Is that what you want?" I asked.

"You want to know what I want?" he kissed my neck, and I leaned my head back so he would have more access to my skin.

I moaned when his lips contacted my warm skin, while I was still wearing my dress that was stuck to my body. It created a whole other level of stimulation; it was getting hard to deal with and be patient about.

"You want me to show you what I want?" His voice was low.

I hummed when he grazed my skin with his teeth and rested his hands on my hips. I could feel their warmth through my dress, I could feel how strong they were, I could feel how confident he was about whatever it was he planned in his head since we walked up here.

I nodded quickly and ran my hands in his dark wet hair.

The moment he got the confirmation he needed from me, he kneeled down. His fingers touched my leg delicately, and he unclasped the straps of my heel and slipped it off. He moved to my other heel as I held onto his shoulders.

When my shoes joined his sweater on the floor, he pressed his lips to my ankle. I thought he was going to come back and kiss my lips again, but he didn't; his lips lingered around my ankle, so slow that if felt like torture until he reached my knee.

His lips burned into my skin, and I forgot all about the rain when he held onto my legs and pulled up the fabric of my dress. With every inch that ridden up, my legs shivered and wiggled, trying to direct him to the place I wanted him the most.

I bucked my hips when he kissed my inner thigh, and then when they went higher to the soft material of my panties.

He pressed one last kiss on my thigh and pulled away to stare at me. "Forget what I said about the rain, I love the rain, and most of all, I love how you look like after the rain."

He stood up and pressed a kiss to my lips and then pushed me back till my back was pressed to the door of his room. He ran his hands over my dress and lifted up to my hips. My body was shivering with anticipation, as he took my hand and stopped it on the fabric he just lifted.

He let go when I held onto the satin around my hips and smirked. "Hold onto it for me."

Before I could ask him why he needed me for that, he bent down and yanked my panties off and threw them aside.

I gasped when he pushed his tongue inside of me while he watched my reaction. My hands were shaking, so I clenched my fists around the fabric when he pushed my legs apart even more and wrapped his arms around my knees to keep me steady. I moved my hips against his head that was buried between my legs and invoked a gentle pressure in my lower stomach.

I moved one of my hands to grip his hair when his lips wrapped around my clit, but he didn't let me go off with it so easily, and moved my hand back to the dress so he could flick his tongue to my sensitive spot.

"William," I cried when I felt the pressure building up in my stomach. He dug his fingers into the skin of my legs and sucked on my clit and that's all it took for my orgasm to wash over me.

He gave me time to gain my breathing back. I let go of the dress when he stood up and held onto me when he noticed my wobbly legs that couldn't stand on their own with the mouth of his.

He licked his lips when he faced me and moved my hair behind my shoulders. "Are you okay?"

"Whatever it is you want to do to me, just know that my answer is yes, it's always a *yes*, so don't be shy." I hummed when he ran his hands down my arms.

He laughed and squeezed my side playfully.

"If I say I want to fuck you against that door?" he asked, "what would you say about that?"

My entire body hummed at his idea and instead of talking, I tried to wrap my legs around his hips to get my center closer to him—but failed miserably.

He chuckled and wrapped both my legs around his hips. His hands slipped under the dress and rested on my ass to keep me steady, and when I rolled my hips to his body I felt his hardness. He pushed his hips into me too, and groaned when I rolled my hips again, harder this time, and met with a throbbing member through his jeans.

He pushed the thin straps of my dress down, but not enough for his hands to reach my bare breasts. "Can you do me a favor, Nora?"

"If the favor is taking off this dress, then yes, I would be more than happy to help you take it off," I mumbled and tried to move my hands to lower the straps, but his strong body kept me in place.

"Next time you wear this kind of a dress, don't walk with it in the rain where anyone could see *these*." His thumb grazed over the fabric that covered my nipples. "That sight is meant only for me."

I whimpered. "What if I was trying to turn you on, and it was all part of my wicked plan?"

He yanked the front of my dress down and cupped my bare breast, hard. "Then your plan worked. I'm more than turned on."

I rasped and arched my back when he wrapped his mouth around my nipple and sucked on it as he tugged on my other one.

My legs tightened around him, and he took that as his chance to strip off his jeans and boxers and kicked them to the floor.

His erection sprung free and he pushed the dress out of his way before he held my hips and pushed into me with one long thrust.

I felt with every thrust and touch of his mouth and hands on my ass and my breasts how much he wanted this, how much he wanted me, how much he loved me. Our flesh clashed with each trust as he picked up the pace when he heard my moans.

"You have no idea how much I love the sounds you make," he rasped and thrusted me with more force.

I pulsed around his dick at his sweet words. "How much?"

"So much that I consider spending every day until spring this way, having walks in the rain, dancing in the rain, doing whatever you wish in the rain, just so we can spend our time later in bed," he moaned. "Or the door, or counter, I don't know, we agreed you're better than planning than I am, and creative."

"I can think of a couple of ideas," I whimpered and felt him move one of his hands from under my ass to behind my head.

"Hold on, Nora."

Before I could ask him what he meant by that, his strokes became harder, faster, deeper—he pushed my body against the wooden door. His hand protected my head from being banged against the door as the rest of my body clashed with his body with each thrust.

I clenched around him and held onto his shoulders as the

orgasm ripped through me. He thrusted a few more times and grunted as he came too. He leaned his head at the crook of my neck and kissed it while his hands rubbed my sides gently. We both panted and took the time to look at each other before William carried me to bed and went to lie beside me.

"So, are you going to tell me what more you want or are you going to leave me hanging?" I lifted a brow.

His shoulders shook from laughter when he looked over me. Besides our hair that was a bit wet from the rain, our bodies felt hot because of our closeness and intimacy.

"Right now, I want you to rest," he said as he kissed my forehead.

"I can handle another round. I can prove it if you don't believe me." I pouted and reached my hands forward to touch him, but he took them and pressed them to his cheeks and hugged me.

"I know you can handle a lot more than another round, but I also know you had an emotional morning. I know you moved on from your ex, and you love me like I love you, but he said some harsh things, you need time to process all that happened."

"I did that already, processed it all," I whispered. "I don't feel ashamed, or guilty or like I'm supposed to live without love because I need to deal with mental things. I feel like I've been processing that since he broke up with me, but only today I came to that realization, I really let it all sink in." I took a deep breath. "He dumped me before one of my biggest exams."

I didn't want to keep dragging this on. I knew William would give me all the time in the world, but I wanted that time to be about us, not about my past. "He got mad at me every time I preferred to stay home instead of going out with friends, he was sick of my stress, he couldn't deal with it anymore so he broke up with me. That's basically what the story is."

"Nora," he brushed my hair, "I'm sorry you had to go through that."

"You should've seen how I talked to him back today, I honestly considered punching him or spilling wine on his expensive suit, but it was still my mother's auction, I didn't want to cause a scene," I laughed at the ridiculous idea. "Besides, I said what I needed to say, I don't need anything else."

"I'm proud of you," he caressed my cheek and covered my body with more of the soft blanket. "*My girl.* I said you had a daring heart, didn't I?"

I blushed when he called me that way. "Your girl, huh?"

He shrugged. "We agreed on the first day we met we weren't going to call each other nicknames other people use. Well, it was more of an unwritten rule between us, but still. I never called anyone *my girl* before."

"So, how was your morning? Did you and your dad settle things?"

"We had some disagreements, some agreements, but I made one very important one," he tucked my strand of hair. "Do you think you could pull off the goodbye party of the restaurant at the end of the month?"

I sat on the bed and looked up at him. "What?"

He chuckled and rested his hands on his stomach. "I told my dad I'm willing to move on, but only if he'll let you be the one to plan an event. What do you think?"

"I think it's amazing, but what about you?" I asked, my heart was beating quickly from excitement. "What are you going to do?"

"I don't know," he answered, and sounded more at peace with that fact than he did yesterday. "I'm on unlimited vacation at the moment, at least until I'll learn what I want to do in life."

"You can be a businessman, you'll look good in a suit," I said.

"Really?" he smirked and traced his hands over my knee.

"You can be a cook," I said.

"You just want me to be in a kitchen more so I can make you more coffee," he squeezed my hip. "Don't you?"

"I don't need you to be in the kitchen all day to make me coffee, all I need is to use my charms." I giggled and to prove to him how quick my charms work, I kneeled back and rested my body over his. I pressed a long kiss to his lips and smiled when he wrapped his arms around my back. "See?" I whispered to his lips. "Charm."

"Oh, you have more than personal charm," he muttered. "I love you for many reasons, you know."

I love you.

I hoped he was going to say that every day, because I got used to him saying it way too fast.

"Or you can be a florist," I suggested. "You already have previous knowledge about flowers, and you love to be around them, it could be perfect for you actually."

"It will definitely make it easier to pick up tulips for you." He rubbed his hand over my skin and stopped at my lower back.

"Well, whatever it is you decide to do with your life, I hope it will help you move on as you wish." I pecked his lips.

When I opened them and looked at his blue eyes, I could see he was close to moving on more than he thought. He just needed time. And in our case, we had all the time in the world.

William

EPILOGUE

THREE MONTHS LATER

When I was a little kid, I had a specific idea of what spring was supposed to look like. I thought that without my grandparents, I couldn't love the spring ever again, or walk in a tulip field ever again. But when I walked with Nora in Keukenhof, surrounded by tulips, I realized *that* was what spring meant for me now, that was how I wanted it to look like from now until forever.

She was wearing a white dress with her hair falling down her shoulders, the wind blew her hair every once in a while, making her laugh like a child as she ran through the tulips and took photos she was probably going to post on social media later on.

I fell in love with her in the rain, when she let the rain fall down on her and danced with me in soaked clothes, and I fell in love with her more in the spring, with flowers in hand and a white dress. I didn't need to think how much more I was about to fall in the summer, I was a hopeless romantic, I knew there was no going back from this, no going back from *her*.

I closed my eyes when I felt the sun on my skin, and when I

opened them, I could picture myself in another universe, where my grandma was standing right there with me, looking at Nora and smiling. "Is that her?"

"Yeah, that's the *one*," I said in blushing cheeks.

"When you said she had green eyes, I didn't picture them that..."

"Beautiful?" I chuckled. "You should see them in the cold weather or when she's looking up at the sky, their color pops up in a whole other way."

"I'm glad you found her," she mentioned.

"Because she made me come here after all this time?" I didn't look around at all the colors, at the tulips or the stress, I wanted to hold on tighter to the image I had in my head of my grandma, if I'd let myself look away she might disappear.

"Because she helped me move on?" I whispered.

"Well, that's a big plus. I couldn't bear seeing you so miserable, forgetting how to live," she said in her familiar gentle voice. "I like her because she takes care of you and takes you to some parties every once in a while, and you know, it's always nice having another person coming to visit the garden."

"It was only one party, let's not exaggerate," I chuckled. "You'll start to sound like Dad soon."

"Don't be mad at him, Will," she said and put her hand under my chin to make me look at her. "It's not his fault, the restaurant wouldn't survive one way or another, nothing could've stopped it."

"I'm not mad at him anymore." I shook my head, though I knew she was right, she always knew when someone was lying.

Yeah, it was three months ago, I already started a new job, I moved on from being a waiter and serving so many customers each day, but I was still mad. Not at my dad, it wasn't his fault as my grandma said, but at the universe, at bigger things than me that controlled this life.

"I'm not," I emphasized. "I accepted reality, I accepted the fact you and grandpa are not here anymore. I may have lied about it in the past, but now I mean it, *I am*."

I turned back to her when she didn't reply, just to find the space near me empty, instead of my grandma I found tulips, more and more tulips.

"Hey, are you okay?" Nora appeared in front of me, her phone wasn't in her hand anymore.

"Huh?" I blinked my eyes. "Yeah, why wouldn't I be?"

"I called your name but you didn't answer, you were looking at the sky for a long time," she whispered.

I didn't need to tell her why, she knew why. She knew it was one of those times I talked with my grandma and asked for advice, I did it much more the last couple of months.

"Maybe we should head back home." She caressed my cheek. "I think you had enough for one day."

"I'm okay." I kissed her hand that was pressed to my warm cheek. "I just needed a second to myself. This place brings back old memories, you know?"

"Would you like to tell me some of them?" she asked carefully.

Nora pushed me out of my comfort zone many times before, but she never pushed me about *this*.

"I would," I nodded. "But first, I think I should take a few pictures of you near those white tulips over there."

"Because they match my dress?" She played with the skirt of her dress. "Or maybe because you want to take a picture of me, print it and put it at your desk at work, so you can look at me every time you miss me?" she asked cheekily.

"Florists don't have desks," I laughed. "I barely have space to write down orders because there are always flowers on the counter."

I stepped closer and pushed a strand of hair out of her face, smiling when I felt her shiver under my touch. "But I do have a picture of you on my phone."

"Which one?" she asked immediately.

"The one where you're drinking coffee in my bed, looking up at me," I said. "You remember that morning?"

"When I slept over at your place for the first time," she smiled. "And you put on some song by The Beatles while making me coffee."

"It wasn't just some song," I muttered.

She rolled her eyes at my seriousness. "I'm nothing like the sun, William."

Something in me broke every time she said that and let the smallest insecurities get to her. Even if it was for a few moments before her confident self-came back to life. It was amazing how she had so many compliments to give, but she never knew how to accept that one compliment from me.

But one day she will, I knew that much.

"You're right." I lowered my head and brushed our lips together. "*You're better.*"

THE END